Heidi Stephens has spent her career working in advertising and marketing; some of her early writing work includes instruction manuals for vacuum cleaners, saucepans and sex toys. For the past ten years she has also freelanced as a journalist and, on autumnal weekend evenings, can be found liveblogging *Strictly Come Dancing* for *The Guardian*. She lives in Wiltshire with her partner and Labrador, Mabel.

Two Metres from You is Heidi's debut novel.

T0017617

HEIDI STEPHENS

TWO METRES FROM YOU

ACCENT

First published in 2021 by Headline Accent
An imprint of HEADLINE PUBLISHING GROUP

4

Cataloguing in Publication Data is available from the British Library

ISBN 978 1 4722 8582 9

Typeset in 11.03/13.67pt Bembo Std by Jouve (UK), Milton Keynes

Printed and bound in Great Britain by Clays Ltd, Elcograf S.p.A.

Headline's policy is to use papers that are natural, renewable and recyclable
products and made from wood grown in well-managed forests and other
controlled sources. The logging and manufacturing processes are expected to
conform to the environmental regulations of the country of origin.

HEADLINE PUBLISHING GROUP
An Hachette UK Company
Carmelite House
50 Victoria Embankment
London EC4Y 0DZ

www.headline.co.uk
www.hachette.co.uk

To Pip and Mabel, with love

CHAPTER ONE
Sunday, 22 March 2020

Gemma had been waiting on the station concourse for over half an hour when the robotic female voice announced that her train was now boarding at Platform 3. She was cold and stiff from sitting on her rucksack, her toes numb inside the flimsy trainers that were designed for treadmills and gym mats and polished studio floors, not draughty London train stations. She pulled her coat tightly around her and wrapped her arms around Mabel, lifting up one of her front legs and burying her nose into the leathery pads of her paw. They smelled inexplicably of earth and digestive biscuits, which Gemma inhaled like it was the furry essence of courage and calm. Mabel licked her face, prompting a weak smile from Gemma, her first in hours. She kissed the top of her head, on the velvety patch right between her ears.

She'd been messaging Caro when the platform was called, letting her know she was OK from behind a curtain of untidy blond hair that hid her blotchy skin and red-rimmed eyes from curious passers-by. Right now she couldn't remember a time in her adult life when she was more in need of a stiff drink, but she didn't dare leave Mabel tied up outside any of the shops. Hopefully there would be a buffet car or a trolley on the train that would sell her wine, no doubt for a rip-off price. Since this was a state of emergency, she'd even consider cider.

She struggled to her feet, scratching the metal tip of her coat belt across the four inches of bare ankle below her gym leggings. The skin was already pink and itchy from the cold, and now it hurt in that special, particularly hurty way that only applies when your skin is semi-frozen. Aside from her shambolic appearance, it was reasonable to assume she smelled less than fragrant. Eau de Boot Camp et Misery. But there was little she could do about it right now and it wasn't like Paddington was busy. It was a Sunday, and besides, people had been avoiding unnecessary travel for a week or two now. Last week the government had formally introduced a new rule that meant you couldn't get closer than two metres anyway.

As if confirming Gemma's suspicion about her current aroma, Mabel's shiny black nose did a covert frisk of Gemma's copious bags and pockets. No treats emerged, so she flumped back down by the pile of luggage and watched her owner wrestle her arms into the straps of the rucksack. Gemma tied Mabel's lead to the waist strap, gripped her train ticket between her teeth and scooped up everything else with both hands: a mix of branded hessian shoppers, supermarket carrier bags and a huge leather handbag that was bursting at the seams with clothing and toiletries and the dangling plug of a BaByliss Big Hair. Everything about Gemma looked like it had been shovelled together against the clock, a chaotic jumble of woman and Labrador and miscellaneous belongings. She felt like a human version of the kids' game Buckaroo, weighed down with humiliation and anger and grief. One more item of emotional baggage and she would flip.

At the ticket gate, Gemma gave the inspector a helpless look and he opened the wide gate so she didn't have to put her bags down to feed the ticket in. Mabel trotted dutifully along the platform, perhaps sensing that now wasn't the time to investigate discarded burger wrappings or strutting pigeons. At the first Standard Class carriage Gemma elbowed the button to open the door and climbed in, trailing Mabel behind her. She piled all the bags under the luggage shelf, then slid the rucksack from her throbbing shoulders and let it fall on to the rack above. Mabel sat and waited while her owner untied her lead, then jumped on to the seat by the window. Gemma rubbed the sore patches on her fingers where the bag straps had cut into them, then fell into the aisle seat and hugged Mabel's head with a sigh of relief.

She thought about how she'd write up today as a first-person experience in a women's magazine, the kind you read as a guilty pleasure at the hairdresser or the dentist. *I went from loved-up in London to HOMELESS WRECK in ONE DAY*. Or maybe *I walked in on my man CHEATING, check out the INCREDIBLE PHOTOS*. Gemma didn't actually have any photos, incredible or otherwise, but the image was imprinted on her retinas for the rest of time.

The tinny voice of the train driver confirmed that Gemma was indeed on the 19.50 service to Bristol Temple Meads, calling at Reading, Didcot Parkway, Swindon, Chippenham, Bath Spa and Bristol Temple Meads. She was only going as far as Chippenham, which the Trainline app had told her was just over an hour. As the train began to pull out of the station, Gemma let out a slow and wavering breath. Despite everything, getting out of London felt like she'd loosened the tiny knots in her stomach; the more miles she put between herself and Fraser, the better.

'Any drinks or refreshments?'

Gemma jolted from her nap, induced by the furry warmth of Mabel's head on her lap and the soporific swaying of the train. She took a second to remember where she was, and felt a momentary wave of sickness.

'Do you have any wine? Or cider?'

'I've got both, my love. Wine is on special offer, two mini bottles for seven pounds. Red or white.'

Gemma mentally calculated how many she'd need to induce oblivion, but not death. 'Can I have six red? And a bottle of water. Do you have a cup? And a Twix.'

The woman passed everything over with the patience and implacability of someone who had witnessed a whole world of tiny dramas in her time. Gemma hesitated for a second before handing over her debit card, then decided she might need the cash for a taxi. It wasn't like she and Fraser had shared a bank account, so there was no way he could use her spending to track her down. *Not that he'd bother*, she thought; Fraser wasn't known for exuberant romantic gestures unless there was a guaranteed blow job at the end of it, and the only thing that would persuade Gemma to be in the same postcode as his penis any time soon was the opportunity to kick it really hard.

She poked four of the wine bottles into her handbag, wiggling them into the crevices between her belongings, leaving the remaining two on the tray table with the water and the Twix. Mabel lifted her head hopefully at the rustle of the foil wrapper, but had to settle for lapping Buxton from a plastic cup and a freezer bag of dog biscuits that magically appeared from Gemma's coat pocket. Gemma drank the rest of the water from the bottle, then unscrewed the first mini wine and poured it into the cup.

It struck her that this time last Sunday she'd been relaxed and replete after she and Fraser had finished their usual Sunday takeaway. They'd walked along Bermondsey Street to collect it together, following their traditional debate about whether to go with Gemma's favourite Lebanese or Fraser's preferred Thai. As usual Gemma had capitulated to keep the peace, even though all the dishes from the Thai place tasted the same and the personal hygiene of the owner made her question the state of the kitchen. While they waited, she had regaled Fraser with funny stories from her coffee date with Caro and Joe earlier, and he'd pretended to laugh despite clearly not actually listening. One week on, she was drinking wine out of a dog cup on a train and eating a Twix for dinner while strings of drool spiralled from Mabel's jaws on to her leg. *Stay classy, Gemma.*

The Sunday coffee with Caro and Joe was a long-standing date; a tradition they'd tried to keep up since they'd all moved to London after university. Sometimes family commitments, holidays, weddings or illness meant it was only two of them, but in the eleven years since they'd graduated they'd never entirely cancelled more than a handful of times, aside from a three-month hiatus in 2014 when Joe was doing a summer DJ residency in Mykonos and Caro had just given birth to Gemma's god-daughter, Bella.

They always met up at 4 p.m. in a favourite café called Dexter's near Borough Market that served up good coffee and squashy sofas, conveniently only five minutes from Gemma's 3 p.m. boot camp, which was run by an ex-Marine called Rob who had arms like Parma hams and a voice like a really angry Barry White. But today Gemma had seen several missed calls from Caro after her class ended; when she rang back, she discovered Caro was cancelling on the basis of a work crisis, and Joe was dying of man flu. He'd been DJ-ing on Saturday night and had probably still been dancing and/or snogging unsuitable men when the sun came up, so crying off at the last minute wasn't entirely unexpected.

Gemma and Caro had chatted for a few minutes about their respective weeks, and after a little coaxing Gemma had mentioned how particularly moody and distant Fraser had been lately. Caro had sympathised, then suggested she surprise him by getting home early, maybe 'spend some quality time together' before taking him out for dinner. 'You mean fuck him then feed him,' laughed Gemma. In the absence of a date with her friends, it had seemed like as good a plan as any.

Twenty minutes later Gemma had arrived home to find Mabel shut in the kitchen and a prime view of Fraser's head wedged between the spread legs of a mystery brunette, which made him look like he had a Tom Selleck moustache. Chaos and screaming ensued, with Mystery Brunette calling Gemma a 'cunt' on her way out, which felt a bit rich when she'd just been grinding hers into Gemma's new Heal's cushions.

The next hour had been a painful blur of shouting, recriminations and slamming doors as Gemma had gathered up as many of her belongings as possible. Most of it went into the hiking rucksack she'd last used for a trip she and Joe had taken around the Greek islands, and the rest was crammed into whatever random bags she could find. After the initial yelling had died down, Fraser had taken to brooding in doorways, watching her empty drawers and cupboards and occasionally proclaiming 'this is fucking stupid' or 'babe, don't do this.' Gemma had ignored him, channelling her misery and fury into getting herself and Mabel out of the flat. Once she was packed, she had pointed a finger in Fraser's face and delivered an emphatic 'Do NOT follow me' before dropping his keys on the mat and closing the front door behind her. She had hurried Mabel to the end of the road, then put the bags down on the pavement and crumpled against a lamppost to call Caro. It took all her remaining energy to whisper *Please help me, I need to get out of London* before the dam broke on tears she'd been suppressing for hours, swiftly followed by those she'd been holding back for days, weeks and months.

Caro had taken charge as usual, ordering Gemma to get an Uber to Paddington and messaging her the train time and the address of the cottage, then staying on the phone until the car arrived. And so here she was, thirty-two-year-old freelance journalist Gemma Lockwood, newly single and heading west to pastures new and unknown. *I walked in on my man cheating and a few hours later I was drinking wine on a train with a dog.* When everything felt less terrible, she could probably make £150 out of that.

The train eased into Chippenham just before 9 p.m., ejecting a handful of passengers on to the cold, empty platform. The wind flapped at Mabel's ears as the carriages slid away to Bath and Bristol, leaving Gemma and Mabel to trudge up the steps in the direction of the station exit and taxi rank. If Gemma had been able to free her hands she would have crossed her fingers; this felt like the back end of beyond, and she had no idea if there would be cabs at this time on a Sunday.

The ticket gates were open and unmanned, spilling out on to a tarmac concourse with a drop-off area, bus stops and one solitary Peugeot in the taxi rank. The driver was leaning on the bonnet, smoking frantically in the frigid air, his free hand tucked under the armpit of his anorak for warmth. He was around sixty and looked a little like Gemma's dead uncle Clive, but Gemma hurried towards him like he was a shimmering mirage in a Wiltshire desert that might fade away at any moment.

The man thumped his cigarette into the gutter and eyed Gemma and Mabel doubtfully. She arranged her face into her most winning smile, trying to look like a sane, professional woman of means rather than an unhinged bag lady with a dog that would almost certainly leave hair and a light film of slobber on his upholstery.

'Can you take us to Crowthorpe?'

'I don't usually take dogs. Allergic.' He managed to add at least four extra r's to the final word, reminding Gemma of Robbie Coltrane's Hagrid in the *Harry Potter* films.

'Please. You're the only taxi, and I don't know anyone locally. I can pay extra.' Gemma tried to access her purse so she could wave banknotes at him, but it was buried somewhere in her handbag and she had less than no hands. She tried another winning smile, this time with teeth.

'Hmm.' He inspected them both for a long moment, then relented. 'Go on then. Get in.'

The twenty-minute journey to Crowthorpe followed the main road out of town, past a tired-looking row of estate agents, takeaways and pubs. A few were open, and Gemma caught a glimpse of outdoor smokers and the flickering lights of fruit machines. The shops gave way to houses – neat rows of Victorian and Edwardian terraces that merged into post-war semis. It reminded her of the town where Aunt Laura had lived in Norfolk, but perhaps all market towns looked the same. After ten minutes and an unnecessary number of roundabouts, the taxi veered off the main road on to a country lane that became increasingly narrow and twisting, lined with shadowy hedgerows punctuated by gated entrances or single-track lanes.

The taxi smelled like a teenage bedroom, and this combined with the hurtling motion and Gemma's wine/Twix dinner was making her stomach do some dangerous churning. She was about to ask the driver to stop so she could throw up into a hedgerow when they passed the sign saying 'Welcome to Crowthorpe' and the taxi slowed. 'What's the address, love?'

Gemma took deep breaths and scrolled through Caro's messages. 'It just says West Cottage, on the corner of Frampton Lane.'

The driver nodded and pulled away, much slower this time, and made his way through the village. Gemma closed her eyes and willed herself not to be sick, and by the time the taxi stopped she was feeling a little less like that time she'd eaten a whole bag of candyfloss at the fairground, then parted company with it on the Waltzer in a centrifugal symphony of pink vomit. Gemma opened the car door, gulping cold air as she pulled Mabel and her handbag out of the taxi. 'How much do I owe you?'

'Twelve pounds,' said the driver, opening the boot and unloading the rest of her bags on to the pavement. He looked at her with an expression of mild concern. 'Are you going to be OK?'

Gemma squeezed out a wobbly smile, pulling Mabel closer to her side. Right now she felt a very long way from OK. 'I'll be fine, thanks.' She sank her arm into her handbag and fished around until she felt the soft leather of her purse and pulled it out, extracting a £20 note. 'Keep the change. Thanks for helping me out.'

The driver grinned and walked back to his car. 'No worries. It's a nice village, this. You'll be right.'

Right about what?

Gemma watched him drive away, then turned to unlatch the wooden gate of the cottage. She remembered Caro's instruction to look for the cast-iron chicken by the door, but there were no street lights in this part of the village and no moonlight anywhere, so Gemma clicked on the torch app on her phone and waved it over the tiny front garden. She spotted the bright red chicken and lifted it up; it was heavier than she expected, but the ring with two door keys was underneath, pressed slightly into the ground by weight and time. Gemma hooked her finger under the keys and levered them out, then jiggled the old mortice key into the lock of the porch. It swung open into a small coat and boot space with a stone-tiled floor, so Gemma transferred all her bags from the pavement before closing the gate and tackling the inner door, which opened with a silver Yale key. Inside was pitch-dark and smelled inexplicably of cheese, but flicking the light switch on the wall yielded nothing.

Gemma looked at Mabel, suddenly overcome with physical

fatigue and mental exhaustion. She vaguely remembered Caro messaging something about the fuse box, but she felt too tired and muddled to work it out now. The only thing that really mattered at this moment was making sure her dog was OK; everything else could wait until morning.

The village was silent as Gemma stepped back out into the tiny front garden and let go of Mabel's lead. While she sniffed around the shrubs and did her business, Gemma used her phone torch to empty the contents of the rucksack in search of Mabel's dog bed, bundling it into the house with the wool picnic blanket Fraser had bought her for Valentine's Day and the four remaining mini bottles of wine. Once Mabel had finished, Gemma scanned her torch over the shadowy rooms. One had two sofas, so Gemma kicked off her trainers, put the dog bed next to the fireplace and told Mabel to settle. As her dog turned in circles in pursuit of the perfect sleeping position, Gemma padded through to the kitchen in her purple gym socks and found a bowl in a cupboard by torchlight, filling it with water from the tap; she put it next to Mabel's bed, then returned to the kitchen for a wine glass. Her final mission was to shine her torch up the creaky stairs in search of a bathroom; when she came back downstairs, Mabel's head was on her paws and her big Labrador eyes were already closing.

Gemma shuffled under the soft blanket, a gift that had been full of possibilities, a promise of picnics and live music and lazy summer evenings under the stars. Since that had turned out to be colossal bullshit, she would now use it to wallow in wine and self-pity in a dark room. She unscrewed all four wine bottles and lined them up on the wooden floorboards by the sofa, tipping each into the glass and transferring it immediately into her mouth. Gemma felt the pain in her shoulders and hands and heart soften and blur at the edges, and closed her eyes to wait for the benevolent mercy of sleep.

CHAPTER TWO

Monday, 23 March

Sometime after midnight, Gemma lay on her side on the sofa, her head pickled with wine but refusing to yield to slumber. Her eyes had adjusted to the intense darkness, and she was able to pick out the doughnut shape of Mabel curled up on her bed, and the pale stone casement of the window reflecting the tiniest sliver of moonlight. The blackout felt soothing, but the quiet was strange; after eleven years living in London, she couldn't remember the last time she had experienced such a fundamental absence of noise. Perhaps if she opened a window or stood outside there would be hooting owls or rustling hedgehogs or the distant hum of the M4, but inside the deadening walls of stone and plaster, there was nothing but silence so profound and heavy it felt like she could hold it in her hand.

It was crazy to think it was only eight hours since she'd walked in on Fraser and the Mystery Brunette; it felt like days had passed. She picked apart her feelings for a while, compartmentalising the anger from the hurt and the humiliation, and came to the conclusion that she was mostly angry about the cheating, but actually fairly dispassionate about Fraser no longer being her boyfriend. If she was entirely honest with herself, the relationship had been on the wane for a while, and Fraser screwing somebody else simply eliminated the emotional inconvenience of ending it herself. Gemma had left with her dignity and her dog, which were the only two things she really cared about. There were books and kitchen utensils and other domestic detritus to be collected and dealt with at some point (Fraser could definitely keep the Heal's cushions), but surprisingly little by way of admin. Fraser owned the flat; she had simply paid him her share of the mortgage and bills each month and thrown some money into the pot for food.

For all his faults, Fraser had always been pretty laid-back about money – not wasteful or frivolous, but not pernickety either. His apparently easy-going nature was one of the things she had liked about him when they'd met at a party a year earlier, along with his mile-wide Scottish grin and the fact that he clearly fancied her rotten. He was only a few inches taller than Gemma's five foot four, with a slim, runner's physique and close-cropped hair in a red so dark it was almost brown, but not quite. His boyish face had gained a scattering of freckles that summer, and in those first few heady months Gemma had entertained the idea that he might be The One. But in the six months since she had moved into his flat in Bermondsey, she'd felt more distance than when they had lived on opposite sides of the river.

It wasn't a single big thing that changed, more a series of tiny fractures in their relationship that seemed to multiply exponentially, like hairline cracks in a porcelain vase. A new tension in his body, less affection, longer periods of moody silence, being cool or dismissive with her friends. In the space of a couple of months, his usually half-full glass had simply drained away. Fraser worked as a property consultant, which meant he contracted himself to property developers, providing sales and marketing support and helping to launch shiny new apartment complexes that cost a bomb and all looked like they were made from the same box of Lego. He talked about things like 'dynamic strategy' a lot, pairing tailored suits with Converse trainers to make him look edgy, and bombing round town in a glossy black convertible Mini that cost a fortune to lease, never mind park. He was a shameless networker, sliding into conferences and seminars and launch parties like he was coated in lube. He was charming, well-connected and, at the height of the London property boom, very much in demand.

But in the past couple of years everything had changed – the uncertainty around Brexit and changes to buy-to-let rules had caused a slump in Fraser's business and, more recently, his mood. He'd talked a good game when Gemma had met him, but she'd soon discovered the colossal chip on his shoulder about being a working-class boy from Clydebank who'd grafted his way up the ladder in an industry riddled with English public schoolboys. But Fraser had put the hours in and success was coming his way; things would get better and he'd ride the wave again.

The previous September he'd gone on a lads' long weekend to the Algarve with some of his property friends, and later he'd admitted to Gemma in a rare moment of post-sex candour that a fancy villa in Portugal was the game plan – retire early, play tennis, take up golf. Fraser's hero was Duncan Bannatyne, another Clydebank boy who'd made half a billion or so and now lived in the same resort they'd stayed in; Fraser had seen him having lunch and reading the *Telegraph* at one of the beach clubs.

Caro had tolerated him at best; she thought he was arrogant and selfish and didn't take care of Gemma after Aunt Laura died. But Gemma had stuck with him, smoothing out the stress, cutting him acres of slack and doing her best to be the Understanding Girlfriend while he was clearly going through a tough time. Right now it burned pretty hard to realise that Fraser was simply screwing somebody else behind her back. *How endlessly fucking disappointing men are.*

The Mystery Brunette intrigued Gemma too – she'd never seen her before, and had no idea where Fraser had met her. She'd been slimmer, more polished and considerably younger than Gemma, with shoulder-length glossy hair and immaculate nude pink nails. It suggested her weekday job was a sensible one – law, finance, most likely property. Entirely different from Gemma, who scrubbed up fine for a special occasion but on an average day opted for a more natural look. Fraser had always said he liked that about Gemma, that she was comfortable with her face and her body; he thought overly groomed women looked like dolls. Well, Fraser had definitely managed to get this one's legs spread to an unrealistically obtuse angle. Presumably she did yoga.

Whoever she was, she'd been surprisingly unbothered at being interrupted by Fraser's girlfriend; other than hissing the c-word at Gemma on her way out, she'd simply put her lacy knickers, black jeans and shoes back on, smoothed down her hair and slipped out the front door. It suggested that this weekend tryst was a purely sexual arrangement, and she had another, more stable set-up to fall back on. Gemma wondered how long it had been going on; whether yesterday was a one-off, or if he'd been wafting the cushions to remove the smell of sex every Sunday for weeks. She briefly considered the possibility that she was one of many, but soon gave up on that train of thought. *That way madness lies.*

In the deepening blackness of her first night in Crowthorpe, Gemma tried to think like a journalist, piecing together the facts to better understand the story. The Mystery Brunette had been wearing flat, baby-blue suede shoes, with no socks – not the kind of thing you'd ever wear on the tube or for a long walk. So she was either local, or keen enough on Fraser to drive south of the river in a global pandemic for an orgasm. No handbag, just a belted cream trenchcoat that she'd draped over a chair, along with her clothes. No coffee mug or water glass, so they hadn't bothered with pleasantries. Fraser had been fully dressed, but in a slightly dishevelled way that made Gemma wonder if they'd already had sex, got dressed, and then she'd half-undressed again. Either for a second round, or more likely because Fraser hadn't finished the job properly first time and they still had another hour or two before Gemma was due back. If this was the case then he would have definitely used a condom, because there was no way Fraser would go down on a woman if his own body fluids were already involved. He wouldn't even kiss Gemma after she'd given him oral sex; it was a weird hang-up of his. Either way Gemma would need to get an STD test as soon as possible, which added another layer of fury and humiliation.

Talking of humiliation, at some point Gemma would have to call her mother and tell her that she and Fraser were finished. She might gloss over some of the finer details; Barbara Lockwood didn't really do soap opera-style drama, and sex talk was an absolute no-no. She'd be upset, not because she particularly liked Fraser (she'd only met him once and her only comment had been 'he's quite pleased with himself, isn't he?'), but because he represented a genuine possibility of Gemma settling down and delivering grandchildren before she entered the eternal reproductive desert. Gemma's sister, Louise, had provided two, but they lived inconveniently abroad.

As Gemma teetered on the edge of slumber, her brain leaping between Fraser and her parents and Louise and Aunt Laura like moving platforms in a video game, she felt a brief moment of calm. Full and final closure would come later, but for now there was a sense of resolution, a line drawn. This cottage was a transit lounge, a temporary refuge where she could regroup for a few days before getting back to real life.

Sleep consumed her just as Mabel abandoned her bed and hopped on to Gemma's legs, like a protector against the return of dark thoughts and night-time torments.

Hello. Hello. Is anyone home? Why would anyone shout that? Either I'm home, in which case you shouldn't be in the house uninvited, or I'm not home, in which case you DEFINITELY shouldn't be in the house uninvited.

A heartbeat of consciousness, then Gemma's left eye flew open. The right eye made a similar attempt, but appeared to be crusted shut with some kind of organic glue her body had produced in the night. The same glue appeared to have coated the inside of her mouth and set like concrete in her skull.

Hello. In the house. The voice of a man. Not a fever dream, but an actual man in the house while she was trapped on the sofa by a crusty right eye, a concrete skull and no feeling in her legs.

Oh God, she had no feeling in her legs. *Do not panic, deep breaths.* Gemma lifted her head a few inches from the cushion, her head splitting open with pain. With her right hand firmly clamped under her right eye, she used the left to peel away the crusty eyelid.

14

Everything slowly came into focus, revealing 25 kilos of yellow Labrador flumped on her ankles. Mabel hadn't even woken up for the shouting, so perhaps it was a fever dream after all. That said, Mabel had a very poor track record of protecting Gemma from terrible men; she could be murdered in her bed and Mabel would probably just snooze through it, then snack on Gemma's corpse in lieu of breakfast. With a groan of agony, Gemma lowered her head back to the arm of the sofa and tried to suppress the waves of nausea and pain racking her body.

'Hello.' A voice from above, and a glimpse of a giant upside-down face with green eyes and a thatch of scarecrow hair.

'JESUS FUCKING CHRIST, FUCK,' yelled Gemma, reflexively hurling Mabel off her dead legs and scrambling to her feet. Hours of restricted blood flow had left her with noodles for limbs, so she floundered back to her knees, her arms flailing to gain some kind of balance and focus on this man, this INTRUDER, who was staring at her with a mix of amusement and confusion. No visible weapons, unless you counted strangler's hands like massive shovels.

Hands and knees, deep breaths. In. And Out. In. And Out. Slowly Gemma's legs stilled and her breathing became more regular. Mabel was now sniffing around the man's dusty boots, on the off-chance they were hiding a small reservoir of biscuits or perhaps a tiny steak, medium rare. *Worst guard dog ever.* Gemma lifted her head and glared at both of them.

'What the fuck are you doing in my house?'

The man gave a short laugh of surprise and folded his arms. 'Unless Caroline has sold it without telling me, which I doubt, it's definitely not your house. The porch was open, the front door was open. I thought she'd been burgled. Obviously I'm sorry if I frightened you.' Gemma gave him a brief once-over. Thirty-ish, well over six foot with rugby player shoulders, paint-spattered shorts and well-worn boots. Clearly cut his own hair and trimmed his beard in the dark. The tiniest trace of a West Country accent. The polar opposite of Fraser, although the last time she'd seen him he'd been wearing someone else's beard entirely.

Gemma's head felt like it was being beaten by stick-wielding toddlers, and she realised she probably looked and sounded a bit unhinged. She sat back on her heels, her hands clamped either side of her nose in some kind of hungover prayer. 'I'm sorry. I'm Gemma. I needed somewhere to stay and Caro said I could come here, she's an old friend. I got here late last night; everything was . . . a bit of a mess.' Her voice cracked, and she realised in horror that she was about to cry.

The man blushed and fidgeted, clearly unsure how to comfort a stranger in this new world of social distancing rules that he'd already broken several times over. He shifted his gaze to Mabel, who was now sniffing at the debris littering the hearth around the wood burner. She was wearing a red collar, which inexplicably still had a lead attached. Man and dog eyed each other for a few seconds, before reaching a mutual understanding.

'I'm Matthew. You seem to be in a bit of a mess, and your dog needs a walk. Get yourself sorted, I'll be back in a bit.'

Before Gemma could organise her muddled thoughts enough to speak, the man picked up Mabel's lead and headed out of the front door, closing it quietly behind him.

Gemma sat for a few minutes, trying to make sense of what had just happened. Either a random friend of Caro's had come in to check on the house, or a huge man had just stolen her dog. Combined with her splitting head and rancid mouth, it all felt like a jumble of jigsaw pieces that didn't fit together. She needed water, and a bathroom.

The blood had finally returned to Gemma's lower limbs, so she tentatively wobbled out of the lounge into what in daylight was clearly a dining room. It was easy to see why the man *(Martin? No, Matthew)* thought she'd been burgled; there was stuff everywhere. Her rucksack was lying on the porch floor, its contents disembowelled into a tangle of clothes and shoes. The hessian shoppers and plastic bags were spewing out toiletries, more crumpled clothes and her laptop; did Matthew say both doors were open? They must have been if he'd just walked in. How could she not have closed them? She was lucky not to have been murdered, never mind burgled.

The smell of ripe cheese felt stronger here, and for a horrifying moment Gemma wondered if it was her. She lifted her left arm and sniffed hesitantly in the direction of her armpit, discovering an eye-watering combination of stale gym sweat, hot train, red wine and sofa sleep. Awful, but no cheese.

The heavy linen curtains on the tiny window were still closed, so she opened them in a flurry of dust motes and stale air. Dirt and stink she could deal with, but first she needed to tackle the most critical things – use the bathroom, clean her teeth, drink as much water as she could stomach and, most importantly of all, find a pen and make a list.

CHAPTER THREE

To Do

- Make a list
- Discover electricity
- Wash stinky body
- Make contact with civilisation
- Find dog

Gemma made her way up the narrow, carpeted stairs into the attic, expecting to find some kind of storage space full of whatever stuff Caro didn't have space for in her flat. Family heirlooms, extreme sports equipment, boxes of school photos showing a serious, dark-skinned girl with untameably fabulous hair. Instead she found it had been converted into a beautiful attic bedroom, with a double bed tucked under the eaves and an en-suite bathroom. In her dishevelled state, the enormous egg-shaped bath and glossy walk-in shower both looked like heaven.

Like every room in the cottage, the bedroom smelled like Stilton, but, as far as Gemma knew, Caroline hadn't been here since a brief visit last summer. Gemma wound the handle on the three skylights, thinking the least she could do was give the place an airing before she moved on in a day or two.

She wandered from room to room through the house, wrestling open ancient window latches to allow the breeze to move the dust around a bit. In a week it would be April, but already there was some spring warmth in the air and the sky was full of morning

18

birdsong. The front windows overlooked the only road through the village, which clearly went nowhere interesting as there didn't seem to be any cars going past. Traffic had much reduced in London over the previous week as more people started to work from home, but here it felt like the world had ended. *Perhaps it has*, thought Gemma. She hadn't looked at her phone since last night and right now wasn't entirely sure where she'd left it.

Aside from the master suite in the loft, there were two more bedrooms and another bathroom on the first floor, then a dining room, lounge and kitchen downstairs. The dining room had a huge open fireplace with an ancient wooden mantelpiece, but there was no grate and the chimney had been boarded up with some kind of polystyrene sheet. The lounge was more promising, which was probably why Gemma had ended up passing out in there last night; a cosy room at the front of the house, with a couple of threadbare sofas, a dusty blue rug and a wood burner laid with paper and sticks. The hearth had a small basket of dry logs and matches, and a poker was propped up against the stonework. *Should have slept with that last night*, she thought darkly. *Could have used it on local intruders.*

The kitchen was at the back of the house, with a natural stone floor, duck-egg-blue cupboards and an enormous, brushed-steel range with seven gas burners and two ovens. Gemma had learned to cook in both of Aunt Laura's beautiful kitchens but had rarely had the chance at Fraser's; if they ate in, he liked to take control of the kitchen and make a huge theatrical performance out of it. But since this village was unlikely to have a deli salad bar, Gemma figured she'd have to work out how to use the range. The kitchen window overlooked a rambling, overgrown garden with a stone and timber building at the far end; she couldn't see if it was part of this property or next door, but resolved to investigate later.

As Gemma went back up to use the first-floor bathroom, she caught a glimpse of her ravaged face in the mirror above the sink. She looked, unsurprisingly, like a thirty-two-year-old woman who had spent hours ugly-crying before drinking the best part of a litre of red wine and falling asleep under a dog. She was still wearing yesterday's sweaty running gear, her blond highlights were growing out and her teeth were furry and wine-stained. She vowed to have a shower as soon as she worked out how to turn on the hot water.

Despite the dust and the pervading smell, West Cottage was undeniably lovely. As far as Gemma knew it had been bought by Caro's parents as a renovation project after their only daughter left for Leeds University. They had both passed away a couple of years ago, Caro's mum from breast cancer and her dad eight months later from a long-standing heart condition; Caro had said that what was left of his heart crumbled after her mum died. Caro had rarely visited the cottage since, although she'd left a few pieces of furniture, a cupboard of linens and some kitchen basics for the occasions when she stayed. All other traces of Caro's family were gone, and Gemma wondered where all their stuff was – certainly not in Caro's flat. Perhaps it was all stored in the building at the end of the garden.

What the cottage lacked, however, was food and internet, both of which were aligned in the basics section of Gemma's hierarchy of needs. In fact, she would probably rather go hungry than sacrifice her online support network, and right now there would be people wondering if she was dead in a ditch. She hunted down her phone, finding it wedged down the back of the sofa with two tiny wine bottles and a few strips of her picnic blanket, which Mabel had clearly snacked on in the night. A fitting metaphor for her wreck of a relationship – once comforting, now in bits.

Gemma swiped the screen to open her phone, and found several WhatsApp messages from Fraser, all variations on 'can we talk?' but in an increasingly wheedling tone. She deleted all his messages, then blocked his number for good measure. The next message was from Caro, sent while Gemma was on the train last night, explaining in detail where the fuse box was and telling her to ask Matthew in a house called The Barn if she needed anything. Well, Matthew had beaten her to it, and seemingly kidnapped her dog. Joe had messaged to say he'd spoken to Caro and could Gemma please confirm the happy news that she'd 'left that cheating fuckhead for good'. Then there was a message from her sister featuring some kind of funny cat video and two missed calls from her mother, who wouldn't know anything about Gemma's situation but called her regularly to give her a coronavirus update according to the *Daily Mail*.

Gemma pressed dial on Caro's number, only to hear the double beep that confirmed there was insufficient signal. She wandered into the kitchen and tried again – the result was the same, repeated in every room of the house including the attic bedroom. Terrific. No signal, no WiFi, stuck in a village in the arse end of nowhere with no car. Gemma couldn't actually drive, but right now that seemed like a curse from the gods rather than something she had never quite got around to.

Food and basic hygiene, then. These she could deal with; the rest would have to wait. She found the fuse box above the door in the porch and flicked the main switch to turn on the electricity. The distant hum of the fridge confirmed that this task at least had been a success. Turning on the hot tap in the kitchen, she heard the boiler spark into life and chalked up success number two – she now had hot water. Her skin itched in anticipation of being clean again, so she climbed the stairs to the loft shower, pausing briefly at the linen cupboard to grab a towel. It had the texture of a Weetabix, but it would do – she'd get a full body scrub as part of the package, and at her usual day spa she'd pay fifty quid for that pleasure.

Soaping her hair vigorously with some shampoo she had tracked down in Caro's bathroom cabinet, Gemma began to feel more human. She rinsed it through and added a golfball-sized blob of conditioner, raking it through to the ends with her fingers and leaving it to work its magical chemistry for a few minutes. She soaped under her arms and between her legs, allowing the hot water to soothe her skin as she parked images of Fraser going full

Magnum P.I. on the Mystery Brunette, focussing instead on the priority tasks for the day. Firstly, find food for her and Mabel, and retrieve her dog from Matthew the Dognapper. Secondly, find somewhere in the village with a phone signal or free WiFi and pick up her emails – there were probably work deadlines she needed to know about. Gemma had two jobs: writing crappy articles for women's magazines and lifestyle websites, and copywriting for Caro's ad agency. The former was more fun, but the latter paid more money. Once all the work stuff was dealt with, she needed to make the house liveable, albeit for a very limited time – she'd give herself a couple of days, then start looking for a new flat.

As always, Gemma felt better for having made a list – despite the madness of the past twelve hours, she was actually an orderly kind of person who thrived on small, achievable goals. As a teenager she developed a list-writing habit – inconsequential day-to-day stuff like 'make the bed' or 'eat breakfast', scribbled into a desk diary in neon gel pens. The habit had stuck into adulthood – every day began with a list, and anything not completed was carried over to the following day until Gemma couldn't ignore it any longer. In the early months Fraser had found this charming; later on it was just another thing that seemed to annoy him. Gemma rinsed her hair, trying not to think about how many things on his bedroom to-do list he'd ticked off with the Mystery Brunette. *What a shit.*

It was after 10 a.m. by the time Gemma had dressed and run a brush through her wet hair; it was the kind that air-dried pretty forgivingly, and she rarely bothered with a hairdryer unless it was a special occasion that required additional volume. It definitely needed a cut and colour though – perhaps she could find somewhere out here in the sticks in the next day or two, then go back to London with fresh hair and renewed purpose. Somehow she hadn't got round to booking in recent weeks; it had felt like there were bigger things to worry about than getting her highlights done.

Gemma jogged down the stairs feeling decidedly better, albeit starving – she hadn't eaten since lunchtime yesterday, unless wine counted as one of the major food groups. She'd lost weight in recent months, having been a comfortably curvy size 14-ish for years. Now Gemma's jeans felt loose around the waist and her bra had been hooked in an extra notch, but she didn't feel any sense of joy in this – firstly she firmly believed that nobody should seek self-worth on the bathroom scales, and secondly she was thirty-two, newly single, and squatting in someone else's house about 90 miles from civilisation. Somehow losing a few pounds didn't feel much like cause for celebration.

The stairs brought her back to the dining room, which was still home to the chaos of bags and clothes that had created a landslide from the porch. Gemma took ten minutes to battle the mess, dragging her huge rucksack and bag of toiletries up to the loft bedroom, and moving Mabel's dog bed next to the dining-room fireplace, where the late-afternoon sun would stream through the windows. She folded the remains of the picnic blanket and tucked it into the bed, then filled the bowl with fresh water and placed it on the hearth. Then she gathered up the empty wine bottles and put them in the recycling bin outside the back door.

So, food. Was there some kind of village shop, or a bus that would take her to a supermarket? Did they even have buses in this part of the world? Could she call last night's taxi? Gemma had no idea, and without a working phone she had no means of finding out using normal methods, so she stood outside the front gate in the morning sunshine, feeling helplessly out of her depth. While waiting for divine intervention, she looked up at the front of Caro's house; it had a very pleasing symmetry, like a child's drawing with four windows and a door, and a chimney at each end. It looked a bit like the cottage in *The Holiday*, her favourite Christmas film unless you counted *Die Hard*, which no sensible person did. The front was covered in a Virginia creeper that was just starting to bud, and a rambling rose grew over the porch. In a couple of months it would look like a cottage from a chocolate box, or one of the jigsaws that had gathered dust in quiet corners of Aunt Laura's care home. Perhaps Jude Law lived next door, or perhaps it was just angry pensioners and curtain-twitching locals.

A stone wall separated the tiny, overgrown front garden from the road, with a small wooden gate in the middle, painted white. On the left of the gatepost, a mailbox had been attached to the wall, presumably because the porch had no letterbox. She opened the flap, but it was empty – no doubt all of Caro's mail was redirected to her house in London. Gemma looked back at the porch, clearly a later addition to a cottage that Gemma now knew was just over 200 years old, as there was a carved datestone between the upstairs windows that read *1815*. The same year that Jane Austen's *Emma* was published, Gemma mused; she was the least favourite of all Austen's heroines, being nothing more than a meddling, self-satisfied busybody who definitely didn't deserve Mr Knightley.

'Are you lost? Can I help?' Gemma was jolted from her literary reverie by an elderly woman with a red canvas shopping trolley. She was mildly stooped, wearing a cardigan over a floral polyester dress paired with tan tights and brown lace-up shoes. Her hair was set in a perfect white halo, like a gossamer motorbike helmet.

'I'm sorry, no. I'm not lost,' blustered Gemma. 'I'm staying here for a few days, but I need to get some food and I don't have a car. Is there a shop nearby?'

The woman ignored Gemma's question, her beady eyes taking in the damp hair and the crumpled clothes. 'I'm Margaret. Don't stand too close, we're all supposed to be social distancing. Are you a friend of Caroline's? Or a relative? You don't look like a relative, she's much darker than you. Her mother was very dark, of course, but her father was Irish, I think. It's a lovely house, shame to see it empty. I've told Caroline to sell it, it needs a family. But she won't listen. Just like her mother. Are you staying long? I hope you haven't brought the virus.'

Gemma didn't know what to say. She just wanted some coffee and the component parts of a bacon sandwich. Why was this woman still talking? It was all too confusing, and she suddenly felt like lying down in the road and waiting for crows to claim her broken body.

The fatigue must have shown on Gemma's face, as Margaret decided to take pity on her, at least for now. 'There's a shop, ten-minute walk down there, other end of the village. In the lane by the church. Closes at one on Mondays.' Margaret gave Gemma a final top-to-toe sweep that she felt in the marrow of her bones, then shuffled off with her trolley towards a clutch of modern bungalows a little further along the road.

Gemma picked out the crenellations of the Norman church tower in the distance, and started to walk. She stopped, remembering that Mabel still hadn't been returned by Dognapper Matthew, so she unearthed a notebook and pencil from her handbag, scribbled GONE TO SHOP and tore out the page. She propped it in the window of the porch and set off again, then popped back for a couple of shopping bags and her sunglasses. Anything that might help her get this job done without drawing attention to herself was worth a few moments of her time. Clearly this village was full of quite intense people; staying under the radar was definitely the way forward.

She'd been too busy trying not to puke in the taxi to look at the village as they passed through the previous night, but now she could see that it was gorgeous. West Cottage was now at the far edge of the village, but when it was built it would have stood alone, separated by quarter of a mile or so of fields or woodland. At various points in the twentieth century the gap had been filled, mostly between the sixties and eighties, judging by the style of the houses. But all the modern homes and gardens were neat and well-kept, broken up by occasional stone farmhouses and old cottages like Caro's. Gemma thought how much Aunt Laura would have loved the tulip-filled gardens and the narrow stone pavements worn smooth over hundreds of years; she was fascinated by local history and would have wanted to know everything about the people who had built and lived in these homes. Gemma walked past a modern primary school with bright red railings, and

25

a café that was closed on Mondays; there were only a handful of people around, pushing babies in prams or unloading shopping from cars. All the schools had closed last Friday, so right now the local kids would be demanding attention from their harried parents, some of whom were probably wondering how long this madness would drag on for.

Gemma passed an ancient, half-timbered pub called the Black Crow, which was in darkness with its red velvet curtains drawn, and spotted the turning for the church. Just as Margaret had promised, it was on the same lane as a hand-painted hanging sign for the Crowthorpe Village Shop. Her instinctive reaction was the same as the taxi driver the night before, to hurry towards it like it might disappear at any moment, but she forced herself to slow down and breathe. This part of the village had barely altered in hundreds of years, and Gemma's unexpected arrival wasn't going to change anything.

CHAPTER FOUR

To Do

- Make contact with civilisation
- Buy all the food
- Find dog

The Crowthorpe Village Shop had found a home in a converted classroom of the old Victorian school, the rest of which was now used as a village hall. It sat on the opposite side of a dusty lane from St Michael's Church, next to the gates of an imposing rectory with two immaculate rows of sash windows. A wooden noticeboard attached to the church lychgate informed her that parts of the church were thirteenth century, but it was substantially restored in the mid-eighteenth century, which was also when the rectory was built. *Another building that wouldn't look out of place in a Jane Austen novel*, thought Gemma. *No wonder so many of the men wanted to be vicars.*

Glancing at the rest of the village notices, there was plenty going on but nothing to get the pulse racing – dates and times for toddler playgroup, Youth Club, something called Autumn Club, organised walks around the village and an upcoming spring plant sale in the village hall. It was unlikely any of this would go ahead under the current circumstances, leaving the village more listless and dull than ever.

The shop entrance was reached via a short flight of stone steps, to which a ramp for pushchairs and wheelchairs had been added.

Attached to the wall at the top of the ramp was a chunky metal ring above a metal bowl of water; for leaving your dog outside, Gemma presumed. The idea that you'd tie your dog up outside a shop in 2020 seemed entirely bizarre to Gemma – if she did that in London, Mabel would be a working girl in a suburban puppy farm by sundown.

She perched on the sunny wall halfway up the ramp and swiped her phone into life. The tiny 4G icon shone like a beacon of hope, so Gemma quickly clicked on her emails before it went away. She deleted half a dozen spam and marketing emails, then scanned the work emails for anything drop-dead urgent. Finding nothing that couldn't wait a few minutes, she skipped to WhatsApp to message her mother to say she was visiting friends in the countryside for a few days and would call her in a day or two. Same for Joe – *I'm at Caro's cottage, I'm absolutely fine, house has no signal but I'll try to call you later.* To Caro she sent a heartfelt thank you, along with reassurance that the cottage was still standing and she had briefly met Matthew. She decided not to mention his intruder and dognapper status; it sounded overly dramatic and would be a good story to tell over a bottle of wine when she got back home. To her sister she sent a laughing emoji in response to the cat video, then added *PS Fraser is a cheating fuckhead, I've left him. In countryside with crap signal, will call you soon Gx.*

Life admin complete, Gemma switched back to her work emails. A few commissions for articles, including some bullshit from a fancy food website about top ten middle-class essentials to stockpile, which made her skin itch but she couldn't afford to turn it down. Likewise 'Can you write a beginner's guide to Zoom etiquette?' from another editor, and something about must-have items for a budget work-from-home wardrobe. She replied and said a weary yes to everything, then dug the notebook and pencil out of her bag to jot down the brief and deadline for each piece. She then dropped an email to each of her editors letting them know about her phone/IT situation; everyone was trying to set up home offices at the moment, so this wouldn't surprise or bother them. The 4G signal in this part of the village was good, so if necessary she could walk here twice a day to send and receive emails or do a quick video conference in the shelter of the lychgate. It still had the original coffin rest, which would make a nice desk.

Gemma briefly checked in on the news and was immediately overwhelmed by the sheer number of pandemic-related articles and the scope of the global drama. She downloaded some headline stuff from the *Guardian* app so she could read it offline later, but couldn't face it right now. Her family were all safe and well – Mum and Dad in Norwich, her sister and her family on a military base in Cyprus. There was talk of a lockdown coming to the UK like they already had in Italy, France and Spain, but no sign of when that might happen. They wouldn't do it without notice, and chances were she'd be back in London by the weekend.

Fifteen minutes later Gemma had a wicker basket of essentials propped on the counter of the shop, and another in her hand as she did a second lap. It was surprisingly well stocked for such a tiny space, particularly at a time when lots of shops seemed to be experiencing panic buying and shortages. There were wooden trays of fresh bread from a local Wiltshire bakery, and judging by the warm, wheaty smell it had been delivered this morning. Meat came from a butcher in Bath; jams and cakes were made locally, and they even stocked jars of Bernard's Bees honey from the hives of a man in the village, who it was reasonable to assume was called Bernard. The shop also had a decent selection of tins and household goods, including some lovely handmade scented candles in glass jars that smelled a lot like the Jo Malone ones she'd very occasionally blow £48 on, but priced at £8.50. She bought two for the cottage, they'd help to get rid of the cheesy smell.

Gemma couldn't help but be impressed – she'd seen much poorer selections in some of her favourite delis, and this was all a fraction of the price. Apparently adding the word 'artisanal' was licence to multiply the price threefold, but they didn't bother with that here, it was just local food. In no time she'd gathered a selection of essentials to keep her going for a few days, including bacon, ketchup and bread for the sandwich she'd been dreaming about since she woke up, and some chicken, rice and fresh vegetables for a stir fry later. She added a pack of ginger biscuits, a small bag of dog kibble and a couple of bottles of wine, then lugged the second basket on to the counter next to the first.

For the duration of her shop, Gemma's every move had been tracked by the woman behind the counter. She was probably only late forties but had adopted a permanently sour expression that made her look much older, not helped by the shapeless beige cardigan and aggressively blunt bob. Gemma mentally cancelled her earlier idea about getting a haircut locally and decided to wait until she was back at her usual salon. Other than the barest hint of a dead-eyed smile when Gemma entered the shop, the woman had observed her with an expression of suspicion and dislike. Despite Gemma's best efforts, eye contact couldn't be avoided any longer.

'I think that's everything.' Gemma grinned triumphantly in the hope of breaking the tension.

'I should think it is. We'll have nothing left for anyone else.' The woman's beady eyes swept disapprovingly over Gemma's two baskets. Her glare rested on the dog biscuits, as if Mabel was personally responsible for food shortages and world hunger.

Gemma swallowed a whole list of snarky responses, mostly about being a paying customer in a rural shop that was probably surviving on a financial knife edge. Instead she maintained a slightly manic smile until the woman started tapping the prices of each item into the ancient till and placing them into the shopping bags, huffing and sighing like Gemma was a huge aggravation in her life right now.

Up until this point it had never occurred to Gemma that they might not take debit cards, so it was a relief to spot the machine tucked in a corner behind the cake stand, which offered homemade coffee and walnut sponge with an inch of butter icing for £1.50 a slice. It was Gemma's favourite so she asked for two slices, and the woman slid them into a white paper bag with a floral-handled cake slice. She almost cracked a smile, which made Gemma suspect that she might have baked it herself.

Gemma put her card back in her pocket and reached for the bags, but apparently she wasn't off the hook yet. 'Staying long,' enquired the woman, dispensing with the upward inflection so it sounded like a statement rather than a question. 'You look like you're settling in for a bit.'

'Just a few days,' muttered Gemma. 'Staying at a friend's house, just for a short break.'

The woman raised her eyebrows in interest. 'Here in the village. Which friend's house might that be.' It was unsettlingly monotone, like a five-year-old delivering their lines in the school nativity. The woman held her gaze, her eyes unblinking.

Gemma felt cornered, like any minute she'd be led into a dark room and this woman would shine a light into her eyes. Margaret with the helmet hair would probably be in charge of thumbscrews and sleep deprivation. She weighed up her options and decided to take the journalistic approach – get the story out, then manage it on her terms.

She took a deep breath. 'OK. I'm Gemma Lockwood. I'm a friend of Caroline Merrick's, and I'll be staying at West Cottage for the next few days. I'm a journalist from London and I'm here with my dog Mabel, although I'm not sure where she is right now. Thanks for your help.' Before the woman could react beyond raised eyebrows and a slightly open mouth, Gemma pushed her sunglasses from her head to her nose, grabbed her bags and spun on her heel. She was more than a match for this village.

Gemma found Matthew perched on the same wall outside the shop that she'd used to check her emails earlier, with Mabel lapping furiously at the dog bowl by the door. Realising her owner hadn't abandoned her for good, Mabel bounced around in a canine frenzy, almost garrotting herself until Gemma managed to put her shopping down and untangle Mabel's lead from the metal ring. Gemma mumbled an embarrassed hello to Matthew, blushing at the memory of the state she'd been in when he'd found her earlier. She tore a hole in the bag of kibble and sprinkled a few handfuls on the grass, watching Mabel go at it like a dog whose breakfast should have been hours ago.

When Mabel had finished eating and calmed down a bit, Gemma turned to reclaim her shopping, only to find Matthew waiting at the bottom of the steps with a bag in each hand. He gave an awkward smile and turned to walk back down the lane towards the main road. Gemma was baffled and annoyed; she'd asked Caro for a place to stay, not a manservant. 'Wait, why are you being so nice to me? You've walked my dog, now you're carrying my shopping. You don't even know me.'

Matthew stopped and turned around. 'You're a friend of Caroline's, and she's a very old friend of mine. Also, you only have two hands, so . . .' He gave a casual shrug and strolled on.

Gemma trotted down the steps to catch up. 'OK, so why haven't you asked me why I'm here? I've met two people in this village so far apart from you, and they've both demanded my life story. Are you not interested, or has Caro already told you?'

Matthew stopped suddenly and looked Gemma squarely in the eyes, his face full of fierce intent. 'Do not, under any circumstances, tell ANYONE in this village your name, why you're here, or anything about yourself. They thrive on gossip, and you'll keep them fed for days. Ruth in the shop is the worst, but they're all vultures.'

Gemma opened her mouth, then closed it again. She was dumbstruck and horrified, until Matthew's face crumpled into a smile. 'I'm kidding. People here are lovely, and they'll make you welcome as long as you're happy to make small talk about the weather, or gardening. You'll be fine.'

Gemma laughed with relief, unable to decide if maybe Matthew was OK, or possibly a total arse. She fell into step beside him as they made their way through the village, Mabel trotting at her heels. The footpath was only wide enough for one, so Matthew walked in the road. There were no parked cars on this side, although they lined the pavement opposite.

'You didn't answer my question,' said Gemma, casually. 'About whether Caro had told you why I was here.'

'I messaged her after I found you in her house, to check you weren't a very convincing squatter. She said you were her best friend, and,' he made air quotes despite having a shopping bag in each hand, ' "fleeing a cheating shit".'

Gemma forced a smile despite a sudden wave of nausea. 'I'm hiding here for a few days, but I'll be gone by the end of the week. Thanks for walking Mabel, I wasn't at my best this morning.'

'Ah, the yellow dog has a name! I've been calling her yellow dog, which she didn't seem to mind. She's very well behaved.' He gave Mabel a smile, and the dog swooned at him adoringly, her foamy pink tongue lolling out of the side of her mouth. *Another one cheating on me*, thought Gemma, uncharitably.

She couldn't tell Matthew why Mabel was so well trained, because then she'd have to tell him about Aunt Laura, and it was still too painful to say her name out loud. It had been three years since Aunt Laura had moved into a specialist care home and Gemma had taken custody of her dog, and only four months since Aunt Laura had died. The pain flared like a hot poker in Gemma's chest, but she was learning to manage it, to not let it overwhelm her when other people were around.

'She's a very good dog unless you have snacks. Then she's a maniac.'

Matthew looked at Mabel suspiciously. 'This is why I'm not a dog person. They steal your heart, then steal your food.'

Gemma laughed, trying to conceal her horror at him not being a dog person. He might as well have said he collected toy clowns or read the *Daily Express*. Probably both of these things were true. She decided to change the subject. 'So I have a question for you. Tell me what you do, why you live here, and how you know Caro.'

'That's three questions, but OK. My main business is making furniture, and I also do odd jobs for people around the village. I live here because it's my home, my family have always lived here – my parents live about a mile that way.' He wafted a shopping bag vaguely in the direction they'd just come. 'I met Caroline after her parents moved here. I've done a lot of work on West Cottage over the years. Caroline and I used to go drinking sometimes during her uni holidays. I don't see her much now, but she's a good friend. I miss her, and her parents.' Matthew's cheeks coloured and his voice faded away; Gemma suspected he hadn't talked much about loss and grief either.

Gemma processed all this new and interesting information. Caro often told stories of people in her parents' village, but Gemma couldn't remember if she'd ever mentioned Matthew specifically. He absolutely wasn't her type. Ever since Gemma had known her, Caro had liked her men sleek and polished; her uni boyfriends had been a parade of immaculate, exotic boys with tiny waists and razor-sharp cheekbones. Nothing had changed since they graduated; Gemma and Joe secretly called Caro's husband, Antonio, 'Dressage Tony' because he was always so well turned out. So if Matthew had been her bit of rough at home, she'd kept it VERY quiet.

The journalist in Gemma had a hundred follow-up questions, but they were back at the gate of West Cottage so they'd have to wait. She asked Matthew to hang on for a second, then shovelled Mabel up the steps, into the porch and through the front door, making a meal of getting the key into the lock. *I bet he's laughing at me*, she thought as she waggled the key furiously; *I bet nobody here even locks their door.* She pulled it shut behind her and returned to the gate. Matthew was leaning on it, looking amused.

'Thanks for your help. I'm sorry you had to come so far out of your way.'

Matthew looked confused. 'What do you mean?'

'You said your family lived a mile that way. Now you have to hike back.'

Matthew laughed. 'I said my parents lived a mile that way. I live in the barn at the bottom of your garden. Shout if you need anything.' He handed over the shopping with a broad smile, sidled along the wall to the side gate, and disappeared round the back of the house.

CHAPTER FIVE

To Do

- Make world's best bacon sandwich
- File crappy stockpile article
- Domestic goddess shit
- Investigate WiFi stealing options
- Reward self with excellent dinner and wine

By 8 p.m., Gemma was glowing from a productive afternoon. She'd mastered the hob and made an outstanding bacon sandwich, then filed one article and drafted another. Then she'd put her hair up into a messy bun and found a hoover and a box of cleaning supplies in the cupboard under the stairs. The cottage got a thorough once-over, including what felt like half a bag of cobwebs from the fireplaces and the exposed beams, as well as a wipe-down of every horizontal surface with a damp cloth and some organic cleaning spray that smelled of clementines. She'd made up the double bed in the loft with fresh linen and put a bundle of dirty clothes she'd stuffed in a bag before she left London in the washing machine. While they buffeted in the breeze on the washing line, Gemma had picked a bunch of tulips from the garden and put them in a ceramic jug on the dining table, then taken Mabel for her afternoon walk.

They'd headed out of the village in the opposite direction this time, discovering a recreation ground surrounded by blossoming cherry trees. Just inside the gate was a small gravelled area with a picnic table, water tap and a huge brick barbecue, marked with a sign saying this was a space for Crowthorpe villagers to use, and could they please take all their rubbish home. Gemma was reminded of the private community garden that backed on to Aunt Laura's house in London – the gardener lit the barbecue on a Friday evening in summer and people would wander over with food and drink to eat with their families and neighbours. Gemma felt too self-conscious to go alone, but occasionally Joe came over and they'd take some steaks and a tub of salad and a bottle of wine. He loved the grandeur of it all, swapping the tiny balcony of his flat in Camberwell for a private garden in Pimlico full of hot dads who'd just finished a few sets of tennis. Everyone assumed he and Gemma were a couple, which caused them much amusement. The first and last time Joe had been anywhere near a vagina was when he exited his mother's womb.

The picnic area bordered a half-sized football pitch and a small playground, so Gemma had walked to the far end under the trees and thrown sticks for Mabel to fetch, keeping her well away from the harried mothers pushing their children on the swings. Mabel was harmless, but if a child showed her any attention she had a tendency towards slobbery kisses, which weren't everyone's cup of tea, particularly at the moment.

Now Mabel was dozing in her bed, the table lamps were on, the curtains were closed and the scented candles Gemma had bought at the shop were filling the lounge and kitchen with a fresh, citrussy scent. The cottage was chilly after a day expelling stale air through open windows, but Gemma didn't dare light the wood burner in case the chimney needed cleaning and she set fire to everything. She grabbed an old jumper and put on an extra pair of socks.

Despite her history of personal relationships being all kinds of messy, Gemma could win medals for cleanliness and domesticity. A military childhood meant her family moved house every couple of years, and the married quarters were never up to her mother's exacting standards. Before a single box was unpacked Gemma and her sister were handed a pair of yellow rubber gloves each and put to work scrubbing and dusting, and two or three years later the process would be repeated in reverse as they marched out to head for somewhere new. Pocket money was earned by completing weekly chores – her bedroom had to be kept clean and tidy at all times, and dishes washed, dried and put away after every meal. When her father cleaned the car, he called his daughters out to hose down their bicycles so dust and salt and grit from the roads didn't damage the paintwork. Gemma didn't remember resenting it; it was just part of her life growing up, and when she visited friends' houses the messiness and dubious hygiene made her skin itch. Once a school friend had dropped a slice of buttered toast face down on the kitchen floor and it had come up covered in cat hair, but she ate it anyway; it made Gemma heave just thinking about it. So last night's dumping of stuff and getting drunk in a heap was very out of character, but it had been a challenging day.

By the time Gemma was thirteen, the number of schools she and Louise had attended was reaching double figures. So when her parents were posted overseas again the decision was taken to send Gemma and her sister to a girls' boarding school in Norfolk. Louise was two years younger and settled in happily, but Gemma hated the draughty dormitories, militant house mistresses and oppressive rules. It was no place for a dreamy loner with a wandering imagination; after a year Gemma became so miserable that she switched to weekly boarding and spent the weekends and half-terms with their mother's sister, Laura, in her house nearby, only returning to her parents abroad during the school holidays.

Aunt Laura's second husband, Clive, had died of throat cancer when Gemma was eleven; he was twenty years older than his wife and they had never had children of their own. Aunt Laura had worked as an actress in the seventies and eighties and had been a patron of a theatre in Norwich for a number of years, but settled into semi-retirement after Clive died despite only being in her early forties. She was delighted to welcome her teenage niece at weekends, and took particular pleasure in introducing her to all her bohemian theatre and artist friends, much to the disapproval of Gemma's mother, who was too far away to do a single thing about it.

After relaxing the cleanliness standards a little at university (although her friends and housemates still called her Mary Poppins), the move to Aunt Laura's second home in Pimlico got her back in the domestic groove. She didn't pay rent, but she was required to cover the bills and keep it clean and well maintained. Aunt Laura wasn't as exacting as Gemma's mother, but it felt only right and natural that she should look after somewhere so lovely. There weren't many twenty-one-year-olds lucky enough to live rent-free in a mews house in London, so she seized the opportunity and taught herself to cook, do basic DIY and maintain the pots and window boxes to a standard Aunt Laura found acceptable, which mostly involved not letting them die.

The first six years in Warwick Mews had been a happy time for Gemma, while she built up her reputation as a freelance journalist and supplemented her paltry income by working as a copywriter for Caro's ad agency, writing adverts for organic baby food, retirement homes and breakfast cereals. She established a reliable circle of friends and entertained the occasional boyfriend, including Johannes, who played the French horn for a second-rate orchestra and had lasted two whole years without them ever contemplating living together. Aunt Laura would often come to stay in London for the weekend to do some shopping, and take the opportunity to treat Gemma to dinner, a trip to the theatre or a spa treatment. Gemma had adored her, which made the loss so much harder to bear.

It was Gemma who first noticed how confused and forgetful Aunt Laura had become, but after months of her aunt dismissing it as nothing more than the menopause, Gemma felt she had no choice but to mention it to her mother during their weekly phone call. The family machine kicked into gear in its usual military fashion, and in a matter of weeks Aunt Laura had a diagnosis of early-onset Alzheimer's. She had just turned fifty-six, but her decline was rapid; within a couple of years she had sold the Norfolk house to cover the cost of living in a specialist private care home, and her four-year-old dog Mabel was relocated to live with Gemma in London.

It surprised none of Gemma's family to learn that the Norfolk house had been mortgaged to the hilt and the money from Clive's estate was long gone; Aunt Laura's spendthrift habits were legendary. Just over two years later Warwick Mews had to be sold too; at that point Gemma had only been dating Fraser for six months, and yet it had seemed natural that they would move in together. But within two months her aunt was gone, her relationship was heading south and everything Gemma cared about felt like it was slipping away. The only upside was moving south of the river, which meant she was much closer to Joe and Caro – Fraser's flat in Bermondsey was a twenty-minute walk from Joe's place in Camberwell, and even closer to Caro's near Borough Market. The two of them had kept her going for the past six months, long after Fraser had checked out of their relationship and presumably into the Mystery Brunette.

Aside from a few personal items, the bulk of Aunt Laura's diminished estate was left to the theatre in Norwich which had enjoyed her patronage for over twenty years, provided they name it after her. Gemma had been delighted by the self-indulgent grandiosity of this; it was SO Aunt Laura. But Gemma's mother was less impressed; she took it as a personal affront that Gemma hadn't been 'looked after', even though Gemma hadn't cared a jot – she'd had nearly two decades of Aunt Laura's unwavering love and generosity, there was nothing else she needed.

As Gemma picked through the memories of Aunt Laura's home in Norfolk, she was reminded of a painting she had done on one of the first weekends she'd stayed there. She must have been fourteen. Aunt Laura liked the idea of expressing herself in retirement through the medium of oil and canvas and turned the garage into a peaceful, airy studio. Sadly, she had no talent for it whatsoever, and Gemma had never seen a finished painting emerge. But Aunt Laura didn't mind Gemma messing around with the paints provided she left everything as she found it, so one day Gemma spent a couple of hours carefully copying an outline of the house from a photograph and writing 'you feel like home' across the bottom in elaborate cursive. She signed it self-consciously and left it on Aunt Laura's bed before she returned to boarding school, then immediately forgot about it for fifteen years until she saw it mounted in a frame on a chest of drawers in Aunt Laura's care home. It sat alongside a selection of childhood photographs in silver frames; laughing black-and-white shots of Laura and her sister with their parents that Gemma had never seen before.

Gemma had been visiting Fraser's family near Glasgow when Aunt Laura died, and by the time she had made it back to Norfolk a couple of days later, Aunt Laura's room at the care home had been stripped of her clothes and personal effects and prepared for the next resident. Gemma presumed her drawing had been thrown away with anything else that hadn't been claimed by the executors or the family.

She was still furious at her mother for not saving more of Aunt Laura's stuff for her, although sometimes it felt like she'd been furious at Barbara Lockwood for thirty years. Gemma had once written a poem that started 'I see the world in colour, but for her it's black and white,' then thrown it away before she died of embarrassment. But the sentiment was true – Gemma and her mother had never been close the way mothers and daughters are supposed to be. Growing up, Barbara had seemed to find her daughter's daydreaming and wandering imagination suspicious, telling Gemma she needed to keep her feet on the ground. In turn, Gemma found her mother cold and unfeeling, and had pointed out more than once that it was hard to keep your feet on the ground when you never stopped moving house.

She hadn't been able to bring herself to confront her mother over the missing picture, and things had been even more strained than usual between them during a brief trip home at Christmas. If Louise hadn't been back from Cyprus, Gemma probably wouldn't have gone at all.

As Gemma stood back to look at the magic wand she had waved over West Cottage, she thought about how both her mother and Aunt Laura would have approved – despite their chalk and cheese personalities, they aligned on the importance of order and cleanliness. By 8.30 p.m. she was starving again, so she headed into the kitchen to make a stir fry with the ingredients she'd picked up in the shop earlier. Twenty minutes later she poured herself a glass of wine and happily ate her dinner leaning against the kitchen counter, Mabel lying hopefully at her feet. She had a clean house, food, wine and a happy dog. Life could definitely be worse.

The gentle knock on the kitchen door made her jump, and it took her a moment to realise that Matthew's face was pressed against the small pane of glass. He pointed and gestured at one of the drawers until she found the key, then stepped into the kitchen with a blast of cool air. His brow was furrowed with concern.

'I just came to check you were all right. I thought you might be in a bit of a stress.'

Gemma immediately bridled. 'Why wouldn't I be all right? I'm not a child, I've lived alone for years.'

Matthew paused, momentarily taken aback. 'You have seen the news, right?'

The blank look on Gemma's face told him she had not. 'I've got no WiFi and no phone signal. There's no TV. I've seen nothing. What's happened?' She put her bowl in the sink, her heart beginning to race. *Fuck, fuck, fuck.*

'Gemma, we're in lockdown for three weeks, starting now. We can't leave our homes, other than for a few specific things. If you want to get back to London, you need to leave now.'

Ten minutes later, Gemma was up to date on the news and heavily into her second glass of wine. Matthew refused her offer, presumably in case he needed to drive her somewhere. The government had announced a 'Stay at Home' policy for three weeks, which meant only essential travel was allowed.

There was no suggestion that Gemma couldn't travel back to London tonight or tomorrow morning. But of course, the big question was . . . where would she go? She didn't have a home in London any more, and none of the letting agencies would be open for viewings. All her friends had tiny flats or a houseful of kids; she definitely didn't want to sleep on a lumpy sofa at Joe's for three weeks, nor did she want to share a bathroom with Dressage Tony. Going back to her parents in Norfolk was out of the question, and her sister Louise was in Cyprus with her husband Jamie and their two kids. And obviously she wasn't going back to Fraser under any circumstances.

Whichever way she looked at it, the least worst option was to stay in West Cottage for the next three weeks. The thought was initially horrifying; she didn't want to be trapped in a village of strangers right now, and the world felt too scary to be so far away from everyone she loved. But halfway down wine glass number three she realised that she really didn't have any choice, and she was no stranger to living alone in someone else's house.

Matthew had remained silent as Gemma had prowled around the kitchen, occasionally muttering 'fuck' and topping up her wine glass. Eventually she remembered he was there and brought him up to speed on her plan to stay for the time being. He nodded, clearly relieved that he wasn't going to have to do a mercy dash to the train station. Before he left, he scribbled 'MPBarn7500Q' on the kitchen chalkboard. 'It's the code for my WiFi, help yourself. If you use your phone or laptop at the back of the house or in the garden you should be able to pick it up. Caroline has used it before; there's a booster plug in the drawer.' He smiled thinly and closed the door quietly behind him.

Gemma took a deep breath, the silence of the house settling around her. She felt oddly disconnected from everything, like it was all a bad movie. With immediate effect, schools were closed, non-essential shops were closed, bars and restaurants were closed, even children's playgrounds. She thought about the mums and kids in the park earlier; they couldn't possibly have known that they were playing on the swings for the last time in weeks. The café in the village that didn't open on Mondays wouldn't open on Tuesday either. How strange that must feel to whoever owned it; they probably had a fridge full of cakes and sandwiches ready to go for tomorrow.

Gemma quelled the bubbles of anxiety – she was safe, she was healthy, and everything else was well beyond her control right now. People had been talking about lockdown happening for weeks – the spread of the virus in other countries had shown the UK what the future held, and the general consensus was that the UK had dragged their feet, hoping vague directions about social distancing and hand washing would suffice. But Gemma hadn't expected the lockdown to come into force without any notice; she thought she'd have time to get her head round the idea, talk to her family, make decisions.

But what difference would that have made? A couple of days' notice didn't change her circumstances, and she still had nowhere else to go. Right now, staying put made the most sense.

It was only three weeks; it would be fine.

CHAPTER SIX

Thursday, 26 March

To Do

- More domestic goddess shit
- Clapping thing 8 p.m.

In the three days since the lockdown was announced, and in the absence of any stimulus or excitement whatsoever, Gemma had settled into the daily routine of an Edwardian housemaid. The weather had been mostly mild and dry, so she'd committed to getting up early, putting on her oldest, most sacrificial clothes, wrapping her hair in a headscarf and spending the morning deep cleaning at least one room every day. She'd started on Tuesday with the loft bedroom and the en-suite, and yesterday had tackled the first-floor bathroom, expelling the final vestiges of ripe cheese in favour of citrus and pine and beeswax. Today was all about the first-floor bedrooms, and (barring unexpected excitement or an uncontrollable need to spend the day on the sofa with a good book and a tube of Pringles), she was hopeful of getting both done since they were entirely empty. The Henry vacuum cleaner that Gemma had found under the stairs wasn't really up to the job, but it was better than nothing and, thanks to a bumper box of spare bags she'd found in the same cupboard, she was gradually waging war on years of accumulated dust and dead insects. Henry's smiling red face was the closest thing she had to company right now; she felt like a domestic servant version of Tom Hanks in *Castaway*.

By lunchtime Gemma had transformed both rooms, sucking away a thick layer of grey dust to reveal the wheat-coloured woven carpets beneath. She wiped the skirting boards and the window frames, vacuumed dead flies out of the casements, and ran the crevice tool along the edge of the carpet to remove hundreds of dead woodlice that rattled up the vacuum cleaner tube like plastic beads. The fireplaces were wiped down and de-spidered, and the light fittings bashed with a feather duster to dislodge a cloud of dust and dead moths that brought on a sneezing fit. She planned to tackle the windows another day, so left the murky glass panes and, instead, braved the built-in wardrobe to see whether it was home to dead mice, as she'd discovered in the cupboards built into the eaves upstairs, or just more woodlice. Her years living in foreign countries had made her hardy to crawly things – their house in Cyprus had been riddled with cockroaches. Gemma was less keen on flying bugs – she'd rather deal with a fat spider than a daddy-long-legs any day.

The cleaning was tiring work, and by lunchtime Gemma's muscles ached and her hands were raw from abrasive cleaning products and anti-bacterial soap. The government advised that everyone wash their hands more often, so Gemma made sure she scrubbed them before and after leaving the house for her one period of government-mandated exercise, which was an extended midday walk with Mabel. She'd started to explore more of the countryside around the village, heading in a different direction each day and following public footpath signs across fields and through woodlands, discovering tiny clusters of pretty houses and remote farms. On a sunny day it was hard to beat England in spring, but the West Country felt very different to the walks she'd done with Aunt Laura in Norfolk. The landscape here was more fertile and undulating, the hedgerows more abundant, the trees bigger and more magnificent. When Gemma was a teenager Aunt Laura used to point out every hedgerow tree and wildflower they passed on their country walks, testing Gemma to see if she could recall the names. Eighteen years on she still remembered them – blackthorn, hazel, elder, beech, stitchwort, rose campion, forget-me-not.

Today Gemma ended her walk by the 4G refuge of the church-yard, in the hope of getting hold of Louise – she had been itching to talk to her sister all week, but Louise had just been assigned to a task force that was implementing lockdown rules on the military bases in Cyprus. All they'd managed was a few WhatsApp messages, so it took her by surprise when Louise actually answered the phone.

'I have exactly ninety seconds before my next meeting. Tell me something fun.'

Gemma laughed. 'Sorry, sis. I'm in a village in the arse end of nowhere and the world's gone mad. No fun to be had.'

'But you're OK, right?' Gemma could hear the concern in Louise's voice, and it made her heart hurt.

'I'm fine, I promise.'

'Not pining for the cheating fuckhead?'

'Definitely not. I have Mabel and we're safe. How are you?'

'I'm fine, but I have to go and do my duty or some other bollocks. I'll call you at the weekend. Text me a joke.'

Gemma smiled. She and Louise had been texting each other terrible dad jokes since they were kids and got their first mobile phones.

'I will. Love you.'

'Love you too, Gummer.' Louise had called Gemma this when she was little, unable to get her toddler mouth around the soft 'g'. Even though they were 2,000 miles apart, some things never changed.

Gemma hung up, then sat and thought for a couple of minutes before opening up WhatsApp and starting a new message to her sister.

How do you stop your car from driving into a pig?

There was a short pause, before '*Don't know*' and a laughing emoji

46

appeared on the screen. Gemma typed in '*USE THE HAM-BRAKE*' before heading home with a new spring in her step.

Gemma spent the remainder of the afternoon catching up on emails and pitching for work, and by 7 p.m. she was done in. She heated up the remains of last night's pesto pasta and curled up on the sofa, Mabel on her feet, with a glass of wine and the day's news highlights on her phone. Everything read like a dystopian movie; they were starting to set up Covid-19 hospitals, converting the Excel Exhibition Centre in London into a specialist unit with the potential for thousands of ventilated beds. There were nearly half a million cases worldwide now, with all eyes on the USA, which already had a thousand deaths and rising. President Trump was determined that everything would be open again by Easter, but anyone with half a brain could see that wasn't going to happen. Gemma felt detached from everything and frustrated that she couldn't help – part of her longed to be in London, supporting her friends and volunteering to help. But then she reminded herself of the realities – nowhere to live, how worried her parents would be, the increased risk of her getting ill, or, perhaps more terrifying, being asymptomatic and spreading it to others unknowingly. It made far more sense for her to be here, at least for the time being.

She turned off her phone and breathed deeply, taking in the nooks and crannies of the lounge, her task for tomorrow. Aside from feeling calmer and more in control in a clean house, Gemma's efforts were mostly about showing her appreciation to Caro for letting her stay. She had called her on Monday night after the lockdown announcement, and Caro had been entirely laid-back about Gemma living in West Cottage for as long as she liked. She didn't want rent, but they agreed Gemma would cover the bills and put some time and TLC into the cottage and the garden while she was there. It seemed like the least she could do, and time was something Gemma had plenty of right now, because work was already drying up. Many of her usual newspaper and magazine commissions were being picked up by staffers or not written at all, as advertising revenues plummeted and the media tightened its belt along with everyone else. Caro's ad agency was struggling too – half the staff were being furloughed on the government's Job Retention Scheme and it could be months before any copywriting work came Gemma's way.

Like millions of others, she'd been nervous and worried about her finances all week, but earlier today the Chancellor had announced a government grant for self-employed people and she'd been able to relax again. The money wouldn't be paid out until May, but in the meantime she had some cash saved from her years living rent-free. She'd planned to use it towards a deposit on a flat at some point, but if necessary it could keep her head above water for six months or more as long as her next place in London cost no more than she paid for her share of the mortgage at Fraser's. Her savings were miles off what she would need for a deposit in London anyway; somehow she'd imagined she'd be settled by thirty-two and pooling her resources with someone else. There'd been a brief moment when she thought that someone else might be Fraser; they'd buy somewhere a little bigger, with a decent garden for Mabel, maybe further out in Beckenham or Sydenham or one of those other Zone 4 hams that were self-contained villages that had been subsumed into London's urban sprawl. The future currently looked a little blurry on the relationship front, but that was the least of her worries right now.

Gemma had heard nothing from Fraser since the initial flurry of messages on the night she'd left, and she didn't expect that to change. She'd blocked his number so he couldn't call or message, but he could have emailed if he'd wanted to. Gemma assumed he'd dusted himself down, as was Fraser's way; he prided himself on his resilience and his ability to bounce back from life's challenges, more energised and focussed than ever. By now he'd probably written a LinkedIn post that compared the stagnant property market to a failed relationship – a chance to regroup and re-evaluate, to plan for the future and learn from past mistakes, to re-think strategic imperatives. Gemma tried to feel some sympathy that Fraser would be entirely out of work right now, since non–essential building projects had completely stalled. But then she reminded herself that he would qualify for the same self-employed support as she would, and also he was a cheating shit who didn't deserve nice things.

At some point she would need to go to his place and pick up her remaining belongings; no doubt they'd be all boxed up neatly for a clean, unemotional handover. The only possessions she truly cared about were the few bits of jewellery Aunt Laura had left her, and these were safely at her parents' house. If she found out that Fraser had thrown everything else she owned in a skip then so be it; there wasn't much she could do about it right now anyway. The only thing she really missed about Fraser was the sex; he was surprisingly animated in the bedroom for a man who ironed his boxer shorts, even if it did sometimes feel like he was waiting for a standing ovation at the end.

She also hadn't seen much of Matthew since their awkward encounter on Monday, other than surreptitiously watching him carry lengths of timber from his van into the barn while she was putting yet another full-to-bursting paper hoover bag in the bin. Even at a distance of 15 metres she could see the hard muscles of his back and arms as he lifted chunks of wood on to his shoulder like they were made of foam. There was a military efficiency about his movements that made Gemma think of her father, and other aspects to Matthew's appearance that didn't make her think of her father at all. Gemma had a word with herself over it – getting a rebound crush on your country-boy neighbour was an embarrassing cliché prompted by nothing but boredom and too many romantic novels.

She idly wondered if she might see him this evening, at the first Clap for Carers. It had been happening in other countries for a couple of weeks, and now someone in the UK had started a movement which invited everyone to stand on their doorsteps at 8 p.m. on a Thursday to give a UK-wide round of applause for NHS staff who were on the front line of the fight against coronavirus. Gemma was intrigued to see whether Crowthorpe would get involved; there was something rather un–British about a spontaneous public show of enthusiasm, so she wouldn't be surprised if nobody here bothered. Still, it would be a good opportunity to get a sneak peek at her neighbours and show her support for her friends, several of whom worked in hospitals or clinics. Even if she was all alone on her doorstep, she'd be clapping. Perhaps her applause would be carried on a wave of noise all the way to London.

Most nights Gemma was in bed by 9.30 p.m., and now that her short-term financial worries were resolved, she hoped she would sleep better, letting herself be swallowed by the darkness and silence of the village. Usually the birds woke her at dawn, pecking at the moss on the roof tiles above her head, presumably hunting for soft bedding to line their nests. She liked to lie in bed and listen to the day start, remembering what she'd read about mindfulness and being present in the moment. The usual routines that dominated her life had been stripped away – no alarm clock, no schedule of meetings, no buses to run for, so she had the opportunity to get off the treadmill for a few weeks and let go of all her old stresses and anxieties. The pressure of city life would return soon enough; she should enjoy the calm while it lasted.

Just before 8 p.m. Gemma put on a giant cosy jumper and stood on the tiny path between the front porch and the white gate. She was preparing herself to do this alone and trying not to feel self-conscious about it, when doors started to open up and down the road and people came out – some alone, some with partners and families. Everyone looked like they were waiting for someone to start, so as 8 p.m. ticked over Gemma began to clap. A few followed, tentatively at first, then others followed their neighbours' leads and joined in. The sound grew and multiplied like a symphony, the noise echoing off the old buildings as a few teenagers added half-hearted whoops and cheers which prompted a few dogs to start barking, so Mabel joined in. It made Gemma's heart feel full and tears prickled at the corners of her eyes; however long she ended up staying here, she knew this was a moment she would remember for a long time.

Gemma looked to her left to see Matthew standing about 20 metres along the road, between West Cottage and the driveway to the next house. He was alone, clapping enthusiastically with those big, powerful hands that Gemma suddenly wanted to get a much closer look at. She wondered why he hadn't stood by her side gate, but perhaps he wanted to avoid potential gossip about the two of them or give her a bit of space. Perhaps he'd decided she was mildly crackers after Monday and didn't want to get into conversation, which would be disappointing but entirely understandable.

As the noise died away, Gemma's neighbours smiled and waved and headed back into their houses. She stood and watched for a while, as doors closed on some and others hung about to chat. It was something she couldn't imagine happening where Fraser lived in London; in the six months she'd lived there she hadn't really spoken to any of his neighbours, other than the German woman upstairs who liked to play Brahms concertos at odd hours of the day and once met Gemma in the stairwell and asked if she minded. Gemma actually quite liked her music, as long as she played it during daylight hours. It was the only time she'd ever seen the woman in six months.

'Hey.'

Gemma jumped and turned to see Matthew leaning on the side gate. It was the first time she'd seen him up close since Monday, when she'd been hungover and mortified and didn't really take in the details beyond the straw-coloured hair and the scruffy beard. He had green eyes and nice teeth.

'Sorry. You looked miles away.'

Gemma sighed. 'I was thinking about an old neighbour who liked to play Brahms concertos over breakfast. I think maybe that's something I'll miss.'

Matthew smiled. 'That was an uplifting bit of community to-getherness. It's nice that you joined in.'

Gemma shrugged, suddenly conscious that she hadn't engaged meaningfully with a mirror since Monday morning and probably looked dreadful. She shuffled back to the door, wondering if the porch bulb was casting her in a soft, flattering glow or lighting up her pallid skin like a bad waxwork. 'Goodnight, then.' She quickly closed the door behind her and turned off the light. Matthew walked down the path to the garden, his brow furrowed and the ghost of a goodnight on his lips.

CHAPTER SEVEN

Tuesday, 31 March

To Do

- Buy more food
- Stop eating all the food

The final day of March felt like a milestone for Gemma, a mental turning of the page to something new and uncharted. April had always been her favourite month of the year, full of purpose and possibility; even living in London you could see nature pushing forward with enthusiastic vigour. Spring showers and sunshine gave the city a different feel, washing away the grime, purging the air of winter and bathing everything in an effulgent light under a huge blue sky. Warm days in April brought everyone outdoors, but the absence of wasps, instant sunburn and sticky humidity gave people the inebriating freedom to bask outside for longer, soaking up vitamin D like human sponges, getting their ankles out for the first time in months.

But spring in London was nothing compared to Crowthorpe; here it felt like Mother Nature had got absolutely wasted and gone on the rampage, stuffing every verge, hedgerow and woodland floor with a verdant chaos of cow parsley, hawthorn blossom and wild garlic. Even the nettles had a youthful freshness about them, and it all looked so impossibly, implausibly green, like everything had its own Instagram filter.

The prospect of March rolling into April made Gemma feel like the end of lockdown was tantalisingly close – at some point in the coming weeks she would be able to go home. Right now she felt like a plane in a holding pattern – floating aimlessly in ever-decreasing circles, waiting for permission to land, slowly running out of fuel. She really needed to draw a line under Fraser and get on with her life, even if that meant adapting to a different kind of London in a bonkers new world.

The new month also marked the end of the project that had been occupying most of Gemma's energy for the past week – deep-cleaning Caro's cottage. Yesterday she had tackled the windows, including leaning precariously out of the loft skylights with a wet sponge to scrub away the green mould and bird poo. Only the outside of the upstairs windows had defeated her, but she was avoiding asking Matthew if she could borrow a ladder on the basis that he'd probably insist on holding the bottom of it, which would give him an incredibly unflattering view of her bum and thighs. She couldn't decide if she was more annoyed that this bothered her, or that she hadn't made more effort to have a less spongy bum and thighs.

Even with dirty upstairs windows, the cottage had been transformed from a dusty, gloomy place that smelled of abandonment and decay, to a home that felt loved and lived in. Every room had been scrubbed and polished, and all the storage cupboards and hidden nooks and crannies relieved of mouse corpses, woodlice and dead flies. Gemma had even borrowed some Danish oil from Matthew and oiled the wooden floors – he'd offered to help, but the banging and power-tool noise coming from the barn whenever she took Mabel into the garden suggested he was pretty busy right now. Clearly the space was divided between his living area and his workshop somehow, but she'd never seen inside.

Now the house was fit for human habitation, it was time to tackle the garden. Up to now Gemma had been avoiding it, mostly because she knew absolutely nothing about gardening and really didn't know where to start. Nobody ever bothered to plant anything interesting in the gardens of military homes, because you'd never be around long enough to enjoy it. Aunt Laura's flat had some dwarf shrubs in containers and window boxes full of seasonal bulbs, but all they needed was water and the occasional prune when they started to look like triffids. The garden in Norfolk had been managed by a local gardener who visited once a week, although Aunt Laura liked to stroll around watering everything in the evening, holding a hose in one hand and a glass of Sauvignon Blanc in the other. Most of the border flowers were destined for filling the house with scent and colour; her preference was blowsy, ostentatious flowers like peonies and irises and snapdragons, with no thought for colour coordination or symmetry. Reds and pinks and oranges would all be plunged into huge jugs of water together; an approach to flower arranging that definitely was not subtle, but delightful in Gemma's eyes. She had wanted to grow some flamboyant blooms in Fraser's tiny garden this summer as a tribute to Aunt Laura, but he'd fobbed her off with 'we'll see, babe', which was code for 'not a fucking chance'.

So the garden was her priority tomorrow, which meant Gemma needed a crash course in what to do with a lawn, apple trees, rose bushes and overgrown borders. She briefly considered calling her mother, who had embraced gardening in retirement as a way to kill time and avoid Gemma's father. But she couldn't face the level of detail, the demand that she write everything down, the unspoken implication that if she'd settled down like a functioning adult instead of lounging around in Aunt Laura's fancy London house she would know all this stuff already. Gemma was actually quite proud of her achievements in her twenties – she could hang a shelf, roast a chicken, get rid of Jehovah's Witnesses and put on a superking duvet cover, all without assistance. These were all important life skills.

Gemma jumped as her phone alerted her to a WhatsApp call. Earlier today she'd taken some photos of the cottage and sent them to Caro, so she wasn't surprised to see her friend was calling her back.

'Hey, Caro. How are you?'

'Awful, everything's shit. But never mind that, I'm ringing to express my undying love for you. My house looks AMAZING.'

Gemma smiled; talking to Caro always made her feel better. 'It's all done. Just the garden tomorrow.'

'Honestly, you're a magician. Those years cleaning up mine and Joe's filth at uni were not wasted. I'm so glad you're there.'

'Me too. I'm off to the village shop in a bit, it's the high point of my day.'

'You'll be on the cover of *Country Life* soon,' Caro laughed as Gemma heard a child scream in the background.

'Do you need to get that?'

'Nah, Tony can deal with it. Only one of them is screaming, that's usually a good sign.'

'Is everything OK with you?' Gemma couldn't imagine how Caro and Tony were juggling full-time working from home with caring for their kids; it sounded like hell.

'No, it's horrendous. But I find it's easier to pretend it's not happening if I don't talk about it.' On cue, a second scream joined the first. 'Oh, for fuck's sake. I have to go. Happy gardening, and thank you for showing my house some love.' Caro blew kisses down the phone and hung up.

Gemma smiled and checked her watch; it was already 4 p.m. and she needed to get to the village shop before it closed at 5. It was only a ten-minute walk, but a week's experience had taught her to leave at least half an hour to get there. She could be waylaid by any number of villagers out taking their government-mandated exercise or tending their front gardens, and they all expected her to stop for a socially distanced chat.

She grabbed her shopping list and a couple of bags and gave Mabel a nudge with her foot. She was dozing in her favourite afternoon-sun patch in the dining room and didn't seem terribly impressed at being woken up, particularly without a food-based incentive. Mabel's exercise levels had increased significantly in the past few days – she now had a walk with Gemma first thing, and another with Matthew after lunch. Matthew had stuck his head in the kitchen door on Friday and offered to take her on his walk each day, which meant Gemma could now go early and not make

Mabel wait until lunchtime. She appreciated Matthew's offer, and Mabel didn't seem to mind either.

This walk counted as a shopping trip, so it was in addition to the four or five miles Mabel had already walked today, which was at least double the exercise she got in London. She was also able to run off the lead here, an opportunity she had enjoyed all the time in Norfolk but wasn't an everyday thing in London – it was really only an option at quiet times in the park, when Gemma could keep her away from the bushes. Once in Burgess Park Mabel had slipped her lead and disappeared into a hedge, emerging a few seconds later with a mouldy baguette and a used condom, which was both mystifying and horrific in equal measure. Thankfully the bushes here contained fewer surprises, so they could let Mabel zoom around the fields and woods chasing magpies and squirrels. More often than not she'd come back when called, especially for a dog treat.

As a result of all this exercise, most days Mabel was ready for an extended snooze by 4 p.m. and wasn't remotely interested in a walk to the shop. 'Don't be lazy, we're going,' grumbled Gemma. 'You're a country dog right now, make the most of it. You'll be back in London soon and then you'll be sorry.' Mabel glared resentfully at Gemma for a few seconds, then huffed her way on to four paws.

As expected, it was after 4.30 p.m. by the time Gemma made it to the village shop. On the way she'd acquired some wildlife wisdom from Barry a few doors down, who had a meandering way of telling stories about woodpeckers and local deer populations that would put even Chris Packham into a coma. She'd also bought half a dozen eggs from Grove Farm that she didn't have any cash to pay for, but Hilary said she'd put her name in the book and she could settle up before she went back to London. She'd exchanged idle corona chat with a woman called Cookie who lived in one of the eighties houses that fronted the main road, her name being short for something Indian that she'd given up spelling years ago, instead telling everyone 'just call me Cookie'. As far as Gemma could tell, the estate had about eighty houses, and seemed to be a mix of private ownership and council tenants. She had always imagined places like this to be full of wealthy retirees, or well-to-do couples who commuted to Bristol or London and sent their children to private schools in Bath. Gemma had seen plenty of those, but the majority of the village population seemed to be pensioners and young families getting by – it was clear that Crowthorpe had its share of rural poverty.

The shop was staffed by someone new today; a man in his sixties who reminded Gemma a little of her father. He had a whiff of ex-military about him, something in his posture and the ruler-straightness of his moustache that made him look like he'd forgotten to take the coat hanger out of his shirt. Gemma wondered if he was Ruth's husband, although they seemed like an unlikely couple.

Things had changed in the village shop in the past week. There was now a strip of black tape on the floor that marked where shoppers had to stand while their shopping was processed, and a perspex screen mounted on the edge of the counter to create a transparent barrier between the shopper and the staff. Since Gemma had to step over the line to tap her debit card and pick up her shopping from the open space at the side of the screen, it all seemed a bit pointless; but this was the new normal in Crowthorpe and presumably everywhere else. The shop had maintained their stocks and kept Gemma in fresh food without her having to get a taxi or bus to Chippenham, so she definitely wasn't complaining.

Since the shop was so tiny only one shopper was allowed in at a time, which meant there was usually a short queue outside. Mabel had learned to milk this for all it was worth, so Gemma gathered her shopping as quickly as possible, conscious that by now her dog would be lying on her back with her paws in the air, inviting strangers to give her belly rubs and feed her God knows what. Some people had issues with the hygiene of touching other people's dogs right now, but more often than not somebody in the queue would oblige, securing Mabel's credentials as the most spoiled dog in the village.

The man behind the counter handed Gemma her receipt and stepped back while she retrieved her bags. 'We haven't met, I'm Gareth. I'd shake your hand but I'm not allowed.'

'That's OK. I'm Gemma.'

'I know, you're quite the talk of the village.'

Gemma laughed awkwardly, feeling the colour rush to her face. 'Nice to meet you, Gareth.' She quickly left the shop, swerving the recommended two metres around the first woman in the queue of four outside the door. Mabel was in a blissed-out state, getting vigorous belly scritches from a dark-haired woman in sleek black running gear with her twin sons, who Gemma guessed were five or six. Gemma had seen the woman out running a number of times early in the morning, no doubt getting her exercise in before her children woke up and she added 'teacher' to her list of roles alongside mother, worker, housekeeper, cleaner, nurse, cook, wife. She'd jogged past yesterday when Gemma was learning about local hedgehogs from Barry, who told her that the woman's husband worked long shifts in a hospital in Swindon. The fact that she was still wearing this morning's sweaty running clothes at nearly 5 p.m. spoke volumes about how much time she'd had to herself today.

As Gemma walked home, wishing she'd brought the hessian shoppers instead of two plastic bags that cut into her fingers, she thought about what Gareth had said about her being the 'talk of the village'. Gemma might have been more astonished at her sudden notoriety had Matthew not given her a heads up – a few days earlier he had stopped by to pick up Mabel, and mentioned with a mischievous tone that Gemma was the subject of much discussion, at least amongst the older residents. They saw her as their very own lockdown refugee, stranded in Crowthorpe with nowhere else to go. Her job was an added fascination; apparently Ruth had done a Google search on Gemma's name and had been reading out some of her articles to anyone who would listen. She'd found it amusing when Matthew mentioned it, but also kind of confounding – she had never been the subject of gossip or intrigue before.

Other than when he picked up Mabel, Gemma had seen very little of Matthew; he seemed to be busy with work and not one for idle chatter. This suited Gemma just fine; men were not her favourite species of mammal right now, and even if she'd been on the market Matthew wasn't her type. Despite being a similar age to her, he had a local-boy innocence about him that was a million miles away from her London life. He was clearly capable and definitely not stupid, just unworldly; she couldn't imagine talking to him about books or travel, and it was hard to imagine what they might possibly have in common. Caro, obviously, and living at opposite ends of the same garden. Maybe walking the same dog, at a push. That was pretty much it.

After much consideration, Gemma had come to the conclusion that meaningful long-term relationships weren't for her; perhaps she'd lived on her own for too long. There had been the usual ill-advised one-night stands and dalliances in her twenties, some of which had lasted a few months. A holiday romance or two, then two years of Johannes just after her twenty-sixth birthday. In the end he had decided to take a job with an orchestra back home in Switzerland, but didn't ask Gemma to go with him. She was only upset for the brief time it took her to realise that living in Zurich with a man who cut his toenails in bed was unlikely to be an environment in which she would blossom.

Gemma hurried back to West Cottage in the late-afternoon sunshine, the heavy bags cutting off the circulation in her fingers. She'd only needed a few things, but as usual had ended up buying a couple of local cheeses, two bottles of wine, a pack of doggy beef strips for Mabel and a sharing bag of Maltesers that she was looking forward to sharing with herself later. There weren't many thrills to be had in lockdown life, so no wonder everyone was eating and drinking more – the diet industry was going to make a killing when this was over. Gemma mentally drafted an article about finding joy in small pleasures in challenging times, then realised no one would pay for it, so gave up. She stopped near Grove Farm to rest her hands, and ended up having a chat with an elderly villager called Reg who had a magnolia in a pot for her if she wanted it. Almost certainly not, but she promised to let him know once she'd tackled the garden tomorrow.

As Gemma unpacked the shopping and put the wine on the coldest shelf of the fridge, Mabel quietly slid the pack of beef strips out of the bag and snaffled them under the dining table. Gemma only noticed when she heard the crackle of the wrapper as Mabel attempted to break into the packaging, wedging it between her paws and tearing at it with her teeth. Gemma sighed and sat on the floor against the wall, keeping Mabel in sight but knowing that chasing her would be futile; right now Mabel knew she was in trouble, but if Gemma chased her it would become a legitimate game. Gemma's only hope was to distract her so she could get the pack back, which required time and patience. She held a handful of biscuits and waited for her moment, wondering how it could be that Mabel was brilliantly behaved 99 per cent of the time, but food wiped all her training from her tiny doggy brain.

After a couple of minutes, Mabel stopped chewing, clearly frustrated that her teeth couldn't pierce the heavy waxed paper. Gemma seized the moment, scattering half a dozen dog biscuits across the wooden floor like meaty marbles. Mabel momentarily lost her mind and relinquished hold on the beef strips. Gemma pounced and snatched them back, then wandered back to the kitchen to put them in the cupboard. Human 1, Labrador nil.

CHAPTER EIGHT

Wednesday, 1 April

To Do

- Call Mum. DO IT.
- Distinguish weeds from flowers
- Pull weeds
- Leave flowers

Gemma stood in front of the bathroom mirror, pulling her hair into a ponytail which, along with her well-worn Spice Girls tour T-shirt, made her look like she was having an early midlife crisis. The T-shirt had been a present from Caro to celebrate twenty years since they'd seen them live on the Spiceworld Tour – they hadn't known each other then, but it turned out they had both been at Wembley Stadium on the same night in 1998. Gemma's hair now had a full two inches of dark roots and desperately needed a cut, but that wasn't going to happen any time soon. She'd seen pictures on social media of friends opting for messy tubes of home dye and highlighting kits, but Gemma didn't dare take matters into her own hands. It would get done when it got done, and in the meantime hairbands and makeshift headscarves were her saviour.

Her daytime walks and time outside cleaning windows had given her face a touch of sun – she looked healthier than she had in years, despite not having touched her make-up bag in nearly two weeks. This was really the only time of the year she could spend time in the sun; in high summer Gemma went from English

Rose to Roasted Tomato in minutes, without so much as a freckle in between. She rubbed on a layer of SPF moisturiser, added a slick of lip balm and decided she would do. It was a garden wilderness in Crowthorpe, not the beautiful grounds at Pemberley.

Her phone buzzed on the side of the sink – a WhatsApp from her mother, saying *Call me when you have a minute*. Gemma could feel the passive aggression from 200 miles away; the subtext was 'You haven't called me in a few days and I can't think why, since it's not like you're busy.'

She briefly considered some kind of April Fool's message – *I'm actually at the hospital having my hand reattached after it got caught in some farm machinery* – but then remembered it was her mother, who had left her sense of humour somewhere in the eighties. The first-floor bathroom was at the back of the house and managed a reasonably good connection to Matthew's WiFi, so Gemma pressed the call icon and listened to the tone as she waited for her mother to answer. Barbara still hadn't quite got the hang of the swipe action on a smartphone, so would no doubt be stabbing at the green button right now and wondering why it wasn't connecting. Gemma sat on the edge of the bath, drumming her fingernails on the porcelain as she waited.

'Hello, darling. I hadn't expected you to call quite so soon.'

Gemma instinctively narrowed her eyes and gritted her teeth, already glad this wasn't a video call. 'Hey, Mum. How are you?'

'We're fine, keeping our spirits up. Your father has an RAF Police Association meeting on Zoom later. We don't even know what Zoom is. Where are you living again?'

For a woman who had never had a job and had spent most of her adult life living in houses she didn't own, Barbara Lockwood had extremely strong opinions about Gemma's living arrangements. As far as she was concerned, the years being housed and indulged by Aunt Laura were the sole reason why Gemma was single and childless – she hadn't needed to get a 'proper job' or find a husband. In contrast, Louise had gone straight from university into Army Officer training and was now settled down with Jamie, an Army dentist, and their two cavity-free children. They were the epitome of what Gemma's mother thought a family should be.

What Barbara didn't know was that Gemma and her sister had gone for a walk in Norwich on Christmas Eve, and Louise had confessed that her marriage was desperately unhappy. While they huddled together on a frosty bench in the gardens of the cathedral, watching the robins hopping from tree to tree, Louise had confided that she actually liked women, but had married Jamie in a crisis of sexual identity. There was nothing to be gained from sharing this particular revelation with their mother right now; the truth (and presumably Louise) would come out in time, and their mother's world would come crashing down for a brief period, before she stopped making everything all about her and embraced her youngest daughter's life choices. Gemma, however, would always be a disappointment, the member of the Lockwood family who would never amount to much.

She headed back to the mirror and carefully tweezed stray hairs out of her eyebrows as her mother prattled on about the inconsequential minutiae of her day, including gossip about neighbours not adhering to social distancing rules and scandalous rumours of people driving to Norfolk's beaches to walk their dogs. Gemma answered a few questions as vaguely as possible – yes, she was still working; no, Caro wasn't going to evict her before the lockdown finished; no, she hadn't heard from Fraser. Gemma had told her mother about their split the previous week, sparing her the explicit details but making it clear it was his fault. 'Let's just say he turned out to be less than I deserve.' Barbara had made a huffing noise, no doubt thinking that Gemma was too picky or too difficult to live with, and mentally cancelling her order for a lovely wedding hat.

After ten minutes Gemma started to wrap the conversation up with the usual promises to call again in a few days. As a final gesture of familial support, she suggested her dad call her if he couldn't get Zoom to work later. Her father was a proud man and would rather die in a ditch than ask his daughter for IT support, but it felt good to offer.

*

Gemma left her phone to charge in the kitchen and pulled on her purple dog-walking trainers before heading into the garden. The day was cool and overcast, but dry – perfect weather for a few hours of outdoor labour. She found gloves, a bucket and a selection of old gardening tools in the shed, along with a push-along cylinder lawnmower that didn't look much like it was up to the task of ankle-deep grass.

The garden of West Cottage began outside the kitchen door with a small sunken courtyard surrounded by a low stone wall. Its east-facing aspect meant that it caught the morning sun, and Gemma could see what a lovely spot it would be for the first coffee of the day. A heavy wooden bench had been placed against the house wall, presumably for this purpose, but it hadn't been warm enough in the mornings to use it yet. On her left was a storage area for the wheelie bins and the small tool shed, and to her right the path curved round the side of the house to the side gate that Matthew had used on the day she had first met him. She wondered if he owned the barn or leased it from Caro; if he owned it, the right of way to use that gate and path must be quite complicated. But she could see that the barn had its own entrance at the far end of the garden, so perhaps he just sometimes nipped through the garden as a shortcut, knowing that Caro wouldn't mind.

In the middle of the stone wall, three steps led up to a path that ran the length of the garden, with a wide stretch of lawn either side. On the left side, the lawn was edged with a planted border of lilac trees and flowering shrubs and a stone wall that overlooked a narrow lane that ran at 90 degrees to the main road; Gemma had walked Mabel down there on a number of occasions and knew that it wound past farms and fields to the tiny hamlet of Frampton about two miles away. On the right, a dense laurel hedge ran the full length of the garden, creating a natural fence between West Cottage and the house next door. Gemma could occasionally hear their children screaming on the garden trampoline, although it was hard to know if this was an expression of joy or a snapped femur. The place was clearly huge and had its own private driveway, so they barely felt like neighbours. Gemma had seen a car going in and out of the electric gates on occasion, but had never met the owners.

She walked to the top of the steps and stood with her back to the house. She could see Matthew's barn at the end of the path about 15 metres away, beyond a couple of gnarled apple trees and a large decked area with a clematis-covered pergola that had clearly been built for al fresco dining in the evening sun. The garden furniture had gone, but a brick barbecue with a rusty grill remained. Even in its untamed state, Gemma could see what a beautiful garden it must once have been, and how much love and thought Caro's parents had put into it. It was easy to imagine a summer party full of friends drinking and dancing, lanterns draped through the trees and the sweet scent of jasmine in the air. Caro had been close to her parents but didn't visit nearly as often as she wanted to once she was juggling a high-powered job with the demands of parenting. After they died, she admitted to Gemma that she'd taken for granted that they'd always be here, and would never forgive herself for how much family time she'd denied them in what turned out to be their final years.

Starting at the house end of the border, Gemma knelt down on the lawn and began to tackle the weeds, working her way around the shrubs and border perennials with a small garden fork. Half an hour on the *Gardeners' World* website last night had given her the basics of spring border management, so she snipped last year's dead growth with secateurs and dug out the roots of dandelions and goosegrass and ground elder with a trowel. It was mindless but satisfying labour as, metre by metre, order emerged from the chaos. Mabel occasionally wandered over to sniff at the soil, but found nothing worth snacking on apart from worms and roots, and even she wasn't that desperate. Every now and then Gemma walked back to the courtyard to empty the bucket into the green waste bin, taking the opportunity to stretch her back and shoulders and toss a ball down the garden a few times for Mabel to fetch before starting on the borders again.

Gemma heard Matthew before she saw him; the clatter of the manual lawnmower almost made her stab herself in the hand. He was wearing his usual paint-spattered shorts and work boots, along with a white T-shirt that drew Gemma's eye to his work-tanned arms and the hard muscles of his back. The effort on his face was visible as he hacked through the long grass; clearly it was a machine designed for much lighter work. Matthew stopped at the end of the first strip and swiftly raked the clippings into a pile on the path, then pushed the mower through again. After three passes, a 14-inch-wide strip of perfect green lawn had emerged, so Matthew moved along to the next strip. He didn't acknowledge Gemma or take his eye off the lawn, so she turned her attention back to digging the borders.

Half an hour later, Matthew had finished the laurel hedge side of the lawn and Gemma's back felt like she'd been ridden by a rugby team. She slipped off her gardening gloves and spent a minute or two rolling her shoulders and stretching her neck from side to side, while admiring the precision of Matthew's mowing – perfect lawn stripes, with all the clippings raked into a neat row for easy collection. Her father would have signed him up to the squadron and given him a medal.

Gemma caught Matthew's eye and raised her eyebrows questioningly, while making the 'T' sign with her fingers. He smiled and nodded enthusiastically, so Gemma dropped the gloves and tools into the bucket and headed into the kitchen. While the kettle boiled she found two clean mugs in the cupboard and added a teabag to each, then retrieved a plastic container of milk from the fridge and a packet of chocolate biscuits. She'd had grand plans to make Aunt Laura's famous shortbread recipe, but flour was one thing the village shop couldn't provide right now. Luckily it had a decent selection of McVities, which would do just fine.

Gemma carried the tray out of the back door and up the steps, to find Matthew carrying two folding chairs to join a metal bistro table he'd already placed under the apple tree next to Mabel. They both sat in silence for a minute, sipping tea and admiring their progress in the garden. The sky was full of birdsong; Gemma had never heard so many.

She broke the silence. 'No work today?'

Matthew shook his head. 'I'm waiting for some parts to be delivered later today – everything's taking ages. I thought I should come and help; it's my fault the grass looks like this. I should have given it a first mow of the season weeks ago, never quite got round to it.'

Gemma nodded. The last few weeks had been strange and uncertain for everyone; she could see how mundane household tasks might fall down the list of priorities. She tilted her head to watch a small brown bird hopping along a branch. Aunt Laura had kept a little guide to garden birds on her kitchen windowsill in the house in Norfolk, but Gemma couldn't remember any of their names. Some kind of finch?

Matthew cleared his throat. 'I'd like to ask you a small favour, if you've got time tomorrow morning.'

Gemma turned back to look at him. *He has a nice face*, she thought. *Even though he looks like he's about to ask for one of my kidneys.* 'Go on.'

'Ruth has asked me if I can do a few hours in the village shop.' Gemma looked confused; she had met several different staff on her shopping trips and assumed they had plenty. 'Ruth manages it, but it's run by volunteers. It's a community shop. But most of the volunteers are retired or have health issues, so quite a few would rather not work in such a small space right now.'

Gemma waited; she was yet to see how this might involve her.

'I think legally we can count ourselves as one household, since my barn could be classed as an annexe of your house and we share a garden. It's a grey area.' He shrugged and gave a small smile. 'So I wondered if you'd come with me. It's not hard and I could do it alone, but everybody who comes in wants a chat and it's knackering. I hoped you might . . . help lighten the load a bit.'

Gemma laughed, imagining being trapped in a confined space with a stream of villagers who hadn't spoken to a living soul all day. She'd definitely want moral support.

'Count me in, it's not like I've got much else on. And I'm OK to assume we're the same household if that makes things easier. I breathed wine fumes all over you the other day, so if I was going to make you sick I probably would have done it by now.'

Matthew grinned at the memory, then leaned back in his chair and stretched his arms above his head as he surveyed the garden. His T-shirt rode up a few inches to reveal an impressive washboard of hard abdominals, and Gemma looked away, momentarily flustered. *Less than two weeks single and you're perving on the garden help. Get a grip on yourself, Lady Chatterley.*

She turned back to find Matthew's green eyes observing her with interest, taking in the Spice Girls T-shirt and her make-up-free face like he was seeing her for the first time. She put the empty mugs and half-empty pack of biscuits back on the tray and carried it back into the kitchen, feeling all of a sudden a little warm.

CHAPTER NINE

Thursday, 2 April

To Do

• Pretend to be shop assistant

By the third customer of the morning, Gemma fully understood why Matthew had asked for her help. If Covid-19 could be spread via idle chat, then the Crowthorpe village shop would be a plague house. Starved of company and conversation, the villagers weren't going to waste the opportunity to speak to a real-life journalist about the headlines from their preferred news source (*Daily Mail*, occasional *Telegraph*, mostly 'I read a thing on Facebook') and speculate on what the next few weeks might hold. Gemma was emotionally and physically drained.

They also seemed to think she had some kind of hotline to UK coronavirus mission control, asking her questions about the Prime Minister's health (Gemma knew as much as they did), whether you could drive somewhere to walk your dog (why would you when you live here?) or whether drinking herbal tea might boost your immune system (no idea, but we have several flavours). Gemma was dying to tell them that far from having a hotline, she didn't even have a phone signal, and the most recent article she'd written was a list of Twenty Lockdown Songs to Live By, including 'Don't Stand So Close To Me' by The Police and 'I Think We're Alone Now' by Tiffany. It was hardly prize-winning journalism.

While all this was going on, Matthew kept busy stacking

shelves and operating the price-sticker machine. She caught a glimpse of him smiling as she got caught up in a particularly thorny debate with a very angry man who'd seen proof (source undefined) that the virus was actually manufactured in a lab in Wuhan and was being spread by 5G phone masts. Since Crowthorpe only had 4G in an area roughly the size of a table-cloth, Gemma didn't think he needed to worry too much. Matthew was definitely going to pay for this later.

When she had taken Mabel out for her walk this morning, she was acutely conscious that she was buzzing a little about spending time with him again, even though the attraction made no sense. Historically she'd liked her men physically and emotionally more fragile and less overtly masculine. On this basis Matthew wasn't her type at all, but nonetheless there was something about him that she found appealing. Perhaps it was his solidity in an unstable world, or perhaps she'd just outgrown needy, frangible men. To call him 'ordinary' felt insulting, but that was definitely part of it; he was easy to spend time with, and not wholly uneasy on the eye if you liked the slightly battered rugby player look, which usually she didn't at all, but was finding quite distracting right now.

The one-customer-only policy had made perfect sense to Gemma when she was a shopper, but as a member of staff it created quite a headache. Small talk took time, and every pause in the shopping mission to chat to Gemma or Matthew was greeted with glaring and tutting from those waiting outside, until their turn came and they did exactly the same. Gemma could see why Gareth had closed the door on Tuesday, but it was much warmer today and the breeze from outside kept the temperature in the shop bearable.

Towards the end of the morning, Margaret came in with her red shopping trolley, and looked delighted to have the opportunity to interrogate Gemma again. They'd shared a few waves in passing but not spoken since the morning of Gemma's arrival when Margaret had given her directions to the shop. Gemma rang her provisions through on the till quickly, hoping she might avoid the Crowthorpe Inquisition.

'So, still here, then,' said Margaret, eyeing both Gemma and Matthew beadily.

'Still here,' replied Gemma, willing herself not to be intimidated, 'cluttering up the village.'

'I'm surprised to see you two here together. I didn't realise your arrangement counted as the same household.' The implication hung in the air like one of Mabel's toxic farts, but Gemma batted it away.

'It definitely does,' she said, glancing at Matthew, 'and we stay two metres apart at all times, just to be extra safe. If I didn't wear contact lenses I couldn't even tell you what he looked like.'

Margaret stared at her, momentarily silenced. She made a sceptical 'hmmm' noise at nobody in particular, then wheeled her trolley away.

'Nosy old bat,' muttered Gemma.

'She's actually my great-aunt,' deadpanned Matthew.

'Oh God, really?' Gemma looked horrified.

'No, not really.' Matthew grinned and went back to stacking tins.

By 12.45 p.m. they had dealt with the last few people in the queue, so Gemma offered to help Matthew fix the door to the largest of the two chiller cabinets. The doors only seemed to seal properly half the time, which ran the risk of it being left open when the shop was closed. If that happened on a hot weekend, there wasn't a scented candle in the world that would get rid of the smell of rancid meat and sweaty cheese. Matthew couldn't repair it, so he sent Ruth a text saying she needed to get someone from the fridge company out to look at it, and in the meantime he'd come up with a very temporary fix.

Gemma listened to Matthew's fascinating explanation about how a door could behave like a door or it could behave like a lid depending on angles and mass and gravity, but all she heard was an incomprehensible buzzing noise. She'd never paid much attention in Physics at school; it didn't seem very open to creative interpretation and her teacher had looked so much like the dog from the Dulux TV ads it had been hard to take him seriously. Matthew saw the baffled look on her face and stopped talking, then tried again.

'If we tilt it back a few degrees and wedge some cardboard underneath, it will stop the door swinging open.'

'Oh. Fine. That makes sense.'

Matthew pushed against the top of the chiller to lean it back, and Gemma folded bits of corrugated cardboard from a box that had once held packets of cereal and stuffed it under the feet. As long as nobody pulled out the cardboard wedges or mopped the floor, it would be fine. They played around with the layers of cardboard for a while, Gemma looking up at Matthew's straining arms as he tested to see if it was stable and tilted at the right angle. She decided it was quite a nice view from down here, and there were definitely worse ways to spend a lockdown Thursday.

Ruth arrived at 1 p.m. to lock the shop for lunch, thanking them both for their help and particularly Matthew for fixing the fridge. She dropped shameless hints about the two of them doing more shifts, but they both managed to remain non-committal – Matthew had quite a lot of work in the pipeline, and Gemma definitely wasn't doing unpaid work in this nuthouse without him.

They strolled back through the village together, chatting about the small ways that lockdown was impacting the village. As far as Matthew knew, nobody here had caught the virus yet; in fact Wiltshire had one of the lowest infection rates in the country. Crowthorpe's pain was being felt behind closed doors – no school for the kids, no play area, no village clubs or community events, no church services. The village had already mobilised the troops to deliver shopping and pick up prescriptions and make meals for some of the older and more vulnerable residents, but people didn't seem ready to switch to online community stuff yet. Change happened slowly in a place like this, and there was no point going to all that trouble if things were getting back to normal in a couple of weeks. All of which meant that people had time on their hands, and no physical evidence of the virus other than what they saw on the news, which hardly anyone trusted these days anyway. No wonder some had turned to conspiracy theories.

The conversation drifted to Gemma's life in London, which seemed to intrigue Matthew. He asked about her job and her friends and her favourite ways to have fun, and she shared a few stories but couldn't get enthused; it all seemed so far away right now, like a life that belonged to someone else. There was nowhere to anchor her memories – her home with Fraser was gone, and Aunt Laura's house was now owned by a Dutch architect and his husband. She'd cycled over to have a look at it a few weeks ago, and there was a planning notice on the front gate to say they'd applied to excavate the basement. It was entirely unreasonable, but in that moment it felt like they were ripping her guts out too. Whatever version of London she returned to in the coming weeks, it would be something entirely new.

They walked in silence for a while, as Gemma watched a woman trying to navigate a pram on the uneven pavement between the parked cars. The gap wasn't really big enough and the pram looked like it weighed a ton – why did prams need to be so huge when babies were so small? Gemma could see shadows like car tyres under the woman's eyes; under different circumstances she would probably have had her mother or sister living with her in these early weeks. It must be hard for parents right now, without their usual support network. Gemma was reminded of the running woman with twin boys she'd seen at the shop on Tuesday. Who was taking care of these women, while they took care of everyone else?

She noticed Matthew looking at her, and her cheeks coloured – there was a solid chance he'd just asked a question, but she hadn't been paying attention.

'Sorry, I was miles away. What did you say?'

'I asked what you miss most about your life in London. If you could have brought anything with you, what would it be?'

Gemma was silent for a moment while she thought about his

question. She definitely didn't miss Fraser, or his flat. He liked everything to be white – towels, bedding, furniture – sometimes it felt like living in a psychiatric hospital. It had taken weeks to convince him on the grey and yellow Heal's cushions, and in a moment of sudden clarity she realised that he'd asked the Mystery Brunette to sit on them so she didn't get body fluids on his white sofa. *What a shit.* She definitely missed the Cypriot café on Bermondsey Street that served sweet and strong coffee with a side order of Eurovision chat – everyone had their guilty pleasures, and Gemma's was the Eurovision Song Contest. She'd watched it since she was a little girl – British Forces television might have had a limited schedule, but it always included Eurovision. She and Joe had talked about going to Rotterdam for this year's Grand Final, but the event had been cancelled now, just like everything else. She dragged her thoughts back to the present.

'I miss my books.'

'Your books?'

'Yes. I like to read. I have some books on my phone, but it's not the same as the paper version. The flat I was living in had a whole pile of books I hadn't read yet, and I didn't bring any of them with me. I'm pretty sure they've been thrown out by now.' Fraser wouldn't keep them, the covers were too abstract and colourful. Also somebody might comment on them and he'd have to admit he hadn't read any of them. Fraser didn't do fiction; he preferred those motivational business manuals about influencing and networking and conjuring money out of your backside, the kind that had words like 'paradox' or 'unstoppable' in the title.

Matthew paused, his brow furrowed with indecision. 'I have books. You can borrow whatever you like.'

'Really?' Gemma looked at him with interest. She couldn't imagine the bookshelves in Matthew's barn had much that would excite her; in her head it was real-life SAS adventures or high-octane thrillers involving brutal murders in backwater American towns. Or perhaps he liked wizards and dragons or fantasy space adventures; you could never tell.

She didn't want to offend, so she arranged her face into an enthusiastic smile. 'That would be great, thank you.'

Matthew looked at his feet, unable to meet her eye. 'I've got to work for the rest of today and tomorrow, but you could come over late on Saturday and have a look if you like. Eight-thirty or so? I can make some pizza or something.'

His voice trailed off, as Gemma felt a flutter in her stomach that had little to do with the fact she'd walked Mabel in lieu of breakfast. She gave him a smile that she hoped communicated friendship and appreciation rather than deeply impure thoughts. 'That would be great, I'd love to.'

When Gemma got home she let Mabel out into the garden and made a mug of tea and a cheese sandwich, using local granary bread and some Cotswold chilli jam that would go down a storm in her local London deli. She carried it through to the dining room and sat at the heavy oak table, while Mabel sniffed around for crumbs. Her dog bed had limited appeal at this point in the day, as the sun wouldn't make it to the windows for a few hours yet, so she settled on her owner's feet instead. Gemma slipped on the chunky cardigan that was draped over the back of the chair and pulled the sleeves down over her fists.

She'd had a pitch for an article accepted yesterday, about the challenges of living together in lockdown – the lack of personal space and me-time, the awkward clashes in routine, the jarring discovery that your partner was an entirely different beast on Zoom calls and talked impenetrable management bullshit about 'cascading relevant information' and 'squaring the circle'. It was a pressure cooker for relationships, and while some would be stronger for the experience, others inevitably wouldn't make it.

She tinkered with it for a while, enjoying the irony that she was writing about the emotional pressures of cohabiting when she'd only done it once in fourteen years of adult life, for a sum total of six months. The reality was that she liked living alone; she'd found comfort in her own company all her life. Before boarding school,

Gemma's childhood memories involved her father always work-ing, her mother distracted by the endless demands of being an officer's wife and always annoyed with Gemma about something, and Louise surrounded by an impenetrable circle of giggly friends, unable to understand why her big sister wasn't more fun. So Gemma retreated to imaginary places inhabited by witches and fairies, and lost herself in magical lands that could only be reached if you climbed a special tree in an enchanted wood.

The boarding school years were purely about teenage survival for Gemma; living for the peace and freedom of weekends at 22 Church Street, Aunt Laura's house in Wymondham. Aunt Laura didn't believe in watching television before dinner, so Gemma would spend the days nestled into her favourite chair by the lounge window, feeling a million miles away from the bitchy cliques of girls her own age, even though school was less than half an hour away in Aunt Laura's clanking Mini Metro. In Church Street, Gemma's friends were stacked in a pile beside the chair; an intri-guing adult world of novels that had taken her blossoming teenage imagination on a journey of adventure, drama, mystery and ro-mance. Aunt Laura's collection of paperbacks was soon exhausted, so Gemma applied for a library card and walked into Wymond-ham on a Saturday morning to replenish her supply. The town library was housed in a mediaeval chapel; Gemma was usually waiting outside when it opened, running her hands over the smooth flint cobbles and imagining them being placed there by people who had stood on this exact spot 900 years before. Look-ing back, she could see that she had been quite an intense teenager; no wonder she was lonely.

Beckett's Chapel became a place of sanctuary and worship for Gemma; lost in the rows of musty shelves that smelled of old paper and damp and furniture polish, she didn't have to think about the misery of school, or the relentless cycle of packing and unpacking at home. In the library she could be fleeing danger across the Yorkshire moors, or tracking a jewel thief in the French Riviera. She could build her own ranch and tame wild horses, or have steamy, wanton sex with a square-jawed man who could pretty much snap his fingers and make her clothes fall off.

Gemma's early reading habits seemed indiscriminate to Aunt Laura, who often laughed at the mix of books she hauled home. It was common to find an Agatha Christie or a P. D. James alongside blockbuster sagas by Shirley Conran or Barbara Taylor Bradford; in one weekend Gemma read *Catcher in the Rye* (kind of tedious, actually), followed by Jilly Cooper's *The Man Who Made Husbands Jealous* (much better, lots of bonking). None of the books went back to school with her – Aunt Laura didn't want them getting lost or forgotten, and anyway it felt important to Gemma that she kept her weekend world separate, for fear her weekday life would creep in and poison it.

She jolted out of her memories, having no idea how she'd drifted from thinking about lockdown cohabitation to Aunt Laura's local library in the old chapel. She turned back to the job in hand, but thoughts of books had given her another nudge, reminding her about going to Matthew's on Saturday to borrow some of his reading matter. It obviously wasn't a date, but the tiny frisson of anticipation in her stomach made it feel like one.

Gemma pushed her laptop aside and grabbed a big envelope from the window seat – a piece of junk mail for replacement windows and guttering that she wouldn't bother sending on to Caro. In times of doubt or confusion, she always made a list, so now seemed as good a time as any.

Reasons not to fancy Matthew

1. Social distancing
2. He's not your type (local man for local people)
3. He's Caro's friend (awks)
4. He might not fancy you
5. He could be gay
6. You'll make an idiot of yourself

7. You're moving back to London soon
8. You're on the rebound
9. You're crap at relationships
10. Men are shits
11. ~~You are 32 and don't look great naked~~

Reasons to fancy Matthew

1. He's kind and nice (underrated qualities, tbc if sexy)
2. He's literally next door
3. He might fancy you too
4. He probably looks great naked (also: good with hands)
5. You're trapped in a small village in a global pandemic, normal rules have gone out the window

Gemma rested her forehead on the table, trying to absorb its strength and stability while her world continued to tilt on its axis. Nothing. She screwed the list up and tossed it into the wood burner, then returned to the article. Right now it felt easier to imagine other people's problems than tackle her own.

CHAPTER TEN

Saturday, 4 April

To Do

- Find hairbrush
- Find make-up bag
- Make self look less like shit
- Books/pizza at M's 8.30 p.m.

Gemma stood in front of the bathroom mirror, paralysed by indecision. If she looked like she had obviously made an effort, Matthew might think she thought this was a date. So in an ideal world she would look great, but also not in any way like she'd *tried* to look great.

Other women seemed to achieve this with ease – a slick of lip gloss, a zhuzh of the hair and boom – instant let's-take-selfies loveliness. But alas, Gemma wasn't one of them. She didn't dislike her face at all, but it wasn't naturally Instagram-ready – her jaw was a little heavy, and her nose had a bump in the bridge from headbutting a climbing frame as a child. Her eyes were a muddy brown, with eyebrows so pale they disappeared entirely without vigorous pencilling, and her hair was currently an irredeemable two-tone split-ended shambles. With full make-up and the glow of two gin & tonics she could look, if not a million dollars, then a decent 500 bucks, but to someone like Matthew who had only seen the fifty-dollar version, the difference would be very noticeable indeed.

So this was the big question Gemma was grappling with – *between*

50 and 500, how many dollars is appropriate for looking at books, eating pizza, and not screaming 'available for no-strings lockdown sex'?

In the end she settled for about 150 dollars – barely-there make-up, hair washed but in her usual messy bun, jeans and a pale blue shirt that she'd purposely not ironed, slip-on flat pumps, no jewellery or perfume whatsoever. It took the best part of an hour to achieve this lack of effort – more time than she'd spent getting ready for Caro's wedding, and on that occasion she'd been chief bridesmaid.

Just before 8.30 p.m. she grabbed a six-pack of local cider from the fridge (less date-like than wine), patted a miffed-looking Mabel on the head and walked down the garden path to Matthew's barn. Even in the gathering darkness of early April, Gemma could see what a difference their gardening efforts had made. The smell of cut grass still lingered in the air, and without the tangle of weeds and dead stems to hold them back, the shrubs and trees felt like they were on the starting blocks of spring, ready to embrace the space. Gemma had never really thought of herself as a gardening person, and was surprised at how satisfying it still felt, even three days later.

Matthew's barn had originally been a large stone outbuilding, presumably for livestock when West Cottage had been part of a bigger estate. Gemma wasn't exactly up to speed on nineteenth-century animal husbandry, but it definitely looked like the kind of place where you might keep some cows. At some point in recent years it had been converted to create a workshop underneath and a living space above, while still retaining the general appearance of a barn. *A fancy cow hotel*, thought Gemma. *Boutique accomMOOdation. Or should that be MOOtique? God, you need to get out more.*

Not wanting to look over-keen by being bang on time, she did a lap of the barn to get a feel for the place. At the left-hand end was the entrance to the workshop, with a big set of sliding doors that faced out on to the lane. The space between the barn and the road was gravelled, and she could see Matthew's silver panel van parked between the doors and the five-bar wooden gate.

The entrance to Matthew's apartment was at the other end of the barn, up a flight of external steps with a wooden handrail to a small decked balcony and an old stable door. Looking up, Gemma could see that the top level was timber-framed, with a gently sloping shingle roof that ended in a central flat section, like a modern take on a Dutch barn. On the far side she could see a flue for a wood burner, but on the side facing the cottage there were only four tiny windows built into the shingle – she imagined it would be cosy up there in the evening, but perhaps a little gloomy in the daytime with so little natural light. Right now the two windows nearest the entrance had the curtains drawn, giving off a rosy glow from within. The other two were in darkness; Gemma assumed these were the bedroom and bathroom.

As she walked towards the steps, she noticed the small table and two chairs that Matthew had carried over to the apple tree two days before. What lay under his T-shirt flickered in her memory, and she quickly batted it aside. *For fuck's sake, Gemma. Behave yourself.*

She climbed the steps and knocked gently on the door. She heard brief kitchen clattering from within, then a few seconds of silence before the door opened and Matthew's shy smile appeared. Gemma was relieved to see that he'd taken a similarly casual approach on the dress code, with jeans and a check shirt with rolled-up sleeves that had also dodged the iron. Blue socks, no holes. But as Matthew moved into the doorway, Gemma also noted that he smelled freshly showered and had given his scruffy beard a trim. His hair needed a cut, but you could say that about pretty much everyone these days.

'You look nice. Come in.' He stood back to give Gemma space to step through the door.

She stood on the mat just inside the door, rooted to the spot in wonder. This wasn't a lonely bachelor pad full of mismatched furniture, or a gadget-filled man cave. It was . . . it was *beautiful*. Gemma's immediate impression was of a super-stylish Alpine chalet or the hull of a wooden ship, full of warmth and texture. But as her eyes adjusted to the soft light, she started to take in some of the details: the exposed timber frame broken up with soft cream walls and a dark ceiling, the natural sisal carpet, the corner unit of two pale blue sofas occupying the right half of the space, angled invitingly in front of the wood burner. To the left was an open-plan kitchen with soft grey cupboards, fitted around a glossy ceramic hob and a brushed stainless-steel oven that was currently cranked up to full heat. It was beautifully designed to make use of the small space, with every element built to fit under the gently sloping eaves of the roof, from the inset lighting to the curves of the granite worktops. Further along the left-hand wall was a small wooden dining table with two chairs, and a door in the wall at the end of the room that presumably led to the bedroom and bath-room. Gemma gasped and handed over the cider, kicking off her shoes to stride purposefully across the room.

With the exception of the bedroom door, the entire wall from floor to ceiling was taken up with books, slotted into a handmade wooden bookcase that followed the angle of the roof on both sides. Aside from the occasional softly glowing cube light, every inch of every shelf was packed with titles that spanned the literary spectrum from Harry Potter to P. G. Wodehouse. Gemma spotted a full set of Agatha Christies, a section of foreign translations in-cluding Marquez, Dumas, Chekhov and Stieg Larsson, a whole shelf of contemporary fiction, a selection of the very best great American novels and another of British classics – the complete works of Jane Austen, George Orwell, Thomas Hardy and Charles Dickens. Every shelf was full of treasures; Gemma hadn't felt this excited by a book collection since the day she had walked into Beckett's Chapel and asked for a library card.

She ran her finger along a row of well-thumbed Lonely Planet travel guides, organised alphabetically by continent. The first sec-tion included Belize, Caribbean Islands, Guatemala, Honduras, Mexico, Nicaragua and Panama. She felt a wave of shame – she had assumed Matthew was a country bumpkin, but he was better read and had seen far more of the world than she had. She gave him a questioning look, and he shrugged. 'I used to work flat out for a year, then take a year off. Did three separate trips doing odd jobs, you can see quite a lot of the world that way. That was the first year, then I did another in South East Asia and the last one in southern Europe.' His words tailed off as Gemma's face reddened with embarrassment. She had entirely underestimated Matthew, based on nothing other than the village where he lived. She squirmed uncomfortably, feeling like she should go home and have a stern word with herself.

The tension hung heavily in the air, so Matthew wafted his hand in the direction of the books and said 'Help yourself' before heading over to the kitchen. He took a pizza out of the fridge and slid it on to the hot stone in the oven, then popped the tops off two bottles of cider and poured them into glasses. By the time he wandered back, Gemma had managed to unclench and pick three books from the shelf – a Zadie Smith and a Julian Barnes, neither of which she had read, and a battered copy of *The Count of Monte Cristo*. It was Aunt Laura's favourite book, and Gemma hadn't read it in twenty years.

'Good choices. Dumas is my favourite.' Matthew handed Gemma a cider and playfully clinked her glass with his own. 'Here's to great books, decent cider and homemade pizza. Our lockdown could be worse.'

Gemma smiled and relaxed a little, and settled into the corner of the sofa with her cider. Her journalistic instinct kicked in, and by the time the buzzer on the oven went off ten minutes later, she'd established that he was an only child, that his father had been a builder and his mother an interior designer, and he had just turned thirty-one. He'd bought the barn from Caro's parents about four years ago, just after he'd returned from his Europe trip. Up until then he'd lived with his parents to save money for travelling and his future home. The renovation had taken just short of two years, with a little help and a great deal of guidance from his parents. They were both now semi-retired, but he saw them regularly – he walked to his childhood home for Sunday lunch most weekends, albeit that wasn't an option at the moment. For now they had to settle for phone calls, and a quick chat on the driveway when Matthew delivered their weekly shopping. By all accounts it was a strong family unit and Matthew had grown up in a loving, supportive home.

Gemma was fascinated by the idea of living in the same place all your life; it was a concept entirely alien to her. She had no sensible answer to the question 'Where are you from?' – she was from countless houses and innumerable schools in half a dozen countries. She'd been born in Germany and lived in Cyprus twice, interspersed with occasional tours back in the UK, living in identikit military homes in Yorkshire or Hertfordshire or South Wales. The choice of a boarding school in Norfolk was her mother's – Barbara Lockwood had grown up in the area, and it was the school she had aspired to but never attended. If the proximity of Aunt Laura's house in Wymondham was seen as a positive factor, her mother had never mentioned it; but it turned out to be a saving grace for Gemma.

They ate the pizza with their hands at the dining table, one of the many items in the apartment that Matthew had made himself – Gemma was gratified by the absence of candles or flowers or other dinner-date detritus. Matthew had never formally trained as a carpenter or joiner; it was a skill he learned while working for his father's building firm and discovered he had a talent for. Eventually he moved on from stud walling and roofing timbers to designing and making furniture, and set up his own small business with a homemade website and a card on the noticeboard outside the village shop. Working for his father paid the bills while he was starting out, but eventually the balance tipped so that the majority of his time was spent making bespoke designs. Old cottages are a mess of wonky walls, uneven floors and odd-shaped spaces – it's often impossible to find a cupboard or table that fits perfectly. So Matthew would work with the customer to design it on 3D software (another self-taught skill) and make it in his workshop. The labour-intensive nature of the work meant it wasn't nearly as profitable as he would like, so he supplemented his income by being the unofficial handyman for the village, which gave him as much work as he wanted. 'I can't do any at the moment though.' He shrugged.

'Is that part of the lockdown rules?'

He smiled, his eyes glittering. 'Kind of. I'm allowed to do emergency repair stuff, but the woman next door breathed her London fumes all over me. So I need to give it a couple of weeks before I go into anyone's house, just in case. Some of my customers are quite old and vulnerable.'

Gemma looked horrified and covered her face with her hands. 'Oh fuck. I'm so sorry.'

'It's fine. It's already been nearly two weeks, so I'll give it one more just to be sure. I've got loads of furniture work at the moment, and there's nothing in the village that can't wait.'

Gemma steered things towards his personal life, intrigued to know what people did for fun around here. In normal times he socialised with old school friends in Chippenham, was part of a local pub quiz team, and regularly volunteered at a homeless charity in Bristol run by an old school friend. When the village started to feel claustrophobic, he ate noodles and worked seven days a week until he'd saved enough to go travelling. Gemma envied him his wanderlust and freedom, then reminded herself that there was absolutely nothing stopping her from doing the same, except perhaps her responsibilities to Mabel.

In turn she told Matthew about her nomadic life growing up, glossing over her dysfunctional family and the year with Fraser. It didn't escape her notice that neither of them had talked about relationships at all; since it was reasonable to assume that Matthew hadn't spent his adult life living like a monk, it felt like a significant omission on both sides.

'And what about Mabel? How long have you had her?'

Gemma took a deep breath, knowing that she was going to have to talk about this eventually. Now seemed like a good time to try saying the words out loud.

'She belonged to my Aunt Laura. I lived in her house in London, and she lived in Norfolk. But then she got sick and had to move into a care home a few years ago, so she asked if I'd have Mabel. She's been with me ever since.'

'And how is your aunt doing?' Even though Gemma had known the question was coming, the pain flared in her chest again. Would it ever go away?

'She . . . died. Four months ago.'

'I'm really sorry.' Matthew looked at Gemma intently, clearly not knowing what else to say. She noticed his fingers twitch, like he'd instinctively wanted to comfort her but then changed his mind. She held his gaze for a few seconds, wishing she could find the right words, then felt naked under the heat of those green eyes and looked away. Matthew cleared his throat awkwardly and stood up to collect the empty plates and glasses, then put them by the sink and returned with the two final bottles of cider. 'Come and see my workshop,' he said, holding out his hand.

Gemma held the handrail tightly as she walked down the outside steps, the imprint of Matthew's hand still warm on hers, even though he had only held it for a few seconds. She watched him take a swig from his bottle as he weaved round the bistro table and chairs and strode across the gravel to the other end of the building, then rattled a key in the padlock. The door rolled open and light flooded the driveway as Matthew flicked a switch. He adjusted a dimmer so it was less stark, casting a glow over the space within.

It was another beautifully designed space, albeit much more functional than the apartment above. Just inside the entrance was a utility room with a toilet and shower, alongside a washing machine and tumble dryer. Presumably the former allowed him to avoid trailing sawdust upstairs, and the latter didn't fit elsewhere. The rest of the space was completely open, with shelf-lined walls for storing timber, tools and carefully labelled storage boxes full of screws and other hardware. The central area had a concrete floor and a large workbench that was currently home to six carefully cut and sanded wooden planks around two metres in length. Gemma ran her hands along one of the smooth surfaces; the heavy wood was almost white, and she could follow the swirls and knots of the grain with her fingers.

'It's an oak dining table, or at least it will be,' said Matthew, moving closer and cupping the edge of the wood in his hands. 'I need to make a couple of benches too. It's for a family in Bath. The wood cost a fortune, English oak is much more expensive than French, but that's what they wanted.' Gemma stared at his hand, and her skin began to prickle. She felt about thirteen, waiting for a boy to ask her to dance at a school disco. She forced herself to meet his gaze. 'It's going to be fabulous.'

Neither of them spoke; Gemma could feel the tension hanging in the air, mingling with the heady cocktail of sawdust and glue and oil. They looked at each other for a few seconds, both of their cheeks flushing in the half-light. Matthew broke eye contact first, putting his bottle down on the workbench with unnecessary force and snapping Gemma back into the real world as he turned to the door. 'You forgot your books. I'll get them for you.'

Gemma stood alone in the silence of the workshop, breathless and confused. What had just happened? Did she imagine that? Was she supposed to follow? Or did he want her to leave? She placed her bottle carefully next to his, her brain flipping through a whole spectrum of emotions, until she heard Matthew's footsteps crunching back through the gravel. He poked his head around the door and waved the three books in her direction. 'Got them. I'll walk you back.'

It seemed ridiculous to Gemma to be escorted a whole 15 metres, but picking her way along the path in the dark gave her a chance to organise her thoughts. It was clear that Matthew acknowledged the chemistry between them, but for whatever reason didn't want to act on it. At the beginning of the evening she had felt the same way, so she could hardly blame him for not being as reckless and impulsive as she was – Gemma had to admit that in the moment she would have happily ravaged him right there on the workbench, with no thought for the consequences. At least one of them wasn't a total idiot.

Matthew handed her the books at the kitchen door, then immediately tucked his hands under his armpits as he shivered in the cold air. Gemma opened the door and put the books on the kitchen counter, turning to mirror his body-hugging stance. 'Thank you for the books, and for the pizza. Your place is amazing.'

He smiled weakly in return, shifting his weight awkwardly from foot to foot. 'You're welcome, it's nice to cook for someone. I'll pick up Mabel tomorrow afternoon as usual.'

Gemma took the hint and gave him a small wave before heading inside, closing the door gently behind her. She stared silently at the pile of books for a minute, her mind racing; the top one was *The Sense of an Ending* by Julian Barnes. She opened the door again and peered out into the gloom, but Matthew was gone.

CHAPTER ELEVEN

Thursday, 9 April

To Do

- Write more lockdown nonsense
- Faff around in the garden
- Call Joe
- Go running
- Try to enjoy running

By 11 a.m. the temperature had climbed enough for Gemma to think about working outside – it was a gorgeous spring day, and it seemed a shame to be stuck indoors. She'd read on the news earlier that the government was worried about people breaking lockdown rules over the upcoming Easter weekend, since for most of the country the weekend forecast was glorious. But with a garden like this, Gemma didn't feel the need to go anywhere; she was looking forward to a weekend of reading, sunbathing and pottering about doing nothing much.

Other than checking the weather, she'd also been catching up on the news. It felt strange to think of the Prime Minister being in the thick of the virus, like something out of a film with an implausible plot. On Sunday she had watched the Queen make an address to the nation, which ended with 'Better days will return: we will be with our friends again; we will be with our families again; we will meet again.' Vera Lynn references aside, it had made Gemma quite emotional; right now her friends and family felt like they were on a different planet.

All the thoughts of family made her long to talk to Louise, who would be off work with her kids this week. Gemma called but got her voicemail, and was feeling a little bereft when her phone pinged to announce the arrival of a WhatsApp message.

Can't talk, up to my neck in kid shit.

Gemma hoped this was metaphorical for Louise's sake and tapped out a reply. *No problem. Shall I tell you another joke?*

She knew that Louise would be grinning right now. *Oh God. Go on then.*

Gemma thought for a minute, looking at the wooden coat and hat rack by the front door.

What's a hat maker's favourite gameshow?

This is going to be awful isn't it? Go on.

WHO WANTS TO BE A MILLINER.

Fucking hell. Go away.

Louise finished her message with a row of laughing emojis, and Gemma felt her mood lift. Maybe today was going to be OK after all.

In the five days since dinner with Matthew, Gemma had got her head into work, pitching a few more article ideas to various publications and scoring a couple of wins, including one she needed to finish today. She'd even called her mother for a proper catch-up, being careful not to mention Matthew's name even in passing; the Lockwood women had a radar for gossip and her mother would be on her like a hawk. She'd taken Mabel for long walks across the fields, and on Tuesday she'd decided to start running again.

Gemma had never really thought of herself as a runner – her boobs were too big and she had a weirdly short stride, which made her running look like more of a wobbly shuffle. Fraser had once told her she ran like she was taking part in a school sack race, then made a hilarious joke about being happy to get her in the sack any day. Fraser considered himself something of a comedian, but always finished a joke by looking around triumphantly, like he was waiting for someone to appear in a puff of smoke and give him a one-man show at the Edinburgh Fringe.

Not long before she'd left London, Gemma had completed a Couch to 5k programme and had been trying to get into the habit of running for half an hour or so three times a week. Now seemed like a good opportunity to get back into it, so on Tuesday she had dug out her most robust sports bra and hustled Mabel on to the lane outside the cottage. Mostly she discovered that half an hour feels like several years when there's nothing to look at but fields and woods, but she had pushed through to the end and today she needed to go again.

Sightings of Matthew had been few and far between this week, other than him popping his head in the door after Mabel's walk on Sunday to ask if he could switch to mornings for a while, so he could put in a solid day's work afterwards. In the warmer weather Mabel had taken to dozing on the patio outside the kitchen door in the mornings, so Matthew often took her lead off the hook by the door and walked her without Gemma even noticing that she was gone. He had a canny knack of coming over while she was in the shower; Gemma suspected this might be on purpose, but she didn't push it. He clearly wasn't interested in anything more than a neighbourly friendship, and she wasn't going to make an idiot of herself over him.

She took the stiff broom from the tool shed and walked to the decked area at the end of the garden, where a purple clematis rambled over the wooden pergola. It was just coming into full flower, so it created a lovely dappled shade on the wooden deckboards. She quickly swept the area clean, then carried the bistro table and one of the folding chairs from the gravel at the bottom of Matthew's steps. She was sure he wouldn't mind, and she didn't want to disturb him to ask. The small table and lone chair looked a bit forlorn on a deck designed for large al fresco parties, but it was the best she could do. She returned to the house and grabbed her notebook, phone and laptop – the battery was fairly new and would be fine for a few hours.

She settled into the chair and organised everything on her makeshift desk, as Mabel plodded over from her favourite spot under the apple tree and flumped down at her feet. For the first time in a few days, Gemma felt a sense of peace – it was a beautiful day, she had work to occupy her mind, and the horrors of the spreading pandemic felt a million miles away. With the UK's daily death toll rising swiftly, she felt glad to be physically and emotionally out of London, even if she'd give her right arm for a Pret crayfish and avocado salad and a decent coffee right now.

Twenty minutes later, Gemma heard the doors of Matthew's workshop roll open; clearly it was getting warm in there, and he needed to let some air in. She heard faint music coming from inside, and by the time it reached 'Rehab' by Amy Winehouse she realised it was a noughties playlist that was one of her Spotify favourites. It took her back to the Friday-night drive home in Aunt Laura's car, when Gemma was allowed to put her *Now That's What I Call Music* CD into the car stereo. Aunt Laura had occasionally joined in with Gemma's singing; in 2002 they had both loved 'Whenever, Wherever' by Shakira and 'Get the Party Started' by Pink, while 2003 had been all about Beyoncé's 'Crazy in Love' and Busted's 'Year 3000'. Neither of them could sing for toffee, but as Gemma got further away from school and closer to the sanctuary of 22 Church Street, belting out Shakira felt like a celebration of freedom, even if it was only for forty-eight hours.

Humming along to Gnarls Barkley's 'Crazy', Gemma realised that the WiFi was better here, presumably because she was so much closer to the barn. She video-called Joe and was immediately uplifted by the sight of his grinning face on the sunny balcony of his flat in Camberwell, wearing nothing but shorts and a baseball cap. His London party lifestyle had been significantly curtailed by the lockdown, so for the first time it was Gemma's Adventures in Farmerland that held the potential for excitement and intrigue. Joe couldn't hide his disappointment at Gemma's reports of domesticity and solitary runs, none of which ended in her being swept on to a horse by a country squire with strong thighs and a sex dungeon. He'd definitely read too much Jilly Cooper.

As with her mother, Gemma didn't say anything about Matthew, but after she blew Joe a kiss and ended the call she realised her mistake. Joe would speak to Caro, Caro would ask if Gemma had mentioned her friend Matthew, and the fact that she had not, even in passing, would be picked apart for its hidden implications. The three of them had shared a flat at university for two years and nobody knew Gemma better; by bedtime Joe and Caro would have assembled all the evidence and confrontation wouldn't be far away. She should have kept it light and casual – *There's a guy next door, friend of Caro's, seems nice but don't see much of him*. Massive schoolgirl error.

At 1 p.m. Gemma took a break for lunch – a tin of tomato soup with a cheese sandwich to dip into it. It had been a weekend favourite at Aunt Laura's, and was still Gemma's go-to lunchtime snack when comfort was needed. Fraser had hated it – he called it 'duck food', a term that applied to any combination of dry food and liquid. The idea of dunking a biscuit into tea made him heave, and he ate his roast dinners dry, spurning any kind of gravy or sauce. He was also the same about hot and cold food on the same plate – a meal like fish, chips and salad was served with the salad in a separate bowl, which Fraser would eat afterwards, like a lettuce-based pudding. Gemma never could understand his love of Thai food when there were only a handful of dishes on the menu that were dry enough for him to eat.

While Gemma swished her sandwich in her soup, her mind drifted back to Aunt Laura, wondering what she would have made of her current situation. With a pang Gemma realised that she would never have been in Crowthorpe if circumstances had been different; on the night she'd needed to escape London, she'd have headed for Church Street instead. Gemma, Aunt Laura and Mabel would have weathered this storm together, eating tinned soup, reading books and making little dolls of Fraser to stick pins in.

After lunch she hung out some laundry and mowed the lawn, a much quicker job since Matthew had hacked through the jungly growth the previous week. She pulled a few weeds and trimmed the shrubs, noticing for the first time a vine on the back of the house that was coming into leaf. She wondered if it would produce grapes, then reminded herself that firstly she wouldn't be around long enough to find out, and secondly she hated grapes unless they were squashed, fermented and bottled. After an hour of needless clipping and faffing about, Gemma was forced to admit to herself that she was hanging around outside in the hope that Matthew would come out of his barn. She could hear the whine and grind of saws and power tools, interspersed with the occasional thud of timber being moved around, but he hadn't left the workshop for hours.

She stood on the path with her hands on her hips, chewing her lip and watching a snail making its leisurely way across the path, its little rubbery horns alert for a dog in the mood for an exotic snack. *Stop this shit, Gemma.* Either she needed to go to the workshop and talk to him, or stop hanging around the garden like a schoolgirl with a crush, waiting to be noticed.

Her mouth formed a hard line as she reached a decision. She quickly put away all the garden tools and headed back into the house to change. It was time to go running.

Gemma pushed through the first ten minutes to a point where her legs no longer felt like lead and her lungs stopped pretending she smoked forty a day. Running was inarguably hideous, and it was no wonder so many people gave it up in favour of baking or knitting or masturbation. She left the cottage and the village behind, Mabel trotting at her heels and occasionally veering off into the verge to forage for litter or fox poo. Gemma supposed she should put her on a lead since the lane was technically a road, but in nearly three weeks she hadn't seen a single vehicle other than bikes and horses. There was a large livery stables about half a mile out of the village, and at least twice a day she would hear horses clopping by. It was something she never heard or saw in London, and she found the sound rather restful.

A bell sounded in her ears, and the voice told her she was halfway through today's run and should turn around and head for home. *What does home even mean?* she thought. If it was just the place where she lived, she didn't have enough toes and fingers to count thirty-two years of homes. What defined the difference between the place where you lived, and the place that was home? Right now she had no answer, and she was too sweaty for big philosophical questions.

She thought for a while about the last eighteen days she'd spent in Crowthorpe. It had gone so fast, and yet in a weird way it felt like she'd been stuck here for ever. She'd settled into her new routine, waking up with the sun and the pigeons on the roof. She was eating better – the village shop was heavy on fresh local produce and very light on ready meals and junk food. She was also carefully monitoring her news intake so as not to overload her brain with things that she couldn't control; it felt like a twenty-four-hour barrage at the moment, and if you were so inclined you could watch a continuous news feed of unfolding global horrors and never sleep again.

After forty minutes of dragging her feet around the lanes, Gemma headed indoors for a shower and a change of clothes; any kind of shaving and underwired bras were a distant memory, but there was no need to go entirely feral. For the rest of the day she stayed away from the garden and Matthew's barn, instead working in the dining room while Mabel dozed by the window, her fur glowing in the afternoon sun. A few days before, she'd created a Word document entitled 'Aunt Laura', and had started writing down anecdotes and stories whenever she remembered them. The tuneless singing in the car, making cupcakes on a Saturday afternoon, the smell of oils and turps and dusty cloths in the unused art studio, the outrageous stories Aunt Laura used to tell about her old days in the theatre (most of which seemed to involve nudity or drugs), Uncle Clive's monogrammed handkerchiefs. Gemma laughed and sobbed and howled as she tapped them all into her laptop, and felt the grief she'd been hauling around for months gently dissipate with every paragraph.

At 8 p.m. she was emotionally and physically drained, but she dragged herself out of the front door to lean on the white gate and join in with another Clap for Carers. Partly it was about being an active part of the Crowthorpe community, but it was also about connecting with something that felt much bigger and more important. She had seen social media videos from her friends that showed the wave of noise sweeping across London, with people shouting and letting off fireworks. Here the initial enthusiasm had settled into something more like polite clapping at a local cricket match, but it was uplifting nonetheless; it felt good to remind herself that her tiny dramas were insignificant in the scheme of things; that people were putting their lives at risk to battle this virus every day.

As the clapping died away, Gemma waved and smiled at her neighbours as they drifted back to their homes. She stayed by the gate for a minute to watch the dying embers of the sunset cast a warm glow over the fields. A movement to her left caught her eye, and she noticed Matthew watching her from the side gate. Gemma wondered how long he'd been there, and whether it would have killed her to pencil her eyebrows and put some lipstick on earlier.

'Hello.' He took a few steps back and leaned on the wall that separated the side path from her tiny front garden. Mabel bounded over and put her paws up on the wall, demanding a head pat. Her tongue lolled about in drooling excitement as she tried to reach him, but the wall was too high so she settled for frantic tail wagging instead.

'Hey.' Gemma's throat had dried up at the sight of him, and now she didn't trust herself to say anything in case she also started drooling with her tongue out.

The silence stretched out between them, so Gemma bolted for the door again, just as she had two weeks before. She gave Matthew an awkward smile. 'Have a good evening.'

Matthew paused for a half-beat, then lifted his hand a few inches off the wall.

'Gemma, wait. Let's catch up tomorrow. I've been stuck in the workshop all week working on that table, I need human conversation. We can sit in the garden and get the barbecue going.'

Gemma looked at him, trying to arrange her face into an expression of calm and serenity while her stomach did a double backflip with an aerial cartwheel and a handspring to finish. 'That would be nice. What can I bring?'

'Can you bring food? I've got loads of drink but otherwise my fridge is bare and I haven't had time to deal with it. About six?'

Gemma laughed. If it was a choice between friendly neighbour Matthew or no Matthew at all, she'd definitely settle for this version; her only face-to-face conversation in the past two days had been Mabel and Henry the vacuum cleaner.

'Sure. I'll see you then.' She walked back into the cottage, suddenly feeling not very tired at all. If she'd had a tail, it would be wagging full speed.

CHAPTER TWELVE

Friday, 10 April

To Do

- Become culinary goddess
- Shave everything

Gemma lay in bed, gently freeing herself from the final, grasping tendrils of sleep. Morning birdsong had reached its peak, and while she was starting to be able to distinguish the different tunes, she still didn't know what bird they came from. She should order a British garden bird book from Amazon, but delivery was taking for ever right now. It was unlikely to arrive before she went back to London, where it would be no use whatsoever unless there was a big chapter on pigeons.

She remembered that today was Good Friday, which in a normal year would be the beginning of a long and lazy weekend with friends and family. Last year she'd spent the day on a date with Fraser, maybe their third or fourth since they'd met a few weeks before. It was the first date that was in the daytime, so they'd strolled hand-in-hand along the South Bank, both of them nervous and feverish in each other's company. In the afternoon they went back to Fraser's flat and had sex for the first time – a tangle of sweaty sheets that Gemma abandoned for a pre-arranged night out with Joe that she refused to cancel despite Fraser's theatrical sulking. She had left at the last possible minute and met Joe at a bar in crumpled clothes and bed hair, reeking of sex and Sauvage by Dior. Joe wouldn't let her order food until she'd shared every last detail, and they'd ended up drunk and giddy in one of Joe's favourite clubs until 3 a.m. On Saturday afternoon she had taken the train to Norfolk to visit her parents, the intention being to spend Sunday at the care home with Aunt Laura. Gemma found her agitated and confused, and didn't stay long. She got the train back to London rather than stay another night with her parents, and spent Easter Monday alone, grieving for a woman who had not yet died, but was already long gone.

Today Gemma felt in a more positive frame of mind. She had another run to do this afternoon, then the barbecue with Matthew. She found herself grinning stupidly at the thought of it, although it was just some food in the garden with a neighbour. In normal times this would feel like a very ordinary thing, but these were very much not normal times, and any break from the routine felt like something to look forward to. The decision to count themselves as the same household made her feel better about spending time with him – it was bad enough that she was having dirty thoughts without them also being illegal.

Gemma loved a barbecue. In Cyprus during school holidays it felt like the whole island smelled of chargrilled meat; the smell always made her think of sitting under a woven straw umbrella on the beach with her school-holiday friends, eating souvlaki stuffed into a pitta bread and drinking Sprite out of a glass bottle. During those holidays she almost felt normal, surrounded by other teenagers struggling with the same volatile, itinerant life. Her parents offered her the chance to leave boarding school and attend St John's, the local British Forces school, but that would mean leaving Aunt Laura and moving schools again before her exams. Even though boarding school was awful, it was at least reliably awful for a full five years.

She lay in bed and mentally planned her day. Her priority was buying some food for the barbecue, the options being whatever the village shop could provide. Matthew had offered to take her to the supermarket in Chippenham on a couple of occasions, but there wasn't anything she needed desperately that she couldn't buy either from the village shop, or online for delivery. She had never been one for overblown, fancy cooking; when you lived alone you learned to treat food like fuel, rather than the foundation of a grand performance. In her experience no dinner ever truly suffered from an absence of Himalayan rock salt or truffle oil.

So food shopping first, then some marinading and a bit of prep. A run with Mabel after lunch, then a shower and change. *I need to shave my legs and tidy up my bikini line*, she thought, then immediately felt a squirm of shame about where her mind was going. Yesterday she'd been embracing her lack of female grooming, and now she felt like she was failing Feminism 101 for a barbecue with a neighbour. Maybe just a tiny strim round the edges, nothing dramatic.

Gemma's mental list-making was interrupted by the vibration of a WhatsApp video call from Caro. It was a bit early even by her friend's standards; clearly Caro was up with the kids and needed to vent about something. She swiped to answer but left the camera off – there was rarely enough signal for video even at the back of the house, and a high risk that Dressage Tony was with Caro. He definitely didn't need to see Gemma in bed at 8 a.m.

'Morning, Caro, what time do you call this?'

'Gem! I've already had two coffees and am about to make a third. I needed to see your face and a house that isn't total chaos. Turn the camera on.'

'It won't work, there's not enough signal in this backward hellhole.'

'For fuck's sake. Go into the bathroom and hold it up by the skylight. It works there.'

Gemma rolled her eyes and rolled out of bed, putting on a big T-shirt and padding into the bathroom. She stood on the toilet seat and pressed the camera button, and a fractured shot of her friend's face appeared. Gemma missed Caro desperately, but wouldn't swap lifestyles for all the money in the world. Caro and Antonio had two children – five-year-old Bella and three-year-old Luca. The combination of Caro's Algerian/Irish parentage and Antonio's Italian roots had without doubt created two of the most beautiful children on the planet, but they were both incredibly hard work. In normal times Caro had the support of a German au pair, but Amelia had gone home to Hanover weeks ago, leaving Caro trying to keep the agency afloat alongside full-time parenting and (to add insult to injury) having to clean her own house. Antonio was some kind of management consultant specialising in IT for the public sector, which apparently required complete seclusion in their home office for at least twelve hours a day. Caro was doing all of the heavy lifting right now, and by any standards looked terrible.

'You look terrible.'

Caro smiled grimly. 'I feel terrible. You look amazing. Why do you look amazing?'

'Because I've just had a decent night's sleep, and I've been running and stopped eating takeout at eleven p.m. I am also free of the burden of terrible men.'

'I'm still sorry about Fraser, what a total fucking shit. Put that DOWN, Luca. Do you want to talk about it?'

'I absolutely don't ever want to talk about it, but thank you.'

'I totally understand. Let's talk about Matthew instead.'

Caro had laid the trap perfectly, and Gemma fell straight in. Her face froze and she paused for just a second too long.

'What do you mean?'

'HAH. I KNEW IT!'

'Caro, stop it. There's nothing to talk about.'

'You LIE, Gem. I can read you like one of your stupid books. Do you like him?'

Gemma rolled her eyes, feeling thoroughly cornered. Caro was so good at this, and Gemma knew she was beaten.

'OK, fine. I like him. He's nice. But there's nothing to tell, I swear. He made me pizza, but that's it. No body fluids have been exchanged, nothing steamy to report.'

Caro narrowed her eyes, mollified for now.

'How disappointing. I'd hoped to live vicariously through your village adventures. Bella, don't hit your brother. TONY. For fuck's

102

sake, where is he?' Caro disappeared briefly and the children's chatter became more muffled as a door closed. 'That's better. Tony's talking about going to Italy to see his parents for a few weeks; apparently it's about their welfare, but they're holed up in their fucking holiday home in Amalfi with a swimming pool and a tennis court. They want Tony and his sister there, presumably so they can all play mixed doubles while I stay in London and look after his fucking children. I'm absolutely divorcing him after all this.'

Gemma smiled; this was something she'd heard from Caro many times. 'No, you're not, you love him really. You told me you'd never divorce Tony because he worships you and makes you come like a dog on a whistle.'

'Fine, then I'll get a vibrator.'

'You don't already have a vibrator?'

'I'll get a better one. He's a shit. All men are shits. Apart from Matthew, he's lovely. Be nice to Matthew.'

Gemma laughed. 'I'll let you get on. And I'll send Matthew your love – we're having a barbecue in your garden later.' She grinned broadly and gave a thumbs up, ending the call before Caro could respond. The smile stayed on Gemma's face throughout her shower; a call from Caro felt like a good start to the day.

At 6 p.m., Gemma picked her way down the path with a tray of meat and vegetable skewers and a bowl of Greek salad. Finding feta cheese and a jar of black olives in the village shop had felt like a major win, although she hadn't been able to find a red onion. It would be fine without and avoided the horror of potential onion breath. She put the bowls down beside the barbecue, which had already been lit – Gemma could see that Matthew had also moved the small table and chairs back to the deck, and laid the table with two plates and cutlery. A blue cooler sat by the barbecue; Gemma lifted the lid for a peek and found it full of wine and cider.

She returned to the house, her long skirt swishing around her ankles. It was gauzy white cotton with a pale grey paisley pattern, something she had bought in Greece years ago; today she'd paired it with a pale green T-shirt that fell off one shoulder, and a pair of ancient flip-flops. Gemma's hair was loose around her shoulders, and the barely-there make-up had been given another outing, this time with the tiniest spritz of Chanel.

She came back a few minutes later, trailing Mabel and carrying a cardigan and a small jug of salad dressing. The day had been unseasonably hot for early April, and even now it was still in the twenties – no doubt it would get chilly later, but for now the air felt blissfully warm on her skin.

Matthew appeared on the steps of the barn just as she arrived and waved a pair of barbecue tongs. He was in shorts as usual, but these ones were free from splashes of paint and wood glue. Another plain white T-shirt, and a pair of black Havaianas. His feet were respectable, which was a relief; Gemma couldn't be doing with poorly maintained man-feet, all hard yellow skin and fungal toenails.

'Hey. Thanks for bringing food. Let's have a drink and then I'll do some cooking.'

Gemma pulled a couple of ciders from the cooler and popped the tops. The bottle opener was tied to the handle with a piece of frayed blue string, which Gemma found rather delightful. She was a million miles from her usual cocktail haunts right now, and it felt quite liberating.

They both sat in the early-evening sun, drinking and chatting about nothing in particular. Gemma told Matthew about her running, and Matthew updated her on the progress he'd made with the table and benches; everything just needed a final sand and a few coats of oil, then the order could be delivered. His customers weren't in a huge rush but Matthew was keen to move on to other things; he didn't like projects hanging around. Gemma mentioned her early-morning call and passed on Caro's regards, which prompted a discussion about Caro's wedding to Dressage Tony, which it turned out Matthew had also attended. Gemma didn't remember him, but there had been over 200 people and it was eight years ago. She idly wondered if he'd taken a date, but didn't ask. They talked about the current lockdown situation, and how it was supposed to end on

Monday but was very clearly going to be extended. Nobody seemed to know how long for, and it felt pointless to speculate.

After two ciders the barbecue coals were hot and the smoke had died down, so Matthew put the skewers on to cook. The smell of sizzling meat gave Mabel a new lease of life, and she parked herself inches from Matthew's feet until the meat was cooked and a few cooled pieces had been put on the deck for her to inhale in seconds. Gemma and Matthew ate their food at a much more leisurely pace, switching cider for a bottle of wine from the cooler. Matthew had wrapped a bag of ice around two glasses, so they were frosted with cold and the wine tasted crisp and delicious.

By 8 p.m. the sky was darkening, so Matthew stumbled over to flick a switch on the side of the barn that lit the gravel area at the bottom of the steps. They were both rosy-cheeked with alcohol and contentment; Gemma couldn't remember the last time she felt this relaxed and happy drunk, as opposed to the wretched misery-drunk of her first night in Crowthorpe. She leaned back in her chair, her head suddenly a little woozy, and looked up at the barn. The windows were all in darkness; it looked cold and stark from the outside, nothing like the cosiness she'd discovered inside.

'Do you ever find it a bit dark in there, during the day?' She turned to Matthew, who had his eyes closed and his head tilted to the sky.

He looked up. 'What, in the workshop?'

'No, in your apartment. Upstairs. It's beautiful, but the windows are so tiny. I wondered if it felt dark in there sometimes.'

Matthew looked confused and didn't speak for a few seconds. 'Didn't . . . didn't you notice the ceiling on Sunday?'

Gemma looked blank. *What about the ceiling? It was dark.* 'No. What's special about the ceiling?'

Matthew jumped out of his chair and grabbed her hand, causing Mabel to leap around in circles in excitement. 'Come with me, I'll show you. Stay there, Mabel.'

Matthew kept hold of Gemma's hand all the way to the top of the steps, by which time Mabel had settled down on the gravel below, looking resentful. He opened the door and pulled Gemma into the strange half-darkness within; she felt giddy and breathless with wine and anticipation, she had no idea what was happening, but it felt wonderful.

Matthew moved behind her and rested his hands on her shoulders. 'Look up.'

Gemma looked up. The gently sloping walls ended in two ridge beams, and the flat ceiling between was made up of two huge glass panels separated by a central tie beam. As the evening sky deepened into night, it was like looking into two pools of glittering purple light; in an hour or two it would be full of stars.

Gemma sighed happily; it was so ridiculously perfect. She imagined how the room would look in full sunshine, with shafts of light casting beams across the furniture. Mabel could simply inch around the room in a moving sun patch. In winter you could look up and watch the rain beating down on the glass, or feel like you were in the middle of a lightning storm. She imagined lying on the sofa and watching it snow, as flake by flake the heavy grey sky was replaced by a ceiling of the brightest blue-white. 'I didn't notice,' she whispered. 'I was too busy looking at your books.'

Matthew didn't reply. He was still behind her, close enough that she could feel the heat of his body, even though only his hands were touching her. She felt the faintest whisper on her neck as he gently moved her hair to one side, his fingers brushing her bare shoulder.

Gemma closed her eyes, her nerves jangling. She felt a deep, dull ache in the pit of her stomach, as Matthew traced his fingers along the line of her shoulder and down her bare arm. His breathing became heavier and she resisted the temptation to grab at him with both hands, not wanting to look like she was frisking him at the airport.

Matthew's lips touched the curve of her neck, and his hands slid down her back and gently circled her waist. She covered them with her own and giggled nervously.

'My legs won't hold me up.' She turned around and he pulled

her tighter into his body, resting his chin on her shoulder. 'Is there any chance you could kiss me?'

Matthew breathed out slowly, like a sigh. 'Gemma, you have no idea how much I'd like to kiss you. But if I do, I'm going to take you to bed, and we're both hammered.' He released her and pulled away. Gemma turned to look at him, confused and fuzzy-headed. Bed sounded great, what was wrong with bed?

He gave her a penetrating stare. 'Don't get me wrong, I really want to. You have no idea. In fact if you came any closer you'd have a very good idea.' He gave a short laugh, and Gemma tried to smile. 'But I don't want to have drunk sex with you. I want sober, clear-headed, unforgettable sex. Can we do this again? Like, tomorrow?'

Gemma's lust-fuelled brain processed his words, and she tried to extinguish her disappointment along with the fire that was still burning through her lower body. The last few minutes had flipped her world upside down, and right now tomorrow seemed like a very long way off. But not seducing drunk women on a first date, however consensual, was definitely a quality she and Caro had attributed to their imaginary perfect man; it had never occurred to her that he might actually exist. Getting in a strop about it was clearly a bad look, so she gave him a smile that she hoped was charmingly flirty, rather than randy and plastered. 'I can absolutely come back tomorrow. Can we do brunch?'

Matthew laughed, and opened the door. 'We can definitely do brunch, although I suspect very little food will be involved. Now go home and sober up, and take your needy dog with you.' His hand stroked her hair back from her face, and he planted the lightest of kisses on her forehead.

Gemma had no idea how she made it down the steps and hauled Mabel back to the house. Halfway up the path she looked back and saw Matthew watching her from the balcony, so she focussed on walking the rest of the way in a straight line. Her final thoughts before closing the kitchen door were that tomorrow really could not come soon enough, and right now a cold shower might not be a bad idea.

CHAPTER THIRTEEN

Saturday, 11 April

To Do

- Feel like shit
- Sulk

Gemma

After you left last night I had a call from my friend Paul, he's the one who runs the homeless shelter in Bristol. He had a break-in yesterday and a load of damage has been done to their external door and food/supplies room; they don't have the funds to pay for tradesmen to fix it so he's asked for my help. I would have gone last night but I couldn't drive (!!!), so I'm going first thing this morning instead.

I wanted to come over last night and say goodbye, but we both know where that would have ended up. I meant what I said about wanting to do things properly, but it's going to have to wait a few days. I'm sorry about today, but not at all sorry about last night, I had a great time.

I'll stay in touch and let you know when I'll be back – I'll be sleeping on a camp bed in the shelter until everything's fixed, so I get to be a security guard as well as the handyman.

I've left a key to my place on the hook by your back door, help yourself to any more books.

Mx

Gemma found Matthew's note when she came down at 7.30 a.m. to let Mabel out – he had slid it under the door, and left Gemma's salad bowl and meat tray on the low wall outside, all clean and tidily stacked, with the skewers lined up like little soldiers.

She sat on the bench outside the back door, still wearing her pyjamas. The goose bumps on her arms gradually turned purple with cold, but she continued to sit, feeling hungover and miserable, looking at the space to the left of the barn where Matthew's van should have been. Gemma had gone to sleep with the fizz of wine and anticipation in her belly, but now she felt like a deflated balloon. Even in her head this sounded childish and petulant, but right now she didn't care. This was supposed to be a special day, something to take her mind off the mess her life was in, never mind the fact that the entire planet was a virus-riddled shitshow. She felt like stamping her feet and throwing things.

For the rest of the morning Gemma wallowed in a big sulk, dragging her feet around the woods with Mabel, whose head hung low in solidarity with whatever had upset her owner. By lunch-time she had exhausted her personal brand of woe-is-me anguish and was thoroughly bored of being miserable, so she lay on a towel in the garden in her bikini, taking the opportunity to transform the bits of her body that currently looked like uncooked pastry into something a little more sun-kissed. The hot and sunny weather was due to break on Monday, so hopefully she could achieve a mottled pink without burning by the time Matthew got back, as long as she kept to the dappled shade of the apple trees. Mabel stayed close, pricking up her ears expectantly every time she heard a male voice walking by. *He's not here, Mabes. What a sad pair of lonely bitches we are.*

After a couple of hours of turning every thirty minutes like a rotisserie chicken, Gemma had finished the Zadie Smith book and needed something new. She padded back to the house to use the bathroom and threw on a stripy T-shirt dress, then unhooked the key to Matthew's place before heading back down the garden and up the wooden steps. Mabel followed, her nose staying close to the ground on the off-chance that Matthew was hiding inside, waiting to give her bits of cheese and extended belly rubs.

The apartment felt entirely different in the afternoon sunlight – it was bright and airy, with shafts of warmth stretching across the sofas. Mabel immediately jumped up and bagged the best sun patch, turning a few circles before settling down with a huge yawn. Gemma had no idea how Matthew might feel about dogs on his furniture, but frankly he wasn't here and she didn't have the energy to move Mabel. Right now she felt scratchy and tired, a combination of too much sun and the poisonous residue of last night's boozing. She ignored the bookshelves for the moment, lying down on the other sofa with her feet in the sun near Mabel's head. It was cool and comfortable and blissfully tranquil, and Gemma felt herself drifting as she listened to the birds in the apple trees and the clip-clopping of horses in the lane.

When she woke up an hour or so later, the feeling of peace and serenity lingered. She stayed stretched out on the sofa for a while, listening to her own breaths and Mabel's feathery snores. Right now there was nowhere she needed to be, and nobody was demanding anything of her. She was free of pandering to Fraser's moods, free from the tension of spending Easter with her parents, and even free from the anxiety and heartache of visiting Aunt Laura in her care home.

It seemed like a betrayal to even think it, but Gemma didn't miss those visits. Even though it was a fancy private facility that specialised in dementia care, the corridors still had that institutional feel, and no quantity of beautiful flowers in tall vases could hide the smell of boiled vegetables and industrial cleaning fluids and people who were decaying from the inside out. She hated the way the staff talked to Aunt Laura in that singsong voice, like she was a child rather than a woman who had graced the stage as Beatrice in *Much Ado About Nothing* and transformed a decrepit theatre through sheer force of personality. In the early months Gemma would get a bus or a taxi from her parents' house with a knot in her stomach, not knowing whether she'd find her aunt lucid and chatty, or frightened and abusive. In the end Aunt Laura had become a shell, her eyes fixed on the birds outside the window, but unseeing and unknowing.

For the first time Gemma put aside her grief and let herself feel relieved that Aunt Laura was gone. She had been taken far too soon, but she had lived with her illness for less than five years. Some people's decline was agonisingly slow, like watching the foundations of a house crumbling by degrees over decades, with no means to even plaster the cracks. Gemma didn't need to worry about her any more, and instead could channel her energy into living her life in a way that would make her aunt proud.

The feeling of steadfast resolve brought Gemma back to the room, and an awareness that dozing on Matthew's sofa without permission was probably not on the Things To Be Proud Of list. It was just so warm and quiet and comfortable, like one of those cosy dens children build under the dining table out of sheets and blankets. She stayed a few minutes longer, rubbing Mabel's back with her foot as she stretched out her limbs one by one like a cat.

For a few delicious minutes she revisited the touch of Matthew's fingers on her skin last night. It felt unreal, like something from a romantic film – of course the sequel was supposed to be an afternoon of wanton fornication, but apparently it had been cancelled due to lack of availability of the lead actor. Gemma could feel the edge of her mood darkening again, so she forced herself to snap out of it – it wasn't like Matthew had gone to Bristol for an orgy; he was donating his time to a homeless shelter. *Have a word with yourself, you spoilt cow.*

She stood up and stretched a bit more, shaking off the final remnants of her afternoon slumber. Before she completed the book-finding task she came up here for in the first place, she quietly opened the door to Matthew's bedroom and slipped inside. She was curious to see where he slept but was careful not to touch anything; she obviously didn't want him to think she'd been nosing around, so it was important to leave no evidence whatsoever.

It was a lovely room, with another big skylight in the ceiling and a double bed with a pale grey duvet cover. There was an old, heavy chest of drawers which Gemma didn't open, but she did lean over to peer at the three framed photos arranged on the top. One was an old photo of Matthew and his family in a delicate oak frame, taken in the mid-nineties if the baggy striped T-shirt and hair curtains were anything to go by. He looked like an awkward child of seven or eight, uncomfortable in his ill-fitting limbs but not yet hamstrung by the crippling self-awareness of puberty. He was perched on a stone wall with his parents, against a backdrop of turquoise water under the bluest of skies – Greece or Majorca, perhaps. All of their smiles were broad and open, like they'd all obliged when the photographer had told them to 'say cheese'. Matthew favoured his father; he had the same nose and chin and thatch of unruly hair. His mother was a beautiful woman, probably no older in this photo than Gemma was now. It was clearly a special holiday that Matthew had fond memories of.

The second photo was Matthew's parents together, taken in more recent years judging by their appearance and the elegant cut of his mother's dress – perhaps a 50th birthday or a 25th wedding anniversary. The photographer had captured them toasting each other with delicate flutes of champagne rather than looking at the camera, and their glance was one of undying devotion and mutual understanding. Gemma could see why Matthew would love that photo; in thirty-two years she'd never seen her parents look at each other that way.

The final picture was Matthew with a group of two men and two women in a pub, holding a silver cup and cheering at the camera, their fists pumped. Presumably this was his winning pub quiz team, and from the picture Gemma could see that Matthew was the youngest by some years. Gemma's usefulness in quizzes was limited to literature and popular culture, but perhaps Matthew had a host of random specialist subjects that made him a pub quiz assassin – rivers of the world, military history, *Strictly Come Dancing* contestants. The frame was an ugly white plastic that jarred with the delicate wood of the others; Gemma guessed that the team captain had printed a copy of the picture for each of them, and bought identical frames for a few pounds each. Gemma could imagine Matthew putting it on the side and hating it, then wondering if he could switch it into a better frame, but in the end deciding that would be impolite and settling for it grating on his nerves every time he looked at it. The only other item in the room was an old wooden chair in the corner, which currently had yesterday's shorts and T-shirt draped over it. She bent down and surreptitiously sniffed the T-shirt, it smelled of barbecue smoke and something indefinably manly.

On the far side a door led to the bathroom; Gemma flicked the light switch and discovered a space that was monochrome and masculine. She scanned the toiletries on the shelf above the sink, and was surprised at how comprehensive his grooming regime was. He clearly preferred the Kiehl's men's range, and the containers of face wash and moisturiser were half empty, alongside a glass spray bottle of a natural sage deodorant and a bottle of Chanel Pour Monsieur that didn't look like it had ever been opened. There was no bath, but there was a huge walk-in shower with a waterfall head and a tiled alcove that held a single giant bottle of hair and body wash. The space felt clean and minimalist and uncluttered without being sterile, and when Gemma used the toilet she found it spotlessly clean. Perhaps he'd also wondered how yesterday's barbecue might pan out, and scrubbed his loo just in case. The thought made her smile.

On the way back to the lounge she sat briefly on the bed and gave a light bounce – it was rock hard and entirely unforgiving. She lifted a corner of the duvet and found the mattress was barely more than a futon, resting directly on a solid wood frame. *That's going to completely fuck up my back*, she thought, as she carefully straightened the duvet and made sure everything was left exactly as she found it.

Back in the lounge, Gemma drifted along the bookshelves, looking for something new to read. They liked a lot of similar authors, but there were a huge number of books here that she'd never read. A travel biography might be fun, some kind of uplifting yarn about someone crossing the Channel in a rubber dinghy or skateboarding across Africa or something. She looked on the shelf below the travel guide books, and a narrow spine labelled 'Europe 2014/2015' caught her eye. She carefully levered it out from the shelf – it was a hardback photo journal, about 20 centimetres square, the kind you designed yourself online and had printed.

Gemma opened the front cover and found a handwritten note written on the flyleaf.

Matthew,

A few memories from the best year ever. Can't think of anyone I would have wanted to share it with more than you. Love you, Claire xx

Gemma froze, desperately wanting to turn the page but knowing she'd instantly regret it. She took the book to the arm of the sofa and flicked the first page over – Matthew astride a green moped in shorts, T-shirt and flipflops. A little younger, a little harder-bodied and a lot more tanned – if he was thirty-one now, he'd have been twenty-five in 2014. The caption said 'Skiathos hot wheels!' Gemma flipped to the next page, Matthew standing beside the same moped with his arm round a woman, a girl really – she couldn't have been more than nineteen or twenty. Claire was slim and beautiful, with a tumbling mass of beachy blond waves and a smile that would stop traffic from half a mile. Gemma's mouth felt dry and acidic, but she flipped again. This time Matthew and Claire outside a small church on the top of a hill, the azure sea in the background – Gemma knew it as the church in Skopelos where they'd filmed the wedding sequence at the end of *Mamma Mia*, she'd been there herself with Joe a couple of years later.

The rest of the book was more of the same – a smiling Matthew and Claire looking blissfully happy together. Their trip had started in autumn of 2014, which they spent touring the Greek islands. Around November they moved to Austria and worked in a pizzeria called 'Barga' for the ski season, then headed to the Adriatic coast in late March, travelling south through Croatia to Montenegro. Summer was spent in Italy and Spain, Claire picking fruit and Matthew doing odd jobs, and their trip finished in the South of France in late August 2015. The final picture was a selfie of the two of them at Marseille airport, both with dark tans and huge backpacks, their arms round each other as they pulled exaggerated sad faces.

Gemma closed the book, a sour taste in her mouth. It was ridiculous to be jealous of a former girlfriend of a man who wasn't in any way her boyfriend, but she couldn't help it. She assumed Claire was no longer on the scene; it felt bad enough to see her in five-year-old photos without considering the possibility that she might still spend time in his bed. Even taking into account the years that had passed, it was impossible not to compare herself to Claire; if this was Crufts, Claire would be the glossy pedigree that won best in show, while Gemma was very much the over-enthusiastic mutt who took a consolation rosette for Dog with the Waggiest Tail. Gemma was clearly a million miles from being Matthew's type; and it was hard not to think that the attraction for him right now was that she was a) conveniently next door and b) very obviously up for it. The thought made her feel sick.

She carefully returned the photo album to the shelf and forced herself to complete the book-choosing mission she had come here for in the first place. She needed comfort reading that would stop her having bleak thoughts, so definitely nothing about jealousy – now was not the time for *Tess of the D'Urbervilles*. She took a chance on *Ordinary People* by Diana Evans, which she hadn't read but had heard good things about, and *The Shadow of The Wind* by Carlos Ruiz Zafón, which was another one of her favourite books that she hadn't read in years.

There were two new things beyond Gemma's control today – Matthew was away, and the beautiful Claire now existed. There was nothing she could do about either of these situations, so for now she would do what she had always done in dark times, and lose herself in a book.

Hey Gemma, hope you've had an OK day. Hot working in here but made good progress. Getting supplies the biggest issue, might have to wait until Tues for some of it as usual suppliers closed for Easter. Pot noodle for dinner, all time low. Mx

Hey yourself, did some sunbathing and read some books, so not a bad day. More of the same tomorrow, high danger of dying of boredom or lack of human contact. Gx

Please don't die of boredom, I will be back soon for as much human contact as you like. Mx

CHAPTER FOURTEEN

Monday, 13 April

To Do

- Buy food
- Stop feeling like shit

By Monday, Gemma had achieved her goal of turning most of her body from pure brilliant white to a mottled pink, like a wall that had been ragged on a nineties episode of *Changing Rooms*. Gaining any kind of natural tan took an entire summer, so this was the best she could hope for.

The weather had changed dramatically this morning – she woke up to a cold, biting wind that rattled through the window frames and matched her cranky mood. Her limbs felt heavy and sore after a forty-five-minute run yesterday, and even showering and dressing felt like too much effort. If she hadn't been required to meet Mabel's basic needs, she probably would have stayed in bed all day.

Gemma had heard nothing from Matthew all day yesterday, although he had sent a *Hey, you OK?* before bed. She'd replied with *All good, bit too much sun today so having an early night, Gx* and received *OK sleep well Mx* in response. It felt overly polite and somehow deficient, but to be fair she wasn't giving him much to work with. She felt like everything was hanging until she could look him in the eyes and truly understand what a man who had dated a woman like Claire wanted from a woman like her. Right now, casual, no-strings sex felt like it might leave her feeling

117

worse, but equally Gemma wasn't sure she wanted the strings either – she didn't know where they led, and that felt knotty and complicated. Mostly she just wanted Matthew to be there, so this weird sense of limbo would end.

Matthew wasn't the only thing in limbo – the initial lockdown period was supposed to be ending today, but everyone was saying at least three more weeks, even though the government weren't confirming either way. Gemma felt like she needed to make some decisions; she couldn't stay here indefinitely, and being so far from her normal life was making her feel twitchy and directionless. She was feeling stifled by this sleepy village – right now the highlight of her day was a walk to the shop, which felt a bit pathetic even by quarantine standards.

She grabbed Mabel's lead and a shopping bag, and put her coat on to walk to the shop. It was only open for a couple of hours today as it was a Bank Holiday Monday, and while bleach and dog biscuits could wait, milk and tea bags could not. Things were bad enough without foregoing the tiny pleasure of a cup of tea; it was the only thing keeping Britain going. She'd had to start the day with an instant black coffee this morning, and was still feeling bitter about it.

As she walked past the estate, Gemma caught the tail end of a screaming row through an open window; a woman yelling at someone that they needed to pull their weight, that she couldn't entertain the kids AND clean the house AND do the shopping AND do her job on her own. Gemma slowed down a little, wanting to check that nobody would start throwing furniture or crockery or punches. She heard a door slam and the whine of a toddler, but no more yelling.

The voice rang in her ears as she continued walking. She couldn't imagine what it must be like to be locked down with an unhelpful partner and a couple of bored kids; the monotony and stress would kick in pretty quickly. It mirrored the conversation she'd had with Caro on Friday, but Caro could afford to buy toys and games and video consoles to keep Bella and Luca amused. The narrow Victorian townhouse that she and Tony owned in Borough wasn't huge, but it had a garden big enough for a paddling pool or a trampoline. Tony had wanted to live north of the river, somewhere smart and leafy in Zone 2, but Caro couldn't bear the idea. 'It's all Bugaboo mums and four-wheel drives, Gem. I feel bad enough having an au pair and a cleaner without living in fucking *Hampstead*.'

As Gemma walked through the village, she waved and smiled at some familiar faces, and stopped for a chat here and there. With the exception of the unflappable cheerfulness of Steve the Postie, who lived on the estate and did the local mail delivery, Gemma's irritable mood seemed to be mirrored through the village. People seemed bored, frustrated and in need of inspiration. She passed a man kicking a deflated football in the front garden with his daughter, a big-eyed, red-haired child of about four who asked if she could pet Mabel. As girl and dog got to know each other, Gemma chatted to the girl's dad; he had two older kids inside but his wife was a pharmacist, so she was currently at work. They'd played with all the toys, watched all the DVDs, and exhausted all his ideas. He joked that after three more weeks of this he'd have to put them up for adoption, just so they'd have a change of scenery. 'What's adoption?' asked the girl, and her dad smiled awkwardly and hustled her into the warmth of the house.

A few houses further down was an elderly woman struggling with her wheelie bin, so Gemma dragged it up the path for her and asked if she wanted anything from the shop. Her name was Joan and she didn't need anything; apparently a shop volunteer rang on a Wednesday morning to take her shopping list, then delivered it in a box that afternoon. Joan and Gemma talked for a while about the things they missed from before the pandemic – Gemma couldn't wait to meet up with her friends in London, and Joan missed the weekly knitting circle at the village café. They'd swap patterns and share leftover wool, so she always had plenty of inspiration for new things to make. Gemma made a hasty exit before she was invited to look at Joan's woolly creations; Mabel was getting bored with all this stopping and chatting and was already eyeing up Joan's sheepskin slippers as a potential snack.

For the rest of the walk to the shop, Gemma's brain whirred. A seed of an idea was taking root, and by the time she reached the shop it was growing branches and leaves. She checked her watch and saw that she had twenty minutes until it closed, so she tied Mabel to the metal ring and fished out her notebook to scribble down some notes.

Ten minutes before closing time, Gemma closed the notebook, gave Mabel a kiss on the head and went into the shop. Only Ruth was there, getting ready to cash up for the day. The smile she gave Gemma was much warmer than the day she'd arrived; clearly staying three whole weeks had earned her the courtesy of being treated like a normal human being. *I've got my temporary visa*, thought Gemma, returning Ruth's smile and gathering her shopping as quickly as possible. She wondered how long you'd have to live here to be considered a resident; maybe you had to be part of the sixth generation of babies born in Crowthorpe or it didn't count.

As she paid for her shopping, she started to casually fish for information. She was a journalist, this was her happy place.

'Ruth, just out of interest, who's in charge of the village hall?'

Ruth looked up. 'Oh. Well. There's a committee, I'm a member. But obviously we're not hiring it out right now. Why do you ask.' Still no upward inflection, it was like this woman had never learned how to ask a question.

Gemma hesitated. Nothing was ever going to happen if this thought only existed in her head. 'I've had an idea for the village, and I think it would help a lot of people. Have you got time for me to run it past you?'

Ruth's brow furrowed for a second. 'Yes, but we can't talk in the shop, it's not allowed.' She scribbled a phone number on a scrap of paper and handed it to Gemma. 'Why don't you walk your dog round the churchyard while we talk on the phone.'

Gemma left her shopping in the shelter of the lychgate and

called Ruth as she began her first loop of the churchyard. By the time they'd finished talking, Mabel was ready for another nap.

Gemma built on the idea for the rest of the afternoon, working through the potential objections and hurdles as Mabel snoozed on her feet. By 6 p.m. she had written up a proposal on five Power-Point slides she could share on the Zoom video call Ruth had organised with the village hall committee at 7 p.m. The fact that this could be scheduled at half a day's notice on a Bank Holiday Monday was testament to how few social engagements people had these days.

She felt nervous and out of her depth – she'd only been in this village three weeks, and now she was asking them to listen to her ideas. She wasn't even sure why she cared; it wasn't like she was moving here for good. What if she came across as some kind of meddling Londoner, trying to change their way of doing things? To make matters worse, she was going to have to do the call in Matthew's apartment, because her WiFi signal wasn't good enough for a video conference. What if the people on the call noticed and thought they were living together? She'd be a meddling Londoner who was clearly shagging the local handyman, which somehow felt so much worse.

At 7 p.m. Gemma joined the call, having arranged Matthew's dining table so her backdrop was an innocuous blank wall. The first ten minutes were spent unravelling various technical complications – *how do I turn on my video, Sue you're on mute, you need to press the microphone symbol, no that's the camera, we can't see you OR hear you now.* Gemma was gratified to see that it wasn't all old men – the committee had seven members, and four of them were women, including the Chair, who was a woman called Erica.

Gemma introduced herself to the group and tried to allay any preconceptions that she was a busybody interloper. 'I know I'm new to the village, but I've been made incredibly welcome, and I've talked to a lot of people about some of the challenges they're facing right now. I guess maybe people find it easier to talk to a stranger? Anyway, I've had an idea that might make a small difference, but I can't make it work without your support.'

She had their attention, so Erica encouraged her to carry on. Gemma clicked the button to share her screen and cleared her throat, suddenly feeling like this was the stupidest idea ever.

Slide 1

The Challenge

Right now everyone has been stuck at home for at least three weeks, and it feels like the monotony of the situation has kicked in.

Kids are bored, parents have run out of inspiration, sometimes it feels hard to get through the day.

It's easy to buy toys and books and games and start new hobbies if you've got plenty of money, but lots of people in the village are struggling on reduced furlough incomes, waiting for their self-employed government grant, or getting by on universal credit or their state pension. For many people, and for a hundred different reasons, things are really tough right now.

Slide 2

The idea

Lockdown Swap Shop

To bring Crowthorpe villagers together by starting a simple swap shop in the village hall – donate your unwanted toys, books or games in a safe, socially distanced way, and pick up something new at absolutely no cost.

What would we take?

1. Children's toys, books, games
2. Adult books – fiction and non-fiction
3. Board games, outdoor games, jigsaw puzzles
4. DVDs and video games
5. Recipe books, baking tins and kitchen accessories
6. Gardening and DIY books and tools, cuttings and plants
7. Craft/hobby books and supplies

Slide 3

How would we make it safe?

We'll run the scheme for a few hours, three times a week – all new items dropped off will be cleaned with anti-bac spray and quarantined in a storeroom in the village hall for 48 hours. Only quarantined items can be given away.

We'll allow one household in the hall at a time, for ten minutes. That household could be one adult, or a couple, or a whole family. People can book their slot in the village shop in person or by email, so they're not hanging around.

Slide 4

What would we need?

1. Donations – I'll get to that in a minute.
2. Tables to display available items clearly – it's important that people don't handle things, so they need to be able to see what's there. It would help to separate items into categories – adult books, children's toys, craft items, DIY, etc.

3. Some kind of barrier so people are held back from the table – reduces temptation to touch (particularly for kids).
4. Three or four volunteers each session – someone to manage the flow of visitors, someone to accept incoming items, and a couple of people to help with outgoing items. These people will have gloves on so they can handle items and answer questions. At the end of each session all volunteers can anti-bac spray and organise any incoming items for the next session and wipe down the hall.
5. Disposable gloves and cleaning materials.

Slide 5

How would we tell people about it?

Day 1: A leaflet drop to every house in the village (via Steve the Postie?). Also village noticeboard and shop, and village Facebook page (?). Fifty or so houses get 2-part leaflet asking them to donate items for first session, everyone else can bring items along on the day.

Leaflet would also ask people to plan their visit to coincide with their daily outing, so it isn't a special journey. All sessions during shop opening hours, so hopefully additional uplift in sales.

Day 2: Collection of donations, to be left in bin bags/boxes outside each house. All taken to the village hall for cleaning and quarantine.

Day 4: First swap shop.

Day 6: Second swap shop.

Day 8: Third swap shop.

Gemma had talked uninterrupted for twenty minutes, and now had nothing more to say. She un-shared her screen and looked at the wall of stern, silent faces. 'Umm, that's it. Any questions?' she asked weakly.

The questions and suggestions began; Gemma was relieved to see that there was general enthusiasm, although some questioned whether this was in line with lockdown guidelines about use of community spaces, or whether people would have stuff to swap. Holes in Gemma's plan were filled, additional refinements made around ways to display, how to involve people who were completely isolated, and what to do with any leftover items at the end of the lockdown. Eventually a vote was taken and passed – pending a call first thing tomorrow to the Council to check that this was permitted, it would be tested for three sessions, then reviewed by the committee.

Gemma would create the leaflet on her laptop tomorrow, email it to Ruth who would print it off on the village hall printer, and deliver to Steve the Postie, who Erica would call immediately. He'd delivered leaflets for the shop before without any issues, so he could drop these through every letterbox in the village on Wednesday.

Somebody asked if they could ask Matthew for the use of his van to collect all the donations on Thursday, and Gemma updated them on his mercy dash to Bristol; she had no idea if he'd be back by then. She'd barely given him a thought since this morning, and wondered what he would think of this mad idea. A different man with a van was suggested – the husband of a committee member called Rachel who volunteered to collect everything with him on Thursday lunchtime, when Ruth and Gemma would be waiting in the village hall with Dettol spray, masks and rubber gloves to sort and clean everything. Which meant the first swap shop could be Saturday morning, if they liked. It seemed like a lot to achieve, but the committee agreed that there was nothing to be gained from hanging on. A team was assembled, and Erica agreed to email round the notes and action plan first thing in the morning.

It was almost 8.30 p.m. by the time the call wrapped up, and Gemma was exhausted but exhilarated. It felt uplifting to have a project and be doing something that was useful. She realised how much she needed her time in Crowthorpe to feel worthwhile – it was what would have mattered most to Aunt Laura, and even her mother would approve. Aunt Laura loved a community project – she had turned a run-down theatre in Norwich into a thriving space that offered free workshops and holiday drama clubs for underprivileged teenagers. When they were posted in Germany, Gemma's mother had started coffee mornings for young, often lonely military wives – a safe and confidential space where they could meet and offload for an hour. For all her mother's faults, having the empathy to see a problem and the creativity to find a solution was something Gemma had always admired, and seemingly inherited. In that moment, the realisation took her by surprise.

She shook off thoughts of family and picked up her phone, which buzzed with a message from Matthew.

Hey Gemma, how was your day? I'm hoping to be back on Thursday. Hope that's good news? Mx

Hey you. My day was pretty great, and that is really, really good news. Gx

Returning to the pages of notes and ideas on the table around her, Gemma decided that, either by current standards or those of her former life, this had been a very good day.

CHAPTER FIFTEEN

Tuesday, 14 April

To Do

- Running (ugh)
- Plan mad village thing
- Clear the decks of everything unrelated to mad village thing

Erica emailed first thing to confirm that she couldn't get hold of anyone from the Parish Council, and the government guidelines were really quite unclear on coronavirus-specific community initiatives. But volunteer activity was definitely allowed, so as long as they were meticulous about safety, they should probably work on the basis of 'ask for forgiveness, not permission'. Gemma was very much on board with this kind of renegade thinking, and cracked on with drafting the leaflet, which explained in words of two syllables or fewer how the scheme would work.

Deciding this would all benefit from a second opinion, she popped back to Matthew's apartment with Mabel and started a video call to Caro – the woman had a desk covered in awards for advertising, she would have opinions to spare. Mabel immediately made herself comfortable in her favourite spot on the sofa, while Gemma propped her phone up against the wall so she could chat and type at the same time.

'Hey, Caro. I need your help.'

'If you're asking for sex tips I've got nothing, it's drier than the Kalahari down there. I think it's healed over.'

'Haha, no. I need your marketing wisdom.'

'OK, that you can have for free. Wait, where are you? That's not my table, and you have proper WiFi. Holy fuck, are you in Matthew's place? WAIT. GEMMA, DID YOU SLEEP THERE?'

Gemma threw her hands up in despair and laughed – this woman should work for GCHQ.

'NO, I did not sleep here. He's been in Bristol since Saturday and left me a key so I could borrow books, so I'm pinching his WiFi. Stop talking so I can tell you what I need.'

'OK, but how does that even work? Do you count as the same household?'

'It's a very good question. We've decided we do, because of the shared garden.'

'Fair enough. Have you snogged him yet?'

'I have not.'

'For fuck's sake, Gem, you'd make a lovely nun. OK, tell me what you need.'

Gemma outlined the scheme to Caro, who clapped her hands with glee. 'This is SO you. You move into my parents' village and immediately start solving everyone's problems. I love it, THEY would love it. I'm so proud of you.'

Caro made a few suggestions and Gemma edited the copy on her laptop while they chatted. Once they'd ended the call, Gemma hung around in the peace of Matthew's apartment for half an hour to finish both versions of the leaflet, the poster, and the copy for the village Facebook page. She attached them to an email and sent them to Ruth and Erica for approval, then turned to a fresh page in her notebook and started making lists of things that needed to be done each day this week. Her priority today and tomorrow was clearing the decks of work, house cleaning, laundry and life admin so she'd be free to focus on the Swap Shop for the rest of the week.

Mabel wandered over to the table and headbutted Gemma's leg until she bent down to scratch between her ears. She was overdue her morning walk, but Gemma wanted to finish her lists before taking her out. It was also a day for running, so it would very much be worth Mabel's while to be patient. 'I'll be half an hour and then we'll go, you'll have to wait.' Mabel eyed her reproachfully and settled down under the table with a huff, which reminded Gemma of her visits to Aunt Laura's when Mabel was a puppy. She had followed her owner round the house like they were joined by elastic, and could always be found lying at Aunt Laura's feet.

Gemma wondered if Mabel remembered her original owner; it had been almost three years since Gemma had had a phone conversation with Aunt Laura's occupational therapist and the move to a specialist care home was confirmed. The fate of her dog had caused Aunt Laura some distress, so Gemma didn't hesitate to offer to take her to Warwick Mews. Of course at the time she had no idea the house would be sold barely two years later and she would be moving Mabel to Fraser's house, where she had been grudgingly welcomed by a man who seemed to be caught in an internal battle between his love of dogs and his passion for white furnishings. Only six months there, and now Mabel was here. In a week or two she would be living somewhere else. *Poor Mabel*, thought Gemma, *she was supposed to live out her life in the comfort of the house in Norfolk. Now she's being moved around like just another piece of my luggage.* She stroked Mabel's head for a few minutes, in time with her contented growls.

By midday Gemma had ticked a half-hour run down the lane off her list, and Mabel was asleep again, this time back in her bed in the dining room of the cottage. Gemma climbed the stairs to shower and wash her hair, thinking it would be good to do it again on Thursday morning before Matthew got back. Not having him consume her every thought felt like a relief; being sad and needy was quite draining. It also inexplicably made her want to eat biscuits.

She had also stopped obsessing about Claire, rationalising that the trip finished five years ago and people's tastes changed. She'd been dating Johannes at that time, and while she had loved that he was creative and interesting and musically gifted, for the life of her she couldn't remember what had kept them together for two years. He had pale, feminine hands with unfeasibly long fingers, no appreciation of irony or satire, and approached sex like one of his musical scores – to be rigidly followed note-for-note, with no artistic interpretation whatsoever. He played her just like his French horn – a little light fingering to warm up, then a deep breath and absolute focus to the end.

So yes, Claire had been young and glossy-haired and beautiful, but maybe she'd also been a right moaning cow throughout that trip and gave REALLY bad blow jobs. The worst kind, all teeth and gagging. The thought made Gemma laugh out loud in the shower, and the noise echoed off the tiled walls. *Uh oh, you've started laughing at your own internal dialogue. You need to get out more.*

Gemma came downstairs with her hair wrapped in a towel and checked her emails. Ruth and Erica had approved her copy and leaflet design, so Ruth would get them all printed and delivered to Steve the Postie later today. Gemma felt tense and nervous about the whole project – perhaps nobody would donate or people wouldn't want to get involved. Perhaps she'd overestimated the need for something like this. Maybe the police would turn up and arrest them all. For the thousandth time in the last twenty-four hours, she asked herself why on earth she had started this, when she could just have opted for a quiet life in the cottage until it was time to go back to London.

The reason, as always, was Aunt Laura. She'd have told her to go for it, and not let obstacles or excuses get in her way. *The future is promised to no one, Gemma; you have to make things happen.* How true that turned out to be; Aunt Laura's future had been curtailed far too soon. Gemma wondered what she would have said about Matthew, but she knew the answer to that too. It was another one of her favourite sayings – *Follow your heart, but take your brain with you.*

Gemma walked into the lounge and opened the wood burner. Crumpled on top of the unlit tinder was the list she had written on the back of an envelope almost two weeks ago, the day before she'd gone to Matthew's barn for the first time. She smoothed the envelope out until it was mostly flat, then grabbed her pen and made some additional notes.

Reasons not to fancy Matthew

1. Social distancing – **bit late for that**
2. He's not your type (local man for local people) – **no longer applies**
3. He's Caro's friend (awks) – **she seems OK with it**
4. He might not fancy you – **indications are positive**
5. He could be gay – **he's definitely not gay**
6. You'll make an idiot of yourself – **guaranteed**
7. You're moving back to London soon – **still true and problematic**
8. You're on the rebound – **still true, less problematic**
9. You're crap at relationships – **still true, can't be helped**
10. Men are shits – **possibly not all men, tbc**
11. ~~You are 32 and don't look great naked~~ – **Can't believe you wrote this, behave yourself**

Reasons to fancy Matthew

1. He's kind and nice (underrated qualities, tbc if sexy) – **can confirm v. sexy**
2. He's literally next door – **sore point right now**
3. He might fancy you too – **see above, indications positive**
4. He probably looks great naked (also: good with hands) – **still tbc**
5. You're trapped in a small village in a global pandemic, normal rules have gone out the window – **still true**

Gemma stabbed the envelope on to the rusty nail above the dining-room fireplace so she could revisit it later. The thought of Matthew made her skin prickle and her stomach do backflips, but the consequences loomed in the corner of her mind like little nagging goblins. Her heart told her to give into the feelings, her head told her to be careful. The relentless battle between the two was at risk of bringing on a migraine, so she turned her attention to more practical matters. It would be nice to put a few groceries in Matthew's flat before he got back, things like bread and milk, maybe a few flowers from the garden. The peonies weren't quite ready – the buds were tightly closed and perfectly round, like pink table tennis balls – but there were still some wild daffodils left. She added a few items to her shopping list, found a blue striped jug in the kitchen and headed outside.

By 3 p.m., Gemma was entirely at a loose end and couldn't settle to anything. All her lists were done, the house was clean, and the jug of wild daffodils was in the kitchen waiting to be transferred to Matthew's place on Thursday. She made a mug of tea and hunted in the cupboard for more biscuits, then remembered she'd finished the last few yesterday. They were chocolate Hobnobs, eaten as a celebration of a successful Zoom call and a very poor substitute for dinner.

She opened the cupboard and took a quick inventory – she'd managed to acquire a small bag of flour from the shop, which Ruth extracted from a locked store cupboard and told her not to tell anyone about, like she was dealing hard drugs or stolen goods. She also had butter and caster sugar – Aunt Laura had made an amazing shortbread with those three ingredients, but Gemma couldn't remember the proportions. She opened WhatsApp and her finger hovered over the green phone icon for a moment before she pressed decisively. Her mother answered after a few rings.

'Hello, Gemma darling, this is a surprise.'

Gemma closed her eyes and focussed on her mindful breathing. 'Hello, Mum, how are you?'

'I'm fine, keeping busy in the garden. Your father is digging, I'm directing operations.'

Gemma laughed; she could just imagine her dad huffing and grumbling in the borders.

'Mum, I need your help. I want to make Aunt Laura's short-bread but I can't remember the quantities. Do you know?'

Her mother was silent, and the moment dragged out long enough that Gemma wondered if she'd been cut off. 'Mum? Are you still there?'

'Yes, I'm still here, I'm just thinking. Hold on a moment.'

Gemma heard her mother open the kitchen door and the creak of her feet on the stairs. Another door opened, presumably a bedroom. Then a brief knocking sound as the phone was placed on a hard surface, followed by the dragging of wood on wood as a drawer was opened. Gemma had heard that sound a hundred times and knew exactly where her mother was right now – kneeling in front of the old wooden chest of drawers in the blue guest bedroom, wiggling open the big bottom drawer that stuck halfway. She couldn't think what her mother was doing in there; she'd slept in that room at Christmas and that chest had contained nothing but offensively floral bedlinen and mustard towels.

There was a sound of squeaky bedsprings as Gemma's mother sat down on the bed, and her voice returned. 'Here we are.'

'What is it? What have you found?'

'It's your aunt Laura's recipe book. She used it to write down favourite recipes, and she's stuck some in from magazines. It used to be in her kitchen in her house in Wymondham. I think the shortbread recipe is in here.'

Gemma knew for sure that it was, she could picture the book perfectly. A large spiral-bound notebook with a pale green cover and unlined white paper, the kind of thing you'd buy in a stationery shop for a couple of pounds and use as a sketchbook. 'Recipes' had been written in black marker pen in the white box on the front cover, and the cardboard back was a mess of swirly scribbles where Aunt Laura used it to check if her pen was working. Gemma had flicked through the pages so many times, some containing nothing more than a few lines of handwritten instructions in Aunt Laura's spidery scrawl, others crisp and heavy with glue and recipe cuttings from *Good Housekeeping* or the *Sunday Times* food magazine. Gemma remembered that the shortbread recipe page was handwritten, the page spattered with smears of butter and tiny hardened blobs of dough. Aunt Laura didn't care; as far as she was concerned sticky recipe books were the sign of devoted use. According to Nigella, anyway, and Nigella was never wrong.

'I know exactly the one you mean. Where did you get it?'

Barbara sighed heavily. 'I helped to clear out her house in Norfolk before it was sold. I suppose it was nearly three years ago now. It seemed like something she might ask for, or perhaps I thought there was a chance she might live independently again. Silly, really. A couple of months ago I unpacked the box and put it in a drawer for you. I thought you might want it.'

Gemma's eyes welled with tears; she hadn't realised just how much she wanted it until that moment. 'I do, Mum. Thank you.' Her mother cleared her throat; Gemma could hear her flicking through the pages. 'Here we are. It's easy enough. Six ounces of flour, four ounces of butter and two ounces of caster sugar. I'm sure you can convert that into your metric nonsense.'

Gemma laughed. 'I definitely can. Thanks, Mum. I'll send you a photo when they're done, shall I?'

'What on earth for? What would I do with a photo?'

Hey you. I made some shortbread today. If you're lucky there might be some left when you get back. Gx

There better had be. I've been eating kettle food for days. I need home cooking, and also you. Mx

You've been out in the big wide world. Don't you need to self-isolate for two weeks? Gx

I definitely do not. But if you'll self-isolate with me, I might consider it. Mx

I'm afraid I've become a mainstay of the village community while you've been away, I'm organising inspiring projects to improve lockdown life and am extremely busy and important. Gx

Hahahahahaha Mx

CHAPTER SIXTEEN

Thursday, 16 April

To Do

- Running again (ugh ugh)
- Change sheets (just in case)
- Scrubber duty 1 p.m.
- Wash village hall out of hair
- Re-shave everything

Gemma woke up with a jittery, nervous feeling in her stomach after a turbulent night's sleep. Whichever way she looked at it, today was going to be a very big day. It was donation sorting day, and at some point Matthew was coming back from Bristol. He hadn't said when, but Gemma expected to be at the village hall all afternoon, so chances were he'd be back by the time she got home. She still hadn't resolved the situation between them in her head, and had made a decision yesterday to talk to him when he got back. She had popped up to his apartment the previous evening to leave a few items of fresh food and the jug of flowers, and had borrowed a few more books. It was unlikely she'd have time to do much reading in the coming days, but at least it was a legitimate reason to be there.

She started the day by taking Mabel for a run and checking her emails; she'd had no new work assignments for a few days, which to some extent was a relief since she had so little time right now, but in other respects was a bit of a worry. She'd considered pitching a story about lockdown village life and her swap shop idea, but wanted to see how it went first and run it past the committee. She didn't want them to think she was an opportunist, selling them out for column inches.

By late morning Gemma had changed the sheets and laid out a change of clothes for this evening – she'd shower and wash her hair when she got back from the village hall, and do some quick personal grooming. She thought about how much Caro and Joe would tease her for such blatant sex preparation, but she'd never known a situation when she'd regretted being prepared, and anyway they'd never know. Only Mabel was here, and she was currently asleep and wouldn't judge.

After lunch Gemma put Mabel on her lead and walked her to the village hall. She had no idea how long this would take and didn't want to leave her at home alone, so she'd agreed with Ruth that she'd bring her along. Mabel would happily settle down in the office at the back of the shop, and Gemma could take her for a quick walk round the churchyard later. As they strolled through the village Gemma returned a few waves and nods of greeting, and smiled at the odd "Lo, Mabel' that came her way. Even if people didn't know her name, they always remembered her dog.

Ruth was waiting in the village hall when Gemma arrived, armed with a couple of bottles of Dettol, a packet of J–cloths, two surgical face masks and some white latex gloves like the ones Gemma's doctor snapped on before giving her a smear test. She made them both a cup of tea in the small kitchen at the back of the hall, and they settled down to wait for the van to arrive. Gemma sat on a table and swung her legs, her hands gripping the table edge. Ruth watched her carefully, her face softer than the first day she'd seen Gemma in the village shop, but still missing nothing.

'What you worrying about now.' Always a statement, never a question.

'Everything. What if nobody donates anything, or nobody turns up on Saturday? It could be a stupid idea and I'll have wasted everybody's time.'

'Most of the slots for Saturday have already gone, you're flap-ping about nothing.'

Gemma looked up. 'Really?'

'Yes, really. I've had loads of people asking in the shop, they seem keen. To be honest, everyone's bored out of their minds, anything for a change of scenery.'

Gemma smiled and relaxed a little. 'I'm sorry. I've never done anything like this before.'

'I can tell. I thought you were a right madam that day you came here, turns out you've got a bit of something about you. You'll fit in just fine here.'

Gemma looked up in alarm. 'I'm not staying. I have to get back to London soon.'

Ruth raised her eyebrows. 'Why's that then.'

'Because that's where I live. It's my home.' Gemma watched Mabel, sleeping in the warmth of the window. Her barrel chest heaved in and out with sleep, and every now and then her front paws twitched. *Perhaps she's finally caught that magpie*, thought Gemma.

'Not right now it's not. Right now you live here.' Ruth paused for a few moments. 'When's Matthew back.'

Gemma smiled wryly to herself, people in this village missed nothing. They'd probably set up neighbourhood watch when she arrived; the barbecue last week must have set off all kinds of alerts, like smoke signals across the garden fences.

'Later today, I think, I'm not sure.'

Ruth made a sardonic huffing noise that was no doubt accompanied by more raised eyebrows, but Gemma wasn't looking – the white van had pulled up in the car park and she was momentarily saved.

For the next half-hour, Gemma and Ruth worked with Rachel and Chris, the couple with the van, to unload a huge pile of bags and boxes, alongside loose items like children's scooters and toddler ride-on toys. It seemed like everyone who had been asked had taken the opportunity to have a clear-out of unwanted items, and Gemma was relieved and gratified by the generosity. The collection volunteers left, and Gemma and Ruth set to work sorting and cleaning all the donations.

Not everything made the grade – some of the toys were cracked or broken, there were games and puzzles that clearly had pieces missing, and someone had given a stack of baking trays that were flaking with rust. Gemma put all these in a crate marked 'tip' – they would be taken to the local recycling centre whenever it re-opened. Everything else was inspected for damage, then sprayed with Dettol and carefully wiped. Books were quick and easy, but some of the toys and games had intricate nooks and crannies that they needed to poke around in, so Ruth went into the shop and came back with a couple of toothbrushes. It was boring, mindless work, but once they were clean, everything was packed into labelled crates and dragged into the storeroom to sit in quarantine until Saturday.

Gemma and Ruth wasted little energy on idle chat; there was a job to be done and anyway the masks muffled their conversation. At one point Ruth observed how thorough Gemma's cleaning was; clearly she had expected it to be more slapdash. 'Cleaning is my superpower,' replied Gemma. 'I learned from a master.'

By 4 p.m. they'd made a decent dent in the donation pile, so Gemma took Mabel over to the church for a walk. It was ostensibly for Mabel's benefit, but Gemma also needed a break – the gloves and mask had made her hot and sweaty, and kneeling on the wooden floor was making her back hurt. The pain made her think of the day she tackled the garden when Matthew mowed the lawn, and she wondered idly if he was back in the barn yet. If so he would have found the food and flowers, and the little parcel of homemade shortbread she had wrapped in baking parchment and tied with brown garden string. Gemma hadn't told him about the Swap Shop yet; it still felt like a dumb idea that was doomed to fail.

The afternoon was warm and the churchyard was quiet and peaceful, so Gemma took a moment to turn her face to the sun and breathe in the fresh air. She picked her way through the ancient, crumbling gravestones to the newer section at the back under a row of cherry trees, and wandered Mabel along each row as she read the inscriptions. She had considered the possibility that

Caro's parents might be buried here, but there was no sign of them in the handful of graves from three years ago. Caro hadn't mentioned them being religious people, and considering her mother was born in Algiers and her father in Donegal, it seemed unlikely they would have gone to the expense of a Church of England burial. Gemma had met them briefly on graduation day, and again at Caro's wedding and Bella's naming ceremony. By the time Luca arrived, Caro's mother was dead and her father was in his final months, so Caro deferred his naming ceremony indefinitely.

Mabel clearly wanted to run off the lead, so Gemma took her to a grassy space at the edge of the churchyard and threw a stick a few times. She stood under the shade of a horse chestnut tree that was just coming into full flower – Gemma had never looked at the huge bells up close before and was delighted by how intricate they were – like a mass of tiny white orchids with pink and yellow spots.

After twenty minutes Ruth's stony face had appeared at the village hall window, like Mrs Danvers in *Rebecca*. Gemma crossed the lane back into the hall and settled Mabel in the office again. Fresh gloves and masks were snapped on, and by the time the job was finished it was getting dark.

Gemma could see the lights in the barn from the kitchen door, so she closed it behind her and dragged a very reluctant dog down the garden path. Mabel had headed straight for her bed after the walk home, and wasn't remotely interested in another night-time excursion. Gemma didn't care for Mabel's objections – they were both exhausted, dirty and probably smelled terrible, but it felt important to see Matthew today; he must be wondering where she'd gone. She ran up the steps and knocked sharply on the door, and within seconds he was there, looking just as he had when she'd last seen him the previous week. He smiled and opened his arms, but Gemma backed away as fast as Mabel hurled herself at him.

'Please don't, I'm disgusting. I've been wiping children's snot and drool off things all afternoon.'

Matthew smiled and raised his eyebrows. 'You don't look disgusting to me. Why didn't you shower?'

'Because I've only just got back and I wanted to see you. I expected to be back hours ago and didn't want you to worry.'

Matthew let out a short laugh. 'Gemma, did you think I didn't know where you were? It's a small village, and they have a WhatsApp group that has nothing better to do right now than gossip. I almost came and joined you for a walk round the churchyard earlier, but apparently you looked . . .' Matthew made air quotes either side of his head '. . . quite zen.'

Gemma rolled her eyes. She should have known none of this would be news to him, but didn't have the energy to be annoyed about it right now. She made a mental note to be pissy about it later.

Matthew opened the door a little wider. 'Come in and have a shower. I'll make you a cup of tea and some cheese on toast. Somebody nice put some food in my fridge.'

Gemma stood under Matthew's waterfall shower and washed away a day of sticky toys and dusty books. His shower gel smelled a bit manly and he had no hair conditioner, but the hot water felt blissful and restorative. Helping herself to his razor for a spot of lady-grooming felt like a bit of a liberty, so she left everything in its natural state. She was too tired to care right now.

Feeling much cleaner, she sneaked a blob of Matthew's moisturiser for her face and wrapped herself in a pale blue towel, then padded through to the bedroom to retrieve the clothes she'd left on the floor. They'd disappeared, but Matthew had replaced them with a red sweatshirt, a pair of white boxer shorts and a thick pair of grey socks. Everything hung off her, but she was clean and warm. Her skin tingled in the cool room and her stomach felt like she'd swallowed a bag of frogs; it was hard to tell if it was hunger or anticipation.

While Gemma ate cheese on toast in the corner of one sofa and Mabel snoozed blissfully on the other, Matthew leaned on the kitchen counter and told her about the project in Bristol. It had been hard and lonely work, but the job was done and Paul was grateful for his help. Matthew planned to go back after the lockdown and run some basic carpentry workshops with some of the residents in the hostel; it might help them get back into work or at least be able to do odd jobs for money.

In return, there was little Gemma needed to tell him about the Swap Shop – he'd already heard about it on the village WhatsApp grapevine, and had found the leaflet in his mailbox earlier. She told him about her day and the kind of donations they had received, and Matthew promised to help whenever he could. It felt nice sitting there with him, eating toast and chatting. Gemma could see why Caro liked him; during her twenties Matthew would have been a beacon of steadfastness in her uninhibited, libertine life. She would have valued his kindness to her parents while she was working all hours in London, and seen him as a breath of fresh air compared to all those vain, coke-fuelled boys she couldn't help but fall in love with. When life got a bit crazy, Caro would have called Matthew for a dose of calm, unruffled reality. Perhaps she still did.

Once Gemma had eaten, Matthew took her plate and made her a peppermint tea in a red spotted mug. He sat on the sofa beside her, lifting her feet into his lap and rubbing them gently through the massive socks, which felt blissful and also vaguely erotic. Suddenly he looked at his watch and stopped.

'I have good news and bad news.'

Gemma looked at him, feeling slow-witted and exhausted.

'The bad news is I have to get off this sofa, because it's time to go and clap for the NHS. But the good news is that all your clothes are in my washing machine, so you get to stay here and drink your tea while I go and clap twice as hard for the both of us.' He stood up. 'I'll take Mabel so she can do her business.' He swiftly put on his trainers, then clipped on Mabel's lead. 'Come on, yellow dog.' Mabel leapt off the sofa with a look of swooning adoration. *She wouldn't have budged an inch for me*, thought Gemma.

She put her mug on the floor and stretched out full length on the sofa, wiggling her toes. She thought about what would happen when Matthew got back; it felt like he'd been away in Bristol for ages and he'd made no attempt to kiss her, even though she'd been butt naked in his shower earlier and was currently wearing his clothes with no underwear. Was he still interested, or had the moment passed? Were they now reduced to friendly chat and a chaste rub of tired feet, but strictly with socks on? And in the end, might that actually be for the best?

When Gemma woke she felt cold and discombobulated. A heavy fleece blanket covered her body, but it had slipped off her legs and left her goosebumpy and shivering. She sat up, realising she was still on Matthew's sofa, under the pale light of the waning crescent moon shining through the skylight. She looked at her watch – it was nearly 1 a.m., and she must have fallen dead asleep before he got back from the NHS Clap. *Super sexy, Gemma. Good work.*

Gemma unravelled herself from the blanket and stood up, her back and shoulders aching from yesterday's cleaning efforts. She ran the kitchen tap, gulping down two glasses of water as Mabel watched her with one eye open. She raised her head a fraction of an inch as Gemma scratched between her ears, then closed her eye again and settled back into the sofa with a contented growl. Gemma stood for a moment in the middle of the room, wrestling with what to do next. She desperately needed the bathroom but didn't want to wake Matthew, and walking back to the cottage in the middle of the night seemed ridiculous.

Being as silent and stealthy as possible, Gemma opened Matthew's bedroom door and crept past his sleeping form. She quickly used the bathroom, deadening any potential tinkling noise with loo paper and quietly closing the lid in lieu of flushing. Her teeth felt furry from not being cleaned before bed, so she put a blob of Matthew's toothpaste on her finger and poked it around in her mouth for a bit, which gave the fur a minty edge but was otherwise pointless. She tiptoed back into the bedroom, pausing to watch

Matthew sleep for a moment. He was on the side nearest the bathroom, facing into the middle of the bed; the other half of the bed was untouched. Gemma wondered for a moment if that was a throwback to sharing the bed with other women, perhaps even the gorgeous Claire with her beachy hair and perky boobs that fitted effortlessly into skimpy triangle bikinis without the need for industrial underwires.

Gemma's mouth formed a determined line as she walked round to the empty side of the bed. She slid off the jumper and socks so only Matthew's boxer shorts remained, then slowly reversed her body into the curve of his, wincing silently at the lack of mattress. He mumbled something incomprehensible in his sleep, then shifted his left arm and gathered Gemma into the warmth of his body, his hand resting gently on her breast. She felt her nipple harden under the warmth of his fingers, but resisted the urge to wake him. She relaxed into the coolness of his pillow, and they both slept.

CHAPTER SEVENTEEN

Friday, 17 April

To Do

- Zoom therapy with Caro and Joe
- More village hall nonsense 1 p.m.

'Gemma. I need to go, I've brought you coffee.' A whispered voice wormed its way into Gemma's subconscious, but she couldn't remember who it was, or pinpoint where it came from. It made her feel warm and happy though, so she decided it could stay.

She opened one eye, her head still buried in the pillow. Matthew was perched on the edge of the bed, fully dressed in his workshop shorts and an old grey T-shirt with holes under the armpits, holding another mug, this time covered in blue spots. He smiled softly as she battled her way out of the fog of sleep. 'Hey.'

Gemma lifted herself up on to one elbow, suddenly aware that she'd fallen asleep with wet and un-conditioned hair last night; right now it probably looked like an enormous wicker basket. She surreptitiously patted it down, mentally calculating its height and girth. 'Where are you going?'

'Downstairs. I need to finish the table and benches. This time last week I had loads of time, now I have to deliver them tomorrow. I need to start oiling.'

'Sounds exciting.' Gemma shifted into a sitting position and winced as the wooden bed frame dug into her hips. She bruised like a peach, and right now it felt like she'd taken up Mexican wrestling. She took the mug from Matthew and clutched it with both hands. It smelled like proper coffee from a machine, the first Gemma had had in the best part of four weeks. If he'd asked her to marry him in that moment, she'd have said yes.

'How do you sleep on this mattress? It's like lying on a door. I feel like Kate Winslet at the end of *Titanic*.'

Matthew laughed and shrugged. 'I like a thin mattress, it stops me lazing around in bed. I lie on it to sleep, and when I've stopped sleeping I get up.'

'So you have a bed that actively repels women,' Gemma teased. 'No wonder you're single.'

'It didn't repel YOU. You definitely weren't there when I fell asleep.'

'I woke up cold and needed the loo. You looked irresistibly warm.'

'That's the nicest thing anyone has ever said about me. And now I have to go to work. I've already let Mabel out and popped into yours to give her breakfast, so no rush. Can I come over later? I'll be done by seven.'

Gemma pretended to think about it. 'I'll check my diary, but it should be fine.' She smiled and hugged her knees to her chin in what she hoped was a vaguely adorable just-woken-up pose.

Matthew walked to the bedroom door, then turned back to look at Gemma. He stared at her for a moment, and Gemma was pleased to see he was struggling to leave. 'You are lovely. I'll see you later.'

As soon as the bedroom door closed, Gemma fell back on to the pillows and squealed as her spine made contact with solid wood. Honestly, this bed was the worst; the mattress was barely more than one of those cushions you put on a pool lounger on holiday. It felt like a masochistic way to sleep – no doubt Matthew was also the kind of man who swam naked in frozen rivers and whipped himself with birch twigs to get his circulation going. Gemma liked furniture that cushioned and cradled her – her bed at Warwick Mews had pillows for reading, pillows for sleeping and pillows that served no purpose other than giving her something soft and comforting to hug.

She slid gently off the edge of the bed and took another quick shower, humming Switzerland's 2019 Eurovision entry (came fourth, should have won) and resisting the urge to bellow the chorus in case Matthew could hear her downstairs. She put on her freshly washed and dried clothes from yesterday and dropped Matthew's T-shirt, boxers and socks in his laundry hamper, then made the bed and washed up her mug. Attempts to hustle Mabel off the sofa to go home were futile; *She's found her happy place*, thought Gemma. *I know how she feels.*

Her watch told her it wasn't quite 9 a.m.; she had a WhatsApp video call scheduled with Joe and Caro at 10.30. She couldn't call yet – Joe was a night owl and considered any kind of human conversation before 0930 to be inhumane, and Caro would probably be trying to force-feed Cheerios into Bella and Luca so she could park them in front of CBeebies and start work. But it was raining outside, so there was definitely a case for calling them from here rather than in the garden. She'd kill half an hour, then try them both at 9.30.

Gemma spent ten minutes working out Matthew's coffee machine, finding ground coffee in a canister and scooping it into the portafilter, then tamping it down like they did in cafés and twisting it into the machine. She pressed some random buttons until it started making all the right noises, then heated half a mug of milk in Matthew's microwave and added a double shot of espresso. It smelled like heaven and tasted even better.

Hugging her mug, Gemma gave the bookshelves another inspection. She liked the way they were organised, by genre rather than alphabetically by author or (God forbid) by colour. A whole section of classics, separated into British, American, other works in English by non-British authors (a lot of Irish writers here, Matthew clearly had a soft spot for James Joyce) and English translations of foreign classics. Modern fiction was a little more haphazard, covering several shelves in the middle section and vaguely categorised into literary, crime, science fiction and Scandinavian, although one whole shelf seemed to be taken up by books that didn't really fit anywhere else, which Gemma loved – have a system, but don't lose your mind over it. Non-fiction, biography and travel filled the space around the bedroom door, with a deep shelf along the bottom that held reference books, carpentry manuals, books that were too big for the other shelves, and a lovely set of coffee table books about classic interior design that Gemma guessed had been a gift from his mother.

Her eyes lingered on the travel section, feeling a twist of guilt and shame that she was blatantly scanning it for more travel journals or photo albums, because apparently she wasn't done with making herself feel like shit just yet. Other than Claire's delightful keepsake album, there were none that Gemma could see. She ran her finger along the edge of a high shelf and found no dust, then hated herself for checking. *Oh God, I'm turning into my mother.*

After fifteen minutes leafing through a beautiful book called *Time* by the British sculptor and photographer Andy Goldsworthy, Gemma decided it was an acceptable hour to call Caro and Joe. She picked up her phone and opened WhatsApp, then quickly wrote a message in their three-person group. *Can we video now? I have WiFi without standing outside. Gx.* A thumbs up emoji appeared from Joe within a few seconds – he lived on his phone and was very likely lacking more attractive offers right now. Gemma stroked Mabel's head and waited for Caro – five minutes later she appeared online and started the video call.

'Sorry, was just putting *Peppa Pig* on for the kids. Bella knows how to skip to the next episode so they'll be fine indefinitely.'

Gemma waved and smiled at them both – Caro's dark hair was wet and her face make-up-free; she had clearly just got out of the shower and was now clutching a mug of coffee. Joe's head was freshly shaved to his skull and he looked like he'd just been let out of prison.

'Wow, Joe. That's quite an extreme look.'

'Desperate times. Could be weeks before I can see my barber, so I took matters into my own hands. I quite like it.' He ran his hand over his snooker-ball head, then shrugged doubtfully. 'It'll grow back.'

Caro's eyes were scanning the background of Gemma's camera feed. 'Wait, Gem. Are you at Matthew's again?'

Gemma smiled sweetly. 'I am. He's in his workshop, and kindly let me use his WiFi again so I could speak to his undeserving friend.'

Joe's eyes narrowed. 'Bit early to be knocking on his door, isn't it? He must be a very early riser.'

Caro snorted her coffee and they both fell about laughing. *God, I miss them both*, thought Gemma. She missed their Sunday afternoon coffees and impromptu cocktails. She missed Joe's 3 a.m. drunk party texts and early Friday breakfasts in Borough Market before Caro went to work. She missed the days when she worked in Caro's office and they bunked off for half an hour to eat huge cinnamon buns from the Nordic Bakery in Golden Square, calling it a 'briefing meeting' so Caro could put them on expenses.

Caro pulled herself together, wiping the tears from her eyes with her sleeve. 'Come on, Gem. We need details. My sex life is a wasteland, Joe is reduced to sending dick pics to strangers. No, hang on, he's always done that. You need to spill the beans.'

Gemma wanted to play along with the fun but didn't know where to start. Right now she had no idea where she stood with Matthew, or how she felt about him. When she thought about it, she found herself feeling confused and anxious.

Joe peered a little closer to the screen. 'Hey, Gem, are you OK?'

She smiled thinly. 'I'm fine, guys, really. Things just feel a bit confusing. The stuff with Fraser, being here on my own. Matthew is lovely but in lots of ways he's really not my type, and I'm really not sure I'm his either. I don't want to make things more complicated than they are already. I'm just not sure this is going to be a fairytale ending, sorry.'

Caro cleared her throat, a sign that Gemma recognised as a lecture incoming. 'When you say not your type, what do you mean? Because honestly, Gem, your track record is an absolute shocker.'

Joe nodded, raising his hands like he was about to launch into a gospel interlude. 'YES, Caro.' Gemma realised this was a conversation they'd already had between them, and a dull pain formed in the pit of her stomach. Brace, brace.

Caro took a deep breath and continued. 'Let's see. The guy at uni, the Philosophy student who wrote you poems and read them to you in bed. Grim, and also weird.'

Joe laughed and waved his hands excitedly. 'Oh God, that guy you met at Bestival who wore clown trousers. Wouldn't stop ringing you afterwards. For, like, MONTHS. And then sent a picture of his ugly cock to your work email.'

Gemma put her head in her hands, dying with embarrassment at the memory. There was no point fighting back, this conversation had been a long time coming.

Caro continued. 'The Swedish guy who bred guinea pigs. That guy who tried to move into your house and get you to lend him money. Johannes. God, Johannes was dull. You know he was dull, right?'

Gemma's head snapped upright. Johannes deserved a mild defence at least. 'I accept he was dull, even by Swiss standards. But he was also gifted and interesting.'

'Museums are interesting, Gem. I find seminars about advertising interesting, Joe is fascinated by early nineties rave classics on vinyl. But neither of us want to have sex with them. Honestly, babe, if you set the bar any lower we'd have to limbo under it.'

'You both said Fraser was a catch.'

'It's all relative. Compared to the other losers you've dated, Fraser was Brad Pitt. He had a job and his own teeth and hair. He wore mainstream clothing and didn't have any weird hobbies. You also told me he licked you out like a dog with an ice cream.' Joe gasped, his face frozen in horror. 'Sorry, Joe, girl talk. But he was also a mean bastard and he cheated on you in the flat you shared, which is a lowlife shitty thing to do. So Gem, forgive me for being blunt, but you need to revisit your type.' The final two words were delivered with bonus air quotes.

Gemma looked up at the worried faces of her two oldest friends. Caro was right, of course – Gemma had spent her adult life choosing men who were easy to win, and painless to lose. Just like her friendships in childhood – *Don't get too attached to anyone, Gemma, you'll be moving away soon.*

She took a deep breath and smiled weakly. 'I like him. Matthew. Even though we've spent three evenings together and he hasn't even kissed me. I slept in his bed last night but nothing happened.' Caro's eyebrows shot up and Joe turned the palms of his hands upwards, clearly confused. Gemma wafted them both away. 'It's a long story. I like him a lot, and that makes it feel complicated. Caro, your parents' village is lovely but I can't stay here; London is home. So if he and I get all attached and in a week or two I leave, then what?'

Caro and Joe both stayed quiet for a moment, Joe because he didn't know what to say, and Caro because she was swallowing another lecture. She gave Gemma a hard stare. 'Gemma, you're already attached. It's obvious to me, to Joe, and probably everyone in Crowthorpe, including Matthew. And honestly, he's the best man I know. If he likes you, you've absolutely scored. For once in your life do something that actually makes you happy. If it's meant to be, it will work out. But you need to stop running away.'

Caro's words rattled around in Gemma's head as she walked Mabel to the village hall. It was still raining, the kind of spring drizzle that lingers in the air and makes you feel like you need three jumpers. Aunt Laura used to say this kind of weather made her bones hurt; when Gemma scattered her ashes at some point in the future, she needed to make sure it wasn't near water. It was a job she'd been putting off for months.

Do something that makes you happy. Stop running away. Caro was right, of course, Gemma had just been too stupid and stubborn to see it. She'd been running away all her life – from friendships, from school, from her parents, from exciting career opportunities, from anything that might at some point be taken away from her. She had removed all risk from her life, and in turn the possibility of reward. For Gemma, the marker of a good day was one that

151

managed to be anything more than mediocre. *Such dizzy heights to aim for.*

With a sad sigh, she realised that Fraser wasn't the reason she'd left London; he was just the final straw on the back of a camel made of shit. There was a whole heap of other stuff she wasn't dealing with – Aunt Laura dying, being furious with her mother for being cold and distant for pretty much Gemma's entire life, not being able to help Louise, the awful situation in the world right now. It all felt chaotic and unmanageable, like that party game where you put on a pair of oven gloves and try to eat chocolate with a knife and fork.

Outside the village hall, Gemma lifted her face up to the rain, feeling it settle like a cooling mist on her skin. She couldn't predict the future, but she could control the now. *Do something that makes you happy.*

Mabel nudged her hand with her wet head, thoroughly fed up with all this hanging about outside having Big Thoughts. Gemma smiled and took her into the shop for a carrot and a sleep.

CHAPTER EIGHTEEN

To Do

- Matthew 7 p.m.
- Do not fuck this up

By 7 p.m., Gemma was as ready for Matthew as she would ever be. Any kind of subtlety had gone out of the window in favour of come-hither candlelight, a lavish spritzing of perfume and a set of black Myla underwear. It was seductively skimpy, even though the bottom half cleaved her in half like cheese wire, and the top half was very much for display purposes only.

She'd bought it before Christmas in the hope of adding a bit of festive sauce to her relationship with Fraser; he had been working long hours on the launch of some executive Lego apartments in Greenwich, and Gemma was just coming up for air after Aunt Laura's death a month before. They'd got back from Christmas at Gemma's parents in the early hours of Boxing Day, both of them heading straight to bed, feeling exhausted and cranky. Things felt just as bleak between them the following morning, so Gemma made Boxing Day lunch and got dressed up for what she hoped would be a restorative hour or two in bed. As it turned out Fraser didn't even notice the underwear; he simply yanked down her knickers along with her black skinny jeans and ignored the silk blouse and lacy bra altogether. Foreplay involved him telling her that he only had eight minutes before Hearts vs. Hibs kicked off on Sky Sports Football, so they needed to crack on.

Gemma had recounted this story to Caro and Joe over pre-New Year cocktails a few days later; they had both been outraged on her behalf, but they'd all ended up screaming with laughter about it. Looking back, Gemma realised that the Mystery Brunette had also retained her blouse and bra; no doubt Fraser was in a hurry to get her out of the flat, or maybe he simply wasn't a boob man and Gemma had never noticed. *What a waste.*

She looked at her watch and drummed her fingers on the kitchen counter. Mabel was walked, fed and settled in her bed. There was chicken in a tomato and basil sauce keeping warm in the oven, and a bottle of English sparkling wine in the fridge. She'd seen it in the village shop and asked Ruth if she could pop it in the chiller; Ruth had given her a knowing look that penetrated Gemma's very soul, but didn't ask any questions.

Gemma assumed the reprieve was down to her hard work this afternoon, preparing the village hall for the first Swap Shop tomorrow. The floors, doorknobs and toilets had been mopped, scrubbed and sanitised, and the tables set up and wiped down. Barry had helped her set up a rope line a metre from each table, and posters had been printed and stuck to the walls with simple instructions – 'please observe social distancing', 'please don't touch anything, ask a volunteer'. All Gemma had to do was be there an hour before people started to arrive, to lay out all the donations on the correct tables and brief the team.

All the slots were booked for tomorrow, and at least half of those for Monday. More rain was forecast, but queueing was the absolute norm these days and everyone would bring an umbrella – in many ways, the British had been preparing for this all their lives. It was still a mad idea, but they were ready.

By 7.10 p.m. Gemma was unravelling. The jittery backflips in her stomach were a mix of anticipation and terror, and it made her realise just how disconnected her previous sexual encounters had been. At thirty-two Gemma had to admit to herself that nobody had ever truly excited her. Her partners had either been efficient and methodical like Johannes, who banged her in time to his internal metronome, or style over substance like Fraser, who demanded feedback after every fuck. Having sex with Fraser felt like going to a café, ordering the soup of the day, then being pressured into leaving a glowing review on Tripadvisor afterwards. It was filling and tasted perfectly nice, but in the end it was just soup.

The honest truth was that the few seconds Matthew had spent brushing his fingers along Gemma's neck a week ago had been the most erotic and sensual experience of her life. What would happen when he touched her properly? She might spontaneously combust. When was going to be the right time to mention that her ex was a cheating shit and she hadn't had an STD test yet? Would he mind, or have condoms? The village shop didn't have any, she'd surreptitiously checked. Nobody ever had to deal with all this admin in erotic novels, and it all felt quite stressful.

Gemma jumped at the light tap on the window and glanced up as the door opened behind her. She caught a brief glimpse of a blue shirt and the scent of something zesty and masculine before Matthew's hands were on her waist, thrusting her back into the edge of the kitchen counter. Gemma gasped as his body enveloped hers, his groin pressing into her hips as Gemma's fingers raked through his damp hair. Matthew pulled her closer, his lips tracing an urgent path from her neck to her mouth; he gave a guttural moan as the tip of his tongue met hers, and it was all Gemma could do to whisper 'Take me to bed' before her knees threatened to give out entirely.

They both lay under the eaves of the loft, Gemma gently tracing a line from Matthew's shoulder to his elbow. She was fascinated by the colour of his hair – it was neither blond nor brown, but a perfect mix of the two. She couldn't work out if it was the glow from the bedside lamp, or simply that Matthew's hair was two different shades, but either way it seemed outrageous that she had to pay a fortune six times a year to achieve the same effect. His eyelashes were darker and unfeasibly long – why did men need long eyelashes? Like her pale eyebrows, Gemma's eyelashes barely existed without mascara.

Her fingernail carved around the edges of his tattoo – a sun formed by a hollow black circle with gently curving tendrils of flame; heavier and darker at the compass points and more delicate in between. Matthew's eyes were closed, and a small smile played on his lips. 'That tickles.'

'Tell me about your tattoo.'

Matthew turned his head to face her, glancing down at his arm. 'Not much to tell. I got it in Spain while I was travelling. Payment for fixing the door of a tattoo parlour in Marbella. It's the only one I've got.'

Gemma smiled. 'I know.' She tried to push away thoughts of Claire, who would have been with him that day. Perhaps she had one that matched; a tiny version on her ankle or wrist, or the base of her spine. Ugh.

'My mum cried when I showed it to her. Something about her baby boy disfiguring his body.'

'I think your body looks just fine.'

Matthew grinned. 'Perhaps you could tell her that.'

She propped herself up on one elbow and took in the full measure of the man in her bed. He filled the space with his huge shoulders and strong legs, a smattering of curly hair on his pale chest and his limbs a mass of dents and scars from twenty years of encounters with splinters and power tools and hard, heavy objects. Gemma wondered if in summer he worked with his shirt off; so the brown skin would turn all those tiny flaws to silver and she'd be able to follow them around his body, like one of those dot-to-dot drawings she'd done as a child. Her stomach rumbled.

'We should eat something.'

Matthew's eyes had closed again. 'That would involve one or both of us leaving this bed, and I'm not ready.' His left hand took hers and slid it slowly under the duvet. She felt the assertive, urgent hardness of him as the same hand slipped between her thighs. Food could wait, apparently.

Gemma lay with her head on Matthew's hard stomach, feeling his chest rise and fall as his breathing steadied. 'You've never told me about your old girlfriends.'

Matthew half sat up, reaching behind his head to fold the pillow in half. 'What?'

'Women. You know that I was dating a cheating shitbag but you've never mentioned any of your other women.' Gemma smiled playfully and rolled onto her pillow, trying to make it look like she was teasing rather than shamelessly fishing.

Matthew laughed. 'There are no other women. There have been in the past, obviously; tonight wasn't my first time.' He smiled, shrugging his shoulders and staring off into the middle distance. 'I don't know. I've had girlfriends here and there. I dated a woman in Bristol on and off for a couple of years, but she was quite a bit older than me and wanted to settle down and have kids. Had a few blind dates set up by friends, some of them went on for a while. I guess I've always liked my independence, haven't met anyone special enough to make me give it up.' He gave Gemma a challenging look that made her feel jittery. 'What happened with your ex, anyway? Did you really catch them at it?'

'I did. It was pretty awful, actually. I don't recommend it.'

Matthew took Gemma's hand and stroked his thumb over the back of it. 'No. I imagine that was a rough day. And then you came here.'

'I did,' said Gemma, feeling her insides turn to liquid. 'What about all your travelling? You must have met loads of women. No holiday romances?' *Subtle, Gemma. This isn't fishing, it's beating a salmon with a hammer.*

'Sure. Thousands of them. Coast-to-coast hot women with backpacks stuffed with tiny bikinis and Daddy's money.' Matthew laughed again and swung his legs out of bed, grabbing his clothes and heading into the bathroom.

Gemma enjoyed the view for a moment, trying not to brood. Why didn't Matthew want to talk about Claire? Maybe something bad had happened; she could be dead, or missing, or the mother of his tiny, blond, green-eyed children. Maybe the heartbreak was still raw and he just couldn't talk about it. Gemma shook her head, internally rolling her eyes. *Perhaps you've read too many novels and the reason he's not telling you is because it's none of your fucking business.*

Matthew's head appeared round the bathroom door. 'Have you tried this enormous bath yet? It's amazing.'

'How the fuck would you know?'

'Haha. Nice try. I fitted it.'

Gemma sank further into the deep water and rested her head against Matthew's chest. Her hair flowed out into the gaps between them as she sculled her hands to tactically position the piles of white foam; a silly thing in view of the previous hours, but old insecurities died hard. The heat penetrated and soothed every corner and crevice of her body; it felt incredibly decadent and entirely blissful.

Matthew reached over the side of the bath and picked up a glass of sparkling wine from the wooden chair he'd moved from the bedroom as a makeshift table. He took a sip, then offered the glass to Gemma's lips before putting it back down next to the bottle. He kept his left hand hanging over the side of the bath, and Mabel sidled over for a scratch between her velvety ears.

'Tell me again why my dog has joined us.'

Earlier Matthew had left Gemma to run the bath with all the foam and expensive oils she could find, while he threw some clothes on and headed downstairs to see if dinner was salvageable. Sadly after several hours in a low oven it looked like a sun-baked cow pat, so he turned the oven off and abandoned it. He let Mabel into the garden while he retrieved the wine from the fridge, but hadn't banked on her refusing to go back to her bed; instead she parked herself at the bottom of the stairs and gave him full puppy eyes until he let her follow him back to the loft. Gemma was already in the bath when he returned, and she listened for a few minutes as he folded his clothes on to the chair in the bedroom, not realising until he came into the bathroom that they had company.

'She looked lonely and asked so nicely. I thought you wouldn't mind.'

'She's got you sussed as a soft touch. I thought you weren't a dog person? I thought they stole your heart, then stole your food?'

'I've decided to make an exception for your yellow dog.'

Matthew's fingers swirled away the foam and gently brushed Gemma's nipple. It immediately hardened in the cold air of the bathroom, and she shivered before batting his hand away. 'Stop it, you'll corrupt Mabel. She's led a very sheltered life up to now.'

'I'll cover her eyes.'

'No, you won't. You won't have any spare hands.' Gemma giggled and intertwined her fingers with his. 'How did the table go today?'

'It was fine. The guy who ordered it hasn't been well; he had surgery a couple of months ago so he's high risk for corona. They've asked me to wear a mask and gloves when I deliver tomorrow. I normally spend so much time with my clients but I've never even met this family. Everything's been done by email and video call.'

Gemma looked at Matthew's hands. They were huge compared to hers, with calloused palms that seemed incompatible with such a gentle touch. It felt nice, lying together like this and chatting about ordinary things, even though nothing felt ordinary these days.

'I watched the daily government briefing today, using the village hall WiFi. It was the Business Secretary, can't remember his name. They can't put a date on the vaccine, it could be years. Sooner or later things are going to have to start getting back to normal.'

Matthew kissed the hair above Gemma's ear. 'I quite like this version of normal.'

Gemma smiled. 'Do you have a TV? I can't remember seeing one in your place.'

'I never got round to it. If I want to watch something I'll do it on my laptop or my phone. I don't need paid-for stuff, I'm not really into sport and big movies and stuff. Would rather read a book.'

'Ah yes, your famous book collection. Tell me more.'

'You ask a lot of questions for someone who has a naked man in her bathtub.' Matthew shifted into a more upright position so his legs were submerged, sliding Gemma up with him. 'OK, if you must know. My mum was the school librarian when I was a kid. She got into interior design later, but for years books were her job. I was an only child and horrendously shy and awkward, so I got into reading really young. Even when I was older I was never that fussed about video games or bands or football; I used to cycle to Chippenham library on my BMX during school holidays like a massive nerd.' He sounded embarrassed, but Gemma was delighted. She told him about the library in Beckett's Chapel, and reading at her aunt's house at weekends during term time, and how English Language and Literature at university seemed like the obvious next step.

'I thought about uni,' said Matthew, 'but by then I'd been working weekends and school holidays with my dad for years and really enjoyed it, so I just cracked on with work and kept reading in my spare time.' Gemma could hear the smile in Matthew's voice as he recounted the memory. 'When I renovated the barn the bookshelf was something I'd imagined in my head for years. I'd been in there loads of times. Caroline's mum and dad used it as a garage and a tool store. I kept drawing pictures on napkins and envelopes of how the place could look, and eventually Dad went over to talk to them about me buying and renovating it. I was scared they'd say no, so refused to ask. That way I could keep the dream alive.' He shrugged, and the water rippled over Gemma's shoulders.

Gemma tried to imagine how it would feel to create your own home, to your own perfect design. It felt like something from a fairy story.

'How did it feel to unpack your books on to those shelves?'

'Honestly, it was the best feeling ever. I had loads of empty space, but that was OK. It just meant I was going to stay for a long time.'

Gemma pulled Matthew's arms tighter around her, resting her chin on his bicep. She imagined her books lined up alongside his, occupying her own little corner of his shelf. Clearly this was the kind of thought you had in a state of post-orgasmic delirium, but in that moment staying for a long time felt like a really nice idea.

CHAPTER NINETEEN

Saturday, 18 April

To Do

- Actually do the mad Swap Shop thing
- Sleeeeeeep

At 7.30 a.m., Gemma lay on her front and gently slithered down to the end of the bed, making an undignified reverse exit from under the duvet on to the floor. She'd been awake for a while trying to work out how to manage it – her side of the bed was wedged under the eaves of the roof, and Matthew was too big to climb over. She'd had no dinner, four hours' sleep and felt like she'd been thoroughly manhandled, and now she was getting out of bed like a burglar backing out of a ventilation pipe.

A croaky voice piped up from the other end. 'You could have asked me to move over, you know.'

'I thought you were asleep. Why didn't you say something?'

'It was too much fun watching you pretend to be a caterpillar.'

Gemma crawled up on to the duvet and pinched Matthew's foot. 'You're a git. I need to get up, I've got to sort Mabel out and be at the village hall by nine.'

Matthew yawned. 'I'm sorry I can't come. I need to get to Bath and deliver this table. Do you want me to come and help later?'

'It's fine, we've got loads of volunteers, and to be honest I can do without the gossip and the knowing looks.'

'Too late for that. I bought the condoms in the BP garage at the crossroads yesterday; the guy who owns it lives next door to Ruth.

The village will have known my seduction plans before you did.' He laughed to himself. 'Still, at least they'll stop nagging me to find a good woman.'

Gemma felt that jittery feeling again. Matthew was talking like this was more than just getting through tough times with great sex and good company. Last night had been a revelation, but they needed to be realistic. She rationalised that now was probably not the time to bring up reality; she was enjoying his cheerful mood.

Matthew shifted down the bed, took Gemma's hand and kissed her palm gently. She felt the warmth that flowed through her body every time he touched her; it was intoxicating and terrifying in equal measure. He moved his lips to the tips of her fingers and looked up at her. 'Can I come over again tonight?'

Gemma fought to control her breathing and got a grip on herself. *Follow your heart, but bring your brain.* 'I'd love to, but I'm going to get back late. I'm already shattered, someone kept me up half the night.' She grinned and prodded his arm. 'Can we do tomorrow instead? I'll be fully recovered and I have no plans whatsoever.'

'Works for me. How about you come over for the brunch we never had last week? I promise not to be in Bristol.'

Gemma smiled, already wishing she didn't have to leave. She gave him a quick kiss and headed for the shower, very aware that everything south of her collarbone was going to ache for the rest of the day.

It was raining hard by the time Gemma arrived at the village hall, the first of the volunteers to arrive. Ruth was busy opening up the village shop, so Gemma headed there first – they had agreed that Mabel could stay in the office again so she could have a walk at lunchtime. Gemma rubbed her down with a towel and settled her in with her blanket and a carrot from the hessian sack. She gave her a belly scratch and a kiss between the ears and returned to the shop for a quick cup of tea; Ruth eyed Gemma beadily, clearly in possession of knowledge that she couldn't confess to.

'You look tired, dear.' *And so it begins*, thought Gemma.

She smiled sweetly. 'I didn't sleep well.'

'No, I'm sure you didn't.'

Gemma wondered what Ruth would say if she just blurted out the details. *To be honest, Ruth, I spent the night being shagged into next week by your village handyman. I can barely walk.* Gemma realised that she was grinning like an idiot at this thought, and Ruth was still watching her. She rearranged her face into an impassive smile and sipped her tea.

By 10 a.m. the tables were laid out with donations, the volunteers were all wearing gloves and masks and everyone was ready, albeit looking like a ragtag band of renegade surgeons. Erica was on the door checking the booking list and managing the flow of one household at a time, making sure they all had a squirt of hand sanitiser in each direction. Barry was taking inbound donations on one side of the hall, explaining patiently that these items weren't available to take today, but they'd be cleaned and quarantined in time for Monday so please book again. The crates for books, old tools and kitchen bits and bobs were already filling up; Gemma had also spotted a book of knitting patterns and an assortment of different coloured wools that made her think of Joan; she would ask Ruth to call her later, once she'd worked out how on earth you sanitised balls of wool.

Gemma was on the opposite side of the hall, manning the outbound donations with Gareth, the shop volunteer who Gemma had met last week. Over small talk she'd discovered he was recently retired from the Royal Navy, which explained the military aura she'd sniffed out during their shop encounter. He reminded Gemma so much of her father, forced to retire at the peak of his career, going from hero to zero in a matter of weeks. They chatted a bit about his background, and Gemma discovered that he spoke five languages fluently, had published several papers on mathematical physics, and was widely regarded as one of the UK's leading experts on nuclear submarines. And now he was describing books, board games and tools to curious customers in a rural village hall. Gemma tried not to laugh as he read out the blurb on a Danielle Steel hardback as if he was briefing the crew of a navy destroyer. She made a mental note to call her dad later, she hadn't spoken to him in weeks.

The first family was a couple with two children under five who relished the opportunity to run around the village hall like whirling birds; the mums didn't seem terribly bothered about their fly-by proximity to other people so Gemma didn't make a fuss. Her experience with Bella and Luca had taught her that you couldn't reason with children this age, so there was no point trying to enforce a two-metre rule. They dropped off a few puzzles and games and a yellow scooter, and picked up a couple of new toys, a skipping rope and some books for the kids, along with a cocktail shaker and recipe book for themselves. *You're going to need it*, thought Gemma, watching the youngest child scale a precarious stack of chairs.

The flow of households was slow and steady over the three-hour session, giving Gemma a fascinating snapshot of the make-up of the village. There were several more well-to-do couples with big-eyed children named Florence or Hugo who inspected the tables solemnly and whispered questions to their parents, tugging gently on their clothing. Older people in couples or visiting alone, handsome dads carrying little ones on their shoulders, dive-bombing siblings to shrieks of childish delight. Mums on a mission, focussed on getting the most out of their ten-minute slot. Gemma was gratified to note that even the glossiest of thirty-somethings had dreadful split ends and needed a manicure – in this regard lockdown was definitely a leveller.

Other families were less easy to categorise – worn-looking mums herding kids while Dad smoked in the car park. Mums on their own, their children crusted with snot that they'd long given up trying to manage, looking for anything that might expand their universe beyond finger food, CBeebies and colouring books. Dads on their own with bored-looking older children, wearing that haunted, exhausted look that screams 'weekend parent'. Older parents who could have been grandparents. Mums who were barely out of their teens. Parents who crouched down to their child's level and explained things quietly, others who ignored them until the noise echoed off the old schoolhouse walls, then told them to 'shut the fuck up'.

Gemma watched and smiled and offered as much help and support as she could from a safe distance. Nothing about this tableau of village life was tugging on her ovaries, but it was nice to do something positive. People seemed pleased with their new finds, and proud that Crowthorpe had taken the initiative – several people told Gemma this was a 'lovely thing' and expressed their thanks to the volunteers, or tried to leave donations. Gemma directed them into the shop, which had a collection tin for Wiltshire Air Ambulance on the counter; hopefully they'd buy a jar of Bernard's honey while they were in there and Ruth would remember not to be a complete bitch.

Two other things kept worming their way into Gemma's consciousness today. The first was Matthew, whose hands and lips she could still feel roaming her body like he was trying to commit every square inch of her to memory. Whenever she relived the highlights from last night, her stomach did another backflip; it had felt like they'd both come to the table hungry and eaten like the food could be taken away at any moment, and for the first time Gemma had experienced what real sexual chemistry tasted like. Whichever way she looked at it, she was still famished and really wanted seconds, ideally followed by dessert. Her head told her this spelled trouble, but her newly unleashed sex drive didn't have the strength to resist. Now she thought about it, she felt the same way about sticky toffee pudding, and she could definitely eat one of those right now as well.

The second thing needling at her was the women in the village – the ones she'd noticed since she'd arrived, and those she'd seen today. In particular she'd been thinking about the single mums, the working mums and the older women, who somehow seemed to be bearing the emotional burden of this lockdown in a way that felt draining to watch, never mind deal with every day. For them social distancing wasn't about being two metres away; it was about being disconnected from their whole support network. The Swap Shop was a fun and uplifting change of scenery for the whole village, but what about these women specifically? What more could she do to help them? She parked it in the corner of her brain where problems were left to unravel, and hoped she'd get a flash of inspiration at some point.

By 1.30 p.m. all the stragglers were gone and the hall was empty. Gemma took Mabel for a damp walk in the churchyard while the other volunteers packed up and stored the leftover donations from today, and by the time she'd put her back in the office, everyone was armed with Dettol spray and cloths to start cleaning the new batch. The pile was smaller than Thursday, so between the four of them they had it finished within a couple of hours, including scrubbing down the hall and all the tables. It had been a successful inaugural day, and the committee seemed delighted by the feed-back. The shop had done a good trade too, which forced Ruth's face into an unnatural muscular arrangement that vaguely resem-bled a smile.

Gemma listened to their enthused chat and thought about how far it all was from her previous life in London; her usual articles took her a couple of hours to write, and had a readership of thou-sands. Here she had invested DAYS of time in an event that would, at best, make an impact on a few hundred people in a tiny village that nobody had ever heard of. Yet it still felt like one of the most satisfying things she had ever done. Aunt Laura would have approved.

Before Gemma headed home, she took Mabel into the shelter of the lychgate to call her dad. The proper phone signal meant she could call her parents' landline rather than using WhatsApp, so there was a better chance that Dad would answer. She pulled out her phone and searched for the number, noting with shame that the last time she'd called it had been nearly a month ago. It rang four times before a gruff voice shouted at her.

'Lockwood. Who is it?'

Gemma smiled. Dad had left the RAF Police nine years ago, but he would remain Group Captain Peter Lockwood until the day he died. He'd joined up at eighteen and served the full thirty-seven years before he reluctantly retired at the age of fifty-five on a full pension; the retirement age was set by the RAF, so he had absolutely no say in the matter. Civilian life was turning out to be a colossal waste of his time and talent, and he'd been bitter about it ever since.

'Hello, Dad, it's Gemma.'

'Oh, hello, darling. Hang on, I'll get your mother.'

'No, it's fine, Dad. I actually called to talk to you.'

There was a brief silence, and her father's voice softened. 'Well, that's very nice. Is everything OK?'

'Yes, of course. I just haven't talked to you for a while. I wanted to see how you are.'

'Well. I'm perfectly fine, apart from all this bloody virus non-sense. Nobody seems to know what they're doing; the whole thing is an absolute bloody disgrace.' Gemma could imagine him reading his *Daily Telegraph* over breakfast, getting more and more furious at the varying levels of competence being shown by the government. 'Your mother has me working like a navvy in the garden every day, apparently there's now a plan to grow bloody vegetables.' *Poor Dad*, thought Gemma. *He hates gardening more than he hates vegetables.*

She heard her father's muffled voice as he covered the handset. 'It's Gemma. No, she wants to talk to me. For God's sake, I'll let you know.' His voice returned.

'I'm back. Your mother tells me you're living in Wiltshire. Nice part of the world, we were stationed there for a while in the eight-ies, before you were born, I think. How are you?'

'I'm fine, Dad. Keeping busy. I'll be going back to London soon.'

He gave a disapproving grumble. 'Hmpf. What's the hurry? London's full of bloody sick people. You're better off staying out of the way for as long as you can.'

Gemma smiled. Despite his brusque exterior, her father worried about her just as much as her mother did. He'd been an imposing but inaccessible presence in her childhood – always working, and away on RAF Police business for months at a time. Unlike other parents who came home from trips bearing airport gifts and stories of their adventures, Gemma's father brought a canvas bag full of dirty clothes, acres of paperwork and silence on all work matters – it was an unspoken rule in the Lockwood family that they didn't talk about Daddy's work. During family holidays he took charge of directing operations, from pitching tents to planning the optimum driving route from campsite to campsite along the Rhine, and spent any downtime reading books. Not the kind that Gemma liked – Peter's literary tastes were limited to military history and spy fiction. If the author made even the tiniest of errors in operational procedure or uniform protocol, her father would write to the author and provide corrections. Gemma wouldn't be surprised if he still did; he had to fill the retirement void somehow.

'Have you heard from Louise?'

'I think your mother spoke to her the other day. No idea what she's doing. Army nonsense.' Louise's decision to take a commission in the Army rather than the Air Force was a sore point – she had graduated from Sandhurst within weeks of his retirement and he took it as a deeply personal insult. Louise had recently been promoted to Major, at a time when women could genuinely strive for the highest ranks of the Army. Gemma felt like she could have been a four-star general and their father would still think Louise had made the inferior choice.

'I'll call her tomorrow, will send your love.'

'Hmm. Well, I need to get on. Do you want to speak to your mother? She's hovering like a fart in a helicopter.' Gemma heard her mother exclaim 'PETER!' in the background.

'I won't, not today. I'm standing in a doorway in the rain so I'll call her tomorrow.'

'Fine. I'll let her know.'

'Love you, Dad, take care.'

'You too.' He hung up, no doubt relieved to escape the minefield of emotional declarations. If there was one thing Gemma had learned about her father over the years, it was that he'd rather direct tactical security operations in some war zone hellhole than tell his daughter he loved her.

The rain stopped as quickly as it started as Gemma walked Mabel home, and the clouds parted to bathe the village in glorious late-afternoon sunshine. Feeling like she was in no particular hurry, Gemma headed off the main road into a small patch of woodland south of the village and let Mabel off the lead for a run about. She bounded in loops off the main path, diving into banks of cow parsley and emerging dotted with tiny white flowers. The air smelled of rain and wild garlic; Gemma picked a few handfuls for the pasta she had planned for tomorrow evening; she could use it to make pesto later.

She did two full circuits of the woods, picking her way through glades of bluebells and dappled tunnels of rhododendrons. She stopped for a moment and watched Mabel run, leaping over fallen logs and lapping fresh rainwater from puddles. The sky was full of birdsong and the light fell in golden beams between the trees. A strange feeling of lightness overcame Gemma – a sudden sense of being in exactly the right place at exactly the right time. It wouldn't last, but right now, in this moment, it would do.

CHAPTER TWENTY

Sunday, 19 April

To Do

- Matthew, all day

Gemma woke up on Sunday to sun streaming through the loft windows, feeling rested and restored. Inspired by her walk in the woods, she had spent the previous evening with one of her favourite books, Daphne du Maurier's *Rebecca*. It was the rhododendrons that had made her think about it, although the delicate pink buds in the woods were nothing like du Maurier's giant blood-red blooms, which were used to symbolise the eponymous dead wife – a looming, malevolent presence at every turn. Aunt Laura wouldn't have them in her garden; she said du Maurier had spoiled them for her, made them evil and menacing. Gemma had borrowed the book from the library and devoured it in a weekend, coming to the conclusion that none of the characters had any redeeming features and they all deserved each other.

Her positive mood had lingered since her walk the day before, after which Gemma had decided to stop this endless wrestling with her feelings and go with the flow a little. At some point soon she needed to return to real life, but for now she reminded herself of her earlier vow to treat this situation like a holiday. It made it easier for her to live in the moment and reconcile the situation with Matthew – he was her lockdown romance; someone who would help her find herself, then wave her off like he had all the other women in his life. It was an arrangement that suited them both, so she could definitely stop over-thinking everything.

Gemma found a pair of denim shorts and a faded pink T-shirt and put her hair up into a messy bun. Aside from the three inches of dark roots, the ends were starting to feel properly ratty, but a decent haircut was probably still weeks away. She had no idea when she'd next get a manicure or pedicure – the previous week she'd stripped off the final remnants of old polish and left them tidy and short but otherwise free of their usual glossy colour.

She was pulling a few weeds from the border under the lilac trees when Matthew wandered over from the barn, wrapping his arms around her in a bear hug and kissing her neck before she could take off her gardening gloves. He sat on the grass for a few minutes to play with Mabel, who rolled on to her back to demand a belly rub. Gemma finished weeding and put the tools away, before joining Matthew on the grass. Mabel went into a state of bliss as a second pair of hands joined the first to scratch behind her ears.

'What shall we do today?' Gemma asked.

'I thought we could go for a walk. A long one. Maybe take a sandwich so we don't have to hurry back.'

'Are we allowed out for that long?' Gemma's news consumption had been sporadic at best; she found the endless conflicting opinions and political point-scoring stressful and unhelpful, and some of the rules seemed a bit open to interpretation.

'I think so. There's no time limit on how long we exercise for, it just says once a day. We just have to stay away from other people, which is my favourite kind of walk.'

It sounded good to Gemma, but before they went anywhere she needed to eat. 'You promised me brunch.'

'Yes, I did. Come this way, it's waiting for you.'

The table in Matthew's barn was set with everything Gemma needed right now – coffee, fresh juice, toast and a fruit salad that he had clearly painstakingly prepared himself. Mabel had resumed her preferred position in the corner of the sofa, and looked like she was readying herself for a short nap.

'Where did you get juice and strawberries? They don't have them in the shop.'

Matthew loaded up the coffee machine and pressed the button. 'I went to Sainsbury's in town yesterday. Bought some nice cheese and olives too. We can take them on our walk.'

Gemma realised it was exactly four weeks since she'd arrived in Crowthorpe, and she hadn't left the village once. Her world had become so small, the idea of a big supermarket felt a bit overwhelming.

'Can you buy everything now, or are people still stockpiling loo roll?'

Matthew laughed. 'Eggs and flour are still tough to find, but otherwise it's fine. I get my eggs from Grove Farm, and Ruth has a secret stock of flour that she keeps in a cupboard for her favourite customers.'

'She sold me a bag last week.'

'Well, aren't you the chosen one.'

Gemma helped Matthew wash the brunch dishes, enjoying the everyday, humdrum normality of it. She was reminded of Fraser's obsession with stacking the dishwasher – if Gemma put anything in, he'd rearrange it to his liking, even though there were only two of them and it was rarely full. With hindsight she'd been so grateful for his lack of financial nit-picking, she'd failed to notice all the other ways in which he was a colossal wanker.

Once the dishes were cleared away, Matthew tried his best to lure Gemma to bed, but he had to settle for some heavy petting against the kitchen sink instead – it was such a beautiful day and it seemed a shame to spend it indoors, even if the prospect of getting Matthew naked was extremely tempting. He grudgingly relented and disappeared into the fridge to find things for lunch, putting everything into a rucksack along with a big bottle of water that they could share with Mabel. Gemma went back to the cottage to grab Mabel's lead and a jumper in case the weather turned, and met Matthew by the side gate a few minutes later.

It was the perfect spring day for a walk – the countryside felt fresh and green and on the cusp of flourishing, without the limp, dusty tiredness that comes with high summer. The hedgerows were packed with wildflowers and butterflies, and Mabel discovered an appetite for goose grass that Gemma had been previously unaware of – it wasn't something you saw a lot of in London. They hiked across fields and through woods with no need for a map; Matthew had walked these paths all his life. Gemma had no idea if he had a particular destination in mind but didn't ask; it felt liberating to just walk, and to put her trust in someone else to lead the way for a change.

As they strolled along they talked about nothing in particular – Gemma told Matthew about her writing work, and he talked about the furniture projects he'd enjoyed most, and some funny stories from doing odd jobs in the village. Gemma told him about her sister, skipping over the bit about her being a closet lesbian in a loveless marriage. Matthew shared the story of a mangy dog that had trailed him around Thailand for so long he'd looked into bringing it home for his parents; even though he didn't like dogs, it seemed worth rescuing. In the end, he'd left it with a British family in Bangkok. Gemma talked about the countless places she'd lived, and Matthew tried to explain what it was like to live in the same place all his life.

They met a few other walkers out and about and were careful to move over and give other people a wide berth as they passed, putting Mabel on her lead if other dogs were around. After a few miles of wide footpaths where they could mostly walk side by side, Gemma and Matthew climbed over a wooden stile into some woods of young ash and beech trees and started to head downhill along a narrow, winding track. The ground was a pungent carpet of wild garlic, not yet flowering although the white buds were appearing here and there. Gemma could hear a stream trickling nearby, but couldn't see it.

At the bottom of the hill they climbed over another stile and walked into a tiny hamlet; just a collection of a dozen or so pretty stone cottages with a single-track road in and out. A meadow of the most dazzling green stretched out in front of them, a swaying mass of daisies and dandelion clocks that would be a sea of wild-flowers in a month or two. Mabel sniffed the air hopefully, and Matthew led them along a well-trodden path through the grass that sloped gently down to the water. He stopped on a grassy bank next to a shallow pool on the bend of the river, fed by a small waterfall from the sluice gates of an old mill. He put down the rucksack and turned to look at Gemma. 'What do you think?'

It was a breathtakingly beautiful spot, with a sandy bank that eased into shallow, fast-flowing water that swirled around patches of half-submerged water plants that Gemma couldn't name. Fur-ther along the bank was a deeper, still pool that Mabel immediately plunged into, paddling happily in circles until her paws found shallower ground. She ran to a sandy island above the water line and shook vigorously, before running back along the bank and throwing herself straight back in again.

'It's gorgeous,' said Gemma, sitting on the grass and starting to remove her trainers. 'How did you know about it?'

Matthew sat beside her, his arms resting on his bent knees. 'I used to come here a lot when I was a kid. Sometimes with friends to swim in the river, and sometimes on my own. I'd ride my bike to the village,' he nodded at the houses behind them, 'and walk here. It was a good place to read a book.'

Gemma smiled. She too remembered the secret places she used to go to read – the ha-ha by the hockey pitch at boarding school, the oak tree in the field behind Aunt Laura's house, the stone lookout point on the cliffs behind their house in Cyprus. A paper-back tucked into the back of her shorts, maybe an apple or a peach in her pocket. Places where she could be somewhere else entirely.

Pulling off her trainer socks and tucking them inside her shoes, Gemma dabbled her toes into the shallow water, watching it alter its course around this new and unexpected obstacle. The water was cold but crystal clear; later in the summer it would be a glorious spot for a wild swim. She and Caro had regularly visited Hampstead Ladies' Pond in the years before Bella and Luca, but it had been a while since she'd been; Fraser wasn't much of a swimmer, and had a particular issue with bodies of water that contained living things that might touch him, like plants or fish. They'd once taken a day trip to Whitstable and Gemma had suggested a dip in the sea, and he'd looked at her as though she was offering him up to the sharks as a light snack.

She leaned back in the grass on her elbows, while Matthew rummaged in the bag for food. She was pretty sure that stopping by a river to eat lunch in the sunshine wasn't part of the lockdown rules for exercise, but right now she didn't care. There wasn't another soul to be seen, and the combination of sun on her face and cold water flowing across her feet was heavenly. Matthew tore a strip of bread from half a baguette, then stuffed a slice of cheese and a couple of olives into the middle before passing it over to Gemma. While she ate, he pulled a plastic box from the bag with the leftover strawberries from brunch, and the thermos bottle of water. Mabel dappled around in the shallows, chasing sticks caught in the flow and periodically hurling herself into the deeper pond to cool off. The smell of food lured her over to Gemma and Matthew, who gave her a lump of cheese. She ignored the water Matthew had poured into the strawberry container for her, having happily quenched her thirst from the river.

Once the bread was gone, they sat contentedly in the sun for a while, Gemma occasionally flicking water on to Matthew's legs with her feet and getting a jab in the ribs in return. It was time to head off; they had a long walk back and the skin on Gemma's arms was starting to turn pink.

Matthew stood up and held out his hand to Gemma, who finished tying the laces on her trainers and levered herself up. He looked across the fields on the other side of the river. 'I thought we'd take a slightly different route back, come in at the other end of the village.'

'Fine by me. You lead, I'll follow.'

176

Matthew cleared his throat. 'It will take us past my parents' house – it would be nice to say hello as we go by.'

Gemma's immediate reaction was to feel wary; why on earth would Matthew want her to meet his parents? Then the feeling turned to panic – she looked like a sweaty mess, with no make-up and hair like pigeons had taken up residence. But within seconds she had a stern word with herself. *This isn't about you, Gemma. He wants to see his mum and dad.* She shrugged and smiled casually. 'Sure, no problem.'

The shadows were lengthening as the tower of St Michael's Church appeared on the horizon, and Gemma was hot, tired and in desperate need of a shower. Mabel looked ready for a very big nap but stayed close to Gemma's heels as they walked along the lane, hugging the hedgerow.

A row of three houses appeared ahead of them, each set a little way up the hill with a large front garden and a driveway that sloped down to the road. They stopped outside the last in the row; it was sixties in style, with large dormer windows in the tiled roof, and what looked like a substantial extension on the side. Gemma assumed Matthew's father had done a lot of work on it over the years.

'How long have your parents lived here?'

'They moved in after they got married; it was a wedding present from both their parents, back in the days when buying your kids a house wasn't completely insane. So mid-eighties, I guess.' Matthew got out his phone and pressed a button, then turned to smile at Gemma while he waited for someone to answer.

'Hey, Mum, it's me. I'm fine, I'm actually outside, we're on our way back from a walk. Thought you might want to pop out and say hello.' There was a short pause. 'OK, see you in a minute.'

Gemma was interested that Matthew hadn't had to explain who 'we' was – had he already told his parents about her? She attempted to smooth the tendrils of hair that had escaped from her ponytail and wiped the dusty sweat off her face with the back of her equally dusty hand.

The front door opened, and a woman stepped out of the door, leaving it open behind her. She was elegantly dressed in flowing linen trousers and a long tunic, with her fair hair wound tightly into a bun that was secured at the nape of her neck. She smiled warmly at both of them as she walked down the drive, stopping a few metres from the garden wall and blowing Matthew a kiss with both hands.

'Hello, love, sorry I can't come closer. What a lovely surprise.' She turned to Gemma. 'You must be Gemma. I've heard a lot about you. I'm Christine.' Her eyes twinkled as she lifted her hand in a wave, and Gemma desperately wished she didn't look like she'd slept in a hedge.

She smiled and waved back. 'Hi, nice to meet you.'

Christine turned her attention to Mabel, whose tail was wagging furiously. 'Hello, Mabel.'

Mabel tugged at her lead until Gemma let her go, then slipped under the wooden gate at the bottom of the driveway and bounded over to Matthew's mother, who knelt down to scratch under her chin. Gemma looked at Matthew in surprise, and he shrugged.

'I've brought her here a few times on our walks. She's made herself quite at home in the garden.' On cue, Mabel turned on to her back and offered up her belly for a rub, like the attention whore she was.

'Your dad is dicing with death up a ladder in the garage, so I don't think he'll be joining us. You both look like you've caught some sun; where did you get to?'

Gemma wanted to beg for permission to run home for a shower and a change of clothes, then come back looking less like Ray Mears. She was annoyed that it bothered her so much – what did it matter if she impressed Matthew's mother? She was hardly interviewing for future daughter-in-law.

Matthew was explaining the route they'd taken, '. . . so we stopped at Oldford Brook for lunch, and Mabel had a swim. And then we walked back.'

'Goodness, that IS a hike. Still, lovely day for it.'

Gemma watched the dynamic between Matthew and his mother

and felt a tinge of jealousy. She couldn't remember ever being that relaxed and comfortable with her parents; conversations always felt loaded, and old resentments died hard in the Lockwood family. The grinding of teeth at family events created a four-part harmony.

She realised she hadn't uttered a word other than a perfunctory greeting, and pushed herself to make the effort. 'Your garden looks lovely.' It was banal, but true. The borders had that casual cottage garden abundance that looks artless and natural but takes huge amounts of planning to achieve; Gemma knew it well from Aunt Laura's house in Norfolk. Right now Christine's garden was holding back, waiting for the warmth of May to unleash a mass of summer colour.

'Thank you, dear, I'm sorry you can't come through and see the back. I've been planting vegetables.' Gemma thought of her poor dad, toiling in the veg and cursing every bloody courgette and runner bean. 'Perhaps you can come and have a proper look when this is all over. Stay for lunch.' Christine looked from Gemma to Matthew and back again, her face full of hope. With a sinking heart, Gemma realised that Matthew's mum knew she wasn't just the woman next door, and had no idea Gemma wasn't planning to stick around.

Matthew smoothed over the awkwardness with farewells and promises to pop by in the week with their shopping, and Gemma called Mabel back from the garden and said goodbye with a smile. They walked back through the village with little to say, Gemma feeling like they needed to talk but not wanting to spoil what had been a wonderful day. With barely a word, she took Matthew home and gave Mabel her dinner, then settled her down in her bed by the window. Matthew watched her, his face a mask of intensity and nervous energy. In silence, Gemma took his hand and led him upstairs for a shower, and they didn't come back down for a long time.

179

CHAPTER TWENTY-ONE

Monday, 20 April

To Do

- More Swap Shop

Gemma and Matthew half-jogged to the village hall, towing a bemused Mabel behind them. They had both overslept after an evening in bed, followed by a very late dinner and a bottle of wine that led to a soak in the bath that ended up back in bed. This morning Gemma's hair was a crispy, tangled mess and her arms and face had an angry sheen of sunburn from their walk yesterday, but she didn't have the time or energy to worry about it.

At the entrance Gemma and Matthew headed off in two directions – Matthew to placate the waiting volunteers, and Gemma to put Mabel in the office at the back of the shop. Barry was in charge today, and momentarily stopped arranging bottles of Mary Berry Pomegranate Salad Dressing into a precarious pyramid when a red-faced and rattled-looking Gemma burst in with a panting dog.

'Crikey. Are you OK?'

'I'm fine, overslept. Just need to put Mabel in the office, can you throw her a carrot and fill that old ice cream tub with water when you have a second?'

'No problem. Look, give her to me, I'll get her sorted. You look like you're about to have a heart attack.'

Gemma smiled gratefully and handed over Mabel's lead, then kissed between her ears and ran back out of the same door she'd entered approximately twenty seconds earlier.

The volunteers were all assembled when Gemma hurtled in and flew straight into action; firstly to make up lost time, but also to deflect attention from the knowing smirks and raised eyebrows being directed her way. Matthew took it all in his stride as usual, so Gemma put him on the door in charge of managing traffic and dispensing hand sanitiser. She allocated Erica and Ruth on the outbound items and positioned herself at the table for inbound donations. Gareth had gone to a family funeral, an aunt who had passed away at a ripe old age. The strict rules around social distancing meant that limits had been put on the numbers of people who could attend funeral services; Gemma couldn't imagine what it must be like to be one of only a handful of mourners in a cold crematorium, unable to hug or comfort each other, never mind share a plate of mini pork pies and a memorial sherry at the local pub. Gareth had offered to pop in later to help clean up, presumably because he had absolutely nothing better to do.

Visitors started trickling into the hall at 10 a.m., one household at a time, and like Saturday it was a mix of families and couples and people on their own; clearly the opportunity to walk to the village hall in the sunshine on a Monday morning was too exciting to resist. There were also more donations for people to choose from, a combination of what was left from the original collection, and the sanitised and quarantined items from Saturday. The atmosphere felt quite upbeat considering this was the end of week four of lockdown; there was a sense of resignation, an acceptance that this was just how life was going to be for the time being, a few faux-chirpy declarations of 'We've just got to get on with it, haven't we?'

As on Saturday, many of the visitors were older, and many wore face masks and gloves like the volunteers. Gemma marvelled at how quickly this new dress code had become normal – a month ago, the only people you ever saw in London wearing face masks were South East Asian tourists. Now the tourists were gone, but the masks were being worn by retirees in English villages. She wondered if they'd become mandatory for everyone soon, and how long that might last.

Almost all the customers paused for a brief chat with Matthew on their way in, and appeared to be delighted to see him. They asked after his parents and sent their regards, which he dutifully promised to pass on. Matthew had told her that his dad had a long history of asthma, so they were staying isolated from the rest of the village apart from a walk together across the field behind their house each day. Matthew dropped off their shopping, and his mum cleaned everything with antiseptic wipes before putting it away. Now they knew he was getting down and dirty with his neighbour, she probably cleaned everything twice.

Inbound donations were slow and steady – lots of fiction and a good selection of cookbooks, a few kitchen gadgets and old tools. One woman in her sixties dropped off a bag of children's colouring books, pens and craft sets, all unopened and unused. Her face was a mask of sadness and grief, and Gemma could only imagine what had happened to her grandchild – at best a family rift, at worst something entirely more devastating. Gemma thanked the woman and she smiled sadly, her eyes lost to memories. 'Good to have someone use them, they're no good to me any more.' She left without looking at the donations table, giving Matthew a half-hearted wave on her way out.

As more families arrived and organised chaos descended on the hall, Gemma found her thoughts returning to the conundrum she'd parked in her brain a couple of days before; how to reconnect people in the village to help with loneliness, isolation, lack of support networks and sheer boredom. She was primarily thinking of the women, but actually everyone could benefit from more talking, more sharing and an opportunity to offload. By the end of the session, an idea that had been bubbling away had taken a little more shape, but it needed Matthew's help and input before she could take it any further.

When Erica locked the door after the last visitor, they agreed a half-hour break before cleaning started, so Gemma grabbed Matthew and Mabel and hustled them outside for a walk. As they strolled through the field behind the church watching Mabel dart in and out of the wheatgrass, Gemma gathered her thoughts on the idea she'd been brewing and shared it with Matthew. She told him about the conversations she'd had with people in the village and the things she'd noticed, recalling her surprise when she looked at the village noticeboard that first day and saw how many clubs and societies there were. Community made a real difference here; people knew their neighbours and cared about what they were doing. 'Sometimes more than they should,' laughed Matthew. So why couldn't they re-start some of those community lifelines online? Lots of places were doing it using video platforms like Zoom, it was becoming the norm. So why not in Crowthorpe? It wouldn't work for everything, but enough that the majority of people in the village had the opportunity to re-ignite those old connections.

Gemma opened a notes app on her phone and they started to make a list of the main groups in the village that would benefit from more support – older people living alone, carers, single parents, teenagers, working parents who were now carrying the added burden of home schooling and living together 24/7. Churchgoers. The list was huge and there was clear crossover between the groups, so they narrowed it down to the biggest and highest priority.

To Gemma's mind the challenge was lighting the first fires – if they could make video meet-ups feel normal and easy, people would start to create their own groups. So a general chat over a cup of tea for mums might spawn a smaller group that wanted to talk about home schooling, or healthy cooking, or just get drunk together after the kids had gone to bed. All they had to do was get the ball rolling with some starter groups, and then let the village do what it had been doing naturally for decades.

'So who's going to run these starter groups?' asked Matthew. 'We can't do everything. I'm still working and you're busy saving the village.' He smiled teasingly at Gemma, who pulled a face in return.

'We're going to get the usual people who run these things to do it. It's the same club they've always led, just online instead of in the village hall or the pub or the café.' Gemma folded her arms, her eyes glittering.

'And how exactly do you plan to convince them to get involved in your mad scheme? Remember, this isn't London. Talking to big groups on video isn't normal; people here are still using landlines.'

'Well, let's see. We need someone known and respected in the village, who's good at charming people.' Gemma smiled sweetly at Matthew, who held his hands up and backed away.

'Woah, Gemma. This is your area of expertise, not mine. I'm not good at the community stuff. I just . . . keep myself to myself.'

'No, you don't. You do all their odd jobs, you've been in all their homes; the people here trust you. All you have to do is make a few phone calls and rally the village do-gooders, elders, whatever. They're probably bored out of their minds right now and would love to hear from you. I'll do all the admin.'

Matthew sighed heavily, a defeated look on his face. He looked at the list on Gemma's phone. 'Just so I'm clear, you want me to call the vicar, the woman who runs playgroup, Yvonne from Autumn Club, Charlie from the pub and Tamsyn from Youth Club.'

'I do. But first we need to iron out a few issues. Let's carry on at my place later, then we'll make the calls in the morning. I'll make you dinner.'

Gemma felt restored and re-energised by the time they got back to the shop; she had another scheme brewing, and an evening with Matthew ahead. She popped back into the shop just as Barry was locking up, and asked him to hold on a second while she put Mabel back in the office. Hopefully the cleaning wouldn't take long, and she could have a quiet nap in the meantime.

The volunteers had re-assembled in the village hall, so they set to work cleaning the latest batch of donations. The addition of Matthew, Barry and Gareth – who'd changed out of his funeral suit and joined them – to the usual team of Ruth, Erica and Gemma, helped make light work of the pile; they rattled through it in less than an hour, and had everything crated up ready to be dragged through to the storage area before a final wipe-down of the hall and tables.

As Gemma gave the village hall toilet some elbow grease and bleach, she heard an almighty crash followed by a shower of tinkling glass from the other side of the wall. Thinking it was one of the windows in the main hall, she sprinted back to check everyone was OK. But other than all the volunteers being frozen in confusion, the huge arched windows were exactly as she'd left them. 'What the hell was that?'

Matthew shrugged, but Ruth hurried towards the door. 'It must have been in the shop.'

Gemma's hands flew to her face as realisation dawned. 'Oh my God. Mabel.'

Ruth rattled the key in the lock as Gemma hopped from foot to foot, unable to breathe as tears and panic bubbled inside her chest. She fully expected to find Mabel dead or horribly injured, so it made her scream when Ruth opened the door and a yellow furry body shot out like a bullet, hurtling across the lane into the churchyard before anyone could even register what had happened. Gemma shouted her name and started to run after her, but Matthew grabbed her arm.

'No, you stay here. She might come back and she'll be scared if it's all strangers. Give me her lead and I'll go and find her.' He squeezed her arm and looked at her intently. 'She's OK, Gemma, she won't go far. It'll be fine.'

Gemma nodded and dug Mabel's lead out of her handbag, then watched Matthew jogging off into the churchyard. She took a few deep breaths to calm herself down, reminding herself that Mabel wasn't squashed under a chiller cabinet with her back paws sticking out like some kind of canine remake of *The Wizard of Oz*, so that was a good thing. Matthew would bring her back, and it would be fine.

The bad news was that Gemma still didn't know what the

185

crashing noise was, or why Mabel wasn't snoozing in the back office. She experienced a creeping sense of dread, then headed into the shop.

'Oh my God. Oh my fucking GOD.'

The shop looked like someone had thrown a rave in an abattoir. The chiller doors were hanging open, with packs of meat either empty or covered in teeth marks where Mabel had tried and failed to rip her way through the vacuum packaging. The hessian bag of carrots had been scattered across the floor, punctuated by small piles of orange vomit where Mabel had eaten her fill, then thrown up and started again. Worst of all, the Mary Berry pyramid had been toppled, creating a river of broken glass and pomegranate salad dressing that flowed from the centre of the shop to the door. For good measure, Mabel had clearly done a few laps of the shop in a panic and taken down a rotating rack of greeting cards and a cardboard display unit of lentil crisps, which she'd subsequently trampled through, bursting a few bags open on the way. All in all, it was absolute carnage.

Gemma looked at Ruth and the rest of the volunteers, all of whom were rendered entirely speechless. How could one dog create such havoc in such a short time? She blew all the air out of her cheeks, trying not to cry.

'This is my fault. I can't have closed the office door properly when I got back from our walk.'

Ruth gave her a stern look. 'It's not your fault. I should have called the fridge man but I haven't got round to it. You can see the cardboard propping up the chiller has got all soggy. Mabel wouldn't have done this if the fridge wasn't open.' Personally Gemma thought that was stretching Mabel's self-control a bit, but right now was prepared to go with it.

Barry gasped. 'It's my fault it's soggy, I mopped the floor before I closed the shop. Ruth told me not to mop around the fridge, but I forgot.'

Everyone looked at Erica, who put her hands up and took a step back. 'This has absolutely nothing to do with me.'

Gareth laughed and broke the tension, then moved into military mode by starting to organise the troops.

'OK, this isn't going to clear itself up, so let's make a plan. Barry, you go and help Matthew, see if you can cover a bit more ground and track Mabel down. She's probably feeling quite sorry for herself. Gemma, you get some rubbish bags and gloves for everyone, we'll need to be careful with all this glass. Erica, can you get a broom, mop, dustpan, whatever's in the cupboard. Ruth, put the kettle on, we all need a cup of tea. Let's get started.'

A couple of hours later the shop looked considerably less like it had been looted by middle-class pirates, and all the spoiled food and chewed packaging was in the big wheelie bin at the back of the shop. Fresh cardboard wedges were propping up the chiller, and all the sticky dressing had been mopped up and the stone floor scrubbed with a stiff brush, leaving a section stained pale pink like there'd been a brutal murder. Gemma suspected the smell of pomegranates and vinegar would probably linger for the rest of time, reminding the people of Crowthorpe of the day her stupid greedy Labrador got high on carrots and twenty-eight-day-aged Aberdeen Angus ribeye and went on the rampage.

Gemma was burning with shame, but also becoming increasingly worried that neither Matthew nor Barry were back. It wasn't like Mabel to run off, but she must have been terrified by the noise of the falling bottles and was probably hunkered down somewhere, feeling sick and scared. When the cleaning was finished Gemma popped outside and called her name in the churchyard for a few minutes, but there was no sign of her. She couldn't get hold of Matthew because he had no signal, so she just had to wait. Evening was falling, and she was starting to entertain horrible thoughts about Mabel being on her own in the dark, her paws full of broken glass, injured and scared.

When she walked back from the churchyard, the rest of the volunteers were standing in the lane outside the shop, looking ready to go home. Gemma apologised to Ruth for the fiftieth time.

'Don't be daft. It was nobody's fault, and no real harm done.'

Gemma smiled weakly at everyone. 'I'm going to stay here and wait for Matthew. I've got a phone signal here so he can call me, and Mabel might come back. You all head off, and thanks for being amazing.'

Gareth shook his head and held up a fistful of rope, cut into metre-long lengths. 'Don't be ridiculous. We're all going to look for Mabel. I've made some leads and worked out a plan so we can cover more of the village. We'll meet back here every half-hour to check in.'

Gemma started to cry heavy, racking sobs, overwhelmed by fear and exhaustion and gratitude. Barry reached out to pat her on the shoulder, then awkwardly withdrew his hand when he remembered he wasn't allowed. Everyone looked at her, clearly desperate to offer comfort but powerless to do anything. Gemma's phone rang, and her heart leapt as she saw it was Matthew. She fumbled to answer it through her tears, putting it on speakerphone so everyone could hear.

'Gemma? I've got Mabel, she's fine. She was in your garden.'

CHAPTER TWENTY-TWO

To Do

- Hug dog
- Wallow in guilt and mortification

Gemma ended the call with Matthew, sobbing with relief. She blew kisses at the volunteers, then ran through the village as fast as she could, not stopping until she was coughing up a lung at the bottom of Matthew's steps. She really needed to do more exercise – sex and light jogging were clearly not cutting it.

Mabel was stretched out on Matthew's sofa, her head in his lap as he gently stroked her head and gave Gemma a huge smile. He'd scoured the village for her for two hours, searching the fields and woods and calling for her until he'd found himself outside West Cottage. He decided to pop into the barn to call Gemma so they could make a new plan, but instead had found Mabel lying on her side under her favourite apple tree, fast asleep and snoring away contentedly. He'd gently woken her up to check for serious injuries, then carried her up to his apartment so he could call Gemma. She'd had a long drink and didn't seem any the worse for her adventures.

Gemma gave Mabel a long hug, sobbing into her furry neck. She couldn't voice how relieved and grateful she was – Aunt Laura had trusted her to look after Mabel for the rest of her life, and something terrible could easily have happened to her. In the past few hours Gemma had worked through endless nightmare scenarios in which Mabel had fallen prey to malevolent cows, become tangled in barbed wire, run in front of a lorry on the M4, thrown herself into some kind of clattering farm machinery, crossed paths with a dog-hating farmer with a shotgun, been stolen by thieves and fallen down an old well. The countryside was full of things that could kill a dog and today Gemma had lived through every one of them. She moved from Mabel into Matthew's arms and he held her tight until she stopped crying. 'It's OK, she's home now,' he whispered, stroking her hair until her breathing calmed.

Matthew carried Mabel back to Gemma's cottage, where Gemma held the dog still as Matthew picked bits of glass and food and twigs out of her fur. By some miracle she didn't seem to have cut her paws at all, and other than a few bramble scratches, a fat belly and a doleful look in her eyes, she seemed to be fine. Gemma called a vet in Chippenham to ask for advice and was told to keep a close eye on her for a day or two and bring her in if she was worried. Matthew carried Mabel upstairs so Gemma could give her a bath, washing away all the mud and pomegranate juice before towelling her off gently and settling her into her bed for what was clearly going to be a very long and restorative sleep.

Once Mabel was settled, Gemma poured them both a well-earned glass of wine and heated up some leftover wild garlic pesto pasta for dinner, then told Matthew about the havoc Mabel had caused in the shop. He wept with laughter when Gemma told him about the teeth marks in the meat packaging, which made Gemma feel a bit better, albeit briefly. Any hope she had that the whole village wouldn't find out about Mabel's exploits was soon scuppered when Matthew's phone started to buzz – seemingly Barry had taken some photos and popped them on the village WhatsApp group, and now everyone was sharing laughing emojis and jokes about Mabel needing a 'dressing-down'. Someone suggested drawing a dog-shaped line around the pink stain on the floor like a crime scene, and Matthew started crying with laughter again. Gemma went off to the lounge to lie on the sofa and die of humiliation alone, and soon fell asleep herself.

When she woke up a couple of hours later, Mabel was still snoozing in her bed and Matthew was standing at the dining table, making notes on countless sheets of paper. One was a list of calls to make in the morning, and another was a list of questions and challenges they'd need to overcome to get the online clubs up and running. So much had happened since their conversation this afternoon, Gemma had entirely forgotten about her idea.

She drifted over to the table and started asking questions, and soon they were both absorbed in the planning again. The biggest challenge was helping older or less tech-savvy residents use the video software so they could join for the first time; obviously the teenagers would be fine, but downloading the Zoom app and managing cameras and speakers could present a challenge to others. On the upside, the crappy phone signal in the village was offset by the broadband speed; it was considerably faster here than Gemma's had been in London. So they were starting from a good place, if they could just find a way to make it easy for everyone to get started.

Matthew suggested the shop, which Gemma didn't even want to think about right now. It was the hub of the village, and everyone used it to some degree or other, particularly the older residents. If they created a simple flyer that had details of the groups on one side, and a step-by-step guide to using Zoom on the other, people could pick up a copy from the shop for themselves, or put it through the letterbox of someone who needed it. Ruth's husband was also delivering shopping to villagers in isolation – people like Joan with her new knitting wool and book of patterns – so they could put a flyer in the delivery boxes too. It felt less wasteful than getting Steve the Postie to put one through every letterbox; this scheme wouldn't be needed or wanted by everyone, and it made sense to start small and let things grow organically.

Even though Gemma had been full of enthusiasm earlier, right now she felt like she wanted to distance herself from the whole thing altogether, to keep her head down and let other people worry about this kind of stuff. There was no sense in hiding how she was feeling, so she waited for a pause in Matthew's note-taking to air her worries.

'Matthew, are you sure this is a good idea?'

'What do you mean? It was YOUR idea.'

'I know, but . . . I just feel like such a dick about today, like I'm some kind of joke. I'd quite like to lower my profile a bit, just until the dust settles.'

Matthew laughed and put his hands flat on the dining table. 'Gemma, everyone's starved of entertainment. You've made their day, given half the village a lift. Nobody died, and Mabel is fine. This is now village legend; people will be talking about it for years.'

Gemma looked horrified. 'Fuck, really?'

'Yes, really. About twenty years ago Barry put an axe through a mains water pipe and completely flooded his garden, and the whole of the street at the front was flowing with water. His house has been called Barry Island ever since. He still gets mail addressed to Barry Island.'

Gemma snorted with laughter, and Matthew grinned. 'You could live here for the next fifty years, and every time you go for dinner at someone's house they will offer you some kind of salad dressing. That's just how this village is, think of it as a sign of affection. Offer to settle up for the food Mabel trashed, be gracious when they refuse to accept your money, and laugh it off with everyone else.'

She looked at Mabel's sleeping form, calculating how much money she'd need to offer the shop to cover her all-you-can-eat buffet. Mabel farted violently, turned over in her bed, and carried on snoring.

They finished the draft plan together, then made a final list of jobs for tomorrow. They were both as exhausted as Mabel, but neither of them wanted to leave her alone all night in case she got sick. Gemma walked her slowly round the garden for ten minutes until she'd done all her business – for now it was fine, but Gemma suspected there weren't enough poo bags in the world to deal with what Mabel was going to produce over the next couple of days. When they came back inside, Matthew carried both dog and bed back up to the loft, where they tucked her in the corner under the eaves. She wagged her tail half-heartedly and tried to give Matthew's face a lick, and they both sat and stroked her until she drifted back to sleep.

After a long kiss that Gemma hoped said a million things about how grateful and relieved she was, she took Matthew's hand and led him to the bathroom, closing the door and leaving the light off so the whirring of the extractor fan didn't spoil the mood, along with the deeply unflattering glare of bathroom spotlights. On this occasion, moonlight would do. They undressed and soaped each other with a kind of curious reverence, Matthew trailing his fingers gently over the curves of Gemma's body like she was an exquisite, fragile sculpture. Gemma realised that he was the first man who had ever made her feel anything other than just ordinary; more than just the woman next door. Matthew listened and made her feel smart and interesting, qualities Gemma had always hoped she possessed but that nobody had ever really noticed. In contrast, Fraser had sometimes looked at her like he couldn't remember her name, or what on earth she was doing in his flat.

Leaning against Matthew in the shower made her want to wrap herself around him like that first night after the barbecue, but she mastered her longing and closed her eyes, shutting out everything but the needle-like drumming of the hot water on her skin and the exquisite agony of his touch. As his hands quickened and his breathing intensified, Gemma backed into the corner of the shower, the darkness consuming her as the world shrunk to nothing other than the cold of the tiles on her back, and the feel of Matthew lifting her legs and pinning her to the wall. It was as close to a religious experience as Gemma had ever known, and in the end even the pounding of the water couldn't stop their cries ruffling the feathers of the pigeons nesting in the eaves of the roof.

In the early hours, Gemma watched Matthew sleep. They must have left a light on downstairs when they carried Mabel up, as a dim glow from the stairwell was casting a yellow halo behind his head. He looked like an angel. Did angels sleep? The lyrics of 'Oh

Little Town of Bethlehem' started playing in Gemma's head, and she worked through each verse she could remember. The lyric she was thinking of was 'while mortals sleep the angels keep their watch of something something', so clearly angels didn't need to sleep. Unless they did it during the day, like vampires, or hamsters. Did angels sleep on the wing, like swifts, or lie down? In which case they'd have to be front sleepers, because those massive wings would really dig in, give you terrible back problems. Gemma turned over, unable to clear her head of rambling internal dialogue. *God, 2 a.m. thoughts are the worst.*

She turned back to look at Matthew, mentally turning off the flow of Christmas carols before 'God Rest Ye Merry Gentlemen' kicked in and she spent the next few hours offering herself tidings of comfort and joy. Matthew slept like the dead, completely still and barely breathing. In contrast, Fraser had thrashed around like an eel in a bucket, and Johannes had whistled through his nose, a side effect of a deviated septum. Gemma had suggested he get it fixed, but he said it didn't affect his ability to play the French horn so it wasn't a problem. On one occasion she'd woken him up to tell him it was like sleeping with Roger Whittaker, but he thought she meant Roger Federer and took it as a compliment.

Gemma lifted her head a little so she could see Mabel, who looked relaxed and comfortable in her bed. Whatever she was dreaming about was prompting tiny growls and paw twitches, and Gemma wondered what she'd got up to in the two hours she'd been missing. Had she gone straight back to West Cottage, or had she had some adventures on the way? Thankfully she'd been spayed, so there would be no surprise baby Mabels in a couple of months. Her impromptu feast didn't seem to have caused any major problems, although she'd generated some fairly noxious gas as they were falling asleep, forcing Gemma and Matthew to retreat under the duvet in a fit of horrified giggles. Matthew said it reminded him why he didn't like dogs, and Gemma told him to prepare himself for an eye-watering twenty-four hours.

She thought about everything that had happened in the past

couple of days – the walk to the river yesterday, meeting Matthew's mum, the carnage at the village hall today. Aside from the two hours he'd spent looking for Mabel, Gemma realised that she and Matthew had barely spent a minute apart since yesterday morning, and yet it didn't feel strange or unusual. Being with Matthew just made her want to be with him more, like a thirst she couldn't quench. The sex was an epiphany, but she'd also enjoyed walking with him, chatting about nothing in particular, watching him with Mabel, working with him on her ideas. He made her feel grounded, like this temporary situation wasn't a waste of her time and her talents. At a time when the world was off-kilter, Matthew's drama-free normality was exactly what she needed, even though they both knew real life had to resume at some point. She'd have to deal with that soon, make a longer-term plan.

'Why aren't you asleep?' whispered Matthew.

Gemma smiled. 'Because I'm awake. Go back to sleep.'

Matthew opened his eyes and looked at her, his face soft with slumber. 'I'm glad you're here.'

'Me too.'

'I'd like to stay like this for a long time.'

'I promise not to kick you out before morning.'

Matthew smiled and drifted away. Gemma closed her eyes and was on the cusp of sleep when a thought flickered that maybe Matthew had meant something else. By morning she'd forgotten the conversation ever happened.

CHAPTER TWENTY-THREE
Tuesday, 21 April

To Do

- Ridiculous video clubs idea
- De-slag cottage
- Find clean knickers
- Call Louise

'Thanks, Alex, that's really good news. Yep. We'll let everyone know and Gemma will email over the details. Great. Thanks.'

Matthew put the phone back in its charging cradle and beamed at Gemma. 'The vicar is on board. He's never used Zoom so he says can you please send him instructions; he'll get his kids to set it up for him. A trial run on Sunday at ten-thirty, see how much interest there is, one hymn only and not too much waffling.' He walked back to the list on his kitchen table. 'OK, I'll try Yvonne.'

So far Matthew had successfully pitched the idea to Reverend Alex and Kate who ran the village playgroup, but Tamsyn from Youth Club had said no – they were already running something similar with quizzes and TikTok challenges for the local teens. Autumn Club had potential, however – in more normal times it had been a fortnightly get-together for the over fifty-fives in the village hall, with tea and biscuits and a regular programme of guest speakers. In the past Matthew had done a talk on winter maintenance for the home, showing people how to lag external pipes and bleed their radiators. To Gemma it seemed like the perfect kind of thing to move online, if they could convince the organisers that using video conferencing wasn't too stressful and problematic.

They had moved their control centre to Matthew's barn because he had a landline; one of those cordless ones with a charging stand, a grey handset the shape and size of an old nineties mobile phone and actual buttons you had to press to dial. It looked charmingly antiquated to Gemma, but she guessed it was essential in a village like Crowthorpe that was a phone signal black hole. Mabel was snuggled into her usual corner of the sofa, so Gemma left Matthew to finish his call to Yvonne and went out on to the wooden balcony with her mobile to call Ruth on WhatsApp. She answered after a few rings and brushed off Gemma's repeated apologies and offers of cash for yesterday. Once they'd got that out of the way, Gemma spent a few minutes giving her a quick rundown on the latest plan and asked if she could print the leaflets in the village hall office and leave them in the shop.

'Goodness, aren't you Little Miss Fixit.'

Gemma stalled, not sure if she'd overstepped some kind of line, particularly in view of yesterday. 'Oh. It's not just me. Matthew said . . .'

Ruth laughed. 'I'm teasing you, I think it's a great idea. Just what people need.'

Gemma laughed nervously. 'I just want to help if I can. You know, while I'm here.'

Ruth's voice softened. 'It will be a sad day when you leave us, my dear.'

Gemma could hear Matthew still on the phone, so she stood on the balcony and WhatsApped Louise. *Oi, sis. You free for a chat tonight?* Gemma would have to walk to the shop for a phone signal if she wanted to chat without Matthew around, but that was OK – she could combine it with Mabel's evening walk.

Matthew's head appeared round the door. 'Yvonne is a yes. She gave me a right mouthful when I asked if she knew what Zoom was. Said she's only sixty-four and her husband used to be an IT teacher, and could I kindly go fuck myself. Rude.' He laughed and held the door open for Gemma to come back in, his hand grazing the back of her jeans as she walked past.

'Oi. Enough of that. We're working.'

'I can't help it, you have a nice bum.'

'I will still have a nice bum when you've called Charlie. I need to get working on the leaflets this afternoon, so I need to know who's on board.'

Matthew pulled a faux-sulky face as Gemma's phone beeped. It was Louise. *Yes please, I need an excuse to take a break from this lot. 7 p.m. your time? Am two hours ahead so kids will be in bed.*

Gemma tapped a quick thumbs up emoji as a reply and turned her attention back to the table of notes. It looked like Autumn Club was going into its usual slot of 2 p.m. every other Monday, starting next week. There would be a Zoom church service this Sunday at 10.30, and the first Parent Pop-In with Kate would be next Wednesday at 11 a.m. Gemma wanted to add two evening clubs to the schedule, which she had tentatively called Lads' Lock-In and Ladies' Lock-In. In her head this was an hour on a Friday or a Saturday when you could bring a drink and log on for a chat, nothing formal or too much like organised fun. Ideally these sessions would be hosted by Charlie and Jess who ran the Black Crow, and Gemma was keen to get them started this coming weekend. They could spread the word using Matthew's village WhatsApp group.

Gemma's phone beeped again, and she saw it was a message from Caro. *Hola Gem. Life here is terrible, tell me you're having amazing sex and loving country life. Cx*

Gemma smiled and sent a laughing emoji, then noticed that Matthew was looking at her, clearly wanting to know what was so funny. 'It's Caro, wanting to know if I'm having amazing sex and loving country life.'

'What did you say?'

'I said country life was great.'

'Ha ha.' Matthew shook his head.

Gemma kissed him gently, her hands sliding up the back of his jumper. 'I'm not giving Caro all the details. At least not until we're both in a fancy bar and I can draw her pictures on a cocktail napkin.'

By late morning Gemma and Matthew had made all their calls and finalised their list, so they agreed to do their own thing until tomorrow. Matthew needed to do a few odd jobs around the village, and Gemma was itching to finish the video clubs leaflet and catch up on some life admin before calling her sister at 7 p.m. She was reluctant to leave the cosiness of Matthew's apartment – it felt like the past couple of days had been a blissful bubble that she didn't want to burst. But Caro's cottage was in need of a clean, the laundry was piling up and she'd get the leaflet finished far quicker without Matthew to distract her with his come-to-bed eyes and wandering hands.

Mabel was even less keen to leave, so Matthew sat beside her on the sofa and scratched her ears. 'I'm sorry, yellow dog. I know you'd rather follow the sun around the sofa while you process all that steak and carrots, but Gemma needs to go home now. It's hard for both of us.' Gemma smiled weakly, unable to stop herself imagining him talking about a move of 90 miles, rather than 15 metres. It made her chest hurt to think about it.

By the end of the afternoon Gemma's mood had lifted, as it invariably did when she'd managed to tick all of the jobs off her list and could enjoy feeling particularly smug about it. The cottage had been hoovered and dusted, two lots of laundry done, the bathroom cleaned and the sheets changed. They'd only been on the bed since Friday but they'd seen quite a lot of human activity since then, and there was no need to let standards slip. She'd walked Mabel on the recreation ground, then finished the design for the leaflet and emailed it to all of the club leaders for them to check times and contact details before Ruth printed it for her tomorrow.

At 6.45 p.m. Gemma clipped Mabel to her lead and walked through the village to call Louise. She couldn't help but notice how many more waves and greetings she received compared to a couple of weeks ago – most people seemed to know her name, and everyone said hello to Mabel, making jokey comments about her exploits yesterday and checking she was OK. Gemma's involvement in the Swap Shops had clearly helped her across the line from 'visitor' to 'one of us', and she had to admit it was a nice feeling. She had never really felt part of a community before; the only place she'd lived in for any length of time was Warwick Mews, and she'd never got to know her neighbours beyond a polite nod and wave. Like Aunt Laura, most of the owners didn't live there much; next door was a Malaysian businessman in his fifties who worked away for weeks at a time, and the other side had been empty the entire time Gemma lived there – she assumed it was owned by overseas investors. Aunt Laura had once told her that Uncle Clive had talked about buying it and knocking it through to make one big house, but he died before that plan ever came to anything. Looking back it was clearly all bullshit; Uncle Clive talked a good game, but he didn't have nearly as much money as he liked to make out.

Gemma sat on the steps outside the village shop with Mabel lying on the path at her feet, entirely unbothered that they were revisiting the scene of yesterday's horror show. The air still had a hint of warmth to it, but Gemma zipped up her jacket – she would soon get cold sitting still outside. She put her headphones in and scrolled through her contacts until she found Louise – the international dial tone sounded a few times before she heard her sister's familiar voice.

'Hey, Gummer. Hang on, I'll go outside.'

Gemma heard a heavy sliding door open, then close again. She could picture exactly where Louise was right now, on the patio of one of the officers' married quarters on the south coast of the island. It didn't matter which one, they all looked the same; the house Louise was living in now was only a few streets away from

200

the one their family had lived in fifteen years previously. The Cyprus air at 9 p.m. in late April would be warm enough to sit in a long-sleeved T-shirt or a light jumper, with the sound of cicadas providing a gentle background hum. In April they would be just getting started – by June the noise would be a relentless, twenty-four-hour cacophony.

'OK, I'm here, we can have a proper chat. How's lockdown life?'

Gemma took a deep breath, not really knowing where to start. Other than their ninety-second chat and a few exchanges of daft WhatsApp messages, she hadn't had Louise's undivided attention in weeks. Her sister knew about Fraser, but nothing at all about Matthew.

Gemma talked non-stop for ten minutes and offloaded every-thing, from how she was feeling about Fraser to the details of her new village life. Then she told her about meeting Matthew, and was just getting started on the plans she'd been working on for the village when Louise interrupted.

'OK, slow down, we need to back up a bit. Just let me get this straight. You've been living in this village for four weeks, have started fucking the hot guy next door, and are now head of the village fete committee or something. Jesus, Gem, you're the re-incarnation of Aunt Laura.'

Louise laughed, but Gemma was confused. 'What do you mean?'

'Don't you remember Mum telling us the story of how she met Uncle Clive?' Gemma's silence told her she didn't, so Louise ploughed on. 'Her first husband was some actor who ran off with his leading lady, so Aunt Laura moved back to Norfolk to lick her wounds. Uncle Clive was the wealthy widower next door; she'd moved into his place within months and started overhauling that theatre in Norwich for something to do. Mum thought her re-bound was indecently hasty; I think she feels women should weep and wail over bad men for longer. How can you not remember?'

The story triggered a vague memory, but Gemma had chosen

not to retain it, along with all the other disparaging tales of Aunt Laura's behaviour that their mother liked to tell, her voice full of bitterness.

'You're right, I'd forgotten. How funny. But this is different, Lou. I'm not going to marry Matthew, it's more like a holiday romance. I've got to go back to London, I can't stay here.'

'So why are you still there? You could have found a new flat by now, even if you can't do normal viewings. What's stopping you?'

'I . . . I don't know. I've been busy with all the village stuff, and I guess I thought I'd wait until . . .' Gemma's voice trailed off.

'Until what? Until people in London stop getting sick? Until there's a vaccine? This is bullshit, Gem. It sounds to me like you're happy living there, and you like Matthew.'

Gemma couldn't deny it. She was happy living in Crowthorpe, and she did like Matthew. But this wasn't home. It was impossible to explain.

'You're right, Lou, but it doesn't make any difference. I don't belong here. At some point I need to go back to London. I feel like I'm in the wrong place, making the wrong decisions, and to be honest I don't know which way is up.'

'Then do it now. Before you end up with a broken heart and take that poor guy down with you. If you're not in love with him you're using him as some kind of comfort blanket, which is a shitty thing to do. And the reason I know this is because I've been doing it for years.'

Gemma was silenced. She'd been so busy offloading, she hadn't had a chance to ask Louise how her life was. 'Oh fuck. I'm sorry. How are things at your end? How's Jamie?'

'Jamie's fine, thanks for asking. He has no idea that his wife is a secret lesbian who should never have married him in the first place. I, on the other hand, am utterly miserable. Work is a fucking nightmare – we've got a curfew from ten p.m. so I've got hundreds of squaddies who are bored out of their minds with nothing to do but make trouble. If you want to go anywhere outside the base, you have to call an automated service and get a text message

202

that gives you permission. The kids are both home from school and all the beaches are closed. None of the married quarters have air conditioning, so if this carries on much longer we're all going to boil in our beds. Basically everything is shit.'

'God, Lou, I'm sorry. My problems feel like nothing compared to yours.'

'That's not true. Mine are circumstantial. Once all this mess is over I'll have a heart-to-heart with Jamie and he'll probably be incredibly supportive because he's the nicest man on earth. We'll resolve shared responsibility for the kids and we'll both be quietly posted back to the UK.' Gemma heard her light a cigarette and inhale deeply; it was a habit Louise had committed to fully as a teenager, but Gemma had always stayed away from. The memory of the final stages of Uncle Clive's throat cancer were enough to put her off, even with the teenage pressure to look cool.

'On the other hand, your issues are much bigger, because you're searching for something that doesn't exist. Some kind of fucking happy-ever-after utopia like the ending of all those fucking books you used to read. Tell me this: what's in London that you can't live without?'

Gemma thought for a moment. 'I don't know, I just can't imagine living anywhere else. It's where my friends are, my job is. It's the only place I've ever properly lived. I don't know how to live anywhere else.'

'I notice you didn't say that living in London makes you happy, or that London is the best city in the world.'

Gemma didn't say anything. Her head felt like it was full of noise.

'It's just a city, Gem. There are lots of them. You've got to find what makes you happy, then live wherever that happiness is. My job makes me happy, so it doesn't matter where in the world I'm based. Dad was the same, Mum learned to live with it. Give it some thought, OK?'

Gemma promised she would, and they talked for a few more minutes about their parents and when they might next see each other. Gemma had a vague plan to fly to Cyprus in September but hadn't booked anything. Maybe it would be OK by then, or maybe Louise would be dealing with a messy break-up from Jamie and wouldn't want her sister hanging around.

'Thanks for the chat, Lou. I appreciate it.'

'No bother. Think about what I said. If there's one thing I've learned it's that you have to stop pretending everything is OK when it isn't. What did Aunt Laura used to say? Follow your heart . . .'

Gemma joined in for the second half, '. . . but bring your brain with you.'

'Yeah, that's the one.' Louise lit another cigarette. 'She really loved you, you know. Far more than she did me. I used to be really jealous about it, took me ages to realise that you needed her way more than I did. I saw an Army therapist for a while after Libby was born and we talked about it. The analogy she used was something about me being happy to set sail and see where the wind took me, whereas you needed to stay close to shore. Aunt Laura was your safe harbour, a refuge when things got stormy.' Louise paused, her voice softening. 'But she's gone. Who's your safe harbour now, Gem?'

Gemma sat on the step and cried for a long time after she and Louise said their goodbyes. She cried for Aunt Laura in a way she hadn't since she died, working her way through the whole spectrum of emotions from fury that her aunt had left her, to the deepest kind of sadness that she'd never get to talk to her again. She cried for her sister, who had a world of pain ahead of her before she had any chance of finding happiness. And then she cried for herself, and this messy situation she found herself in. There were no safe harbours any more; one way or another, Gemma was going to have to learn to sail her ship alone.

CHAPTER TWENTY-FOUR

Thursday, 23 April

To Do

- Make a plan?
- Look at flats?
- Hate everything

Gemma lay in bed and stared at the empty space beside her; it looked cold and unwelcoming. She ran her hand over the unwrinkled duvet, feeling the comforting softness of linen that had been washed and dried a hundred times, worn thin from years of warm, sleeping bodies. Fraser had preferred crisp, Egyptian cotton in the highest thread count he could find, like you'd find in a fancy hotel. He ironed it too, so the pillows retained the sharp creases of multiple folds on the ironing board. He used to make his side of the bed while Gemma was still in it, which always felt like a passive/aggressive dig that she was still in bed while he was up and smashing the day. In books couples lazed in bed on Sunday mornings with coffee and papers, but Gemma had never done it in real life.

She rolled over to the pillow and breathed in the clean smell. It was a shame the warm bulk of Matthew's body wasn't there, but he hadn't stayed over last night; he had to pick up some timber from a yard somewhere up in the Cotswolds. Chipping something, far enough away that he needed an early start. Finding materials was proving challenging for Matthew — a lot of his suppliers were either closed or running a reduced service to protect their staff. He needed some green oak to make a coffee table for a new client, and Chipping Whatever was the nearest he could find that could supply at short notice. He'd invited Gemma to go with him but she hadn't really fancied the 7 a.m. start; now she was awake at 6.45 and wished she'd said yes, it would be nice to get out of the village for a few hours. She briefly considered seeing if she could catch him, but decided not to be annoying. He was probably on his way out and didn't need her faffing around, holding him up.

It seemed like she might as well get up anyway, since she was awake. It would be a good day to take Mabel out for a long walk and do some admin – maybe start looking at flats in London and make some kind of plan. The thought made her feel heavy and lethargic, but she dragged herself into the shower and was dressed in leggings and a long jumper within ten minutes. Not the most glamorous look, but nobody was going to see her today.

Matthew was in the kitchen when she came downstairs, sitting on the floor playing tug with Mabel. He was wearing old jeans and his usual work boots, along with a heavy flannel jacket in blue and black check, hovering somewhere between a shirt and a coat. Underneath was his usual white T-shirt; the whole look was very lumberjack chic. Mabel's jaws were clamped around a red rope toy, which she yanked at with a series of faux-menacing growls. Gemma watched them for a second, torn between annoyance that he kept walking into her house without knocking, and an uncontrollable urge to get him out of those clothes as soon as possible.

'Hey, you. I thought you were off somewhere?'

He looked up and smiled, his hair still wet from the shower. 'I am, but I was just about to leave when I saw the light in the shower and knew you were up. So I thought I'd give you a second chance to come with me, in case you changed your mind. It's a nice drive. Mabel can come. You want to come, don't you, Mabel?'

Gemma laughed. Mabel was a shameless traitor and would follow Matthew to the ends of the earth. She leaned against the door frame and considered the offer. 'I suppose I could, but I need urgent coffee first.'

Matthew stood up, and Gemma was once again struck by the sheer size of him. Even with the length of the kitchen between them, he seemed to fill the available space like expanding foam. 'I'll go and make you one, I've got one of those thermos cups. I'll meet you by the van in ten minutes. Bring a jacket and some shoes you don't mind getting muddy.' He grinned and left through the back door, Mabel trailing behind him.

Gemma went into the dining room and gathered a few bits for Mabel – her lead, and a walking pouch that contained poop bags, dog treats and a bottle of water. She left everything on the side in the kitchen and went back up to the loft to put her hair into a bun, pushing the stray bits back from her face with a pair of sunglasses and adding the bare minimum of make-up so she didn't look like living death. Returning to the bedroom, she pulled a large green box from under the bed that contained a pair of knee-high brown leather and suede boots, the kind of thing you might wear to ride a horse. She hadn't brought any wellies from London and had seen half the women in the village wearing this particular style; it seemed to be very much *en vogue* for walking your dog in the countryside. Aside from being sleek and beautiful they looked super-comfy and practical, so Gemma had googled 'brown leather country wellies' until she found them in a *Sunday Times* article entitled 'The best wellington boots for spring'. They were made by Dubarry of Ireland with a £329 price tag that made Gemma gasp, but by then she'd already imagined herself wearing them, which meant any resistance was futile. In Gemma's experience once you'd made the emotional commitment to an item, you already owned it – actual physical purchase was just admin.

She'd also bought a black padded gilet from the same country goods store – her London coats were impractical for dodging into hedgerows to let tractors pass, and she liked the idea of being warm but still having her arms free. Both had been ordered a couple of weeks ago but only arrived yesterday; lots of things were taking ages to be shipped and delivered right now. She'd been undecided about whether to return them; neither would ever be worn once she was back in London, she'd look like a dick. But there was an opportunity now, and she rationalised that she could keep them for trips back to Norfolk to see her parents.

Mabel was waiting for her outside the back door when she came down, and she could see Matthew watching her as she walked down the path with Mabel trotting at her side. By the time she reached the van he'd broken into a giant grin.

'What are you laughing at?'

'You've gone full Cotswolds, and you look fantastic. Those boots are the sexiest thing I've seen all day.'

Gemma rolled her eyes and snatched the silver thermos cup from his hands. 'It's barely seven a.m. They're comfortable and waterproof, which is all I care about.'

'You look like you're off to the stables. Can you ride a horse?'

'Actually, yes, I can. Stop ogling my new boots, you pervert.' She gave him a light kiss as she climbed into the van, slapping away his roving hands. There was a bench of two passenger seats, upholstered in faded grey and black fabric and smelling of damp timber and wood oil. Gemma shuffled over to the seat nearest the driver's side, settling Mabel into the footwell nearest the door.

Matthew walked round to the driver's side and jumped in, full of childlike enthusiasm. It was one of the things Gemma liked about him – his total lack of self-consciousness, his guileless relish in something as simple as a drive out in the countryside. It was hard not to find it infectious. *And refreshing*, she thought.

They turned left out of the driveway on to the lane, then left again towards the village past the front of West Cottage.

'Wait, can you stop?'

Matthew slammed on the brakes, causing Mabel to slide sideways into the back of the footwell. 'What's up?'

'There's something in the mailbox, the flap hasn't been closed properly. I just want to grab it.'

Gemma climbed over Mabel and opened the door, then jumped down into the road. She extracted the envelope from the mailbox and briefly glanced at it, before closing the flap and running back to the van. She'd expected it to be for Caro, but it had nothing but Gemma's name on it.

'Sorry, I just didn't want to leave that sticking out all day.'

Matthew raised his eyebrows. 'Anything interesting?'

Gemma pushed the note into her pocket. 'No idea, I'll read it later.'

The village was still and silent at 7.30, with just a handful of locals out walking their dogs and the odd jogger passing through. Matthew waved at a couple of people, who raised a hand and gave them both a smile. After a mile they passed his parents' house, but the curtains were closed and there was no sign of life. At the cross-roads the van slowed next to the BP garage, purveyor of condoms and local gossip, then turned left towards the motorway. Matthew smiled, reading her mind. 'I bought a big box in Sainsbury's.'

Gemma smiled back and shrugged. 'I got some from Amazon.'

After a few minutes they crossed the M4 and started to head north. Every few miles verdant hedgerows and views across open countryside gave way to another impossibly pretty village, tightly packed with wisteria-covered cottages and flourishing gardens. Some were just hamlets – a small farm or a handful of houses; others had a crumbling old pub and a church or a tiny village green scattered with ducks. Some they didn't drive through at all; Gemma could see a small town nestled in a valley away from the main road, with stands of pink and white horse chestnuts following a ribbon of river glinting in the sunshine. After exactly a month within the confines of Crowthorpe, it made her want to sing 'Jerusalem' with the windows down.

'It's gorgeous. Everything's so . . . green.'

'You're seeing it at its best right now, there's been so little rain. The farmers aren't happy, but it does look pretty.'

They drove on, the terrain becoming more undulating as the road weaved through buttercup meadows and fields of sheep trailing newborn lambs. Just past Kemble they joined a bigger road to Cirencester; Matthew ignored the ring road signs and drove through the centre so Gemma could see the ancient market town, the streets lined with ancient Cotswold stone houses, half-timbered pubs and imposing Georgian architecture. Even though most of the shops were closed, Gemma could see the kind of places they were – expensive boutiques, artisanal delis and little tucked-away homeware and antique shops. Aunt Laura would have loved it.

'It looks like an expensive place to live.'

Matthew shrugged. 'It is, I guess, compared to other bits of the West Country. But nothing compared to London. You can pick up an old cottage nearer Chippenham for a reasonable amount if you're prepared to fix it up.'

Gemma looked at him. 'Is that what you want?'

He smiled shyly and glanced at her. 'Sure. The barn is great but it's pretty small. It would be nice to have more space, be able to invite friends over. Maybe grow some food, keep some chickens.' He laughed nervously, like Gemma might mock him, but she could easily imagine it – Matthew hammering away at the roof of a crumbling old house, married to a wholesome English rose who was permanently sexually available despite their clutch of sturdy children and her relentless baking. She brushed the thought aside. *Too much Laurie Lee, Gemma.*

Beyond Cirencester they headed north on the straightest road Gemma had ever seen – it pierced the landscape like a silver arrow as far as the eye could see. Matthew explained it was the Fosse Way – an ancient Roman road that connected Exeter and Lincoln via Bath, Cirencester and Leicester. Some bits of it were just farm tracks now, but most of it was overlaid with modern A-roads. The landscape seemed so empty to Gemma compared to London – just miles and miles of grazing farmland, rolling meadows, winding rivers and tiny chocolate-box villages. She noticed that the colour of the cottages was changing – south of Cirencester they were a creamy pale yellow, but here they were darker, more honey-coloured. Everything was so relentlessly, delightfully, ridiculously pretty; Gemma couldn't quite take it in.

'Where are we going again?'

'Chipping Campden. It's about half an hour away.'

'Isn't that where David Cameron lives?'

'Nope, that's Chipping Norton. That's a right turn in Stow-on-the-Wold, we're turning left.'

'Of course we are.' Gemma relaxed into the seat, holding Mabel close. She had climbed on to the seat for a better view once they were on the Fosse Way and the van stopped lurching along windy roads. Gemma had hooked the spare seat belt through her collar to keep her safe, and now Mabel was watching the world go by like she hung out in Matthew's van every day, the breeze through the window flapping her ears. Gemma felt another tinge of guilt – taking Mabel back to south London would mean no more snoozing under the apple tree, no more chasing squirrels through the woods. She'd make sure her next place was nearer some green space.

The timber yard was on the outskirts of Chipping Campden, another ridiculously beautiful Cotswold market town packed with honey-stone cottages, boutiques and cosy pubs. Gemma wondered what a place like this would be like on an ordinary sunny day in July when everything was open; probably packed with tourists, so perhaps now was the best time to see it. Matthew parked near the market hall in the town centre so Mabel could stretch her paws and take advantage of the grass – they had twenty minutes before he was expected at the yard. As Mabel chased her tail and rolled around in the buttercups, Gemma was suddenly struck by a long-forgotten memory.

'Fairy gold.'

Matthew looked up. 'Fairy what?'

Gemma shook her head. 'Sorry. I just remembered a story my aunt once told me. Forget it.'

'I can't now. You have to tell me.' Matthew smiled playfully and nudged her shoulder.

Gemma tried to piece the bits together, but the memory was woolly. She and Aunt Laura had been out for a walk in the sunshine when Gemma was fourteen or fifteen, probably to the farm shop or the post office. They'd passed a field of buttercups with horses grazing in it, and Aunt Laura had asked with a glint in her eye if she knew where buttercups came from.

'OK, I think I've got it. There's a story in fairy lore, about a man who was crossing a field carrying a big sack of gold. The fairies asked him for help, but the miserly old git wouldn't give them any.'

'What did fairies need gold for?'

Gemma looked at Matthew, momentarily confounded. 'Do you know what, I have no idea. Castle repairs? New wings?'

Matthew laughed. 'Maybe they needed to melt it down for fairy furniture. Expensive tastes. Sorry, carry on.'

'ANYWAY, the old man was too mean and selfish to give the poor fairies a bit of his gold and walked off. So the fairies poked a hole in his sack and the gold scattered across the field. To hide what they'd done, they turned it into buttercups, which meant everyone could now share his gold for ever.'

'So basically some fairies mugged an old man.'

'No. Yes. There's a moral about sharing your emotional and physical wealth, but I can't remember the details.'

'So that's why buttercups are fairy gold.'

'Exactly.'

'Or old man gold, looted by socialist fairies.'

'OK, STOP.' Gemma punched him playfully as they reached a marker stone laid into the pavement, with a carving of an acorn at the centre and a spiral of place names around the outside, like the rings of a tree.

Matthew knelt down to look at it more closely. 'It marks the beginning of the Cotswold Way. If you follow the path for a hundred and two miles, it ends up in Bath.'

Gemma read the inscription that formed the outermost ring. '*Now the light falls across the open field, leaving the deep lane shuttered with branches, dark in the afternoon.*' She'd never been much on poetry and didn't recognise the quote. 'T. S. Eliot, I think,' said Matthew casually; Gemma suspected he knew exactly which poem it was, and could probably recite the whole thing from memory.

She looked in the direction of the wooden fingerpost, also inlaid with the tiny acorn symbol. It made her think of the Yellow Brick Road from *The Wizard of Oz* – there was something quite magical about having the path laid out before you, the destination clear-cut and unambiguous. All you had to do was keep walking and trust the signs, and eventually you would arrive. If only real life was like that. 'Have you ever walked it?'

'Not the whole thing, but I've done bits of it. From here to Broadway is nice, and it passes through Painswick, which isn't far from the Slad Valley if you like Laurie Lee.' Gemma blushed at the memory of her earlier thoughts of Matthew and his wholesomely fuckable wife. 'There's a section along Cleeve Hill in Cheltenham with the most amazing views. We should take Mabel there when the weather warms up.' His voice faltered, and Gemma saw that it was Matthew's turn to blush. He turned away slightly, staring at his feet.

Gemma's heart sank. It felt like a cloud had drifted over both of them, casting the carved marker stone beneath her feet into shadow. *I won't spoil today*, she thought grimly. *But I can't leave this much longer. I'll make a plan tomorrow and talk to him on Saturday. Whether I want to or not, it has to be done.*

CHAPTER TWENTY-FIVE

Matthew wandered off to where Mabel was sniffing around and sat down on a stone wall, his feet planted solidly on the grass. Mabel loped over and sniffed him for treats, then sat down against his legs with her head on his knee. Gemma watched them for a moment, suddenly consumed with an overwhelming tiredness. She walked over and sat beside him on the wall; her feet didn't reach the ground, so she swung her new boots a few times to get his attention. Gemma could see the trace of a smile on his lips.

'I've had an email from Erica, they definitely want to continue the Swap Shops. Taking a break for two weeks, then back the week after that. Yesterday went really well.'

Matthew turned his head to look at her, his face full of pride. 'That's really good news, Gem. It's a great idea. Every three weeks keeps it fresh and takes the pressure off the volunteers.'

Gemma noted the shortened version of her name, really only ever used by Caro, Joe and Louise. He'd never called her that before, and it felt nice. 'That's what Erica said. And we've got the first Ladies' Lock-In tomorrow, so that's happening too.'

'Does that mean you'd like to come over to use my WiFi?'

Gemma wrinkled her nose and looked a little sheepish. 'Yeah, if that's OK. Sorry. But I also need you to make yourself scarce for an hour or two so you don't frighten the locals.'

Matthew laughed. 'Fine. I'll go to the workshop and write some dirty jokes for my Lads' sesh on Saturday or something.' He paused and thought for a moment. 'Tell you what, I'll do you a deal. You can use my WiFi tomorrow if I can cook you dinner tonight. We'll stop and get some food on the way home.'

Gemma stood up and turned to face him, manoeuvring herself between his legs. His seated position made their faces almost level, so she leaned in and kissed him. 'You drive a very hard bargain, but it's a deal.' Matthew pulled her closer, slowly unzipping her gilet so he could slide his hands inside, feeling the heat of her skin through her jumper. She felt him stir against her hip and make that low guttural moan in his throat that made her stomach flip, so she pulled back from the kiss to whisper in his ear.

'I'm not sure this is appropriate behaviour for this part of the Cotswolds.'

Matthew gave a deep, breathless laugh. 'Best I get you home as soon as possible then.'

Gemma waited in the van while Matthew was in the timber yard. Mabel's head was resting on her lap, so she stroked her gently between her ears until she drifted off into a blissed-out sleep. She remembered the note in her pocket and slipped it out of the envelope – the paper was heavy cream, with an old-fashioned cursive written in black ink from a fountain pen.

Dear Gemma

We haven't had the pleasure of meeting, I live in one of the houses over the road from yours and I see you walking past regularly with your dog. I used to have an Airedale Terrier but he sadly passed away last year, he wasn't as well behaved as yours, although of course I did hear about the dreadful incident in the shop. It's so important to keep dogs safe if you have to leave them alone.

I wondered if perhaps once this is over we could go for a drink? Or perhaps you can cook us both dinner, I'm afraid I'm not much use in the kitchen.

In the interests of full disclosure, I should tell you that I am a few years older than you, although of course I don't know your age so I'm guessing! But I'm fit and healthy and open to having a woman in my life, particularly when she looks as lovely as you.

I wouldn't normally be this forward but these are exceptional times and at our stage of life you need to 'grasp the nettle'! Since you seem like the kind of woman who likes adventure, I hope you'll consider me favourably.

With regards,
J. Dunn

By the time she had finished, Gemma's eyebrows were sky high – if she'd read this right, she was being propositioned by a man in the village who suggested she might like to cook him dinner. She didn't know whether to be amused or deeply insulted.

When Matthew had finished loading the timber and climbed back into the van, she handed him the note. 'Can you shed any light on this?'

He read it quickly, his face breaking into a smile. 'Jeremy, you dirty old bugger.'

'Who's Jeremy?'

'He lives across the road from you, in the house with the red door. He's a widower, I guess he must be about sixty? He used to hang around with my dad when they were younger, so they must be a similar age. Dad said he used to be something of a player back in the day, but he tried to cop off with my mum at a wedding about ten years ago and Dad has barely spoken to him since.' Matthew started to laugh, his shoulders shaking. Gemma punched him on the arm.

'Stop it. Am I supposed to be flattered?'

'I hate to disappoint, but he's propositioned every unmarried woman in the village since his wife died about fifteen years ago, and most of the married ones. He's playing the numbers game – if he casts the net wide enough eventually someone will take the bait.'

'Wow, how charming. Why is this so funny?'

'I'm sorry. I'll fight him for you, defend your honour.'

'Fuck OFF, Matthew.' Gemma folded her arms, pretending to be annoyed.

He wiped away the tears with the back of his hand and started the engine. 'OK, I've stopped laughing. Let's go home.' He leaned over and kissed her cheek, then added a bonus kiss to the top of Mabel's head. 'You've both got forty-five minutes until we get to Cirencester to think about your perfect dinner. Forget the village shop, today we're going to Waitrose.'

After a month of only eating food from the limited selection in the village shop, Gemma raided Waitrose like this was her final meal on death row. They gathered the ingredients for pan-fried salmon with asparagus and baby potatoes, along with individual pots of tiramisu and cream and a bottle of English sparkling wine, plus a meaty beef bone for Mabel.

When they got back to Crowthorpe they put everything in Matthew's fridge, then agreed to do their own thing for the rest of the day – Matthew needed to unload and stack the timber from the van, and Gemma had some life admin to catch up on. She cancelled a dental appointment, sent a few work emails, had an unproductive but dutiful call with her mother and messaged Louise to say thank you for the chat on Tuesday. She'd missed a couple of calls from Caro but didn't want to talk to her about her return to London until she'd talked to Matthew, so fobbed her off with excuses about bad internet and a promise to call on Sunday for a proper chat. In the long shadows of late afternoon, she put her boots and gilet back on and took Mabel for a long walk across the fields and around the woods, enjoying the novelty of being appropriately dressed for the environment for the first time in weeks.

By seven she was showered and changed into jeans and her favourite slouchy jumper, so she walked Mabel back to Matthew's. He'd also showered and changed into clean jeans and a faded denim shirt, and true to his word he cooked her dinner while she relaxed on the sofa with Mabel and a glass of wine. They washed up together, and as they put the last few dishes away Gemma

217

playfully nudged him with her hip as she asked what he'd like to do next.

'Well, it's a little early for me to take you to bed,' said Matthew, blushing a little. 'But I thought maybe we could lie on the sofa and . . . read?'

It wasn't the answer Gemma expected, but the suggestion delighted her. It was her secret idea of a perfect evening, although if anyone asked she'd obviously say cocktails and dancing or something less overtly nerdy. Matthew put some background music on – some kind of Café del Mar Ibiza chillout compilation – and brought the wine over to the coffee table by the sofa.

By the time darkness fell she was well-fed and warm, lying with her head on Matthew's lap, reading Dodie Smith's *I Capture the Castle*. It was another book that Gemma had first discovered on Aunt Laura's bookshelf, and it had been her favourite of all the coming-of-age novels she'd read in her late teens. She identified with the book's narrator Cassandra – another precocious, bookish teenager who was neither effortlessly popular nor a proud misfit, but felt the invisibility and loneliness of the wasteland in between. Despite being younger than Gemma, Louise reminded her of Cassandra's older sister, Rose – prettier, more confident, more driven. Louise had always had a plan, and she never took her eyes off it for a second. Passing the Army Officer Selection Board, aceing her A-levels, then heading to Sandhurst to begin her Army career. The biggest obstacle was their father, who spent months trying to persuade Louise to join the RAF instead – first with incredulity, and later with bitterness and anger. Gemma was at university by then so couldn't help her sister stand up to him, but Louise never even blinked. Gemma remembered being so proud of her; come to think of it, she still was.

Matthew was nestled into the elbow of the corner sofa reading *Cider with Rosie*, his legs stretched out at 90 degrees to Gemma's and Mabel flumped across his feet. Apparently today's trip had reminded him that he hadn't read Laurie Lee's autobiography in years, and couldn't remember much about it. Gemma had studied it for A-level, and had found the tales of Lee's Cotswold childhood both charming and horrifying in equal measure. Up to that point, all the books she'd read about twenties life in Britain had been about the upper classes – *Brideshead Revisited*, *Mrs Dalloway*, *Lady Chatterley's Lover*; Gemma had never dipped her toe into rural poverty, disease and feral little boys. She remembered being confounded by the West Country dialect and horrified by the casual way Laurie Lee had talked about the plans the local boys made to gang rape one of the village girls. Her handwritten essays about the juxtaposition of childhood idylls and male violence had been punctuated with tiny holes where she'd stabbed her pen through the paper in teenage feminist outrage.

Matthew wriggled down further into the sofa, pulling Gemma deeper into the crook of his arm. He frowned at her pink socks, patterned with tiny unicorns. They had been a Christmas present from Louise.

'Shame you didn't bring the new boots.'

She punched him playfully on the arm. 'They're for outdoor wear only.'

'Talking of which, you didn't tell me where you learned to ride a horse.'

Gemma laid down her book and took his hand, weaving her fingers into his. 'Remember I told you about my Aunt Laura, and how I stayed with her at weekends during term time when my family lived abroad? Her town had the library in the church.'

'I remember.'

'One of the first books I borrowed was *Riders* by Jilly Cooper.' Gemma smiled at the memory. 'Not exactly highbrow literature, but I was fourteen and my mum would NEVER have let me read it. It's mostly sex and horses.'

'Two of my favourite things. I'll order a copy.'

'You should. Anyway, the plot revolves around these two show jumpers, and I thought the whole thing seemed incredibly sexy and glamorous. All the girls in the book had long swingy hair and looked great in jodhpurs, so when I next went home to Cyprus I asked if I could have riding lessons. There was a military saddle club that I could walk to from our house, so my parents packed me off on pony camp. It was my school holiday obsession for a few years. I started way too late to be any good at it; most of the kids there had been riding since they were little. But I loved horses and liked hanging out at the stables, although I never quite managed long swingy hair or looking great in jodhpurs.' Gemma laughed awkwardly. 'I did lose my virginity in one of the stables after a competition when I was sixteen. Came back to the party with glowing cheeks and straw in my hair, just like in the book.'

'OK, this story is just getting good.'

'Ha ha. What about you? What classic literature inspired you to ride around the country on horseback?'

'It wasn't a book, it was a job. There's a stables about half a mile out of the village, we walked past it the other day. It's a livery yard mostly; people pay to keep their horses there. I got a job there when I was fifteen or so; mucking out horses before school, doing odd jobs at weekends. I used to ride some of the horses out sometimes, nothing more than hacking in the lanes or out in the fields, but that's how I learned to ride a horse.'

Gemma thought about how different their lives and experiences were at that moment in time. Matthew here in Crowthorpe, a shy, surly teenager fixing stable doors for cash and the chance to canter over the fields for an hour here and there. Gemma in Cyprus, finding calm and solace in horses, and revelling in the rigid structure and precision of show jumping in her smart black jacket and hard hat. Matthew hoarding his hard-earned wages, Gemma pinning rosettes for best-turned-out pony on the cork board above her bed.

'Do you still ride?' The thought had morphed into Matthew as Mr Darcy, thundering across the grounds of Pemberley. She filed the mental image as something to spend some quality time with later.

'No, not for years. You?'

'No. Occasionally on holiday, but it's a pretty expensive hobby when your parents aren't paying.'

They settled down with their books again and read without speaking for half an hour or so, then Matthew's hand drifted down to stroke Gemma's hair. It felt delicious, so she let her book flop on to her chest and closed her eyes. Matthew said nothing, but continued with the rhythmic caress for a few minutes. Gemma wondered if he was looking at her, or still reading his book.

'Gem . . . do we need to talk?' His voice was barely a whisper, every word tightly drawn with tension.

Gemma silently processed the question, keeping her eyes closed to hide the flutter of panic. Of course they did, but she desperately didn't want to spoil this moment.

'Yes. Soon. But not now. Right now I just want to be here, with you.' She opened her eyes and tilted her head to look at him, her eyes wide. 'Is that OK?'

Matthew half-smiled and breathed out slowly. 'Sure.'

She sat up and swivelled round to face him, taking in his recumbent body, Mabel asleep on his feet, the wide, soft sofa. 'Come on, Mabel.'

Matthew looked panicked, but Gemma smiled. 'It's OK, we're not leaving. I'm just putting Mabel in the bedroom. Don't move an inch.'

Gemma grabbed a disgruntled Mabel by her collar and hustled her into Matthew's bedroom, where she immediately jumped on the bed and settled down with a huge sigh. Gemma closed the bedroom door gently and returned to the sofa; Matthew had sat up a little but was still where she'd left him, looking a little wary and confused.

Gemma sat astride him, her knees spread to their full extent to take in the expanse of his hips. She began to unbutton his shirt, leaning down to whisper gently in his ear, 'Don't think. Just be here.'

Matthew lifted his arms above his head, letting them flop on the back of the sofa as Gemma silently pushed his shirt open, her delicate fingers whispering across his chest and down his stomach. She watched his face carefully, allowing her hands to linger whenever his eyes closed and his breath caught. A feather-light touch on his collarbone, a sweeping stroke down the curve of his side, a touch more pressure with a fingertip from the bottom of his ribcage to the button of his jeans. Gemma wondered how long he could take it, but he didn't move, so she twisted open the button and slowly pulled down the zip, taking hold of him with both hands. For a moment she marvelled at the intoxicating power she held over the man pinned beneath her, until Matthew murmured her name and gathered her up in his arms, flipping her over on to the sofa and burying his head in her body. She heard a muffled 'Oh God, Gem, I . . .' but the rest of his words were lost in a tangle of clothes and limbs and a breathless need to shut everything out but each other.

CHAPTER TWENTY-SIX

Friday, 24 April

To Do

- Stop being a twat and make a plan
- Call Joe
- Book virtual viewings of shitty flats
- Ladies' Lock-In 8.30 p.m.

Sit down, Gemma. Make a list. Everything feels better with a list. Maybe a cup of tea first? Why are you looking at me like that? Fuck, even the dog is judging me today.

Everything felt complicated and onerous today, like climbing a hill with a backpack full of rocks or wading through custard in lead boots. Gemma's brain felt like it was full of bees; it was easy to blame it on wine and sofa sex, but that was just ignoring the facts: a plan for a return to real life needed to be made, and she simply didn't want to do it.

She made a mug of tea and grabbed a packet of ginger biscuits, returning to the dining table feeling resolute. Getting started was always the hardest bit.

Her mind wandered back to the previous evening at Matthew's — it had been pretty special; the kind of night she'd read about in books but never experienced first-hand. Romance had never factored highly in her previous relationships — none of her previous boyfriends had ever gone to the trouble of music, wine, food and snuggling on the sofa, or shown any indication that they might welcome such a gesture from her. Matthew had asked her to stay over but she'd said no – ostensibly on the basis of them both having an early start, but in reality because she couldn't face spending the night in his rock-hard prison bed. Apart from that first night when she'd crept in to use him as a hot water bottle, she'd managed to engineer all sex to take place either in her bed or on his sofa. Her spine would thank her one day.

Gemma sipped her tea and ate a biscuit. Making a list would help her feel more in control of the situation, but maybe it would help to get some context first. There was her situation in this village, but also the wider situation in London and the UK, and the rest of the world. She clicked on to the *Guardian* website and chose their at-a-glance news round-up from the previous night, and immediately wished she hadn't.

Looking at the figures made Gemma's heart feel heavy – this crisis was so very far from over; the impact was going to be felt for years throughout the world. Unsurprisingly, a huge proportion of the UK's cases were in London, with Southwark particularly badly hit. She still felt bad for running away, but equally not hugely enthused about going back.

But what was the alternative? Staying in Wiltshire, filing the odd article when she could find work, joining the Women's Institute and learning to make jam? *Don't make work your excuse, Gemma – it's not like you've tried particularly hard over the past couple of weeks.* This was true – she'd been so busy with village stuff that she hadn't actively pitched for any work, although she'd done whatever had come her way. And the stuff she was writing was absolutely not dependent on her living in London, at least not for now.

She grabbed two sheets of paper and wrote a heading in capital letters at the top of each:

REASONS TO STAY

REASONS TO GO

She stared at the headings for a bit while she ate another biscuit then started to make a list.

REASONS TO STAY

1. It's safer here than in London
2. The cottage is nice and (currently) rent-free
3. Mabel likes the countryside
4. I like the countryside – green space/air quality
5. Nice community/village stuff
6. Only an hour on train from London
7. I really like spending time with Matthew

Gemma's pen hovered over the final line, unable to find the right words. *I like spending time with him. Being with him makes me happy. I like him a LOT. Oh fuck, I love him.* The realisation hit her like a punch in the gut; she put her pen down and covered her face, pushing the heels of her hands into her eye sockets. *Fuck, fuck, fuck.* Falling in love with Matthew had never been part of the plan, and she hadn't seen it coming. But now she'd said the words out loud in her head, it was so obvious. She thought about how different she felt with Matthew compared to Fraser, how much more alive she had felt in the past few weeks. Matthew had flicked every one of her switches and lit her up like a Christmas tree, and even now she was thinking about when she could see him again. *Oh Gemma, you stupid fucking idiot.*

She lifted her head and looked at the other sheet of paper. *Do it, Gemma. It needs to be done.*

REASONS TO GO

1. London is home
2. Eventually this lockdown will end, and you'll wonder why you're still here
3. You came here to get over Fraser, not to get with someone else
4. You'll be nearer your friends

5. You live in a house with no phone signal and no WiFi
6. You won't be Miss Havisham when he dumps you

Gemma took a deep breath. The facts couldn't be ignored; she'd been here far too long and had been avoiding making a decision because it was easier not to. Just as Louise had said, she'd been using Matthew as a way of avoiding real life; he deserved better, and she needed to face up to it like an adult. She resolved to talk to him tomorrow – she was using his WiFi for the Ladies' Lock-In tonight, but wouldn't stay afterwards; it would be too late for a heavy chat and she'd probably just end up taking him to bed to avoid talking, like she had last night. Her mind strayed to thoughts of where his hands and lips had strayed and she flushed with a sudden heat. She brushed the thoughts aside – *Focus, Gemma.*

She galvanised herself into tackling her to-do list – first do a search for a flat share and book some virtual viewings as soon as possible – in-person viewings might not be available for weeks, so she'd have to make do with a virtual live tour and cross her fingers that it wouldn't smell like a gym changing room in real life. Her ideal place was south of the river, cheap, dog-friendly and available immediately, although not sharing with serial killers was also preferred. Living in her own little place would be amazing but financially unrealistic, so it was going to have to be a flat share. It felt to Gemma like a lot could go wrong with this plan, but it didn't seem like she had much choice.

After that she needed to call Joe, in case she and Mabel needed to stay at his for a night before she could pick up the keys, or to beg him to be her emergency back-up if she turned up at the new place and found it was inhabited by terrible people. It was entirely against the lockdown rules so he might say no, but she'd only ask Caro as a last resort. If she called her today she'd give her the third degree about Matthew and she couldn't face that right now.

Gemma made another cup of tea and let Mabel out into the garden. She could hear Matthew clattering around in the barn and it took every ounce of willpower not to go down there and take refuge in the comfort and sturdiness of his arms. The air outside was warm, but she felt chilled to the bone; her knuckles were white as she clutched the hot mug like a lifeline. Maybe she should have a bath, or maybe she should get back to her desk and stop procrastinating.

Back at the dining table, Gemma looked at the list and decided to call Joe first, wanting to hear his voice and get a second opinion on her plan, which felt shaky at best. She climbed up to the bathroom where the WiFi signal was best and used WhatsApp to call him, feeling her heart lift when he answered straight away.

'Yo.'

Gemma rolled her eyes. 'Joe, you're a thirty-two-year-old white man. Stop it.'

'Sorry. What do you need? I'm mega busy.'

'Really?'

'Fuck, no. I'm watching *Drag Race* on Netflix.'

Joe's day job was sales manager for an events company which specialised in fancy weddings, of which precisely zero were happening right now. So he'd been furloughed, and was spending the time cycling around London, teaching himself to cook courtesy of the set of Nigella recipe books Gemma had given him for his thirtieth birthday, and watching a great deal of TV. Gemma felt a rush of fondness for him, thinking of the many nights they'd watched *Ru Paul's Drag Race* together in his flat or Aunt Laura's house, a bottle of wine on the go and Mabel snuggled up on the sofa between them.

She took a deep breath. 'I'm looking at flats, hoping to be back in London sometime next week.'

'Really? Is everything OK?'

'It's fine, just time for me to head home.' One thing Gemma loved about Joe was he didn't ask questions; unlike Caro, who had read the MI5 interrogation handbook. 'I'm hoping to book some virtual viewings and get a place sorted in the next couple of days, but I might need to stay at yours for a night or two depending on timings. I know it's a big ask.'

'It's fine, don't worry about it. But listen, are you sure you want

227

to move into a place without seeing it first? What if it's a shithole?' Joe sounded concerned, and it made Gemma's resolve waver.

'I don't have another option, you can't do in-person viewings yet. I'll try to get a short lease so I can bail out if it's awful. But please don't tell Caro I'm coming back; she's got enough on her plate without worrying about me. I'll call her tomorrow.'

Joe was silent for a moment; all Gemma could hear was traffic in the background, so he must have the windows open. 'Ohmygod, Gem. I've had an idea. I was chatting to my neighbour earlier, he shares the other half of my balcony. His name's Leon, he's a Swedish graphic designer and hot as fuck. Straight, but they all say that.'

Gemma sighed, itching to get back to her laptop and start flat-hunting. 'Joe, are you going anywhere with this?'

'Yes, sorry. He's going back to Sweden next week, I think he said Thursday. His dad has been sick, not corona or anything, but he's coming home from hospital. Leon's going home to help his mum look after him.'

Gemma straightened up, dimly seeing where Joe might be heading. 'Go on.'

'He said he was going for at least a month, maybe longer. He's working from home anyway so he can easily do that from Sweden. Do you want me to ask him if you can rent his flat?'

'Oh my God, yes.' Gemma's heart was racing, this would solve so many of her problems right now. A temporary place to live until she could do proper viewings, with the added bonus of being next door to Joe. 'Does he mind dogs?'

'No idea, I'll go and give him a yell on the balcony now. I'm sure he'll take the extra cash while he's away, and if he hates dogs I'll live in his flat and you can live in mine. Give me ten minutes and I'll call you back.'

'Joe, I love you so much.'

'Of course you do. You're only human.' Gemma could hear the smile and the wink in his voice as he hung up. She sat on the edge of the bath and breathed out slowly; there was nothing more she could do now until she heard back from him. The room suddenly felt strange and foreign, like she'd briefly experienced time travel; for the past ten minutes she'd been lost in the familiar neighbourhoods of south London, and now she was back in Caro's old cottage in Crowthorpe. It felt like two very different worlds, but she'd made her choice about where she belonged. One way or another, in less than a week she would leave Crowthorpe, and all she had to do now was tell the only person who would care.

'Maggie, you're on mute. Turn your microphone on.'

'Steph, we can't see you. You need to turn your camera on.'

Gemma relaxed into Matthew's sofa with a huge glass of wine, smiling at the usual chaos of getting a bunch of people on to Zoom. The system wasn't designed for twenty-five women all talking at once; it was supposed to be for sensible business meetings. But Jess the landlady was in charge of this session and was doing an admirable job of herding cats, so Gemma waited quietly for everyone to settle.

Matthew had been fine when she saw him earlier – preoccupied with his current commission, which looked like a simple coffee table on paper, but in reality was a bespoke design with some complex joints and hidden drawers that he needed to get his head around. He'd given Gemma a kiss and Mabel a belly rub, then headed off to the workshop. They'd arranged to take Mabel for a walk together tomorrow afternoon; the weather was forecast to be warm and sunny, so it would give them a chance to get away from the village. Matthew had his first Lads' Lock-In tomorrow evening so they had no shared plans beyond the walk, but Gemma suspected that he wouldn't want to see her anyway once she'd told him about her impending departure. Joe had called back earlier to confirm that Leon was fine for her to rent his flat for a month, and he'd leave the keys with Joe before he left for Stockholm on Thursday morning. She reminded herself that it was better this way and pushed aside the feelings of desolation.

The Lock-In chat warmed up once the wine started flowing, and there was lots of talk about when this might all be over, and where they'd all be going once they could hit the pubs and clubs again. It was clear that the Black Crow was well attended in normal times, with a monthly quiz night and a big beer garden out the back where the local netball and five-a-side teams gathered after Tuesday-night practice. Lots of people asked if Charlie and Jess were planning on doing takeaway pub meals, but it appeared their head chef was Lithuanian and was spending a few weeks with his family in Vilnius. When he came back, Jess promised they'd start Friday Fish Night again. Gemma's mouth watered at the thought of eating vinegar-soaked fish and chips out of a box on her lap; it had been months.

The women on the call ranged from late twenties to early fifties, as far as Gemma could see, but everyone seemed to have similar experiences. Anxiety about the future, worries about money, missing family and friends but also feeling thoroughly fed up with those they lived with. A few people offloaded their specific problems to a chorus of sympathy, and Gemma wondered what they would say if she piped up. *I've only been here a month but I've been screwing your local handyman and now I've fallen in love with him. I'm going back to London next week but I haven't told him yet; it's all a bit awks, frankly.* Gemma laughed bleakly to herself at the thought; perhaps now wasn't a good time to air her village laundry.

There were small niggles too – having to learn how to cut their children's hair, disastrous attempts to do their own highlights, no flour or yeast anywhere, queuing in the rain at the post office. But there was also support and solidarity – *I've got some yeast you can have, I'm going to the post office tomorrow, leave your parcel on my doorstep.* It gave Gemma a warm feeling – these women would look out for each other long after she'd gone; they would get through it as a village. *Who will do the same for you in London, Gemma? Joe can barely look after himself.*

By 10 p.m. everyone was thoroughly well oiled and the session was declared a huge success. They talked about things they could do in the future – maybe a quiz night, or a drinking game, or a watch-along of a film using Netflix Party. As Gemma hoped, a few splinter groups emerged – one woman was a hairdresser and offered to do a session giving tips on cutting children's hair, and one of the teachers at the village school volunteered to help with home schooling and routines for children. Jess offered to set up a Ladies' Lock-In WhatsApp group to make it easy for everyone to see what was planned. Gemma waved at all the smiling faces, lying that she'd see them next Friday. It made her feel sad to think that this was the only Crowthorpe Lock-In she'd ever be part of, and she'd have to leave the WhatsApp group before it had barely started.

CHAPTER TWENTY-SEVEN

Saturday, 25 April

To Do

- Tell Matthew you're leaving
- Feel like shit

It was early afternoon when Matthew and Gemma headed down the lane in the sunshine, both of them needing to put some distance and space between themselves and the village. After a few minutes Matthew slipped through a gap in the hedgerow and over a stile, into a field with a rough footpath running along the edge. Tiny shoots of wheatgrass were pushing through the hard soil, creating a carpet of green that looked like a snooker table.

Gemma followed closely behind him, unclipping Mabel from her lead as soon as she had belly-crawled safely under the stile. The dog surged ahead, diving into the ditch under the hedge to sniff out the elusive nocturnal hangouts of foxes, rabbits and badgers.

Matthew and Gemma walked side by side for a few minutes, watching Mabel and making small talk about their respective Lock-In events. His was scheduled for tonight, and he was looking forward to it. Gemma gave him the lowdown on hers, without naming any names – most of the male attendees tonight would be married or living with the women she'd spent the evening with yesterday, and she didn't want to feed them any gossip.

Matthew laughed at her stories and seemed to relax a little. Gemma noticed that he shortened his stride to match hers so they could walk side by side, which struck her as rather sweet, and something she'd never seen her father do when he walked with her mother. Peter Lockwood only had one pace, which was a brisk, purposeful march; Gemma couldn't remember ever seeing him stroll or saunter or amble. In her memory, her mother was forever scuttling along in his wake, her legs a good eight inches shorter and not in nearly so much of a hurry.

Gemma was lost in family memories when Matthew reached out to hold her hand; when she had time to think about it later, that was the only justification she had for her insane overreaction. She snatched it back like he'd just trapped it in a sandwich toaster, jumping back a step and glaring at him in horror. He looked shocked, turning to face her and holding his hands up in defence.

'Gem, I'm sorry. I thought . . .'

Gemma tried to clear the buzzing from her head. She felt stupid and embarrassed, but there was no going back now. 'I'm sorry, you took me by surprise.'

'I just touched your hand. It's not the first bit of you I've touched, to be fair.' Matthew's voice was deadpan, which he was entitled to under the circumstances, but it annoyed Gemma none-theless. She took a deep breath and plunged in.

'I'm leaving. On Thursday. I'm going back to London. I made the decision yesterday.'

Matthew put his hands on his hips, looking at his shoes. He breathed in and out slowly, but said nothing. In the absence of any reaction, Gemma kept going.

'Being here, the village, meeting you, has been amazing. But I can't stay, I need to go home. And the longer I stay, the harder that's going to be.'

Matthew looked up at her, his face set into a grim mask. 'Why?'

She shook her head. 'Why what? Why is it going to be harder?' *Oh God, please don't ask me that.*

'No. Why can't you stay? What are you going back for?'

She wiped a hand across her face. It was a good question, but somehow the crappy list she made yesterday didn't feel like it was

233

going to cut it. *Because I've fallen in love with you and my heart isn't strong enough.*

'Because London is my home, just like Crowthorpe is your home.' She waved her arms in the direction of the village. 'I'm just being realistic. It's been great, but . . .' Her voice trailed off, having run out of sensible things to say.

Matthew stood up straight, his arms folded. 'I understand. Being here has been like rehab for you, and now you need to get back to the real world.' His voice was emotionless, and his face impassive.

'No. Yes. Maybe. I don't know. I just know that the longer I stay the harder it's going to be to leave, and I DO need to leave. I'm sorry.'

'You don't have to apologise, Gemma.' She noticed with a wince that the full version of her name was back. 'I'm sorry you're going, but I understand.'

Gemma hadn't known how Matthew would react, but somehow this felt like the worst of all the possible options. Of course she didn't want tears and wailing and declarations of undying love (*OK, maybe a bit*), but anything would be better than this grim, dead-eyed nothing.

Mabel appeared panting at their feet, her fur dotted with cow parsley and hawthorn blossom. It looked like confetti, which made Gemma want to cry. Her break-up with Fraser had left her furious and panicked, but right now she just felt overwhelmingly sad. Her heart hurt in a way that she hadn't experienced since Aunt Laura's funeral.

She looked up and was surprised to find that nothing had changed; they were both still in this field, the sun was still shining, and Matthew was still there with his arms crossed, watching Mabel snuffle in the wheatgrass. The breeze ruffled his hair and made him look like a boy, and it took all of Gemma's willpower not to reach out for a hug. She breathed deeply and forced out a half-smile. 'Let's go back.'

They retraced their steps through the field, over the stile and back along the lane towards the cottage. Both were lost in their thoughts, and neither of them spoke other than banal observations about the sudden burst of wildlife. As Gemma reached out to open the front gate, Matthew stopped in the road. 'Gem . . . wait.'

Gemma turned to face him, her hand still on the gate. Realising they weren't moving, Mabel sat on the step, looking first at Gemma, then at Matthew. He took a step towards her, closer but still out of reach. He looked towards the village and Gemma followed his gaze; she could hear a car approaching, but it was a way off yet. 'I don't want to leave things like this. Like the last few weeks have been nothing.'

Gemma sighed and forced herself to look him in the eye. 'Of course it hasn't been nothing. But it feels like when you meet someone on holiday, or go travelling with someone.' She watched him carefully for a glimmer of acknowledgement, but there was nothing. 'Eventually you have to accept that this isn't real life. Right now I'm pretending to be a country girl, living in a lovely cottage, being part of the community, wearing fancy fucking boots.' He cracked the tiniest smile and didn't interrupt, so she kept going. 'But it's not real. It's not my cottage, I'm not even paying rent. I live in a very non-fancy part of London and have to make sure Mabel doesn't eat poo in the park in case it came out of the arse of a crack addict.' Matthew's eyebrows shot up in horror, and Gemma suspected this may have been an unnecessary level of reality.

They held each other's gaze for a long moment, then Matthew turned his palms upwards, preparing to launch into a speech. At that moment the blare of a car horn interrupted, and Gemma caught a glimpse of a huge black car as it slammed to a halt beside them, kicking up a cloud of dust and gravel from the gutter. Matthew stepped on to the pavement and looked questioningly at Gemma as the door opened, but she was momentarily dumbfounded. A man in a pink shirt, a grey cashmere jumper and perfectly ironed jeans emerged with a huge smile on his face, and assumed a wide-legged power stance between them. To Mabel's eternal credit, she didn't even move.

'Hey, Gemma. Did I interrupt something?'

The man turned to Matthew and held out a hand. 'I'm Fraser. Ah, sorry, we're not supposed to do hand shaking, are we?' He took a huge theatrical step back, and in that moment Gemma didn't think she'd ever despised a human being more.

She looked at Matthew, then at Fraser. *What the fuck is he doing here?*

'What the fuck are you doing here?'

'No need for language like that. I came to bring you home after your little . . .' he looked Matthew up and down like he'd just shat on his brogues '. . . holiday.'

Gemma snorted. 'I'm sorry, what? Bring me HOME? Are you out of your mind?' She pulled Mabel tighter to her side, short-ening the leash in the unlikely event she tried to rip his throat out. The step gave Gemma the height advantage over Fraser, who wasn't very tall on the best of days, and she could tell he didn't like it.

'Come on, babe, this is stupid. I was stupid, it was a stupid thing to do, OK? If you want me to say sorry, I will. I've had time to think about it and I think we should forgive and forget, give things another go.' He stopped and looked at Matthew. 'Sorry, pal, are you still here?'

Matthew took a step towards Fraser, his fists clenched. Gemma put her arm out between them. 'Matthew, it's fine, I'll be OK. Go home, I can deal with this. Take Mabel, please.' She held out the lead, and Matthew unclenched his fists. Gemma was struck by the contrast between them – Matthew a huge scruffy bear of a man, his green eyes full of thunder; Fraser shorter and more delicate, looking like he'd just been dry cleaned. He could have stepped off the terrace of a fancy bar in Italy; only his pale skin and the tinge of red in his dark hair belied his Scottish heritage. She noted that he was using the absence of haircuts to try a longer, more swept-forward style, presumably to hide his receding hairline. It looked ridiculous.

Matthew glared at Fraser and trudged off to the side gate,

Mabel at his side. He looked back at Gemma as he passed down the side of the house; she gave him the tiniest nod and he disappeared. She turned back to Fraser, who was chewing the arm of his sunglasses and looking around the village like he was trying to identify the bad smell.

'Why are you here?' she spat.

'I told you. To ask you to come home.' He turned his palms up in a gesture of openness and took a step towards her. Gemma held her hand up.

'It's a fucking lockdown, Fraser. You're not supposed to travel, and you're definitely not supposed to bring your fucking germs to this village.'

'It felt like necessary travel to me. I tried to call, but you seem to have blocked me. And I'm fine, I haven't been near anyone apart from some old woman in the shop.'

'You went to the SHOP? Oh, fucking marvellous.'

'I found out the name of the village, but I didn't know which house. Apparently it's this one. Nice.' He looked up at West Cottage with a discerning eye. *I bet he's thinking about how much it's worth, the fucker.*

'What do you mean, you found out the name of the village? How?'

'It was easy. Your dad told me. I pretended to be your editor, said you'd left me a voicemail but I couldn't hear the name of the place you were staying. He told me where you were.' Fraser looked hugely pleased with himself, and Gemma could have happily crushed his face into the mailbox. She took a few calming breaths, noting that the curtain on one of the houses opposite was twitching, and another had opened their front door a fraction.

'OK, so now you're here, and if I'm hearing you right you want us to get back together. Am I right?'

'Exactly.' He grinned like a gameshow host who was about to award the star prize. 'I've missed you, and I'm willing to give things another go.'

Gemma started to laugh. He was such a piece of work. 'Fraser,

237

last time I saw you, you were muff-deep in some woman. On my Heal's cushions. Why the fuck would I want to give things another go?'

'Because we all make mistakes.' He nodded in the direction that Matthew had just disappeared and shrugged his shoulders. 'Looks like I'm not the only one, hey, babe?'

It was a low blow, and it hit hard. Gemma gripped the gate behind her and wondered if she could karate-kick him in the face from here without risking him covering her in blood and spit. Breaking his teeth would be great, but it wasn't worth getting sick over.

'OK, listen carefully.' Gemma pointed a finger towards his face. 'You are a lying, cheating shit. You never loved me, and I know for sure that I definitely didn't love you. Go back to London, fuck who you like, never give me another thought. Throw away all my stuff, I don't care. I don't ever want to see you again.'

Fraser took a step back, his face drained of colour and his bravado gone. He gestured feebly to the car, a black Range Rover Sport that looked brand new. 'I hired a car and drove all this way to bring you home. Does that not count for anything?'

Gemma glared, fighting the urge to laugh and roll her eyes. He'd decided that a drive to the countryside required him to hire a Range Rover, which was beyond pathetic. 'Go home, Fraser.' She folded her arms, her face arranged into the most withering killer death stare she could muster. She'd learned this one from her mother.

Fraser blinked at her for a second, breathing through his nose like a bull with narrowed eyes and his mouth set into a thin snarl. He shook his head slightly, put his sunglasses on and stomped back to the car. He opened the door and climbed in, then leaned out so he could have the final word. 'You'll regret this. I made this effort for you, and you'll regret sending me away. I admit I'm not perfect, Gemma, but I'm the best you'll ever do.'

Gemma stood on the step, watching his thunderous face while he executed a laborious three-point turn in the lane before gunning the engine and speeding back towards the village in a second cloud of gravel. As the dust settled, a woman's head appeared in the open doorway opposite; Gemma recognised her from the Lock-In on Thursday but couldn't remember her name. Pippa, maybe? She shouted, 'You tell him, girl!' from across the street while giving Gemma two thumbs up, then disappeared again as the door closed.

She turned slowly to walk through the gate, her head full of anger and confusion, but stopped as Margaret shuffled around the side of the house from the lane. *She'll be sorry to have missed that*, thought Gemma, as Margaret smiled conspiratorially and gave her a wink. 'You're worth ten of Mr Fancy Pants, my dear. And for what it's worth, Matthew is much better looking.'

Hey. Are you OK? Mx

I'm fine, he's gone. Thanks for putting Mabel in the house. Sorry for . . . well, everything really. Gx

You still don't have to apologise. You have to do what's right for you, I totally understand. Mx

Hope the lock-in goes well. Gx

Thanks. Mx

CHAPTER TWENTY-EIGHT

Sunday, 26 April

To Do

- Church Godcast 10.30
- Wallow in self-pity

How was the lock-in? Gx

By 10 a.m. Matthew hadn't replied to Gemma's message, so she took Mabel out into the garden on the pretence of doing her business even though they'd just got back from a walk. Mabel sniffed around the base of the apple tree, clearly hoping that treats might fall out of it. Gemma could see that it was going to produce lots of fruit, although there was no way of knowing what kind of apples they were. She could hear crashing and banging in Matthew's workshop, so he'd clearly decided to work through Sunday. She couldn't blame him; if she had any work on her list, she'd be doing the same.

She checked her phone again since she was in the garden and had better internet. Caro had sent two messages, the first asking if Gemma fancied a Sunday-morning chat, and the second asking if she was OK. The short answer to both those questions was 'no', but she couldn't get into it with Caro now. She claimed terrible period pains and promised faithfully to call in the morning.

She wandered back into the cottage and made a cup of tea. She'd told Reverend Alex that she'd pop into his online service this morning, mostly as technical support although she could tell he was hopeful she might join his congregation on a longer-term basis. Gemma had mumbled something non-committal, not wanting to disappoint him. Her church attendance was strictly weddings and funerals and she wasn't a huge fan of either. She had very limited patience for standing about making polite conversation, and that seemed to be a major feature of both. A couple of years ago she'd stood around for nearly two hours in a shade-free stately home garden in 30-degree heat, while the bride and groom had about two thousand photos taken. By the time the guests were allowed into the marquee Gemma had a scarlet face from too much sun and champagne, and feet that were so swollen from the heat she didn't dare take her heels off in case she couldn't get them back on again. She vowed never to go to another wedding unless it was someone who would genuinely give a shit if she was there or not, and that list was very short indeed.

Just before 10.30 she took her laptop to the bottom of the garden and climbed to the top of Matthew's steps, sitting cross-legged on the small wooden balcony outside the door to his apartment. She needed decent internet but couldn't face walking to the village shop after yesterday; no doubt everybody would know about Fraser's visit by now and she didn't have the energy for even more knowing looks. This was as close as she could get to Matthew's WiFi without letting herself in, and even though the door would undoubtedly be unlocked it felt bad-mannered, particularly under the circumstances.

The signal was strong here, so she logged on to Zoom and joined a parish turnout of twenty or so, which seemed like a lot to Gemma until she reminded herself that about five hundred people lived in Crowthorpe. Most of the parishioners were older residents, but there were a couple of families too. The biggest and most welcome surprise for Gemma was that the Reverend Alex Morton was black; this wasn't exactly the most diverse community she'd ever lived in, and she'd expected somebody pasty and weak-chinned like Mr Collins in *Pride and Prejudice*. Instead she discovered the local vicar had an outstanding jawline and a wonderfully soothing voice for a Sunday morning.

She provided direction to those who struggled with turning on cameras and turning off microphones, thinking that Zoom really needed to introduce a beginners' version as soon as possible, then settled down to listen to the opening prayers and Alex's sermon. He talked about the importance of acknowledging the big picture and praying for those suffering around the world, but also focussing closer to home, on the small things you could do to support your neighbours and yourselves. He also talked about kindness, and how it was an infinite resource that we held within ourselves, but that we should remember to be kind to ourselves as well as others. It felt oddly personal on Zoom, like he was talking directly to Gemma without the echoing vastness and gloom of the church.

With Gemma's support the congregation turned their microphones back on and sang a hymn, led a cappella by Alex, who turned out to have a lovely baritone. Gemma thought 'Be still for the presence of the Lord' was an appropriate choice – Alex had kindly emailed over the words for her the previous day, so she read them off her phone and fumbled through it with everyone else. The session wrapped up with a few final prayers, then Alex confirmed that he'd be around for the next hour or so if anyone wanted to message or call for a chat about spiritual matters. Gemma was tempted just for the soothing voice, but was pretty sure her domestic dramas were unworthy of his time, or God's for that matter.

After the service she closed her laptop and wandered around the cottage at a bit of a loss. She lay on the sofa and tried to read for a while, but the story began with a tragic death and she couldn't make it past page four. She contemplated ringing her parents, but they observed a rigid Sunday brunch schedule and wouldn't appreciate the interruption. Right now her mother would be serving up poached eggs on toast with coffee and juice, with a small bowl of freshly chopped seasonal fruit to follow. Her father would slowly eat everything while reading the *Sunday Telegraph* and the *Mail on Sunday*, entirely ignoring his wife until he'd finished eating and retired to the conservatory to continue tackling the papers until Barbara brought him a cup of tea and half a sandwich at around 1.30 p.m. Then he'd take a walk for an hour before pottering aimlessly in the garden or shed until Barbara served a roast dinner at 5 p.m. – they rotated between beef, chicken and pork all year round, other than during spring when lamb was occasionally thrown into the mix. After years of life's schedule being dictated by the Royal Air Force, Peter Lockwood found comfort and order in these little rituals; Gemma occasionally wondered if her mother felt the same, or whether she ever had days when she wanted to leave her apron on the back of the door and eat a massive pie and chips in the pub on her own.

Gemma slid on to the lounge floor and scratched between Mabel's ears, her book tossed aside on the sofa. This was where she had first met Matthew a month ago; what a shambles she must have looked. She cringed at the memory, wishing she could turn back the clock and present a less unhinged version of herself. With hindsight the idea that she would only stay a few days was laughable. *Where were you going to go, Gemma?*

She thought about Fraser, and his ridiculous performance outside the cottage yesterday. Something had clearly happened to make him decide to get Gemma back – perhaps the Mystery Brunette had dumped him, or he'd realised he couldn't stay afloat without Gemma's half of the mortgage and bills. Perhaps he was just furious that Gemma had left, and wanted to prove to himself that he still had some level of control over her. Or perhaps he was simply a narcissistic, deluded arsehole who genuinely didn't think he'd done anything wrong. After he'd left she'd thought of a thousand things she wished she'd said to him, most of them extremely clever and particularly withering. Now she'd never get the chance, but it was enough to know that he would have spent the two-hour drive back to London in a savage fury, blaming everyone but himself for Gemma not being in the car with him. Hopefully he'd got a speeding ticket for good measure.

After slapping some cheese and chilli jam in a sandwich and not bothering with the soup, Gemma took Mabel out for a run. She'd been gradually increasing her distances over the weeks, and was now running for an hour, albeit still looking like her ankles were chained together. It felt good to play some mindless dance music and plod through the lanes with Mabel at her side, emptying her mind of everything but the music and the rhythm of her feet.

Today she went further, retracing the route she and Matthew had walked exactly a week before to the meadow by the river in Oldford Brook. She took a couple of wrong turns and at one point had to take a short detour to avoid a field of cows, but eventually she found the wooded path that descended to the village and headed towards the sunny glint of the river. By the time she arrived she was hot and exhausted, so she stripped off her trainers and socks and stood knee-deep in the water, her toes sinking into the water plants and stirring up the sediment. Mabel skipped and splashed around her, waiting on the island for Gemma to throw a stick into the deep pool, then retrieving it and returning to the bank to shake vigorously.

Once Gemma had caught her breath, she sat on the bank and let the water dapple over her feet, just as she had the week before. She knew it would feel like a cruel punishment to come here without Matthew, but somehow she needed today to be as awful and miserable as she could make it. It was a tactic she deployed at boarding school too – if she was lonely or depressed or being bullied by the other girls, she'd go and stand in the rain or the snow, the theory being that if things couldn't be any worse, they would have to start getting better. Some girls self-harmed by starving themselves or carving their arms up with the pointy end of a compass; Gemma just made herself feel as terrible as possible until her emotions hit rock bottom and had nowhere else to go but up.

Today she just wanted a hug – from Louise or Caro or Joe ideally, although she'd even take one from her mother since these were desperate times. The irony was that even if these people were here, Gemma wouldn't be able to hug them; right now that felt like one of the cruellest consequences of this awful situation. The only person she could hug was Matthew, and that would be the most selfish act of all.

After half an hour of literal and metaphorical wallowing, Gemma summoned Mabel from her watery playground and started to walk back to the village. She had intended to run, but her legs felt like lead; instead she trudged, replaying yesterday's conversation in the field with Matthew and the encounter with Fraser like a looped film in her brain. How had she wasted a year of her life on someone so worthless?

It was almost 5 p.m. by the time Gemma got back to the cottage, the dust from the fields clinging to the sweat on her legs. She felt gritty and tired, in need of a soak in the bath and a glass of wine. Mabel immediately emptied half her water bowl then settled down on her bed with a dramatic yawn, ready for a huge nap after a four-hour walk.

Gemma poured a large glass of wine and recovered her abandoned book from the sofa – she'd give it another go in the bath; perhaps it would feel less bleak if she was immersed in soapy bubbles. She was halfway up the stairs when the doorbell rang, so she put her book and her wine on the stairs and walked back through the dining room, assuming it was a delivery driver. As usual Mabel hadn't moved; doorbells were not a matter she needed to concern herself with at this time. Gemma opened the front door and was surprised and horrified in equal measure to see Matthew's mother standing by the front gate.

Gemma's immediate response was panic – why did she only ever meet this woman when she looked like shit? Annoyance quickly followed – why did people in this village just turn up? Nobody in London would consider just rocking up at your house without messaging first unless it was part of an elaborate birthday surprise involving balloons and champagne and an impromptu picnic.

Once she'd processed the fact that she was here, curiosity kicked in – as far as she knew Matthew's mum hadn't visited him at all during lockdown, so what was she doing on Gemma's doorstep? She arranged her features into something resembling a polite welcome and opened the door to the porch. Christine stayed where she was, leaning on the gate.

'Hello, Christine. How lovely.'

Christine smiled. She bore very little resemblance to Matthew – her nose was more aquiline and her eyes were brown rather than Matthew's green. Today her hair was pulled back into a half pony-tail, and she looked stylishly nautical in navy leggings, a striped jersey tunic and white canvas shoes. Gemma guessed she was in her late fifties, but she looked a good decade younger. Aunt Laura had always said that women had to make a choice in mid life between face and figure – staying slim came at the cost of looking older. Christine seemed to have managed to achieve both, which Gemma put down to either good genes or an exceptional facelift.

'Hello, Gemma. Have you been out? You look a little hot and bothered.' It was clearly a mild observation rather than a snarky dig, so Gemma tried not to take it personally.

'I'm just back from a run. I was just on my way up for a shower.' A shower sounded functional, whereas a bath might make her look like the kind of woman who drank wine in the bath at 5 p.m. on a Sunday. She smiled politely. 'Were you looking for Matthew? I think he's in his workshop.'

Christine stepped back from the gate a little, looking mildly uncomfortable. 'Actually, no, I was looking for you. I was passing by for a walk and thought I'd say hello.'

Gemma folded her arms and leaned against the door frame, suddenly feeling apprehensive. Had Matthew talked to her? Visiting other people's houses wasn't technically allowed, so she must have good reason.

Christine gave a nervous laugh. 'Actually that's not entirely true. I heard on the village grapevine that you had a bit of an altercation with a man in a black car, so I wanted to check you were OK.'

Gemma stayed silent, processing Christine's words. It seemed unlikely that she was fishing for gossip, even less likely that she actually cared about Gemma's welfare. So why was she here?

'Did . . . did Matthew send you?' Gemma unfolded her arms and stepped out of the porch. Christine's position at the bottom of the steps put her on a level below Gemma, even though she was several inches taller. Just like Fraser yesterday, Gemma had the height advantage.

Christine stepped back, looking flustered. 'No, of course not. I spoke to him earlier and he seemed upset, but wouldn't say why. I just thought . . .'

Gemma could feel her anger rising. Was there anyone in this village who didn't know her business? Was there some kind of gossip network, or had Matthew said something during his lock-in last night? It would have been tempting to share the story about the wanky cashmere Londoner in his fancy car, and how Gemma had sent him packing with a flea in his ear. The village guys would have loved it. Matthew's dad was probably on the call. *No. Matthew wouldn't have done that. Would he?*

Gemma's head was buzzing again. She locked into Christine's distressed look and kept her voice as tight and polite as she could. 'Christine, I appreciate your concern, but with the greatest respect none of this is your business. You'll be glad to hear I'm going back to London on Thursday and taking my drama with me. Could you perhaps share that with a couple of locals, so everybody knows?' Gemma wafted her arm in the general direction of the village, then turned on her heel and walked back into the house. She shut the door quietly, despite the urge to slam it like a teenager.

She stood in the dining room, taking deep breaths. Mabel hadn't moved an inch; in her world the last five minutes hadn't happened. Giving her head a small shake, Gemma headed back up the stairs, pausing halfway to pick up her wine glass and down the contents. She walked back to the kitchen to grab the bottle out of the fridge, then went to get pissed in the bath.

Sorry I missed your message, have been working. Lock-In was good fun. How was your day? Mx

247

CHAPTER TWENTY-NINE

Monday, 27 April

To Do

- Call Caro

Dear Gemma

I wanted to apologise for yesterday. I shouldn't have just turned up like that, it was rude of me. I hope you'll give me the chance to explain, then you can go back to being angry with me.

Matthew came over yesterday, I suppose while you were out for your run. He sat by the gate and we chatted for a while, but when I asked after you he said you were going back to London soon, then changed the subject. I heard about the man in the car from Margaret who lives in one of the bungalows along from you. Nothing much gets past her. For what it's worth, she said you (and I quote) 'kicked his backside from here to Swindon'.

So I suppose my main reason for coming to see you was curiosity; to see if it was true that you were leaving. I'd got quite hopeful, you see – my son is 31 years old, but I've never known him talk about a woman the way he talked about you. He's had girlfriends, of course, but none of them ever quite made the grade. Every time he went off on his travels I crossed my fingers that he'd come back with the girl of his dreams (or guy, I live in the modern world), but he never did. By the time he went on his final trip I'd quite given up hope; on that occasion he took his cousin on her gap year travels around Europe. We told him not to, said it would spoil his trip, but he did it as a favour to my younger brother, who was worried about Claire travelling alone. It's the kind of person Matthew is, but I'm sure you already know that.

I hope you can see why I was hopeful when I heard about you. You sounded funny and smart and interesting and kind, and Matthew told me you love books. In truth you've done more for this village in a month than some people have done in a lifetime. But I'm sure you have good reasons for going back to London, and it's not for me, Matthew or anyone else to tell you where you belong.

Mostly I'm writing to tell you that he never said a word about your situation yesterday, and he also didn't know I was coming to see you. No doubt he'll be furious with me when he finds out. He's a good man, Gemma. Please don't judge him for the bad behaviour of his mother.

Best wishes for the future,
Christine Thorpe

Gemma sat on the sofa with Christine's note, her heart heavy with sadness.

Christine had beautiful handwriting, full of elegant loops and flourishes. She had taken some time over it, clearly happier to express herself in writing than she was in person. Gemma knew exactly how that felt – a pen in her hand gave her a style and an eloquence that she could never match in a face-to-face conversation.

She squirmed a little over Claire, acknowledging that her imagination had got the better of her there. Claire was just a young girl who found a chaperone in her kind and patient older cousin. At any point Gemma could have asked, 'Did you go on your travels alone, or with other people?' and Matthew would have told her, but instead she chose to find a narrative to fit her own insecurities and her preconception of the kind of man Matthew must be, because all men were like that. Gemma remembered the dedication in the front of the photo album – *Can't think of anyone I would have wanted to share it with more than you. Love you, Claire.* Gemma had assumed it was romantic love, but of course there were other kinds that she'd chosen not to consider.

And obviously Matthew hadn't said a word about Fraser to his mother or anyone else, because he wasn't that type of person. But he'd clearly talked about her a lot; Christine seemed pretty well informed on what Gemma liked, and what she'd been doing in the village. It gave her a momentary warm feeling to think that Christine had wondered if Gemma was 'the one' – how disappointed she must be right now. She'd never met Johannes' parents, and her only experience of Fraser's mother had been the ill-fated trip to Clydebank the previous year, the one she had to cut short because of Aunt Laura's death. She was a beady-eyed, tight-lipped woman who seemed to find Gemma very disappointing; but Fraser was her blue-eyed boy who could do no wrong, and Gemma assumed he could have brought home a duchess and she still wouldn't have made the grade.

Gemma re-read the letter. *It's not for me, Matthew or anyone else to tell you where you belong.* This line made her head spin a little. *Where do you belong, Gemma?* It was an impossible question; she'd never belonged anywhere.

She folded the letter carefully and picked up her phone, feeling a touch of guilt that she still hadn't answered Matthew's message from last night. *How was my day? Well, I mostly felt like shit, walked Mabel's paws off, then had a go at your mother before getting drunk in the bath. How was yours?*

She chewed her lip and thought for a while, then tapped in a reply. *Sorry for delay. Yesterday was busy, lots of sorting out to do. Would be nice to see you for a cider before I go. Gx*

It was the worst kind of reply, really – dry, indifferent, chilly. It wasn't at all how Gemma felt, but she needed to keep Matthew at arm's length if she had any hope of getting through the next few days. She genuinely wanted to see him before she left, but also needed to make it clear that her agenda was a drink and a hug goodbye, rather than spectacular sex against the cold tiles of the shower under a torrent of hot water. Gemma shivered at the memory – had that really only been last week?

She looked at her watch; she couldn't put off calling Caro any longer, but the signal in the house wasn't really up to a proper chat and she couldn't exactly stand in the garden where Matthew could hear. She decided to walk to the shop – she could take Mabel for her afternoon walk after talking to Caro, then log back on for the first Autumn Club online meeting at 2 p.m. in case they needed any technical support. She stroked Mabel's head for a few moments, then nudged her out of bed. Mabel glared at her resentfully, then plodded through the kitchen to sit by the back door. Gemma felt another pang of misery and guilt. *He's not coming, Mabes.*

The sun was fully up by the time she walked through the village. It was forecast to start raining tomorrow, so this would be the last day in what had felt like weeks of unseasonably warm and dry weather for April. It felt only fitting that the clouds would roll in just as Gemma was readying to leave, and she found herself welcoming the change – she didn't want to be shut in a tiny flat if it was sunny outside. Cold and wet meant she could hunker down with Mabel and read books until this was all over.

The shop was open when she arrived, so she avoided her usual perch on the step and took Mabel to the churchyard instead. It was deserted, so Gemma did a lap until she found a patch of grass with a good signal and sat down. Mabel sniffed around the graves nearby, then turned a few circles and settled in the sun a few metres from Gemma. The churchyard was quiet and tranquil, and for a long moment Gemma sat with her face angled towards the sun and soaked up the warmth and peace, delaying this call with Caro for as long as possible.

'Gem! Thank God. I thought you were dead in a ditch.'

'Don't be a drama queen. I've been busy.'

'Hang on.' Gemma heard a chair scraping, doors opening and closing and muffled voices before Caro returned. 'Right, that's better, I've hoofed Tony out of the office for a few minutes. How are you? Matthew hasn't been returning my calls either, so I'm guessing you've both had your mouths full.' Caro howled at her own joke, and Gemma rested her head on her knees. *Pull the plaster off, Gemma. It's going to hurt either way.*

'Caro, stop. Please. It's not happening. I'm coming back to London on Thursday.'

Caro was silent for a moment. 'What? Why?'

'You know why. I can't stay here. I appreciate the loan of the cottage and it's been amazing, but I need to get back to real life.'

There was another silence, longer this time. Gemma could hear Caro breathing, the muffled noise of shouting children somewhere in the background. 'Wow. Where are you going to live?'

'In the flat next door to Joe. The guy who owns it is going home to Sweden for a month. After that I'll rent somewhere.'

'Right.' Gemma caught the edge in Caro's voice, clearly pissed off that Gemma had spoken to Joe, but not her. 'What about Matthew?'

Gemma sighed. 'It isn't going to happen, Caro. It's been a great lockdown romance, but neither of us are the settling-down type, and putting ninety miles between us isn't going to help. I'm sorry. I know he's your friend and he's been great, but there's no future in it.' Gemma realised she'd been preparing this speech for days, it came across like she was reading from an autocue.

'Fucking hell, Gem, when did you become the ice queen?'

Gemma's eyes filled with tears, and she furiously blinked them away. 'I'm sorry. It's self-preservation. I don't know what else to say.'

More silence; all Gemma could hear was Caro's pen tapping on her desk, and her own heartbeat. Mabel loped over and lay beside her, her head on her knee, and for a minute it felt like Aunt Laura was there beside her.

Caro took a deep breath. 'OK, there's something you need to know. I wasn't going to tell you but I can't see any other way.'

Gemma sat upright, her nerves suddenly on edge. *What was this?*

Caro continued. 'I knew Fraser was cheating on you when I rang that day. I made a last-minute decision to join you for your class but realised I didn't have my phone and couldn't remember

252

which gym.' Gemma rolled her eyes; this was classic Caro. 'So I ran to yours on the off-chance you hadn't left yet. You clearly had, because there was some random woman on your doorstep as I turned into your street; I saw Fraser open the door and pull her in like he couldn't wait to get her kit off, then give her arse a feel for good measure. I had to sprint home to get my phone, then I rang Joe to work out what to do.'

'You rang JOE? Why didn't you ring me?'

'Because you'd have made excuses for him, given him the benefit of the doubt. You'd have let him talk his way out of it.' Gemma winced at what was probably the truth. 'So we plotted to get you home early so you'd catch him out.'

'Which I did.'

'Which you did. Joe was hiding in the doorway opposite ready to take photos in case she left before you got back, but our plan worked and you caught him at it.'

'I really did. Going at her fanny like a Cornetto in a heatwave.' Caro hooted, and Gemma couldn't help but join in. 'Did I tell you he turned up here on Saturday?'

'WHAT? NO! Oh my God, tell me more.'

'In a minute. Tell me more about this plan you hatched.'

Another pause, shorter this time. 'OK, but this is the bit you're not going to like.' Gemma could hear the tension in Caro's voice, and her eyes narrowed in suspicion.

'Getting you to Crowthorpe was part of the plan. I'd been thinking about it for a while. Fraser was SUCH an unworthy prick and I just thought getting you away from him for a bit might help you see it. Which is why I dropped all those hints, saying that you could use the cottage any time, if ever you needed to get away.'

Gemma thought back to the times she and Caro had talked about West Cottage. She hadn't noticed at the time, but it was always offered to Gemma as a bolthole, never to her and Fraser as a romantic weekend. It was the first place she thought of when she left Fraser's flat, because Caro had planned it that way. *What else had she planned?* Gemma's voice tightened.

'And Matthew? Was he part of the plan?'

The silence gave Gemma her answer, and she resisted the temptation to throw her phone into the long grass. 'Caro?' She repeated the question through gritted teeth. 'Was Matthew part of the plan?'

Caro tried to maintain her bravado, but Gemma could hear the tinge of shame in her voice. 'Yes. Look, I just thought you'd be perfect for each other. I've thought it for years, but I didn't see any point introducing you when you were living in Laura's house – neither of you are the long-distance type. But the shit with Fraser presented an opportunity, so I took it. I didn't tell Matthew and obviously I didn't know about the lockdown; that was a bonus. I just hoped you'd get out of this shithole and fall in love with the village, and maybe Matthew at the same time. You're both a shambles when it comes to relationships and it didn't seem like there was very much to lose.'

Gemma's head felt jumbled, this was all too ridiculous. 'I thought you hated this village. You never come here. Why would you send me down here like some kind of desperate spinster?'

Caro laughed. 'Oh, Gem, I don't hate Crowthorpe, I love it. I never go there because I never want to leave. But I can't live there, it's too far to commute every day and Tony would hate it. He'd be rabidly jealous of Matthew, for a start, can you imagine?' Gemma could absolutely imagine the face-off between Dressage Tony and country-boy Matthew; she'd willingly pay for a ticket and bring popcorn. 'I just can't bring myself to sell it, it's all I have left of Mum and Dad. So I thought of you. You're a country girl at heart, just like Laura.'

Gemma winced at the second reference to her aunt. Caro had spent many weekends in Norfolk with Aunt Laura during university, and later had regularly made up a party of three for dinner or a theatre trip when Aunt Laura was in London. Aunt Laura had called her 'Sweet Caroline', which was something of a joke as there was nothing sweet about Caro, but she had admired her spirit and ambition. There weren't many black women in the upper ranks of London advertising, but Caro had fought her way to the top on pure merit and hard graft.

That said, this particular campaign had been completely out of order and Gemma wasn't going to let her off the hook. 'This is bullshit, Caro. You can't just throw Matthew and me together like some kind of fucking experiment and cross your fingers everything falls into place. And more importantly, we're both your friends and we have feelings. I don't know about Matthew, but I feel like utter shit right now. It's not your job to sort my life out.'

'I know, I'm sorry. It's just you're my friend and I love you, but you make really bad fucking choices all the time. Seeing Fraser with that woman made me so furious, but it also gave me a chance to show you a different kind of life. I had a feeling you'd be happy in Crowthorpe, so it seemed like it was worth the risk.'

'I was happy. I am. But I can't stay. I just can't.'

'Of course you can. You can rent the cottage for less than a shitty flat in London. You can learn to drive, work from home, jump on the train to town whenever you need to. Nothing is stopping you but your own stupid fear of being happy.'

Gemma gasped in fury and started to protest, but Caro interrupted. 'I'm going to go now, there's nothing left for me to say. I'm sorry I interfered, but please just think about it, Gem. You have choices, lots of people don't. Don't waste them.' Caro hung up, and then it was just Gemma in the churchyard, with a sleeping dog at her side.

A cider would be lovely, but I'm afraid I'm not very good at goodbyes. Maybe better to remember the good times and leave it at that? Mx

OK, you're probably right. Gx

I'm kidding. I'm coming over now. I don't have any cider, but we don't need it. Mx

Matthew strode through the kitchen door, scooped Gemma up like she weighed nothing and carried her through to the lounge, his face full of animal intent. He closed the door to keep Mabel out, pulled the curtains so violently Gemma thought he'd bring the wooden pole down, then pushed her gently but firmly back on to the sofa, his eyes glittering with something unfathomable between fury and lust. He leaned over her, one hand creeping under her skirt and up the inside of her thigh, and the other burrowing under her T-shirt. Gemma could hear the urgency of his breathing as he whispered in her ear.

'Do you want this?'

'What? I . . .' She opened her legs a little further, willing his hands not to stop.

'Do you want this? I'll leave now if you don't.' The fingers simultaneously edged under the lace of her knickers and brushed over her nipple. 'Up to you.'

She barely had time to cry 'Fuck, yes' before he buried his face into her neck with a groan and plunged his fingers inside her. Gemma was floored by how intense the sensation was; she felt like she'd been stripped back to nothing but muscles and nerves. She closed her eyes as Matthew's hands and lips roamed every inch of her body with a relentless fervour that didn't abate until they were both burned out and breathless. Matthew rolled over to face her, a slow, sleepy smile on his face. 'If you run a bath and find us both a drink, I'll apologise to your dog.'

CHAPTER THIRTY

Tuesday, 28 April

To Do

- Absolutely no plans whatsoever

Gemma lay on her side, her face inches from Matthew's shoulder. His slow, steady breaths told her he was still asleep, but she couldn't resist trailing her hand down his back to his waist, then gently sliding her hand around his torso and pulling herself into the warmth of his back. The view through the skylights showed her a morning that was grey and heavy with rain, and the room felt cold. She pulled the duvet tightly over both of them and snuggled in a little further.

That Matthew was here at all was entirely unexpected, and Gemma still didn't quite know what to make of it. His message last night had sent her into a whirlwind of confusion, followed by one of the most mind-blowingly intense experiences of her life. In the final post-bath, post-wine moments before sleep pulled her under, she had wondered if she might wake up with regrets. But today she had none. It hadn't felt irresponsible or complicated or desperate on either part, but more like ending things on a high. Rather than feeling sad that her lockdown stay in Crowthorpe was ending, Gemma felt full of gladness that it had begun.

'Don't stop.'

Gemma hadn't realised she was stroking Matthew's arm, her body moulded as best it could around his broad back. 'I thought you were asleep.'

257

'How could I possibly be asleep when you're that close?'

Gemma paused, resting her hand on the warm skin of Matthew's shoulders. She needed to clarify that they were both in the same place, just for her own peace of mind. 'You know I'm still leaving, right?'

Matthew gave a short out breath through his nose that told Gemma he was smiling. 'I know. It's fine. I'm not going to beg you to stay. But you're not going until Thursday, right?'

'Yes. I need to pack and clean this place tomorrow, and check in with the first Parent Pop-In. Then I'm getting the train on Thursday morning.'

'So what are you doing today?'

Gemma paused, mentally running through her to-do list. There was nothing on it. 'I don't know. I hadn't really thought about it.'

'I don't need to work today, I'm a bit ahead of schedule. So maybe we can go somewhere, get out of the village for a bit.'

'It's cold and raining.'

Gemma could hear his eyes rolling. 'Then we'll wear weather-appropriate clothing. Honestly, you city girls.'

Gemma felt inexplicably happy. 'Where are we going?'

'Wait and see. There's something I want to show you.'

It was late morning by the time they made it to Matthew's van, having been waylaid by practical things like toast and coffee and walking Mabel, but also their unwillingness to break the spell they'd woven around each other since last night. Even getting dressed took Gemma for ever, as Matthew removed items of clothing as quickly as she could put them on. By the time she finally managed to get her boots on and slip out of the back door with Mabel in tow, Gemma's face hurt from laughing. She'd grabbed the first T-shirt in the clean pile, which happened to be the commemorative Spice Girls one she'd worn in the garden four weeks before.

Matthew smiled appreciatively as she climbed into the van. 'Nice T-shirt.'

Gemma crossed her arms self-consciously and prepared to defend her first love. 'I was a huge fan back in the day. Caro bought me this, we were both at the same gig even though we didn't know each other then.' The Wembley shows had been at the end of the European leg of the tour, after Geri Halliwell had left the band, so only four of the Spice Girls featured on the T-shirt. She swallowed this fascinating fact, reasonably confident that Matthew wouldn't care.

'Not their best album, though.'

Gemma looked up. 'I'm sorry?'

'*Spiceworld.* Wasn't their best album. *Spice* was better. It has "Who Do You Think You Are" and "Say You'll Be There" on it, which are obviously the best Spice Girls songs.'

Gemma was momentarily dumbfounded, both by the outrageous omission of 'Stop' as the best Spice Girls song, and by the sudden realisation that the last five weeks had clearly been a lie and Matthew was definitely gay. He started the engine and slowly rolled the van towards the lane.

'I will concede that those two are in the top three. You are full of surprises, Mr Thorpe.'

Matthew hit the brakes and turned to look at her. 'Why would you call me that?'

Gemma's brain frantically spun through the letter from his mother, which she had definitely signed Christine Thorpe. 'It's your surname. Isn't it?'

'It's my mum's maiden name. She used it for her interiors business because her married name is Painter, which created some confusion in the interiors world. She still uses it, just out of habit. I'm Matthew Painter.' He stared at Gemma intently, as her face turned from white to pink to a deep crimson. 'How did you know my mum's surname?'

In the absence of a remotely convincing lie, Gemma had no choice but to tell him the truth. She replayed their conversation on the doorstep and admitted that she hadn't been very polite. Then she told him what she remembered of the letter she'd received yesterday. Matthew didn't say anything, but his mouth formed into a grim line as Gemma recalled the bit in the note that said he'd be furious.

'I AM furious. It was none of her business.'

'I think she cares about you. Any mother would do the same.'

'Even so, it's not on.'

'Let's not let it spoil today. It started so well.' Gemma smiled and took his hand, in a gesture that she hoped would make some kind of amends for her insane overreaction in the field on Saturday.

Matthew's face softened and he stroked the back of her hand with his thumb. 'OK, I'll let it go until I see her next. I meant to ask, how did Autumn Club go yesterday?'

'It was great, actually. A really good turn-out, and Yvonne's IT husband managed all the technical challenges. Not much for me to do but smile and wave.'

'What did they talk about?'

'They had a nurse, I think his name was Sam? Talked about hygiene, safety and mental health. It was actually really interesting. Then everybody had a cup of tea and a nice chat about how they think this is all China's fault . . .'

Matthew rolled his eyes. 'Gotta love old people. Sam's a nice guy, he's on my pub quiz team. Knows more about the Eurovision Song Contest than anybody I know.'

Gemma raised her eyebrows. 'I am happy to rise to that challenge.'

'Really? Oh God, you guys have to meet.' There was an awkward silence and Matthew blushed, but Gemma glossed over it.

'It's beautiful here. Tell me again where we're going?'

'I never told you the first time.'

'Damn, you're good.'

After twenty minutes of increasingly narrow and winding lanes Matthew pulled the van into a muddy lay-by next to a metal five-bar gate. There was nothing on the other side that Gemma could see other than overgrown shrubs and brambles, dripping with rain. He turned the engine off and grinned. 'We're here.'

'Is this going to ruin my lovely boots?' Gemma looked down at the glossy leather, still gleaming after only a few days of wear.

'It's going to give them a little of what they're designed for, before you take them back to London and never look at them again.' He looked at them lustfully. 'What a waste.'

Gemma jumped down from the van and stood back so Mabel could slide under the gate and disappear into the undergrowth. Gemma watched Matthew wrestle with the padlock on the gate – she could see the white knuckles of his cold hands trying to manipulate the key. Eventually it turned and the padlock fell away, so he gathered up the heavy chain and wrapped it round the top bar of the gate, closing the lock again. 'Come on, it's this way.'

Matthew walked ahead, pushing wet branches and brambles aside to clear a path for Gemma, Mabel weaving in and out of their legs. The rainwater crept into the collar of her gilet, running in freezing rivulets down her neck. Gemma could see the remains of an old track or bridleway underfoot; on the right-hand side a stone wall created a border between the track and a wooded, sloped bank covered in spindly trees and a carpet of wild garlic. It was in full flower and the smell was overpowering after the heavy rain – Gemma wanted to bury her face in handfuls of it.

After a couple of minutes the path widened and the greenery fell away to an open space in front of a wreck of a cottage. It was in a terrible state, with missing glass in the windows, crumbling stonework around the front door and a hole in the ancient tiled roof big enough for Gemma to climb through. As she stood looking up at it, two pigeons fluttered out of the hole in response to Mabel's frenzied barking and didn't return.

The space around the cottage was equally chaotic – the driveway had once been gravelled but was now a mess of tufts of grass, rocks and random items like a roll of chicken wire, a car hubcap and an ancient rusty wheelbarrow. The surrounding trees and shrubs had encroached on the space, covering the ground with creeping elder, bindweed and goosegrass. Mabel dashed off to sniff everything, emerging from behind the wheelbarrow with a mouldy tennis ball that was split down one side.

Matthew stood with his arms folded, looking at Gemma with a challenging glint in his eye. 'What do you think?'

'I don't think it's quite ready for you to move in yet. Maybe a lick of paint?'

He grinned, clearly delighted that she was on his wavelength. 'But you can see the potential?'

'Of course. It used to be beautiful, it could be beautiful again. But it would be so much work. It could take years.'

'It absolutely will take years, but it's going to be amazing. The plot includes the house, the access road and the garden, and there are some outbuildings round the back. Come and see.'

For the next half-hour Gemma and Mabel followed Matthew around the house and garden. He opened the front door with a heavy key, although neither of the downstairs front windows had any glass and they could have easily climbed in. The house had the original stone floors downstairs, coated in what appeared to be several centuries of dust and dead woodlice. There was a cosy, low-ceilinged lounge with an open fireplace and a huge leaded window, and a spacious kitchen with an old range and a wood burner. Exposed beams riddled with woodworm held up precariously wonky ceilings, with holes in the plasterwork so big it looked like something had taken bites out of the walls.

A creaking staircase led to three good-sized bedrooms upstairs, all with oak floorboards that were missing in places and eaten away in others. The attic held two tiny cell-like rooms that Gemma immediately decided needed to be knocked together to create a cosy office or snug. It turned out the room with the big hole in the roof was a bathroom, with an old Victorian rolltop bath that was plastered in pigeon droppings; any remaining birds had vacated the premises the moment Mabel had put a paw on the staircase. The whole place stank to high heaven, and Gemma could hear rats or other scampering creatures run for cover every time they walked into a room. Behind the house was a large, over-grown garden that had seeded itself with weedy, waist-high grass, bordered on one side by a row of crumbling outbuildings that looked like stables for tiny horses. 'Pig sheds,' said Matthew, reading her mind, 'they'll make a lovely workshop.'

Matthew's enthusiasm was infectious, and it was hard not to get caught up in his vision for the place. The doorways and stairwells were far too small for someone of his size; he had to hunch to walk in or out of every room. And yet somehow he seemed entirely at home.

'Do you think you could buy it? Is it even on the market?'

Matthew smiled. 'It's definitely not on the market. My parents and I bought it a couple of years ago.'

'Really?'

'Yep. It's part of a country hotel estate that belongs to a guy called Nick – the hotel is about a mile that way.' He pointed in the direction of some thick woods behind the cottage. 'This is an old estate cottage that was empty when he bought the place, and he always intended to renovate it but never quite got round to it; it's too far away from the main house to put guests in. He used to be my dad's biggest client; some years Dad did nothing but building work on Nick's properties; he's got loads of them. They became really good friends, and Dad asked Nick to give him first refusal if he ever decided to sell this place. A couple of years ago we did the deal. Nick sold it to us for peanuts – he's pretty sick and not long for this world, and I think he wanted us to have it before his kids inherit his estate and immediately sell it all off.' He looked at Gemma, a smile of triumph on his face. 'So I guess I already own it. Or at least half of it.'

Gemma felt genuinely delighted for him, and she could absolutely see Matthew turning the place around, then settling down with this wholesome, muffin-baking wife. She felt a brief burn of jealousy, but quickly brushed it aside. *Not now, Gemma.*

'How come you haven't started working on it?'

'I'm saving up. It won't be safe to live here for a while, and I need to keep the barn to use as a workshop for as long as possible to make any structural stuff. It's why I'm taking on so much work at the moment; I'm saving every penny.' He walked over to the rusty wheelbarrow and heaved it to the edge of the plot; the tyre was flat and the supports had sunk into the ground. 'Dad and I should be able to start here in the next few months, renovating the pig sheds first to make a workshop and a space for me to live on site. Then I'll sell the barn and buy out my parents' half of the investment, and use the rest of the money to finish the renovation. If I work on it full-time for a few years and eat nothing but soup and lentils, it will all work out.' He turned to look at her, his face earnest. 'Do you like it?'

'I love it. It's incredible. You'll do an amazing job of it.'

Matthew shrugged and shuffled his feet into the dirt. 'I'm excited about it. I've already done a lot of sketches and planning. It's not much to look at now, but . . . one day.'

They walked back through the dripping trees to the lay-by, Mabel snuffling hopefully at Matthew's pockets for hidden treats. Gemma waited in the van while Matthew locked up the gate, trying to make sense of her feelings. She was envious of Matthew; not for his tumbledown house or his lifestyle or his non-dysfunctional family, but for his vision. He knew where he was going, and what he had to do to get there. Like the Cotswold Way, the route was signposted and he just had to follow the path to the end. In contrast, Gemma was a boat in a storm, drifting aimlessly in search of that safe harbour Louise had talked about. She was fine with day-to-day planning, but what was it all building towards?

Gemma scratched between Mabel's ears, trying to find the answer. She spoke aloud in the empty echo of the van. 'What's it all FOR, Mabes? What are we working towards? What's the dream?'

Mabel huffed and settled her head on Gemma's leg. She didn't know either, but it definitely involved biscuits.

CHAPTER THIRTY-ONE

Wednesday, 29 April

To Do

- Clean everything
- Pack everything
- DO NOT FORGET TO PAY EGG BILL

Gemma stuffed the bedlinen and towels in the washing machine, adding detergent and softener. She wouldn't have time to do another wash before she left tomorrow, but hopefully Caro wouldn't mind if it had just been slept in one night. It wasn't like Matthew was coming back tonight; they'd said their goodbyes yesterday in a way that made her feel a bit broken and forlorn, but also resolved to move on and get back to normality. He'd hugged her for a long time, his face buried in her hair, then pulled away to give her a hard, searching look, his hand on her face. 'Take care, Gem, OK?' She had smiled and nodded, trying not to cry. 'I will. You too. Good luck with the house.' Then he'd walked out of the same door he'd come in all those weeks before, and not looked back.

Despite a patchy night's sleep, Gemma felt at peace with the way things had turned out. There was no right or wrong answer in this situation; it was about making a decision that moved her life forward and sticking with it. Matthew had big plans for his country renovation, while she was going back to London to cultivate a new version of herself. More assertive, more confident, more focussed; she would be a happier, better person for this experience.

By eleven Gemma had hung out the washing and was ready to

walk Mabel to the shop so she could join the Parent Pop-In online meeting. It was still cold and showery, albeit yesterday's relentless rain seemed to have temporarily burned itself out. Gemma put her boots and coat on, pulling up her collar to keep out the biting wind, and headed into the village. She found that her impending departure made her want to look at everything more closely, to lodge the details in her mind – the fat, pink rosebuds rambling across the front of one of the cottages; they would be in full bloom in a couple of weeks, and Gemma could only imagine how incredible they would look. The front garden scattered with plastic children's toys and bikes lying on their sides, looking sad and dejected after a night in the rain; Gemma resisted the urge to tidy them up, leaving everything in a neat row ready for the next sunny day. The handwritten sign outside Grove Farm saying 'We have eggs! £2.40 doz., leave money in box.' She slipped in an envelope with enough cash to settle her egg bill, wondering how long it would be before she saw another honesty box. They weren't big in South London.

The rain had started again by the time Gemma reached the shop, so she tucked herself into the lychgate. The first Parent Pop-In started on time and was the most well attended of all the groups Gemma had joined. It was mostly mums, but there were a handful of couples and a few lone dads. Everyone looked tired and in need of a haircut, which was pretty much the entire country these days; Gemma had given up fussing about her hair weeks ago, it would just have to wait. Eleven a.m. seemed to be the perfect time – it was a common time for baby naps, and older children seemed to take a break from schoolwork and could be popped in front of a screen for twenty minutes.

The session was joyfully chaotic, with lots of interruptions and comings-and-goings, but also uplifting and full of laughter and solidarity. Most parents were juggling more than usual, but resigned to make the best of it. What else could they do? Gemma loved how everyone seemed to know each other, and those newer to the village or parenting were made welcome and included in the conversation; it was something Aunt Laura had hugely valued about her small-town life in Norfolk, but Gemma had never really experienced until now.

The session lasted barely more than half an hour, which was all most of the parents could realistically manage – lunch, fresh air and exercise were calling. Another was planned for the following week, and several people asked Gemma to confirm if the Ladies' Lock-In session would be happening again this week. She confirmed that it would but didn't mention she wouldn't be there. What was the point? Life in the village would carry on just fine without her.

As she walked back through the village, she waved at Steve the Postie, who was doing his usual daily round. He did a short mime to communicate 'I need to speak to you' then made a theatrical diversion across the road, stopping halfway to avoid getting too close. He had a West Country accent so strong it was almost comical, like it was 50 per cent his own voice and 50 per cent a Wurzels impression. Apparently he grew up in Somerset, a fact which Ruth shared with Gemma like Somerset was an entirely different planet, rather than the county next door.

'I had a gurt big parcel for you; it needed a signature so I've left it in the porch.'

'Great, thanks. Who signed for it?'

'I did.'

Gemma looked confused. 'OK. Are you allowed to do that?'

Steve shrugged. 'Village life, my love.' He grinned and winked, then turned and headed back to his round.

Who had sent Gemma a parcel? She hadn't ordered anything. She mentally ran through the options, and decided it was probably Fraser sending back the remainder of her belongings. Despite the postage cost, he would get a huge kick out of knowing how inconvenient it would be for her to lug it all back to London on the train. It was exactly the kind of petty thing he'd do, just to have the final word. Pathetic.

She hurried back through the village, Mabel trotting at her heels. They were both cold from an hour outside, so Gemma welcomed the dry warmth of the porch and the opportunity to get out of her wet coat and boots. Mabel had a good shake, then headed straight for her bed for a nap.

Gemma picked up the parcel from the floor of the porch – it was a large, brown cardboard box from John Lewis, similar in size to the one her boots had been delivered in, but significantly heavier. It had clearly been re-used, as the John Lewis label had been plastered over with a white handwritten address label. The handwriting was unmistakeable; Gemma had known it all her life. The parcel was from her mother.

She put the box on the dining table and went into the kitchen to make a cup of tea. She couldn't remember the last time her mother had sent her anything, and for her to have gone to the trouble of finding out the address, presumably by calling Caro, it must be something significant. What could it be? She walked back into the lounge with the mug and a vegetable knife and sliced the tape along the side of the box. Inside was a chunky rainbow jumper that Gemma immediately recognised as Aunt Laura's; it was one of her favourites for reading on a cold day. Gemma carefully unfolded it, seeing that her mother had used it to line the box and cushion the other contents – a selection of flat, brown paper parcels in various sizes, and a white envelope.

Gemma extracted the jumper and put it on. It was warm and cosy in the damp chill of the dining room, and still smelled of Aunt Laura's favourite perfume: Trésor by Lancôme. She ignored the parcels for now and took out the heavy cream envelope, the kind her mother always used for handwritten letters. Inside were three sheets of paper in her mother's small, tight script.

Dear Gemma

I won't lie to you and tell you I'm writing out of the blue; Louise called me a few days ago and told me your life has been turned upside down once again. She said you feel like you're in the wrong place, making the wrong decisions, and don't know which way is up.

I know how that feels, my darling girl. It was my life for 25 years, from the day I married your father until the day he retired and I convinced him that we should move back to the town where I grew up. When I turned the key in the lock of this house, I felt like a bird in a cage that had finally been set free. I was about to unpack our boxes for the very last time, and you girls would finally have a place you could call home. But of course it was too late for you and Louise, because you'd both already gone.

I wish I'd convinced him sooner that a more settled life would be better for all of us, but the RAF Police was his whole world. It helps for me to remember that he was part of some important security missions during those times, that ultimately made the world a safer place. You should ask him about it sometime, although I don't suppose he can tell you everything.

Here's something else that might come as a surprise. All those weekends you stayed with us so you could visit Laura in the care home, I wonder if you knew that I went to see her every weekday? Her long-term memory remained for some time, and we shared a lot of happy stories from our childhood. In the final months she often confused me with you; she must have thought you were visiting seven days a week. How happy that must have made her.

I was also with her the day she died, although by then of course she was heavily medicated and I don't suppose she knew I was there. I saw the painting you did for her all those years ago, the one that said 'you feel like home'. I saved it for you, along with a few other things I thought you might like. Now feels like q good time to send them to you, since it's impossible to know when we might see you again.

I regret the life we gave you, Gemma. It suited Louise, but it never suited you. Your sister was happy to drift, but you needed an anchor. I hoped Norfolk might come to feel like home, like it was for me; your father wanted you to go to a military school, but I wanted you to be near Laura. She was the only member of our family who knew how to stay in one place.

My sister and I were very different people, but she adored you and gave you the stability you so desperately needed. I admit the strength of your relationship caused me pain at the time, and I said and did things I'm not proud of. I wish I could have my time again, but I've left it too late to make my peace with Laura. I hope it's not too late for you and me.

So first of all I'd like to ask for your forgiveness, for not taking the time to understand you better. Not everyone is suited to the travelling life; in that respect perhaps we're not so different.

Secondly, I would like to share some motherly advice, which you can take or ignore as you wish. Stop trying to find home; home is a place that finds you. Home is wherever you are safe, respected, loved and cared for, a place where you can truly be yourself. It's a place where you can hang that painting, and you'll know when you've found it. Perhaps you already have.

And finally, I would like to tell you that I love you. It has been far too long since I told you that.

With love,
Mum x

Gemma wiped away her tears with the sleeve of Aunt Laura's jumper and put the letter on the table. She hadn't realised it was possible to feel so many emotions at once – happiness, sadness, shame. She felt like her heart had broken into tiny pieces and then been stitched back together again, stronger and more knowing than before.

At no point in her selfish, narrow life had Gemma considered what military life must have been like for her mother. Barbara Lockwood had spent twenty-five years in the shadow of her husband, following wherever his job sent him, then being left alone for months at a time. No life outside the base, no career, no friends who weren't the wives of her husband's colleagues, no opportunity to be anything other than Group Captain Peter Lockwood's wife. What a lonely existence that must have been; no wonder they had sent Gemma and Louise to boarding school for some kind of steadiness. Her mother had apologised, but Gemma owed her an even bigger one in return. She resolved to go to Norfolk as soon as lockdown ended for a long walk with her mum. To talk about her life, her dreams, those final months with Aunt Laura, ask her to add to her collection of memories. There was so much Gemma had never thought to ask, because she was only thinking about herself.

She blew her nose and turned her attention to the pile of parcels, all carefully wrapped in brown paper. The first was Gemma's painting – she recognised the shape of the frame and opened it first. She remembered how confident she'd felt when she'd lined up the paints and brushes on the small wooden table, pinning the photograph to the edge of the easel like a proper artist, swirling paints with youthful enthusiasm and determination. Capturing 22 Church Street had felt like such a good idea, but of course it had been much harder than she expected, and Gemma remembered that she'd started to feel embarrassed by it long before it was finished. The message was an afterthought; a way to turn the primitive rendering of the house from the main event to an illustration of a bigger, more important thought. The sentiment was real, she just hadn't realised she was going to write it when she started.

The second parcel was Aunt Laura's recipe book, its pages stiff and heavy with memories. Gemma flicked through slowly and carefully, revisiting meals they'd had together, biscuits they'd baked together, the time Gemma had attempted to make Aunt Laura a birthday cake but forgotten to put eggs in, so ended up with two chocolate frisbees. Aunt Laura had called it a cow pat cake, and helped Gemma make icing that was twice as thick as the sponge. They'd eaten the lot and giggled about it all weekend.

The third parcel was a small pile of books, with a slip of paper that read 'These were the books that Laura took into the care home, thought you might want them. Mum x'. The first was Aunt Laura's battered Penguin Classics version of *The Count of Monte Cristo*, which felt so familiar in Gemma's hands. Two more were novels by Isabel Allende, one of Aunt Laura's favourite writers. The final book was her tiny copy of the *Collins Gem Guide to Garden Birds*; Gemma riffled through the pages and spotted the tiny pencil notations where Aunt Laura had written the date every year when she'd spotted each bird for the first time. There was a robin and a blue tit in January 2019, but nothing after that. The handwriting looked unfamiliar – perhaps one of her carers had written the date for her.

The final parcel felt like a small picture frame, and Gemma unwrapped the brown paper and tissue layers to discover a photograph of her and Aunt Laura together. It had been taken at the theatre in Norwich; Gemma remembered it was an opening night, but she couldn't remember what the play was. Aunt Laura was laughing at something or someone, her head half turned away from the camera. Gemma was sixteen or seventeen, looking up at her with flushed cheeks and a smile of pure happiness. She'd been so excited to be invited, and Aunt Laura had let her try champagne for the first time. She hadn't liked it much but drank it anyway.

Gemma took the two frames – the drawing of Aunt Laura's house and the picture of them both together – and put them on top of the mantelpiece. She stood back and looked at them for a while, wondering what Aunt Laura would say about the plan she had made. Gemma laughed wryly to herself. *You know exactly what she'd say.*

Am all packed. Just wanted to say I'm glad I was your lockdown romance. Might write a book about it one day. Gx

Me too. Can you make the book version of me rich, good with horses and maybe the most handsome man in England? Mx

OMG are you reading Riders? Gx

MAYBE. Mx

CHAPTER THIRTY-TWO

Thursday, 30 April

To Do

- Taxi 11.00
- Train 11.26
- Don't look back

Gemma slept badly again, her mind a jumble of stern lectures from the women in her life who mattered most – her mother, Caro, Louise and the ever-present ghost of Aunt Laura.

In the early hours, she forced herself to acknowledge some painful truths. She wasn't leaving because she desperately wanted to, she was leaving because she was terrified to stay. Her happiness here was inextricably linked to some kind of relationship with Matthew, and at no point in the past week had he actually said he wanted her to stay, or indicated that his feelings in any way matched hers. Matthew had told her himself that he'd never met anyone worth changing his life for. To assume that she had swept into the village and transformed his world in the space of a few weeks was ridiculous. Men didn't turn their lives upside down for women like Gemma.

She thought about all the relationship advice she'd ever read, in articles in *Psychologies* or problem pages in fashion magazines. The advice was always to communicate more – to tell the other person how you feel, to be open and honest. It was easy advice to give, but much harder to do in real life. How could she tell Matthew that she'd fallen in love with him, but had already done a risk assessment on the likelihood that she'd end up broken-hearted, and decided it was safer to quit while she was ahead? He'd think she was off her head.

Gemma showered and dressed, then let Mabel out into the garden while she worked her way down from the top of the cottage; pulling curtains and blinds, closing windows and doors, and checking drawers and cupboards for stray belongings. Compared to the night she left London, Gemma had packed in a much more orderly way, freeing up plenty of space in the rucksack for the books and photos her mother had sent her. She had kept a hessian bag to one side, lined with Aunt Laura's rainbow jumper, to take the two picture frames – for now, both were still on the mantelpiece.

By 10 a.m. Mabel had had her final walk along the lane and Gemma was ready to go, wishing she'd booked a ticket on an earlier train. She hadn't been able to resist looking at the barn as she'd passed the entrance, but everything was still and silent. She couldn't blame Matthew; if the situation was reversed she'd be keeping her head down too. Real life wasn't like the films; there was no last-minute dash to Chippenham station to declare undying love and share a passionate kiss on Platform 2.

She sat at the dining-room table, browsing the news, Twitter and Instagram aimlessly. The headlines were depressing – recession in France and Italy, spiralling unemployment in Germany, the creeping spectre of the virus in Africa. What positivity there was felt contrived – people doing silly dances on TikTok, charity singles, sponsored events. Gemma knew she wasn't being fair, but she felt spiky and sour, suspended in this emotional hinterland between Crowthorpe and London where time seemed to have stopped entirely. She stared out of the dining-room window at the empty road, willing something to happen.

Matthew walked past, making Gemma jump out of her chair so suddenly she knocked it over, which prompted Mabel to start barking. She moved towards the door, waiting for the knock. But it didn't come, so she rushed back to the window in time to see Matthew open the door to the porch and slip a note on to the mat inside. He caught her eye and gave a half-hearted wave, his face pale and unreadable. Then he hurried around the corner and disappeared down the lane.

Gemma hadn't moved so fast since one of her classmates set fire to her lab coat in GCSE Chemistry. She was back in the house with the envelope in her hand in world record time, pulling at the seal frantically, her heart pounding. There was a letter and a small, sealed package that felt like it had folded paper inside – she put it aside for a second and scanned Matthew's note. It was considerably less legible than the note he'd written when he'd had to go to Bristol, suggesting he'd written it in a hurry.

Dear Gemma

Forgive me if I make a mess of this, I've never done it before and it's actually kind of terrifying. The thing is I seem to have fallen for the woman next door, and now you're going to leave and I'm worried that if I don't say how I feel, I might regret it for the rest of my life.

I think you're running away, because that's what you've been doing your whole life. So I want to tell you that you don't need to, that I can help you make a home here. I can't promise to save you, since in some ways I'm as messed up as you are, but maybe we can save each other a bit? You're a good person and I think I'm a good person too, even though I don't pay nearly enough attention to things like clothes and haircuts.

But here's the thing: since you arrived, everything feels better. The sun came out 39 days ago and hasn't gone back in, and yours is the only dog I've ever liked in 31 years. Surely that's a good omen? Although just to be clear your dog is nothing like the dogs in The Omen.

Tomorrow a new month of lockdown starts, and I'd really like you and me and Mabel to spend it locked down together. I honestly can't think of anything nicer. So I'm asking you to stay, even if it's just for another week, then maybe I can ask you to stay a bit longer. Maybe eventually you'll want to stay without me asking.

Was this the right thing for me to do, or should I have just let you go? I've made some notes on the attached, maybe that might help?

M.

Gemma scrambled to open the enclosed package, and almost threw up when she saw the 'reasons not to fancy Matthew' notes she'd scribbled on the back of an old envelope. Her brain whirred back to the night they first slept together, when Matthew had come downstairs while she was running the bath, and returned with a bottle of wine and Mabel. He must have taken it off the rusty nail above the fireplace, he'd have seen it as soon as he came down the stairs. Her stomach turned inside out with horror and embarrassment, as she forced herself to flatten out the envelope and read the additional annotations he'd made in red pen.

Reasons not to fancy Matthew

1. Social distancing – **bit late for that**
   Couldn't stay away if I wanted to, which I don't.
2. He's not your type (local man for local people) – **no longer applies**
   OK, we need to talk about this. What on earth did you think of me?
3. He's Caro's friend (awks) – **she seems OK with it**
   She is, but I wouldn't care if she wasn't. She's not the boss of me.
4. He might not fancy you – **indications are positive**
   I love you, you massive idiot.
5. He could be gay – **he's definitely not gay**
   Can verify. Love gay people, but ideally not in my bed.
6. You'll make an idiot of yourself – **guaranteed**
   I'm OK with that. See point 4.
7. You're moving back to London soon – **still true and problematic**
   Please don't. See point 4.

8. You're on the rebound – **still true, less problematic**
   Think of me as man rehab.
9. You're crap at relationships – **still true, can't be helped**
   SAME. Let's be crap together.
10. Men are shits – **Possibly not all men, tbc.**
    Can confirm, as can my mum.
11. ~~You are 32 and don't look great naked~~ **Can't believe
    you wrote this, behave yourself**
    *Can confirm you look great naked, although also hot in country
    boots and/or Spice Girls T-shirt.*

Reasons to fancy Matthew

1. He's kind and nice (underrated qualities, tbc if
   sexy) – **can confirm v. sexy**
   Thanks, I do my best.
2. He's literally next door – **sore point right now**
   Did you write this while I was in Bristol? I came back!
3. He might fancy you too – **see above, indications
   positive**
   See point 4 above. Don't make me say it again.
4. He probably looks great naked (also: good with
   hands) – **still tbc**
   I await your verdict with stomach pulled in and pecs flexed.
5. You're trapped in a small village in a global pandemic,
   normal rules have gone out the window – **still true**
   *I agree. It's a mad world right now. Can I refer you back to
   Point 4? . . .*

Whole minutes passed before Gemma moved. She read the two
pages again, slower this time, just to check they still said the same
thing. She put them down on the table and looked at Mabel, then
at the pile of bags by the door, then picked the notes up and read
them again. She stared at the two frames on the mantelpiece, still

waiting to be packed. Mabel loped over and put her head on Gemma's lap, and Gemma stroked her head. She suddenly remembered what Matthew had said when he'd found Mabel in the garden after she'd run away from the shop. *'It's OK, she's home now.'* Gemma had been too upset to register it at the time, but now it rang in her ears. He'd known then, and Mabel knew it too. But it had taken her until now to realise it.

She stroked Mabel for a while longer before reaching into the bag and putting Aunt Laura's rainbow jumper on. It felt warm and safe and familiar, like the knitted essence of happiness. She took a deep breath and walked out of the back door towards the barn, Mabel following at her heels.

Matthew opened the door as soon as Gemma knocked, like he'd been pacing the room on the other side. He looked bleak and exhausted, his eyes searching her face for any indication of what she was thinking. He managed to squeak out a 'Hi' before he had to clutch the door frame for support.

Gemma took a step towards him, her hands fidgeting with nerves inside the sleeves of the jumper. 'Your bed makes my back hurt, it's awful. So maybe you could come home with me, and then we can pay off my poor taxi driver, get into bed and talk about what happens next.'

Matthew broke into a huge smile, searching Gemma's eyes for any trace of doubt. He saw nothing but a fiery certainty in her eyes as he reached out for her. 'I think that's a really nice idea.'

Gemma took Matthew's hand, feeling the solid warmth of his fingers as they intertwined with hers. As he reached down to give Mabel a scratch between the ears, she looked across the garden at the open door of the cottage, then turned back to look at Matthew. *You feel like home*, she thought, as the three of them walked down the steps and into the dappled sunlight of the apple trees.

Acknowledgements

Writing your first novel is a strange thing, and writing a novel in 2020 was even stranger. I was furloughed from my proper job in marketing on 1 April, and on 2 April I fired up a Word document and started to write. Incidentally later I switched to a medium more suited to writing a book but (to quote the Book of John) in the beginning was the Word. So I suppose I ought to thank Rishi Sunak for facilitating a few months of dedicated writing time, without which this book would probably never have happened. I'm reasonably confident this is the only time I'll ever put Rishi Sunak in my list of acknowledgements, but these are weird times and nothing is impossible.

My next thanks must go to my boyfriend Pip, who never once asked 'why?' Thank you for the coffees, the breakfasts, the words of support, the times you took Mabel for a walk in the rain so I could unravel a thorny chapter, and the unwavering encouragement. Likewise my children, Sam and Emma, who returned home for the early weeks of lockdown and didn't bat an eyelid at mum tapping away at the kitchen table. Everybody with a dream needs champions, and you three have always been mine.

I'd also like to thank my mum, Joy, my stepdad, Brian, my sister, Ange and my brother, Jon, for their advice on military ranks and protocols – between them they have 110 years of service in the British Army, the Royal Air Force and the Ministry of Defence, and I am hugely proud of all of them. Any mistakes are almost certainly down to me not listening properly.

Crowthorpe is based on a real village where I used to live, albeit it has a different name. While many of the landmarks in the fictional Crowthorpe will be familiar to the locals, none of the characters are based on real people and any similarity to persons living or dead is entirely coincidental. West Cottage is based on a real house too; apologies to John and Sue next door for wiping out your lovely house to make fictional space for Matthew's barn. You were amazing neighbours and we miss you both.

Thanks to Sarah Burr for always believing I could do this, and to my TITS girls and the Guardians Of Pop for keeping me together during an insane year – you didn't know it at the time, but your love and positivity and humour spurred me through the days when this all seemed like a giant waste of time. I'd also like to send love and thanks to the new writer community online; I never introduced myself but you were a source of brilliant advice on finding a literary agent and understanding a bit about how this industry works. I knew nothing; I still don't know much. I'll do my best to pass it forward at some point.

Talking of literary agents, huge thanks must go to Caroline Sheldon for spotting my first three chapters in her mountain of unsolicited submissions and asking to see the rest – 6 July 2020 remains one of the most exciting and panic-stricken days of my life. You have held my hand through this whole process and I couldn't have wished for a kinder and more encouraging guide and mentor. Thanks also to Bea Grabowska at Headline Accent for your boundless enthusiasm, dedication and editorial support. I feel lucky in more ways than I can count.